# THE WELL

JAKE WYATT

CHOO

:01

First Second
NEW YORK

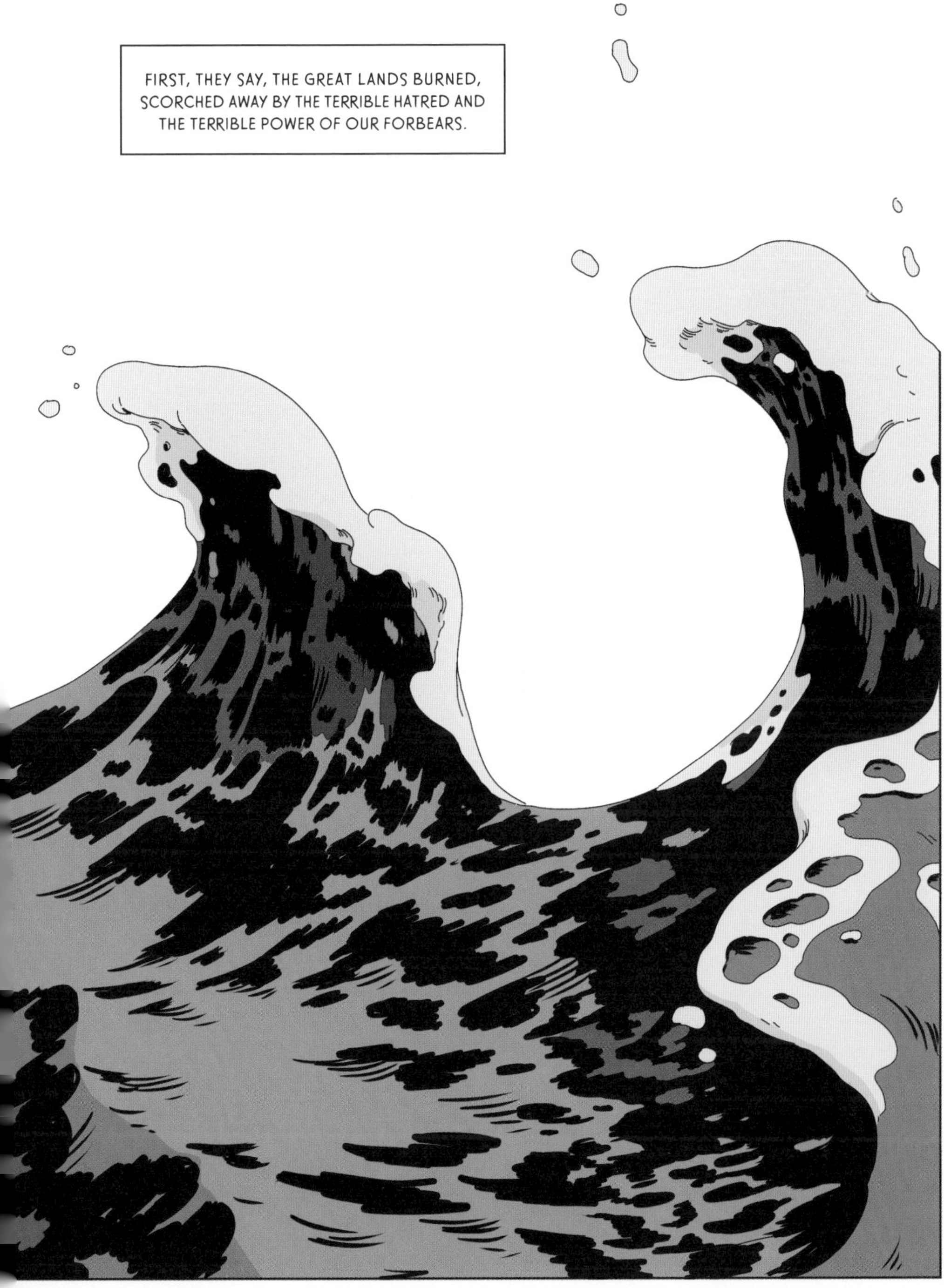
FIRST, THEY SAY, THE GREAT LANDS BURNED, SCORCHED AWAY BY THE TERRIBLE HATRED AND THE TERRIBLE POWER OF OUR FORBEARS.

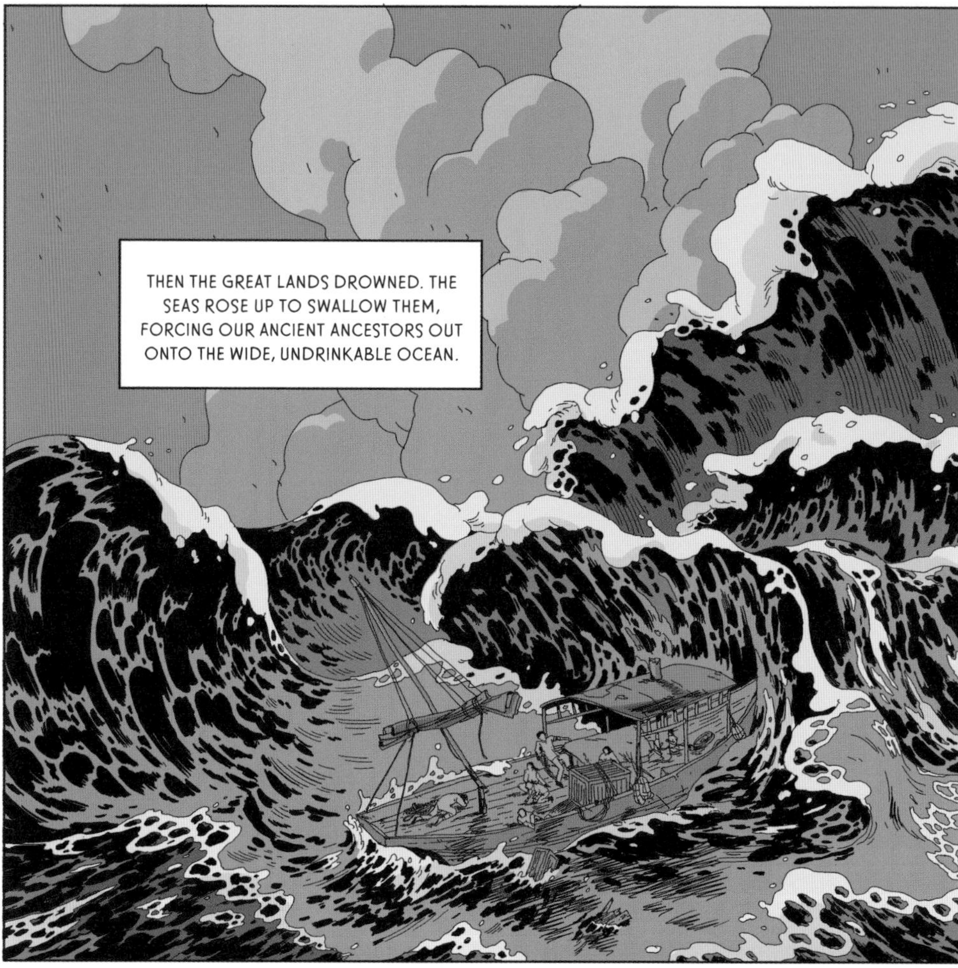
THEN THE GREAT LANDS DROWNED. THE SEAS ROSE UP TO SWALLOW THEM, FORCING OUR ANCIENT ANCESTORS OUT ONTO THE WIDE, UNDRINKABLE OCEAN.

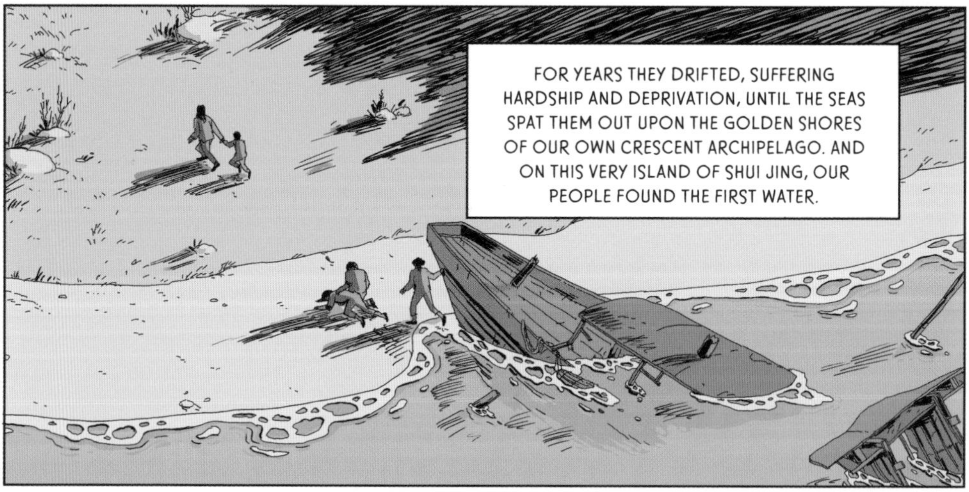
FOR YEARS THEY DRIFTED, SUFFERING HARDSHIP AND DEPRIVATION, UNTIL THE SEAS SPAT THEM OUT UPON THE GOLDEN SHORES OF OUR OWN CRESCENT ARCHIPELAGO. AND ON THIS VERY ISLAND OF SHUI JING, OUR PEOPLE FOUND THE FIRST WATER.

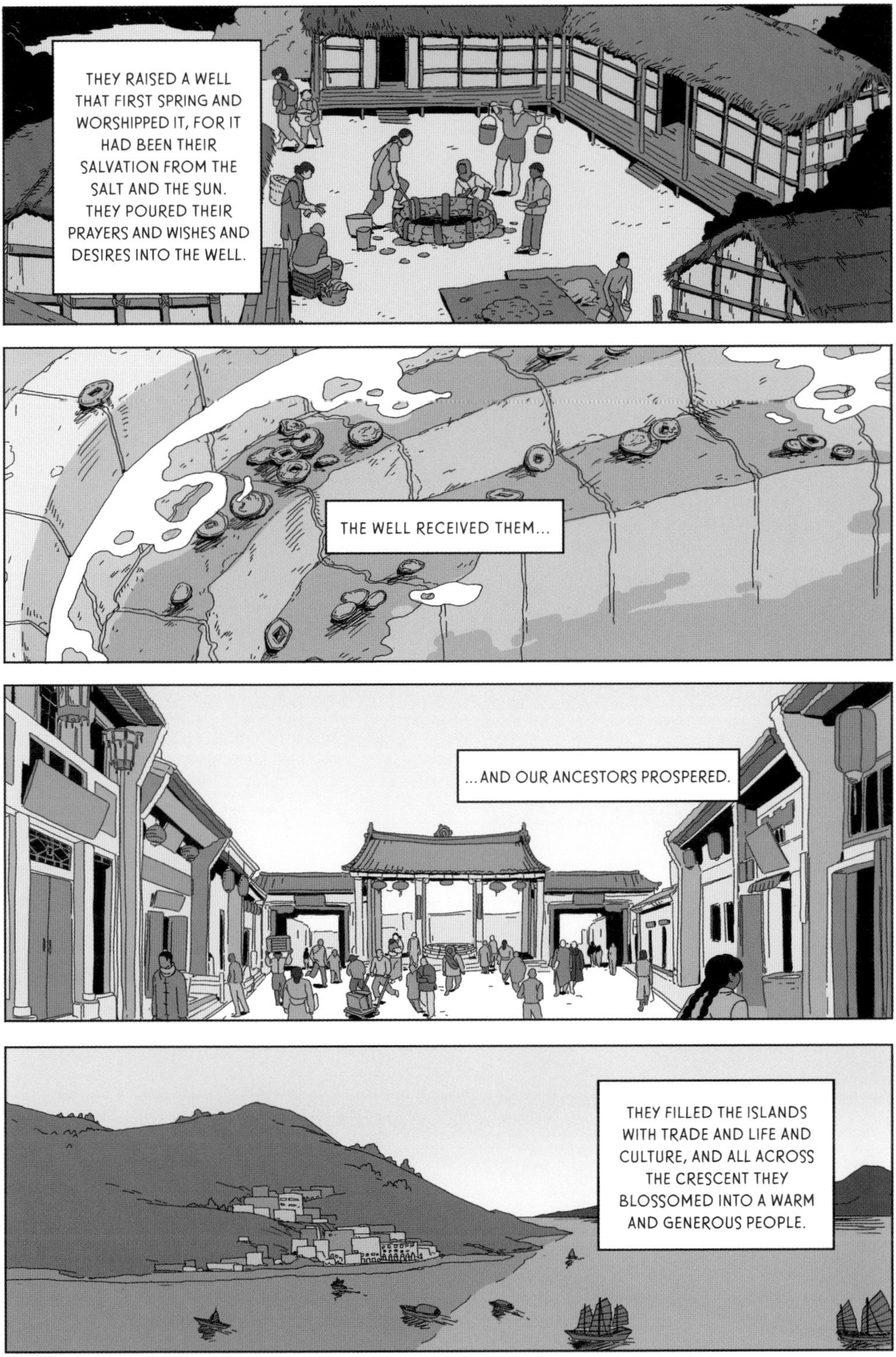
THEY RAISED A WELL THAT FIRST SPRING AND WORSHIPPED IT, FOR IT HAD BEEN THEIR SALVATION FROM THE SALT AND THE SUN. THEY POURED THEIR PRAYERS AND WISHES AND DESIRES INTO THE WELL.
THE WELL RECEIVED THEM...
...AND OUR ANCESTORS PROSPERED.
THEY FILLED THE ISLANDS WITH TRADE AND LIFE AND CULTURE, AND ALL ACROSS THE CRESCENT THEY BLOSSOMED INTO A WARM AND GENEROUS PEOPLE.

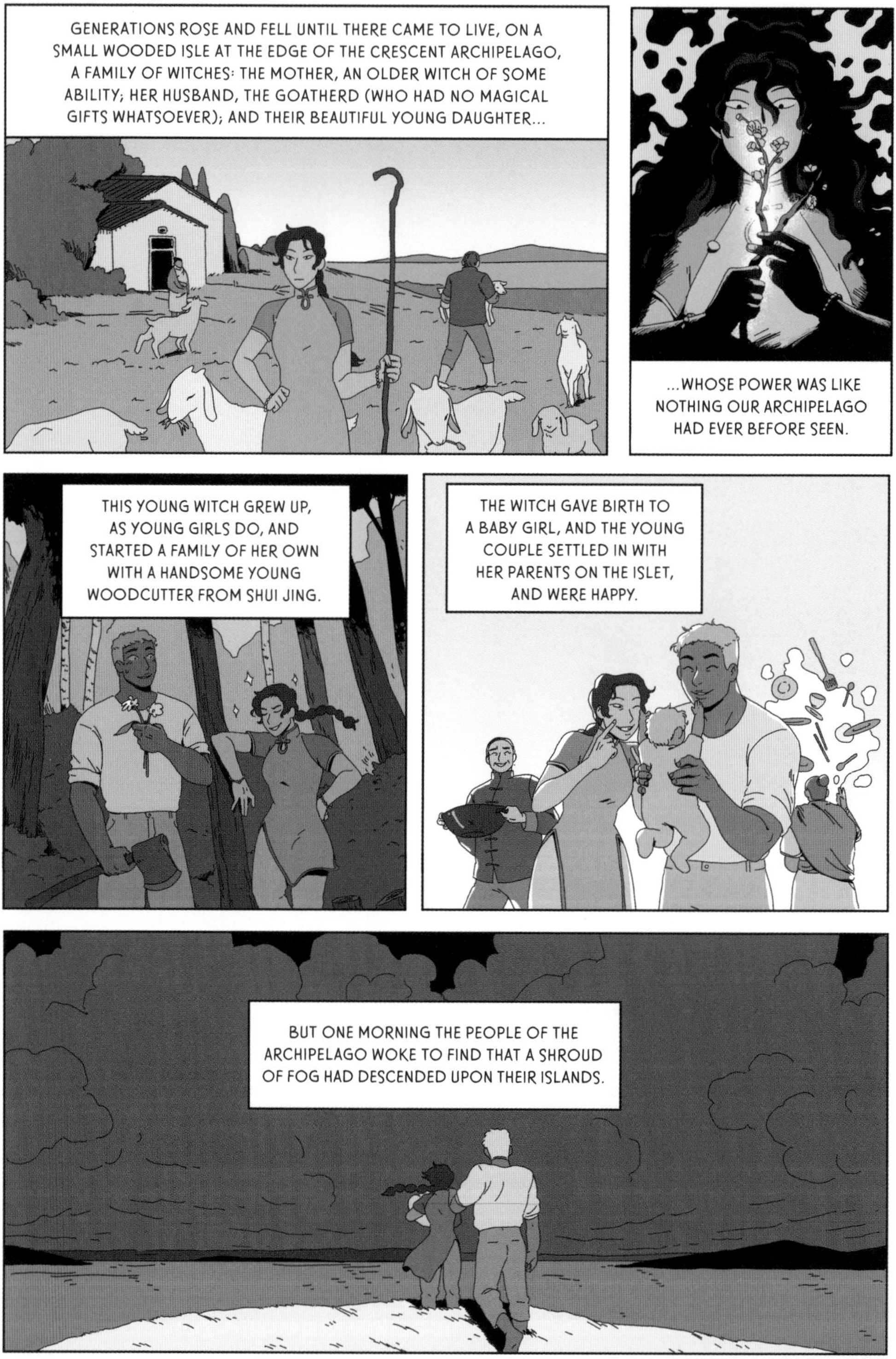
GENERATIONS ROSE AND FELL UNTIL THERE CAME TO LIVE, ON A SMALL WOODED ISLE AT THE EDGE OF THE CRESCENT ARCHIPELAGO, A FAMILY OF WITCHES: THE MOTHER, AN OLDER WITCH OF SOME ABILITY; HER HUSBAND, THE GOATHERD (WHO HAD NO MAGICAL GIFTS WHATSOEVER); AND THEIR BEAUTIFUL YOUNG DAUGHTER...
...WHOSE POWER WAS LIKE NOTHING OUR ARCHIPELAGO HAD EVER BEFORE SEEN.
THIS YOUNG WITCH GREW UP, AS YOUNG GIRLS DO, AND STARTED A FAMILY OF HER OWN WITH A HANDSOME YOUNG WOODCUTTER FROM SHUI JING.
THE WITCH GAVE BIRTH TO A BABY GIRL, AND THE YOUNG COUPLE SETTLED IN WITH HER PARENTS ON THE ISLET, AND WERE HAPPY.
BUT ONE MORNING THE PEOPLE OF THE ARCHIPELAGO WOKE TO FIND THAT A SHROUD OF FOG HAD DESCENDED UPON THEIR ISLANDS.

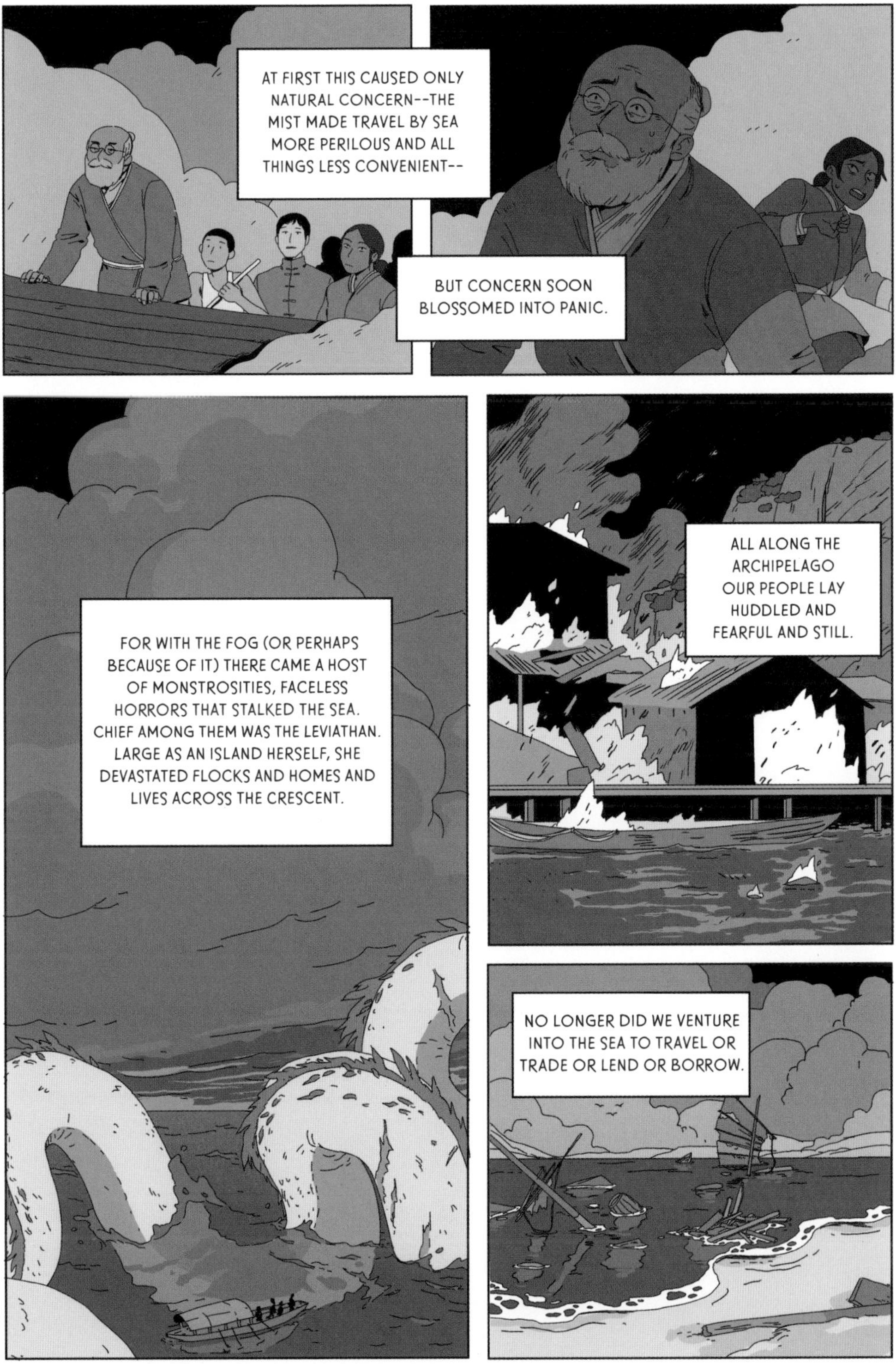
AT FIRST THIS CAUSED ONLY NATURAL CONCERN--THE MIST MADE TRAVEL BY SEA MORE PERILOUS AND ALL THINGS LESS CONVENIENT--
BUT CONCERN SOON BLOSSOMED INTO PANIC.
FOR WITH THE FOG (OR PERHAPS BECAUSE OF IT) THERE CAME A HOST OF MONSTROSITIES, FACELESS HORRORS THAT STALKED THE SEA. CHIEF AMONG THEM WAS THE LEVIATHAN. LARGE AS AN ISLAND HERSELF, SHE DEVASTATED FLOCKS AND HOMES AND LIVES ACROSS THE CRESCENT.
ALL ALONG THE ARCHIPELAGO OUR PEOPLE LAY HUDDLED AND FEARFUL AND STILL.
NO LONGER DID WE VENTURE INTO THE SEA TO TRAVEL OR TRADE OR LEND OR BORROW.

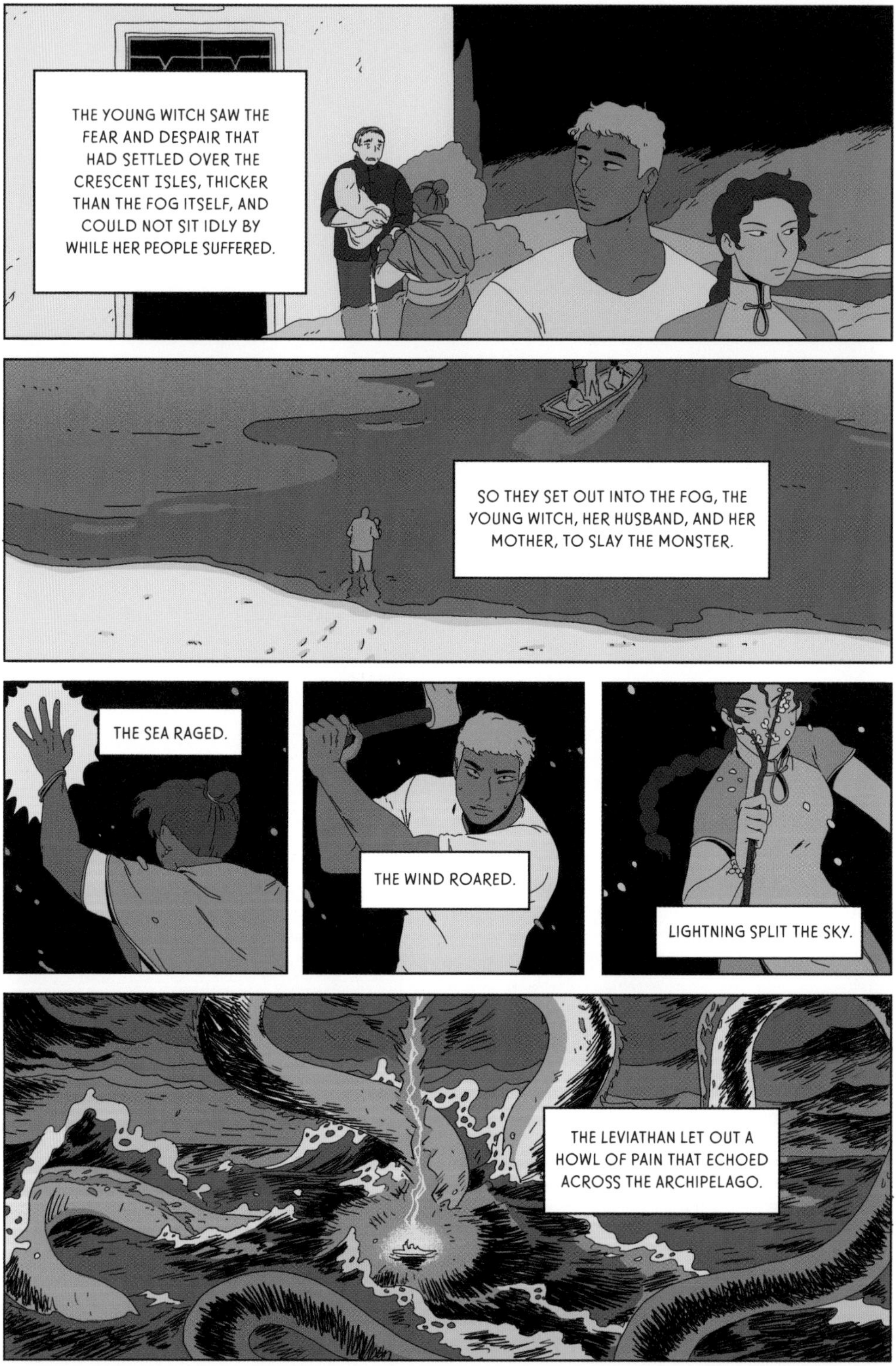
THE YOUNG WITCH SAW THE FEAR AND DESPAIR THAT HAD SETTLED OVER THE CRESCENT ISLES, THICKER THAN THE FOG ITSELF, AND COULD NOT SIT IDLY BY WHILE HER PEOPLE SUFFERED.
SO THEY SET OUT INTO THE FOG, THE YOUNG WITCH, HER HUSBAND, AND HER MOTHER, TO SLAY THE MONSTER.
THE SEA RAGED.
THE WIND ROARED.
LIGHTNING SPLIT THE SKY.
THE LEVIATHAN LET OUT A HOWL OF PAIN THAT ECHOED ACROSS THE ARCHIPELAGO.

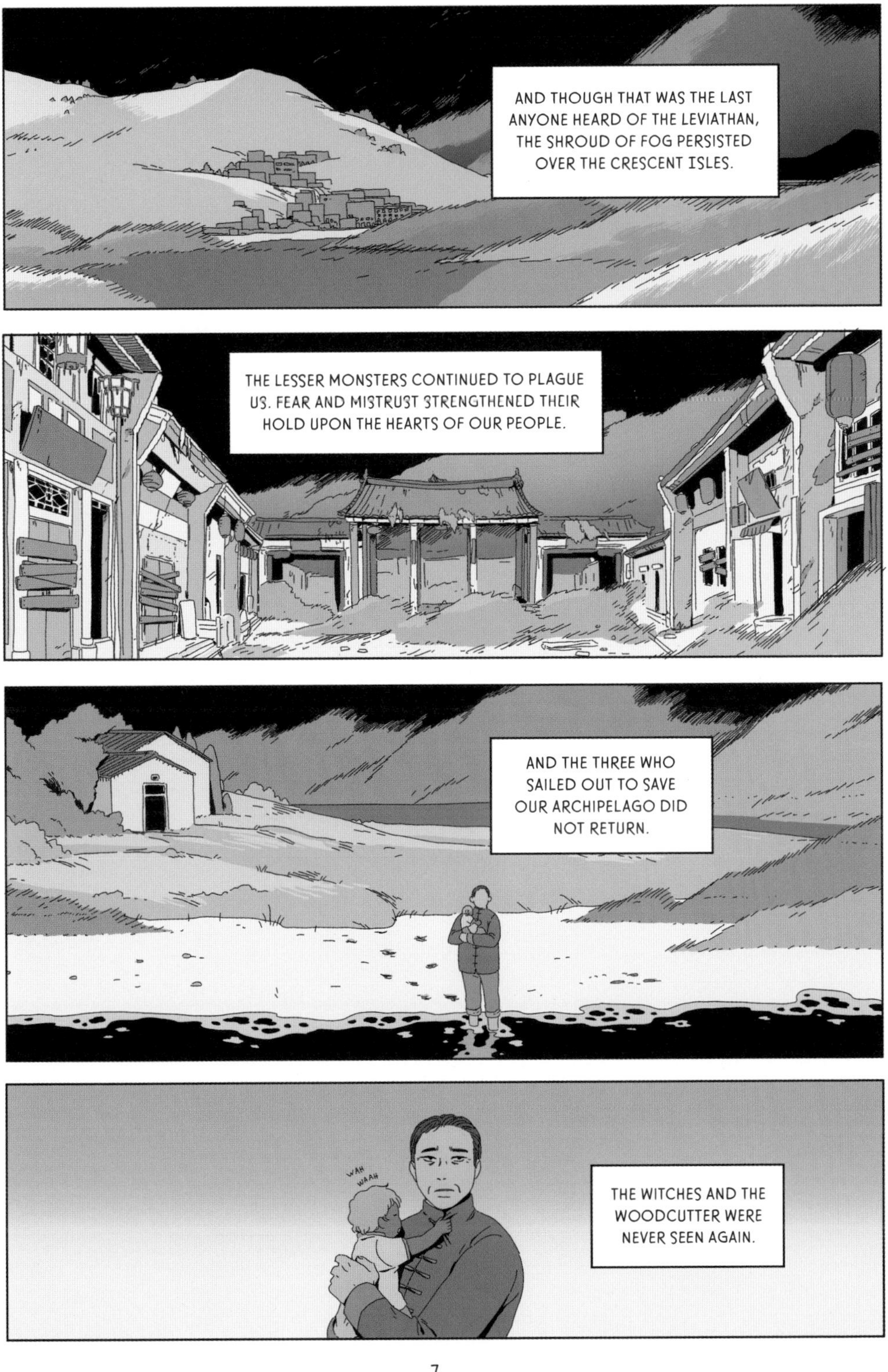
AND THOUGH THAT WAS THE LAST ANYONE HEARD OF THE LEVIATHAN, THE SHROUD OF FOG PERSISTED OVER THE CRESCENT ISLES.
THE LESSER MONSTERS CONTINUED TO PLAGUE US. FEAR AND MISTRUST STRENGTHENED THEIR HOLD UPON THE HEARTS OF OUR PEOPLE.
AND THE THREE WHO SAILED OUT TO SAVE OUR ARCHIPELAGO DID NOT RETURN.
WAH WAAH
THE WITCHES AND THE WOODCUTTER WERE NEVER SEEN AGAIN.

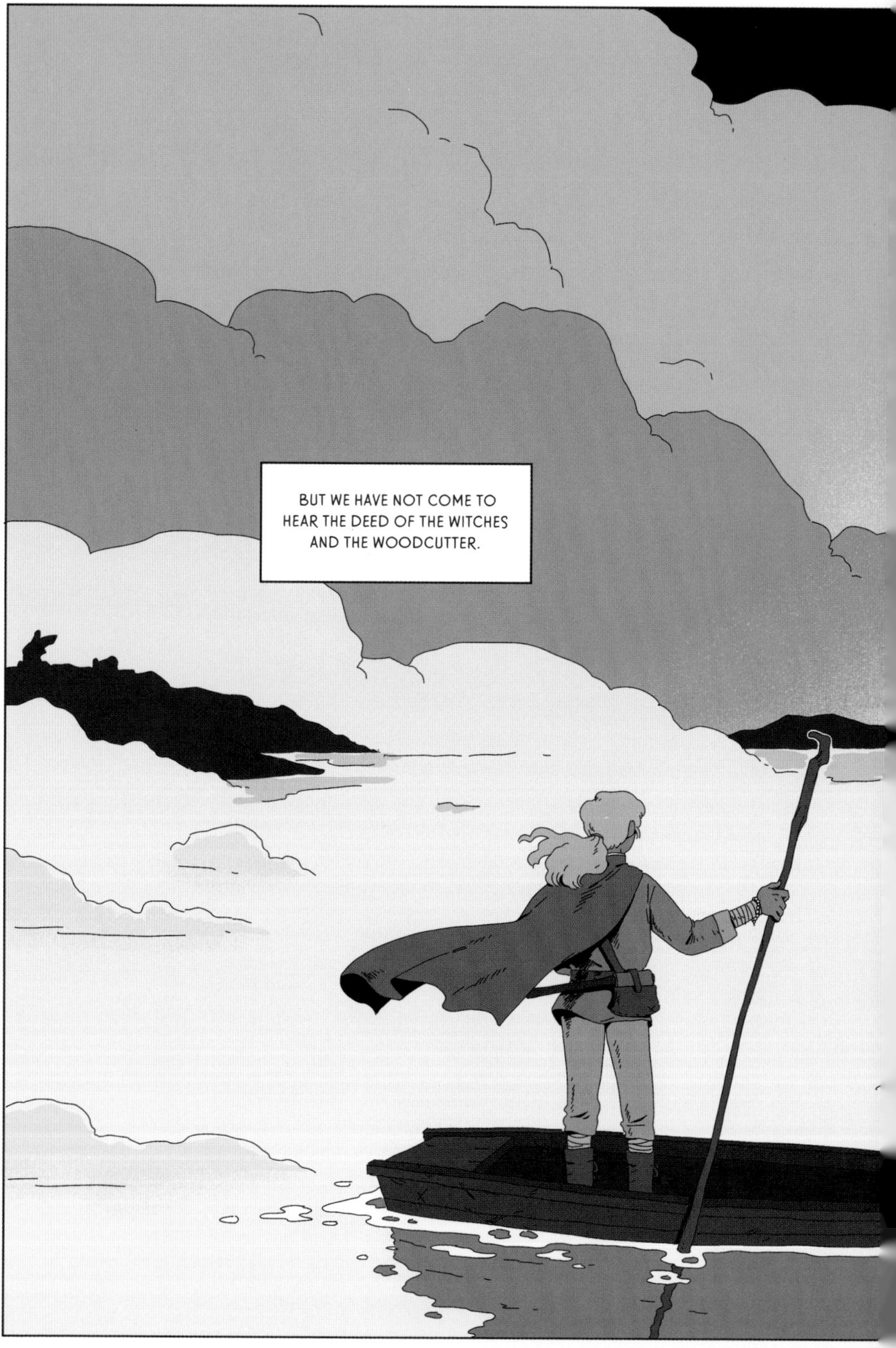
BUT WE HAVE NOT COME TO HEAR THE DEED OF THE WITCHES AND THE WOODCUTTER.

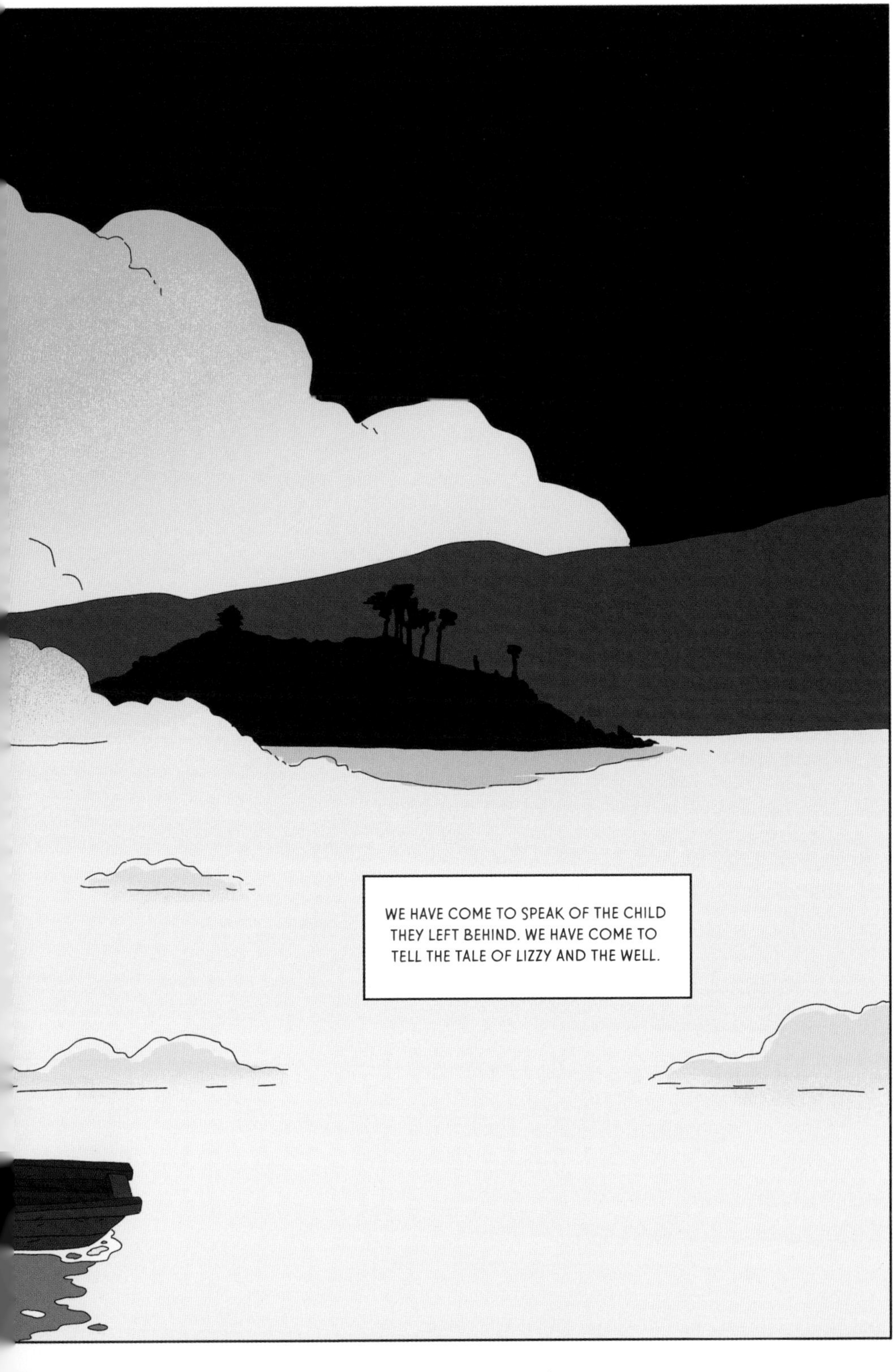
WE HAVE COME TO SPEAK OF THE CHILD THEY LEFT BEHIND. WE HAVE COME TO TELL THE TALE OF LIZZY AND THE WELL.

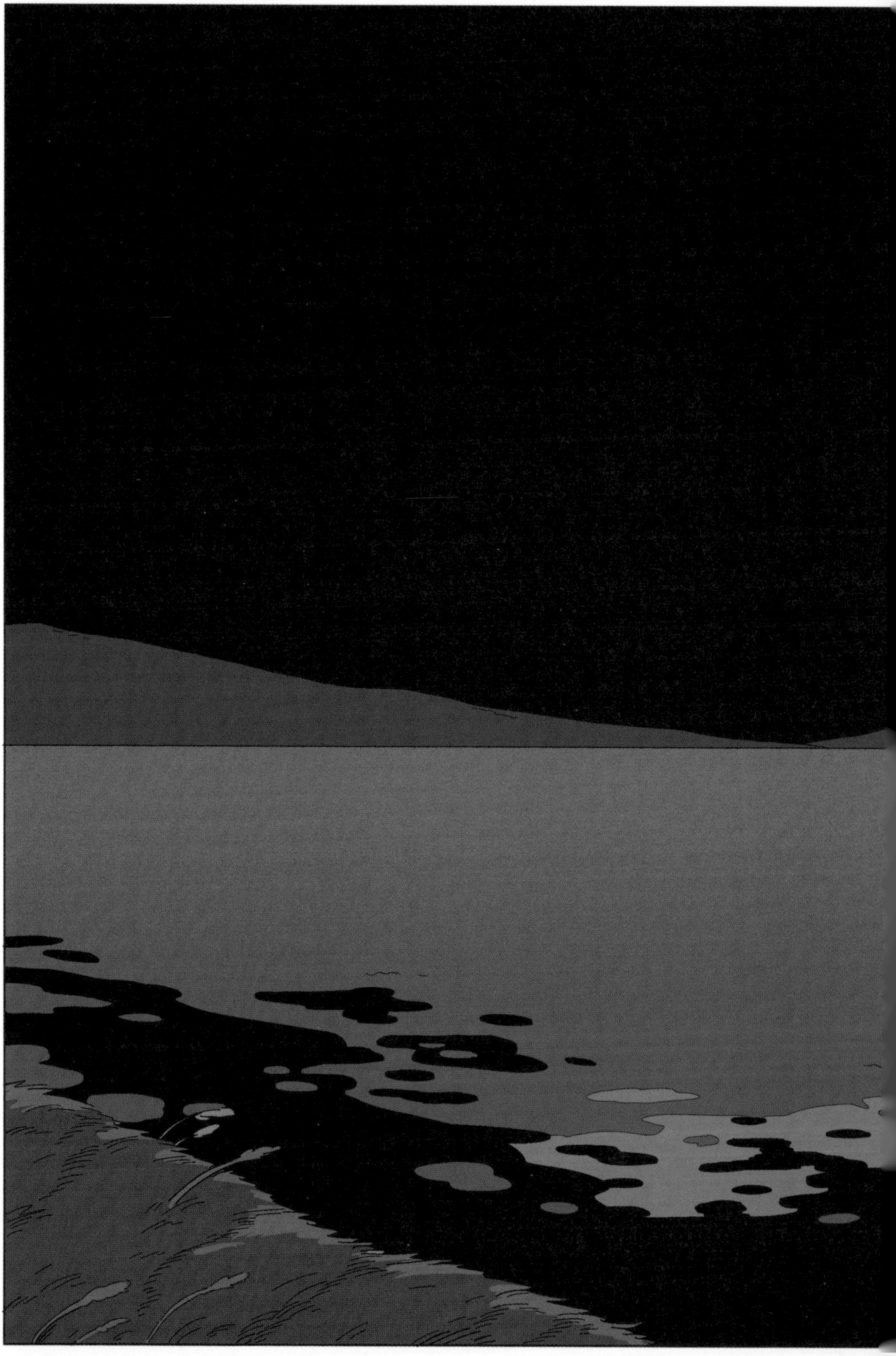

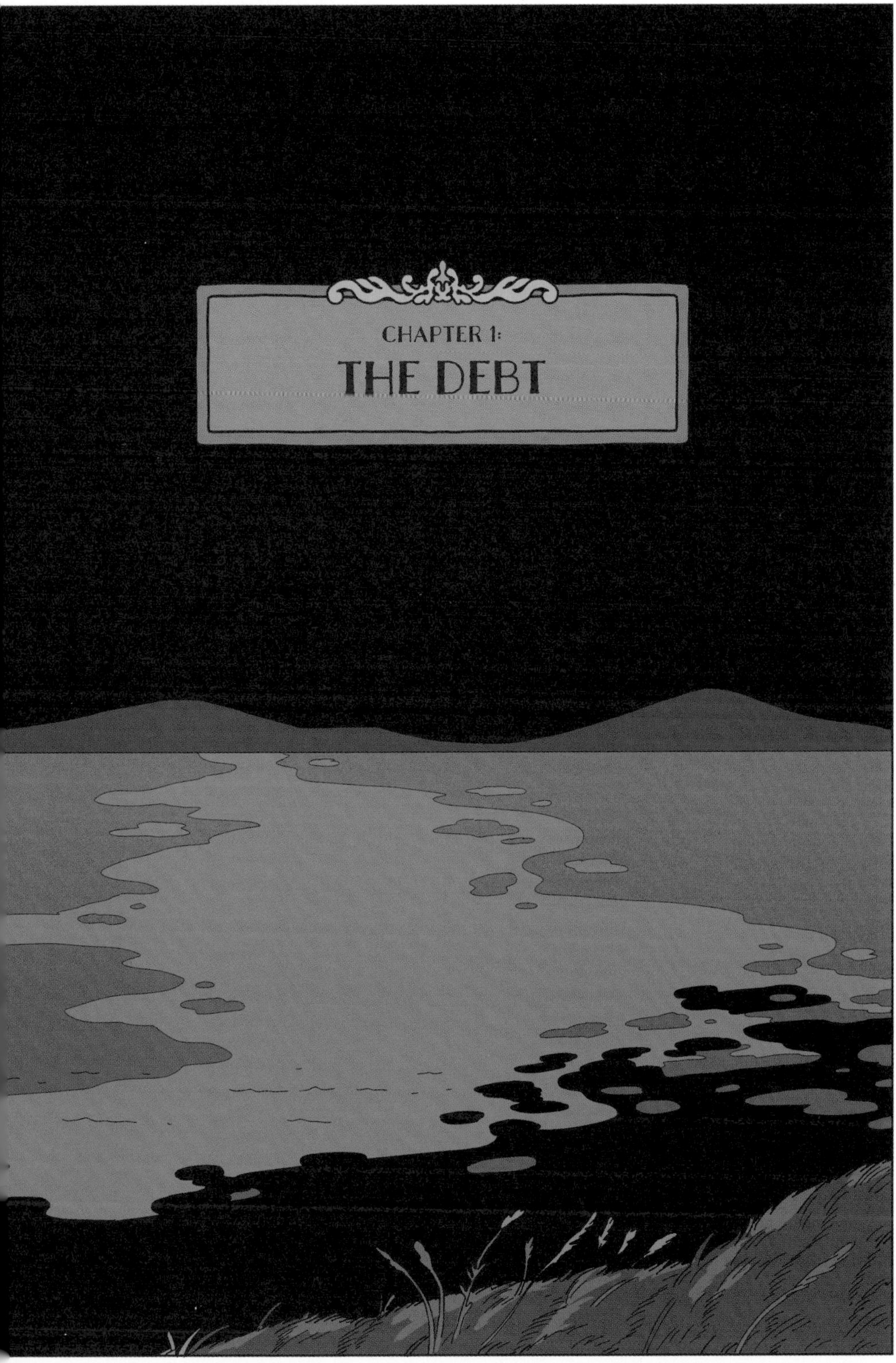
CHAPTER 1:
THE DEBT

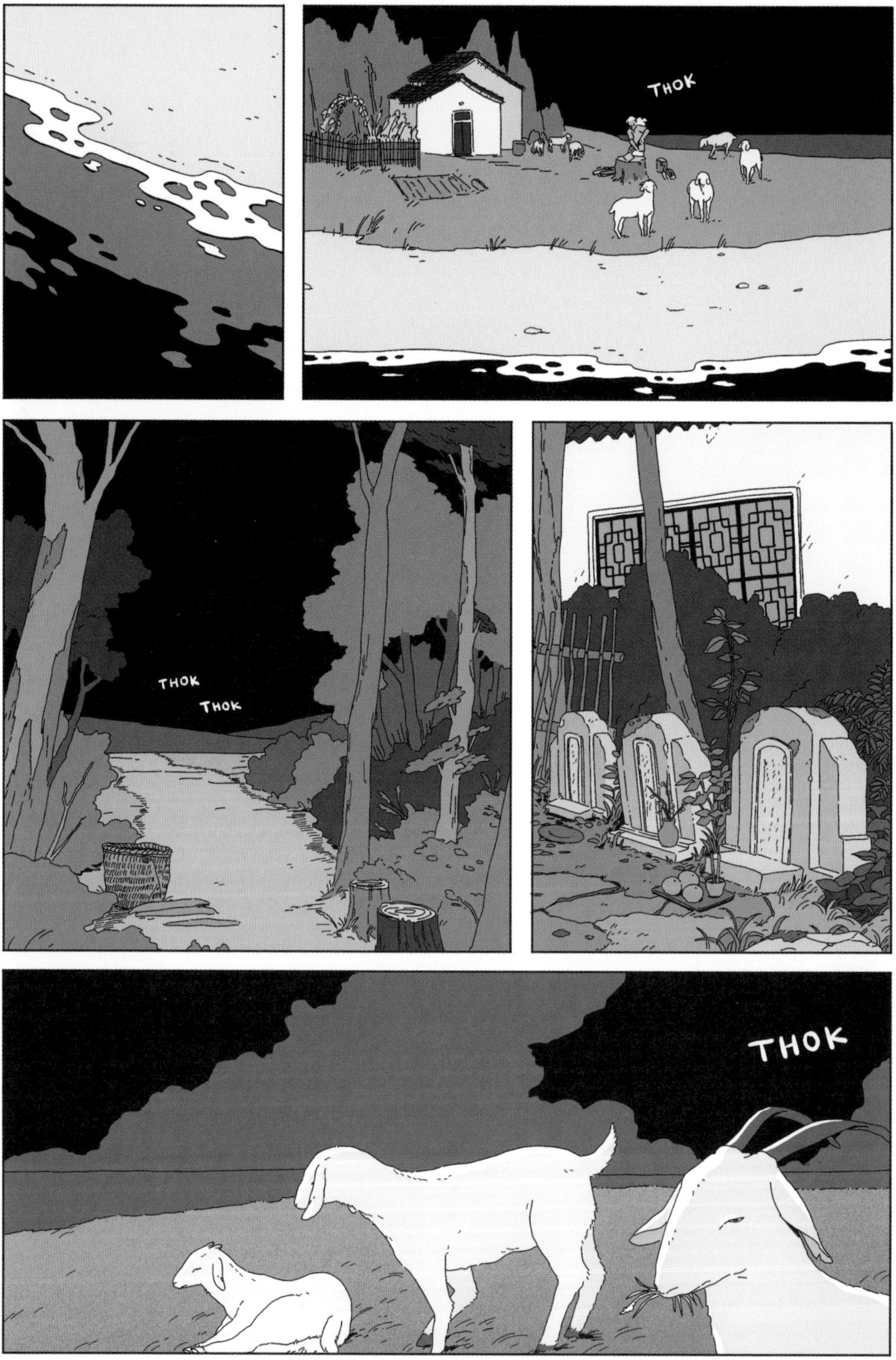
THOK
THOK
THOK
THOK

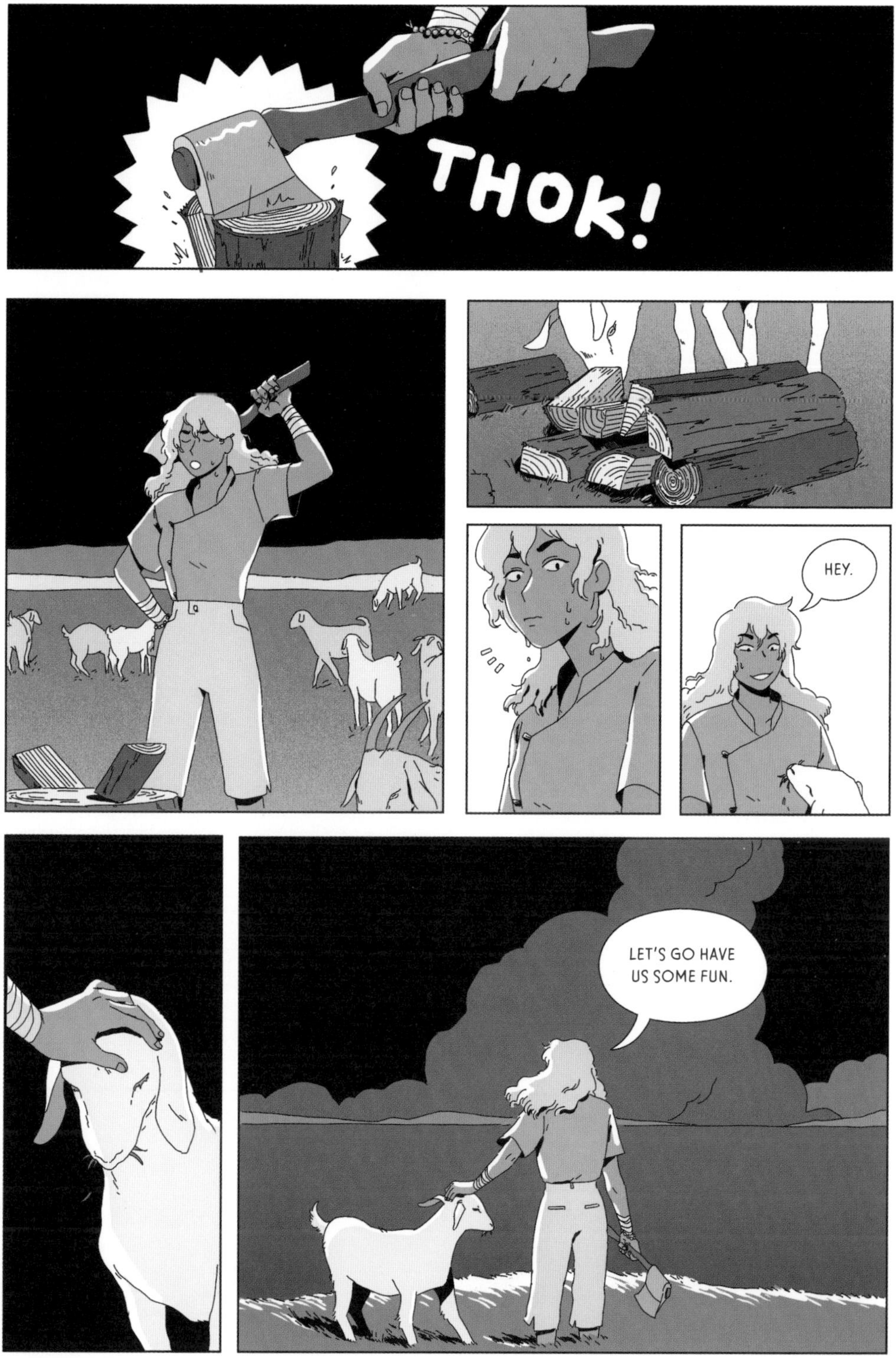
THOK!
HEY.
LET'S GO HAVE US SOME FUN.

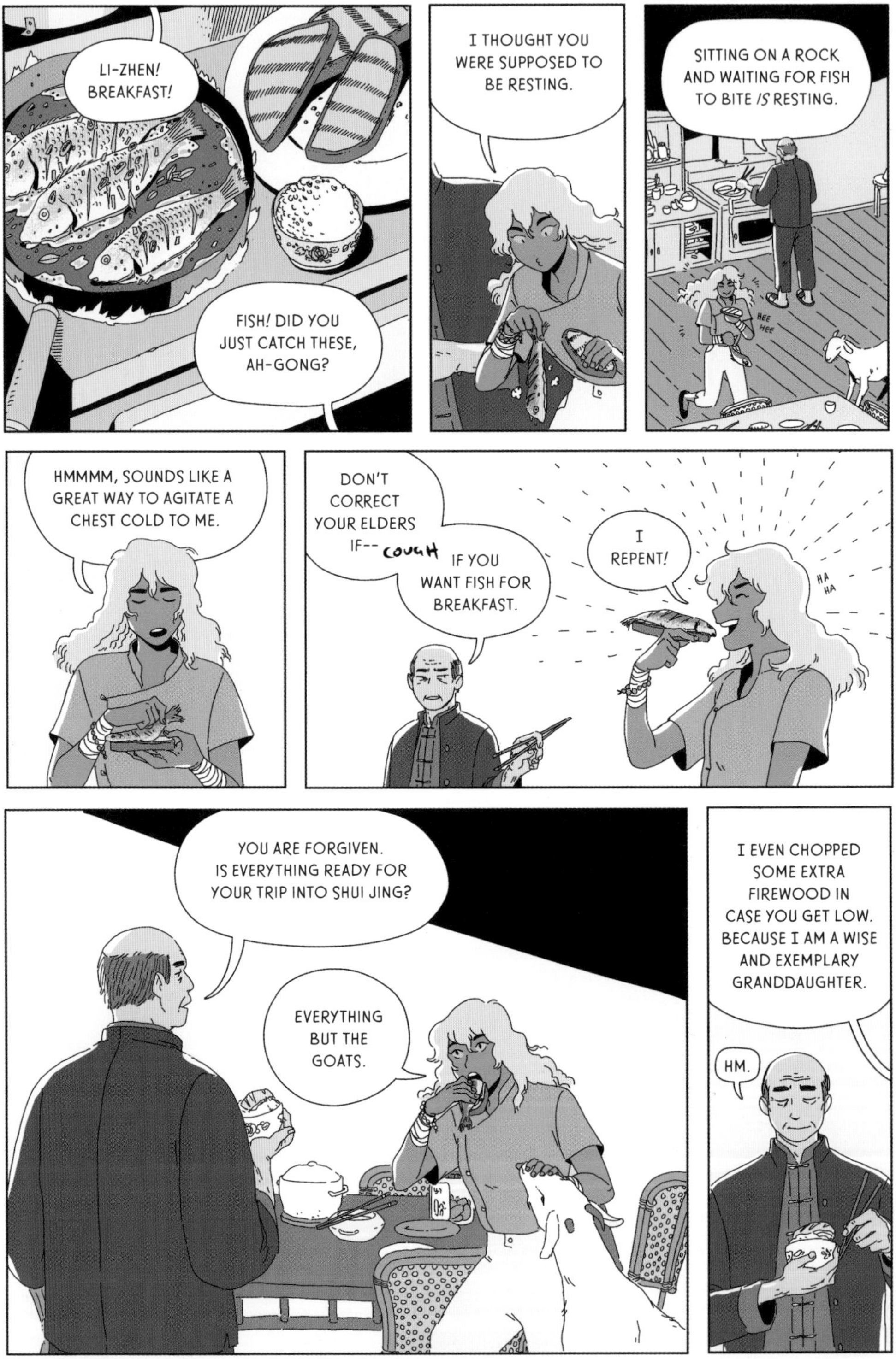
LI-ZHEN! BREAKFAST!
FISH! DID YOU JUST CATCH THESE, AH-GONG?
I THOUGHT YOU WERE SUPPOSED TO BE RESTING.
SITTING ON A ROCK AND WAITING FOR FISH TO BITE *IS* RESTING.
HEE HEE
HMMMM, SOUNDS LIKE A GREAT WAY TO AGITATE A CHEST COLD TO ME.
DON'T CORRECT YOUR ELDERS IF--
COUGH
IF YOU WANT FISH FOR BREAKFAST.
I REPENT!
HA HA
YOU ARE FORGIVEN. IS EVERYTHING READY FOR YOUR TRIP INTO SHUI JING?
EVERYTHING BUT THE GOATS.
I EVEN CHOPPED SOME EXTRA FIREWOOD IN CASE YOU GET LOW. BECAUSE I AM A WISE AND EXEMPLARY GRANDDAUGHTER.
HM.

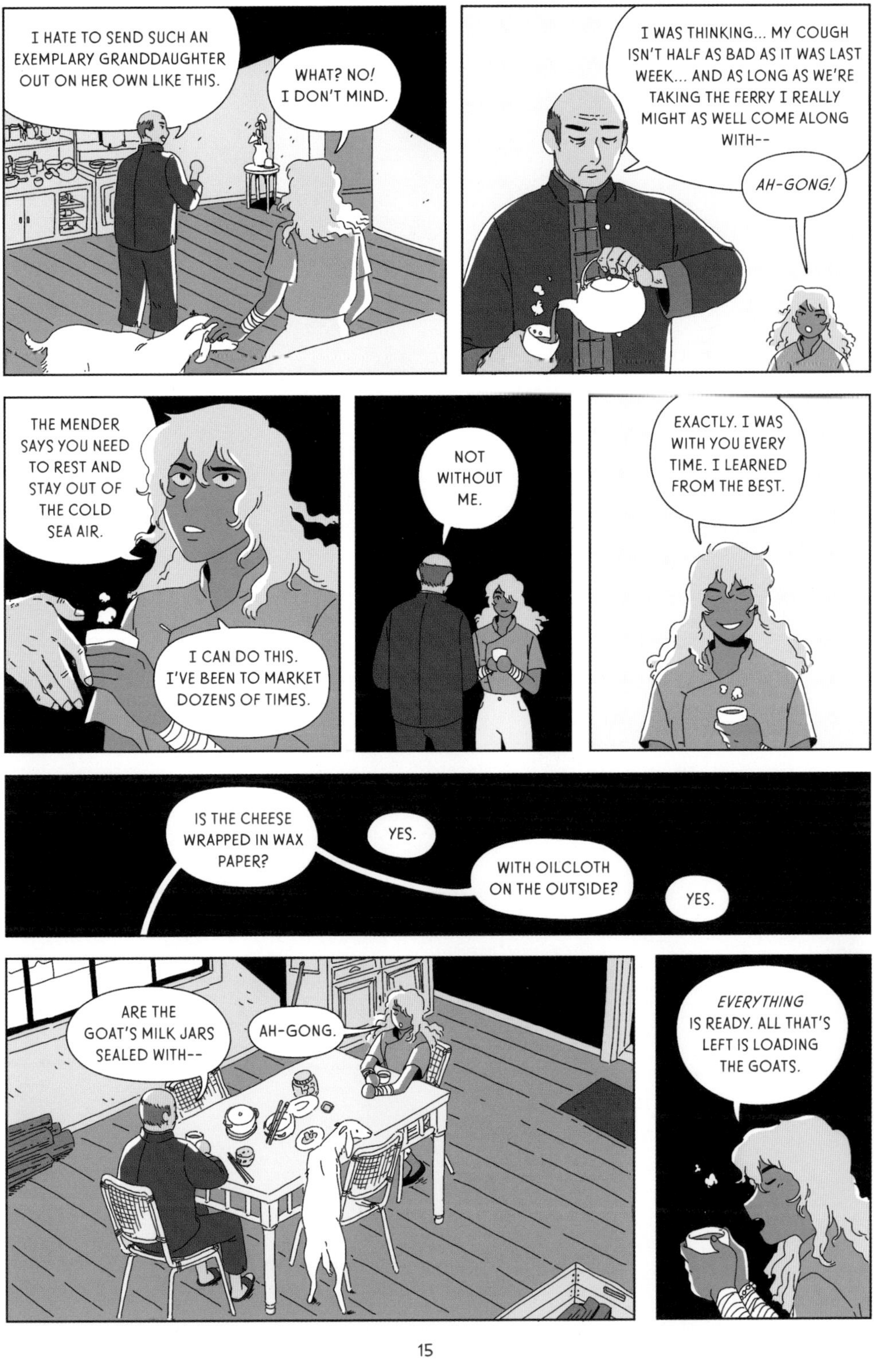
I HATE TO SEND SUCH AN EXEMPLARY GRANDDAUGHTER OUT ON HER OWN LIKE THIS.
WHAT? NO! I DON'T MIND.
I WAS THINKING... MY COUGH ISN'T HALF AS BAD AS IT WAS LAST WEEK... AND AS LONG AS WE'RE TAKING THE FERRY I REALLY MIGHT AS WELL COME ALONG WITH--
*AH-GONG!*
THE MENDER SAYS YOU NEED TO REST AND STAY OUT OF THE COLD SEA AIR.
I CAN DO THIS. I'VE BEEN TO MARKET DOZENS OF TIMES.
NOT WITHOUT ME.
EXACTLY. I WAS WITH YOU EVERY TIME. I LEARNED FROM THE BEST.
IS THE CHEESE WRAPPED IN WAX PAPER?
YES.
WITH OILCLOTH ON THE OUTSIDE?
YES.
ARE THE GOAT'S MILK JARS SEALED WITH--
AH-GONG.
*EVERYTHING* IS READY. ALL THAT'S LEFT IS LOADING THE GOATS.

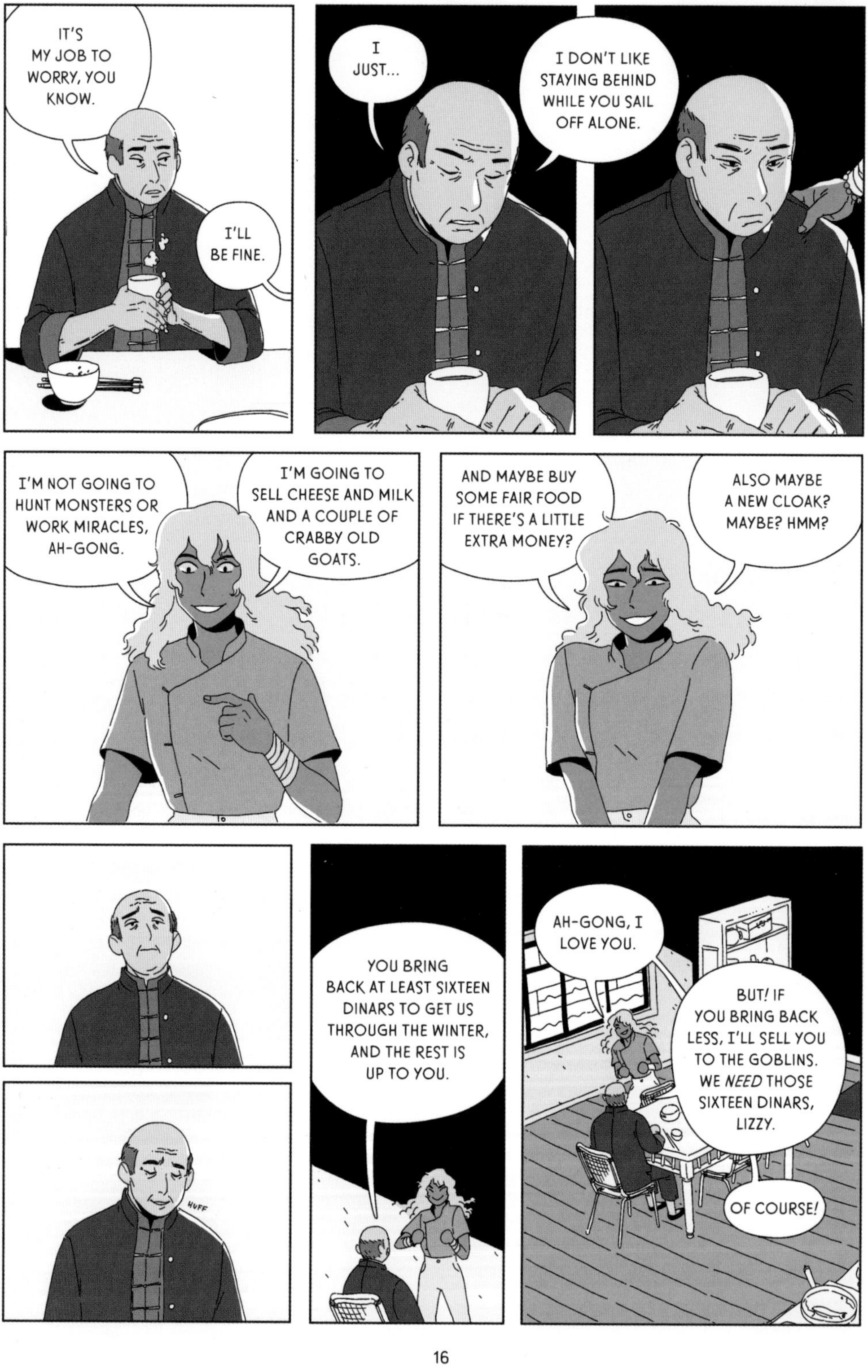
IT'S MY JOB TO WORRY, YOU KNOW.
I'LL BE FINE.
I JUST...
I DON'T LIKE STAYING BEHIND WHILE YOU SAIL OFF ALONE.
I'M NOT GOING TO HUNT MONSTERS OR WORK MIRACLES, AH-GONG.
I'M GOING TO SELL CHEESE AND MILK AND A COUPLE OF CRABBY OLD GOATS.
AND MAYBE BUY SOME FAIR FOOD IF THERE'S A LITTLE EXTRA MONEY?
ALSO MAYBE A NEW CLOAK? MAYBE? HMM?
HUFF
YOU BRING BACK AT LEAST SIXTEEN DINARS TO GET US THROUGH THE WINTER, AND THE REST IS UP TO YOU.
AH-GONG, I LOVE YOU.
BUT! IF YOU BRING BACK LESS, I'LL SELL YOU TO THE GOBLINS. WE *NEED* THOSE SIXTEEN DINARS, LIZZY.
OF COURSE!

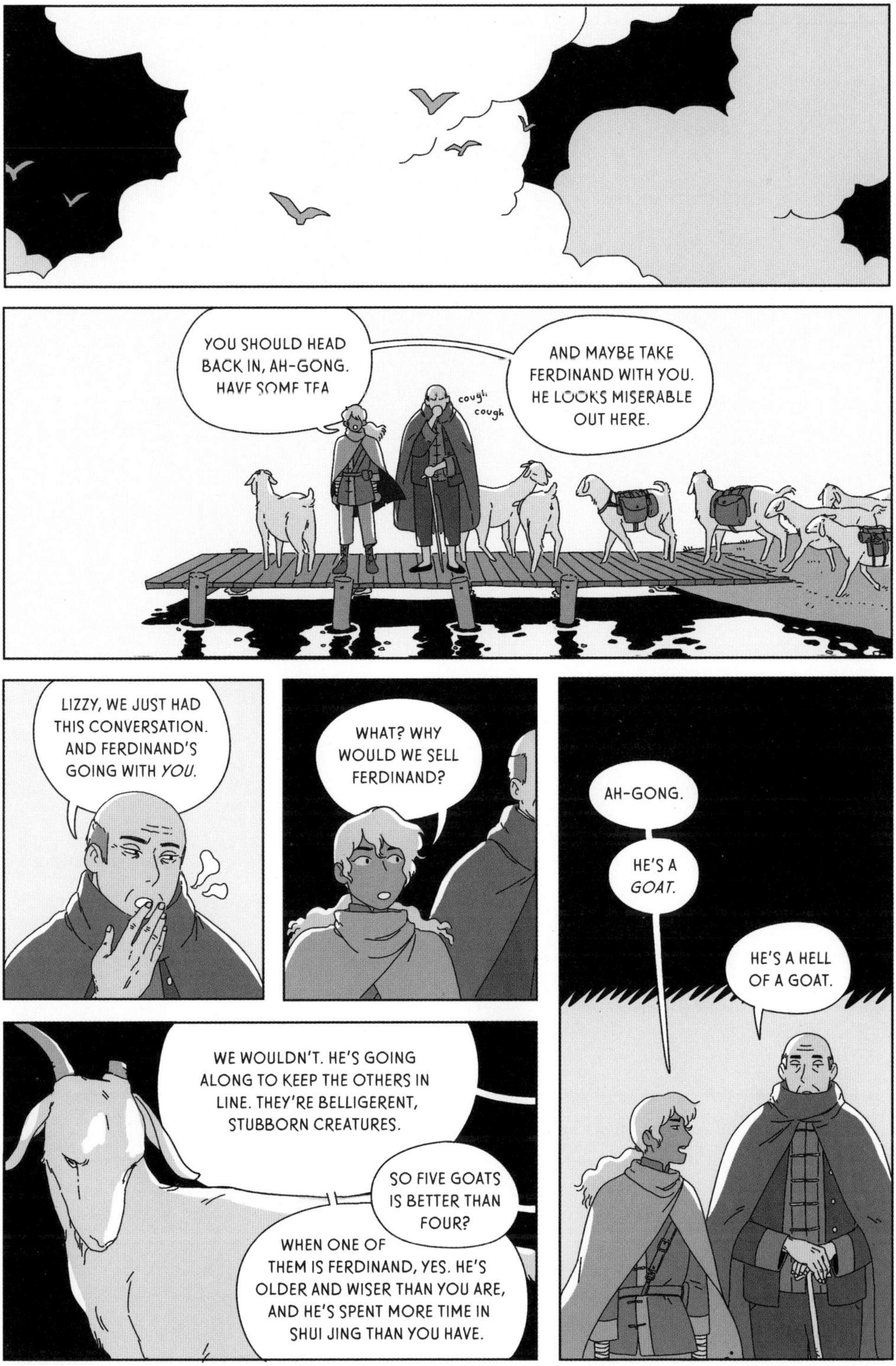
YOU SHOULD HEAD BACK IN, AH-GONG. HAVE SOME TEA
cough cough
AND MAYBE TAKE FERDINAND WITH YOU. HE LOOKS MISERABLE OUT HERE.
LIZZY, WE JUST HAD THIS CONVERSATION. AND FERDINAND'S GOING WITH *YOU*.
WHAT? WHY WOULD WE SELL FERDINAND?
AH-GONG.
HE'S A *GOAT*.
HE'S A HELL OF A GOAT.
WE WOULDN'T. HE'S GOING ALONG TO KEEP THE OTHERS IN LINE. THEY'RE BELLIGERENT, STUBBORN CREATURES.
SO FIVE GOATS IS BETTER THAN FOUR?
WHEN ONE OF THEM IS FERDINAND, YES. HE'S OLDER AND WISER THAN YOU ARE, AND HE'S SPENT MORE TIME IN SHUI JING THAN YOU HAVE.

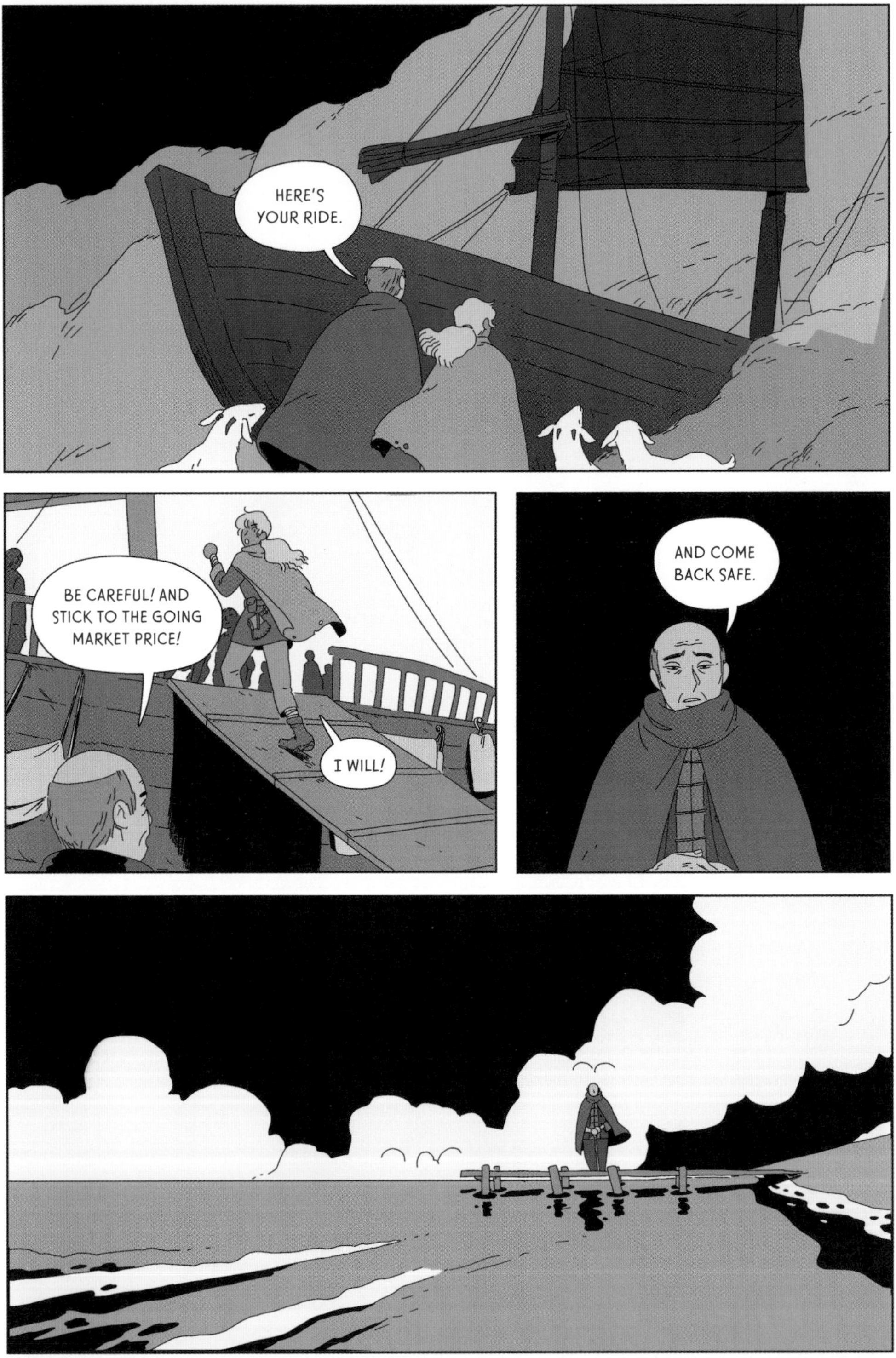
HERE'S YOUR RIDE.
BE CAREFUL! AND STICK TO THE GOING MARKET PRICE!
I WILL!
AND COME BACK SAFE.

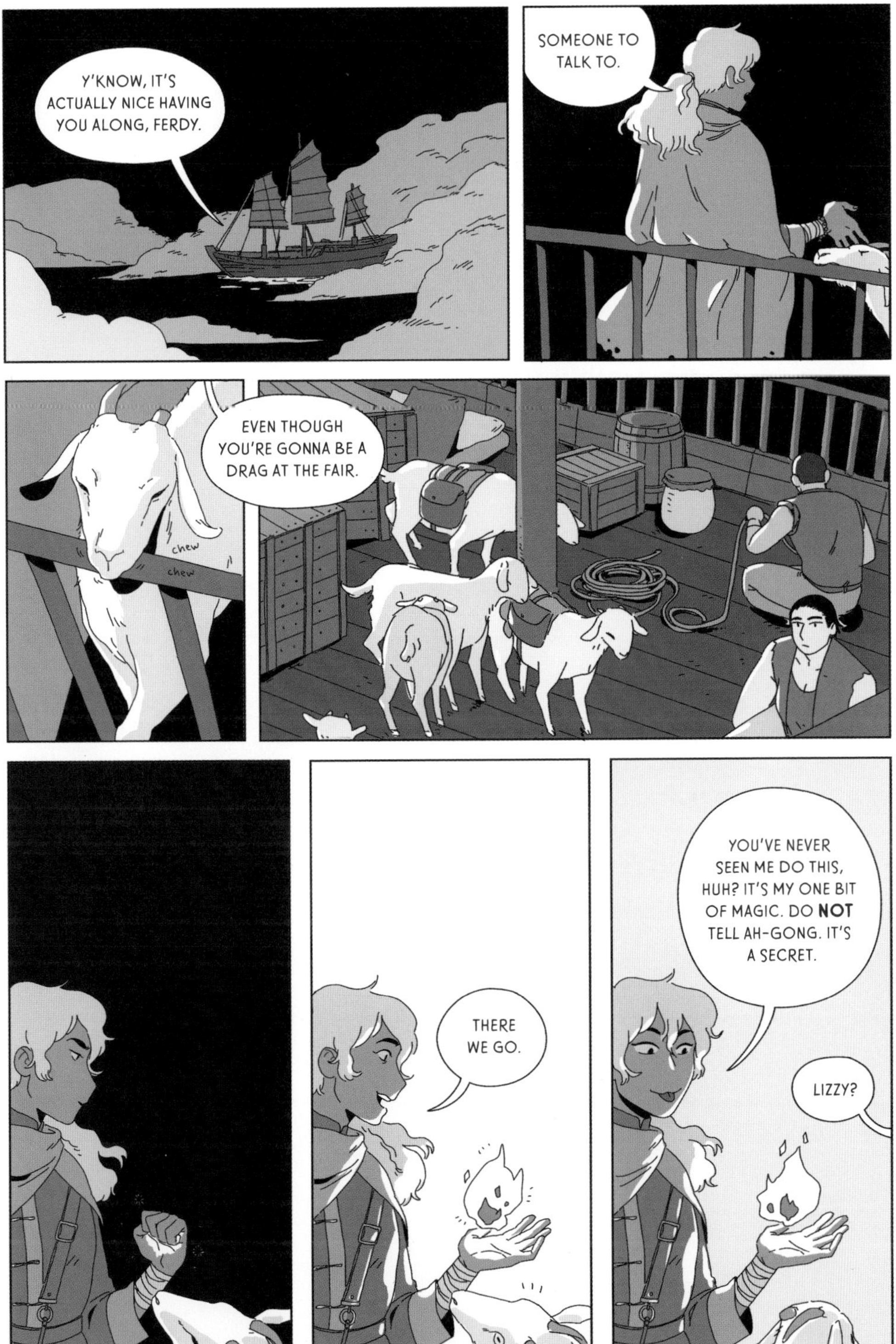
Y'KNOW, IT'S ACTUALLY NICE HAVING YOU ALONG, FERDY.
SOMEONE TO TALK TO.
EVEN THOUGH YOU'RE GONNA BE A DRAG AT THE FAIR.
chew
chew
THERE WE GO.
YOU'VE NEVER SEEN ME DO THIS, HUH? IT'S MY ONE BIT OF MAGIC. DO **NOT** TELL AH-GONG. IT'S A SECRET.
LIZZY?

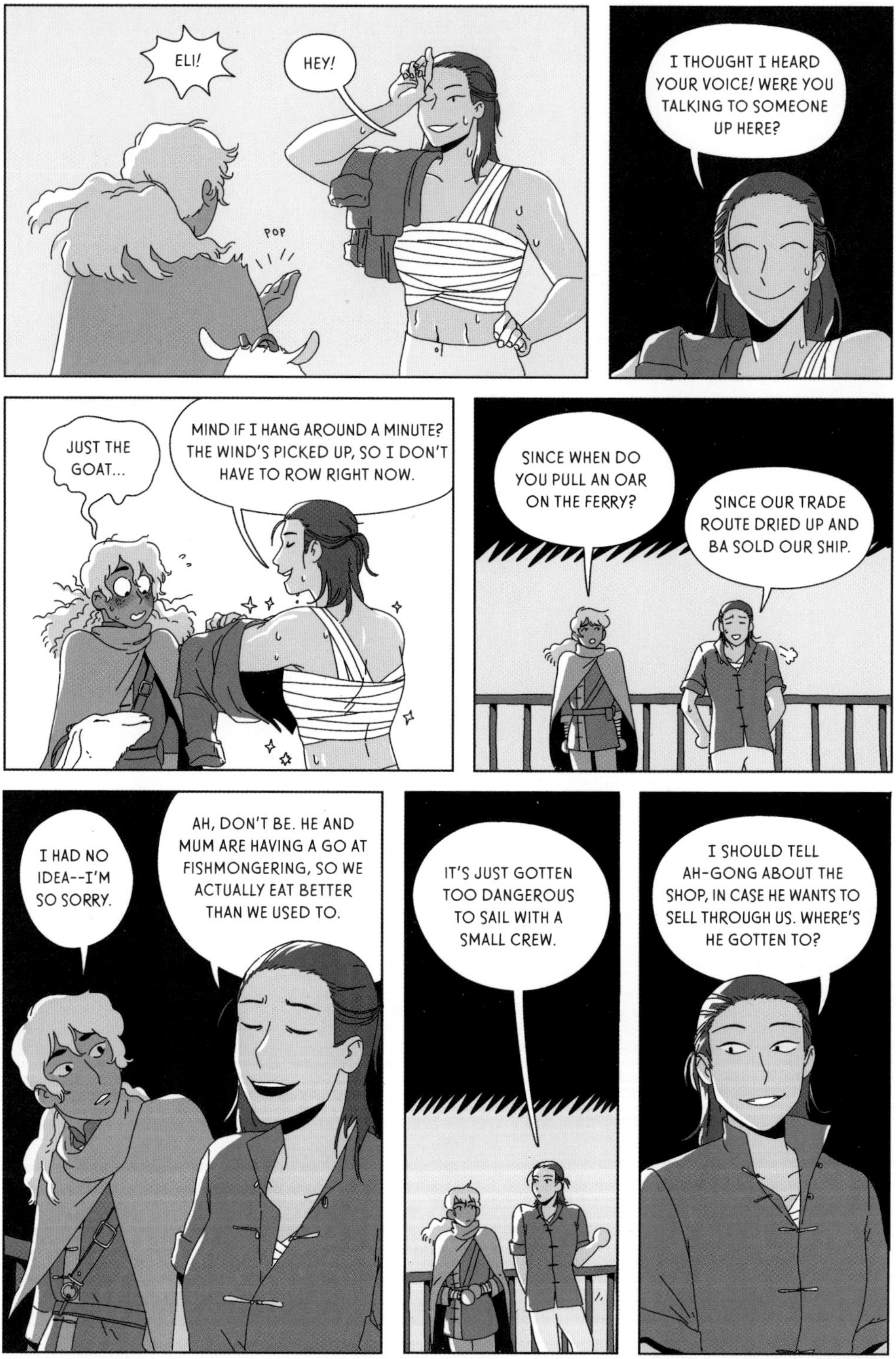
ELI!
HEY!
POP
I THOUGHT I HEARD YOUR VOICE! WERE YOU TALKING TO SOMEONE UP HERE?
JUST THE GOAT...
MIND IF I HANG AROUND A MINUTE? THE WIND'S PICKED UP, SO I DON'T HAVE TO ROW RIGHT NOW.
SINCE WHEN DO YOU PULL AN OAR ON THE FERRY?
SINCE OUR TRADE ROUTE DRIED UP AND BA SOLD OUR SHIP.
I HAD NO IDEA--I'M SO SORRY.
AH, DON'T BE. HE AND MUM ARE HAVING A GO AT FISHMONGERING, SO WE ACTUALLY EAT BETTER THAN WE USED TO.
IT'S JUST GOTTEN TOO DANGEROUS TO SAIL WITH A SMALL CREW.
I SHOULD TELL AH-GONG ABOUT THE SHOP, IN CASE HE WANTS TO SELL THROUGH US. WHERE'S HE GOTTEN TO?

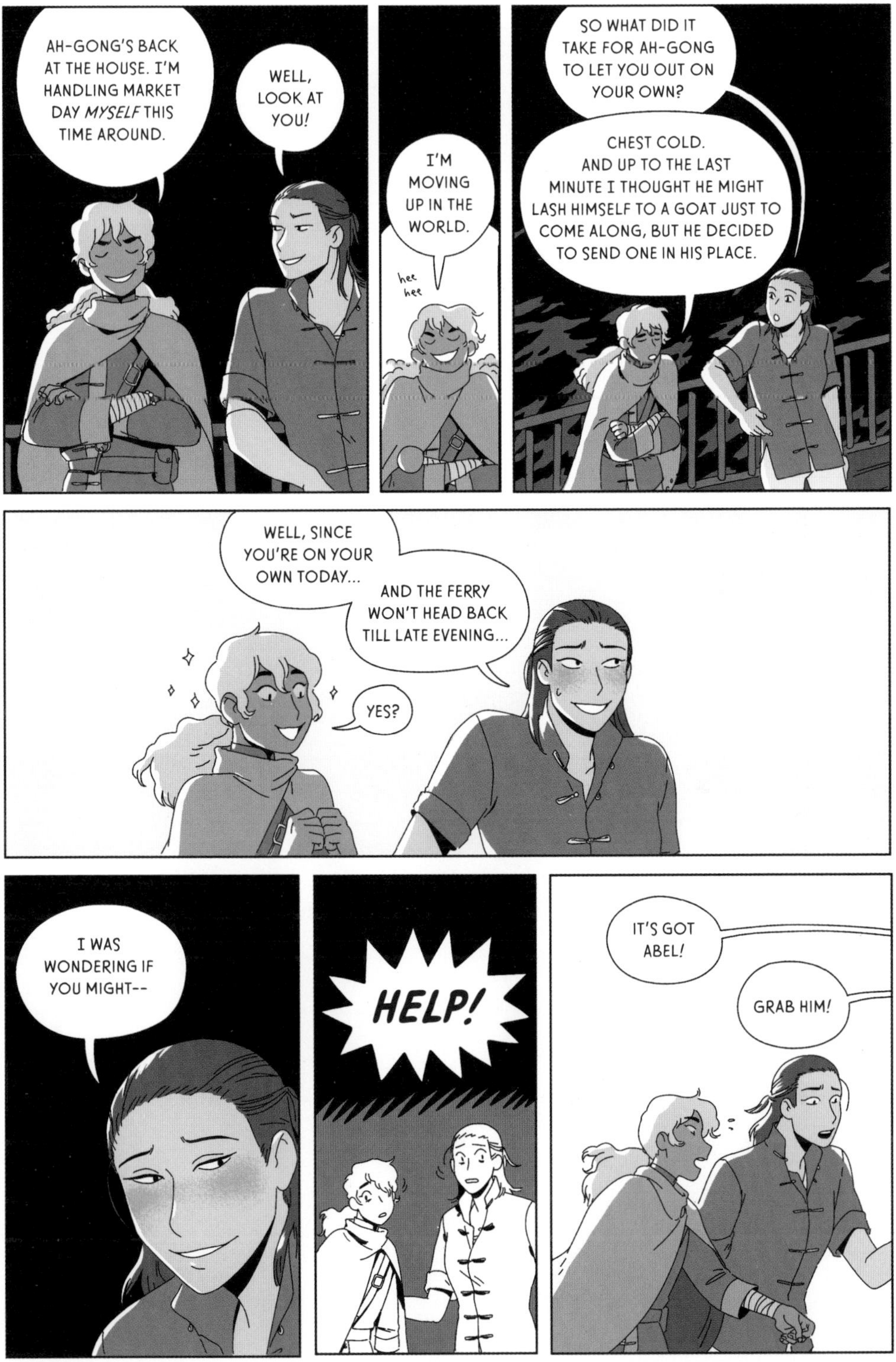
AH-GONG'S BACK AT THE HOUSE. I'M HANDLING MARKET DAY *MYSELF* THIS TIME AROUND.
WELL, LOOK AT YOU!
I'M MOVING UP IN THE WORLD.
hee hee
SO WHAT DID IT TAKE FOR AH-GONG TO LET YOU OUT ON YOUR OWN?
CHEST COLD. AND UP TO THE LAST MINUTE I THOUGHT HE MIGHT LASH HIMSELF TO A GOAT JUST TO COME ALONG, BUT HE DECIDED TO SEND ONE IN HIS PLACE.
WELL, SINCE YOU'RE ON YOUR OWN TODAY...
AND THE FERRY WON'T HEAD BACK TILL LATE EVENING...
YES?
I WAS WONDERING IF YOU MIGHT--
HELP!
IT'S GOT ABEL!
GRAB HIM!

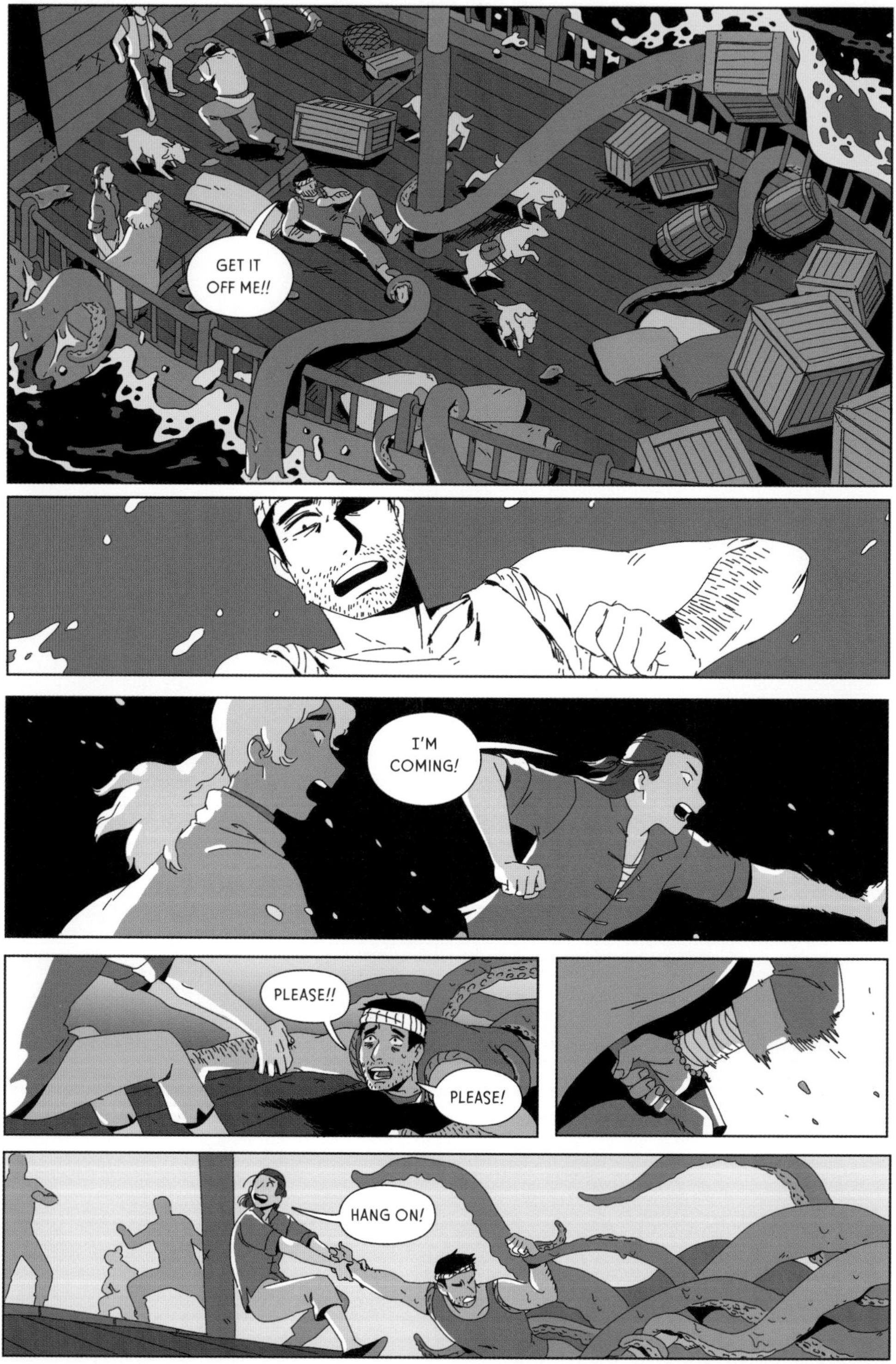
GET IT OFF ME!!
I'M COMING!
PLEASE!!
PLEASE!
HANG ON!

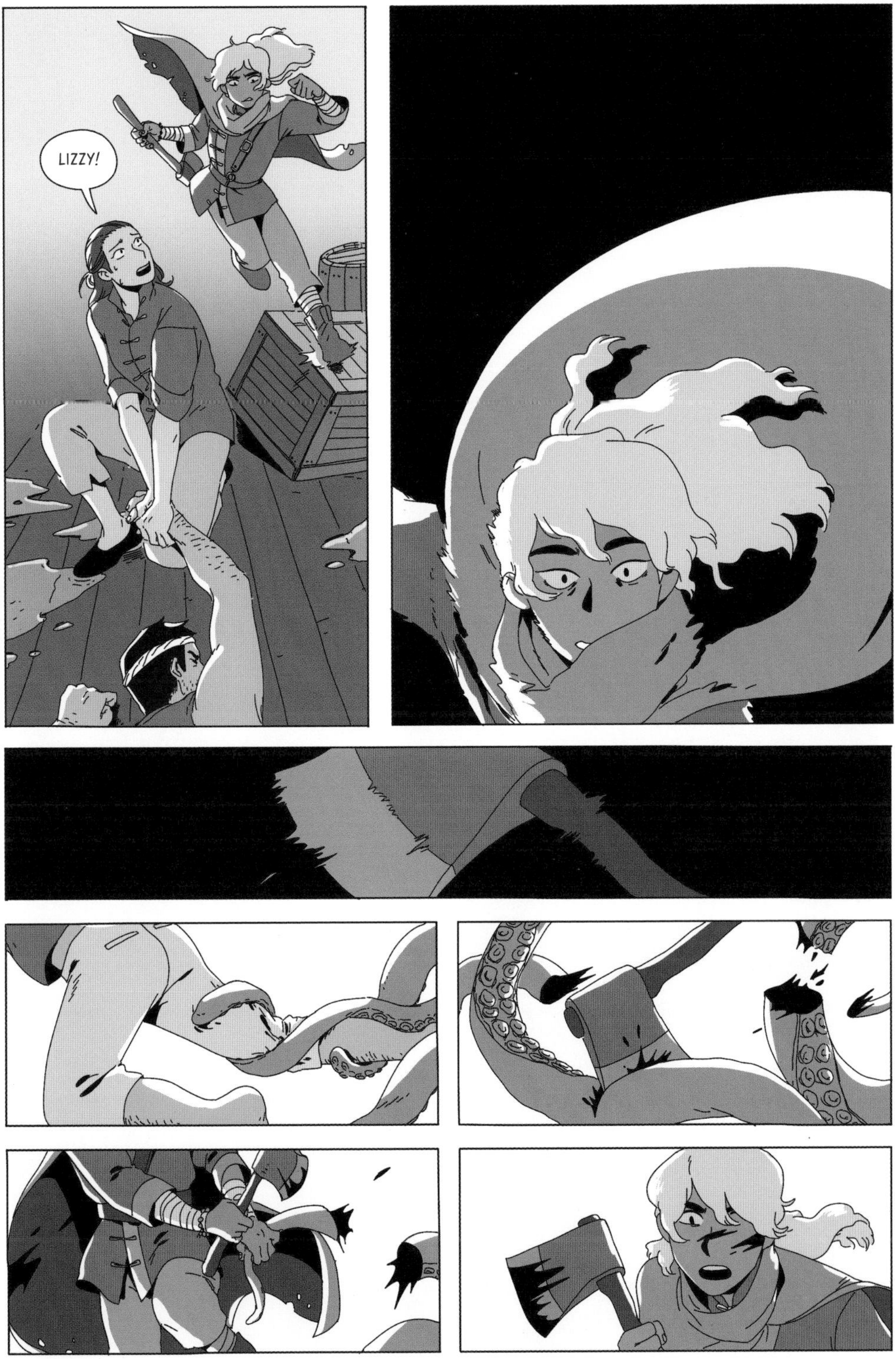
LIZZY!

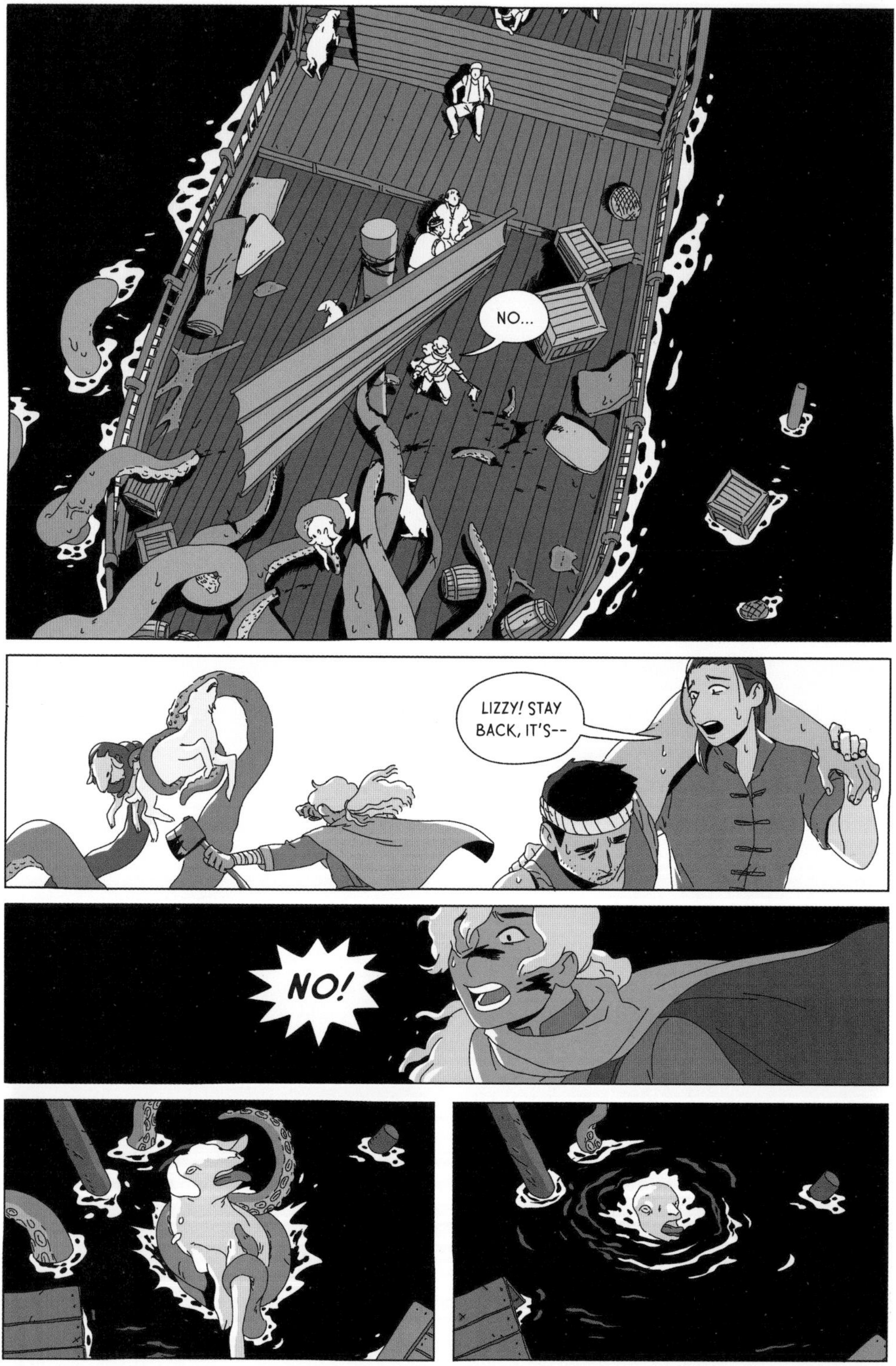
NO...
LIZZY! STAY BACK, IT'S--
NO!

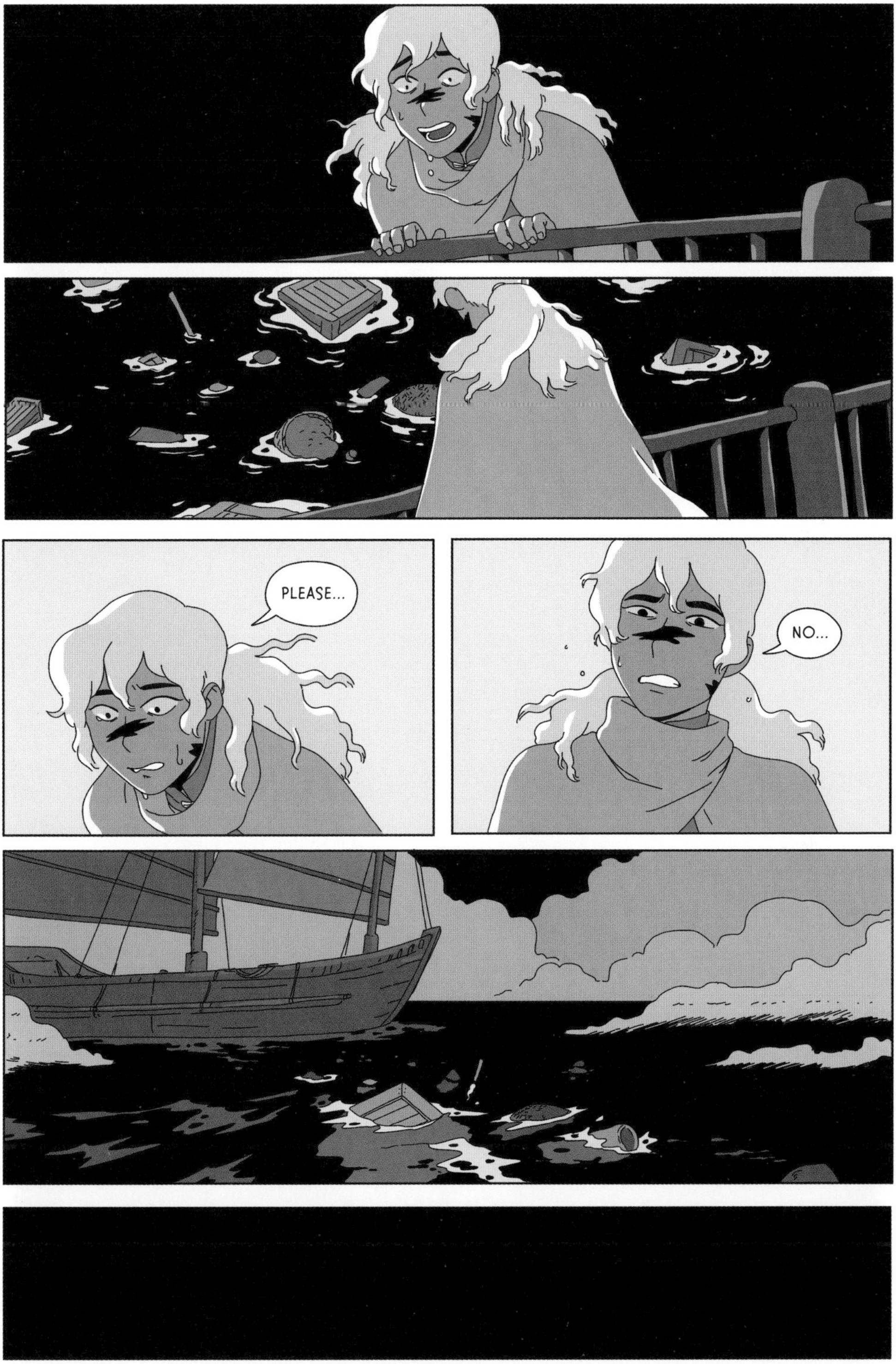
PLEASE...
NO...

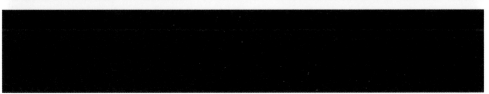

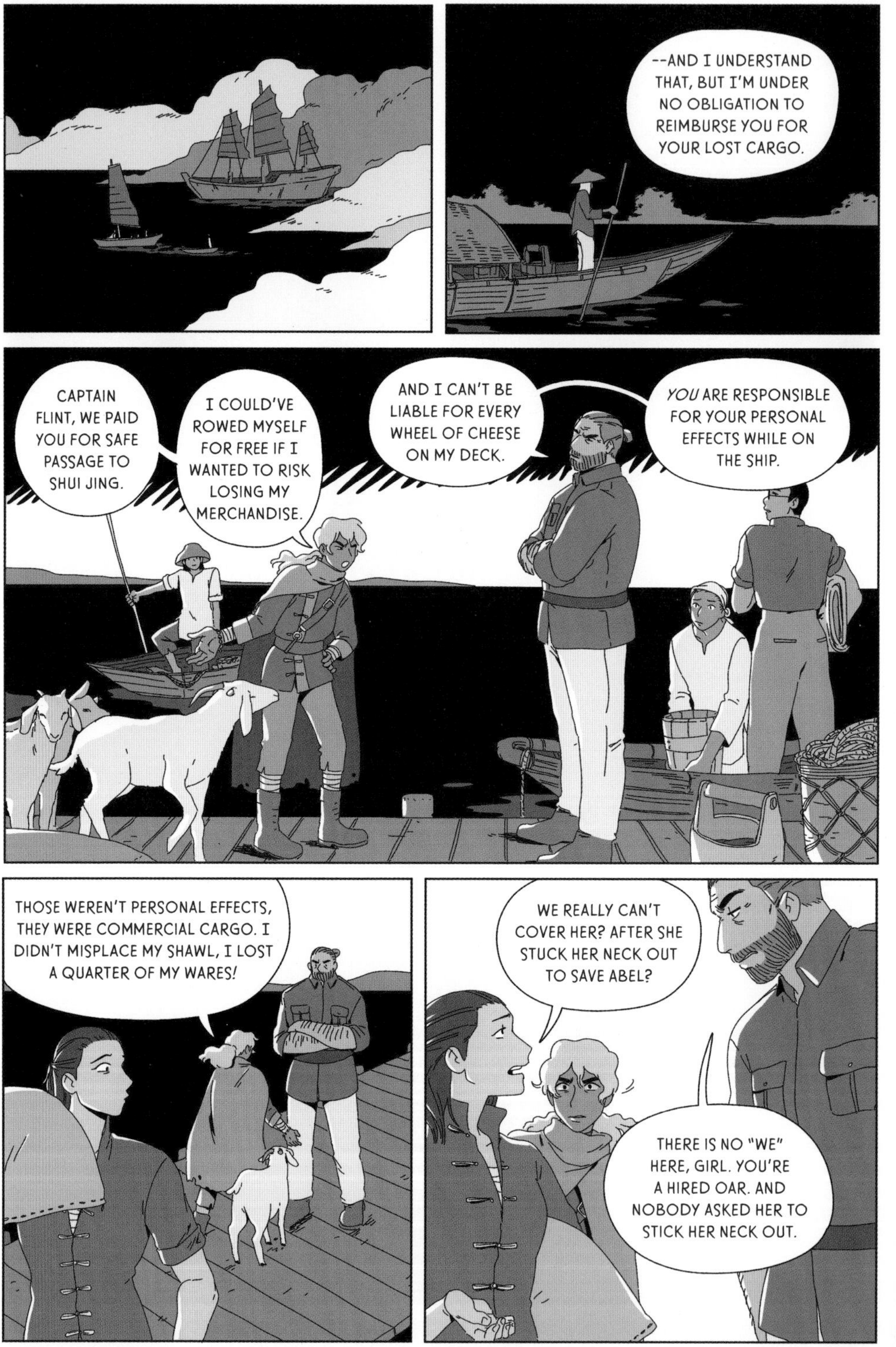
--AND I UNDERSTAND THAT, BUT I'M UNDER NO OBLIGATION TO REIMBURSE YOU FOR YOUR LOST CARGO.
CAPTAIN FLINT, WE PAID YOU FOR SAFE PASSAGE TO SHUI JING.
I COULD'VE ROWED MYSELF FOR FREE IF I WANTED TO RISK LOSING MY MERCHANDISE.
AND I CAN'T BE LIABLE FOR EVERY WHEEL OF CHEESE ON MY DECK.
*YOU* ARE RESPONSIBLE FOR YOUR PERSONAL EFFECTS WHILE ON THE SHIP.
THOSE WEREN'T PERSONAL EFFECTS, THEY WERE COMMERCIAL CARGO. I DIDN'T MISPLACE MY SHAWL, I LOST A QUARTER OF MY WARES!
WE REALLY CAN'T COVER HER? AFTER SHE STUCK HER NECK OUT TO SAVE ABEL?
THERE IS NO "WE" HERE, GIRL. YOU'RE A HIRED OAR. AND NOBODY ASKED HER TO STICK HER NECK OUT.

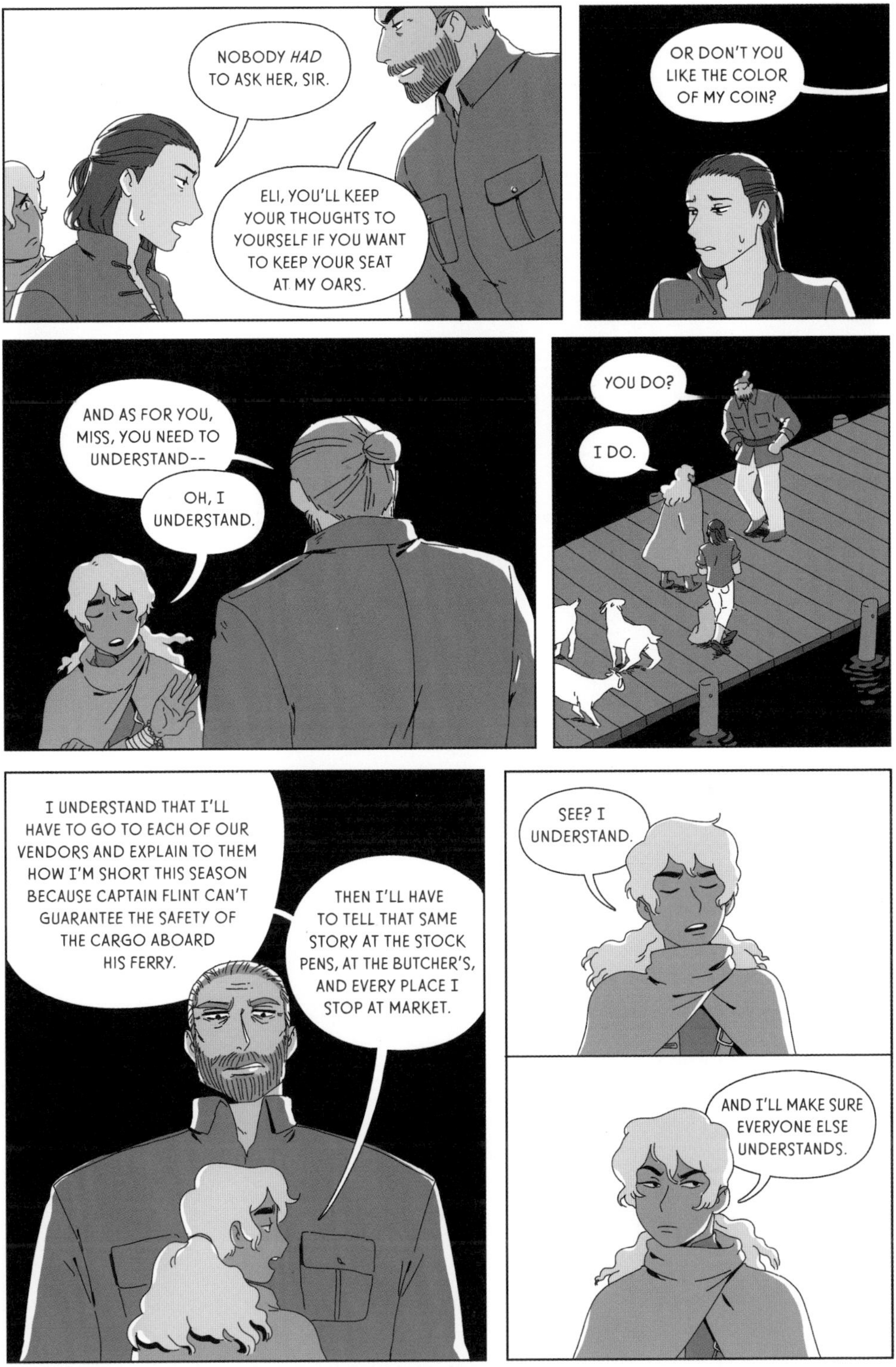
NOBODY *HAD* TO ASK HER, SIR.
ELI, YOU'LL KEEP YOUR THOUGHTS TO YOURSELF IF YOU WANT TO KEEP YOUR SEAT AT MY OARS.
OR DON'T YOU LIKE THE COLOR OF MY COIN?
AND AS FOR YOU, MISS, YOU NEED TO UNDERSTAND--
OH, I UNDERSTAND.
YOU DO?
I DO.
I UNDERSTAND THAT I'LL HAVE TO GO TO EACH OF OUR VENDORS AND EXPLAIN TO THEM HOW I'M SHORT THIS SEASON BECAUSE CAPTAIN FLINT CAN'T GUARANTEE THE SAFETY OF THE CARGO ABOARD HIS FERRY.
THEN I'LL HAVE TO TELL THAT SAME STORY AT THE STOCK PENS, AT THE BUTCHER'S, AND EVERY PLACE I STOP AT MARKET.
SEE? I UNDERSTAND.
AND I'LL MAKE SURE EVERYONE ELSE UNDERSTANDS.

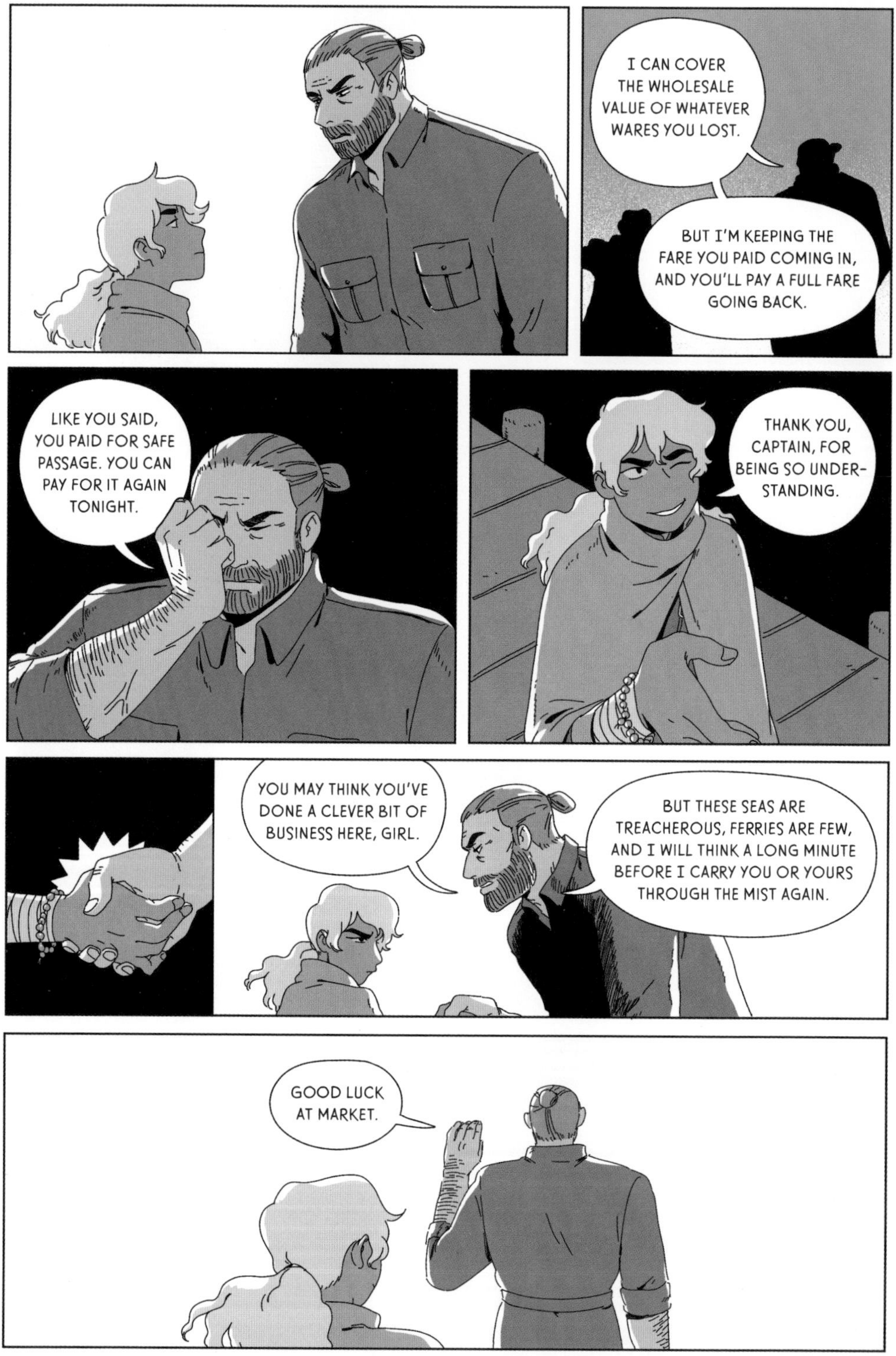
I CAN COVER THE WHOLESALE VALUE OF WHATEVER WARES YOU LOST.
BUT I'M KEEPING THE FARE YOU PAID COMING IN, AND YOU'LL PAY A FULL FARE GOING BACK.
LIKE YOU SAID, YOU PAID FOR SAFE PASSAGE. YOU CAN PAY FOR IT AGAIN TONIGHT.
THANK YOU, CAPTAIN, FOR BEING SO UNDER-STANDING.
YOU MAY THINK YOU'VE DONE A CLEVER BIT OF BUSINESS HERE, GIRL.
BUT THESE SEAS ARE TREACHEROUS, FERRIES ARE FEW, AND I WILL THINK A LONG MINUTE BEFORE I CARRY YOU OR YOURS THROUGH THE MIST AGAIN.
GOOD LUCK AT MARKET.

...FOURTEEN, FIFTEEN...

...SIXTEEN DINARS FOR AH-GONG, TO GET US THROUGH WINTER.

AND THE REST...

...ALL MINE.

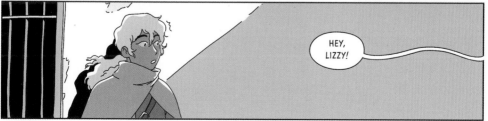

HEY, LIZZY!

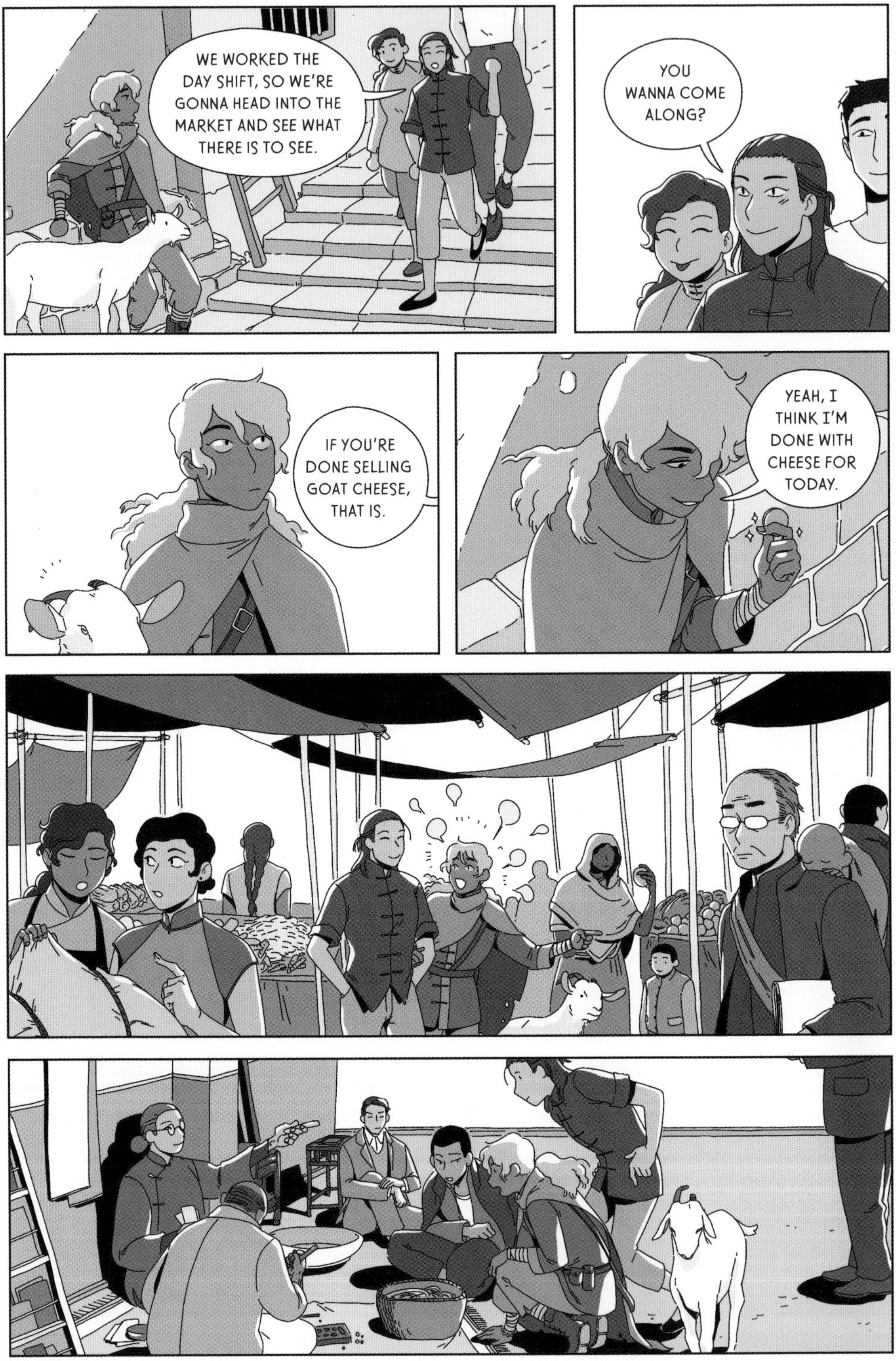
WE WORKED THE DAY SHIFT, SO WE'RE GONNA HEAD INTO THE MARKET AND SEE WHAT THERE IS TO SEE.
YOU WANNA COME ALONG?
IF YOU'RE DONE SELLING GOAT CHEESE, THAT IS.
YEAH, I THINK I'M DONE WITH CHEESE FOR TODAY.

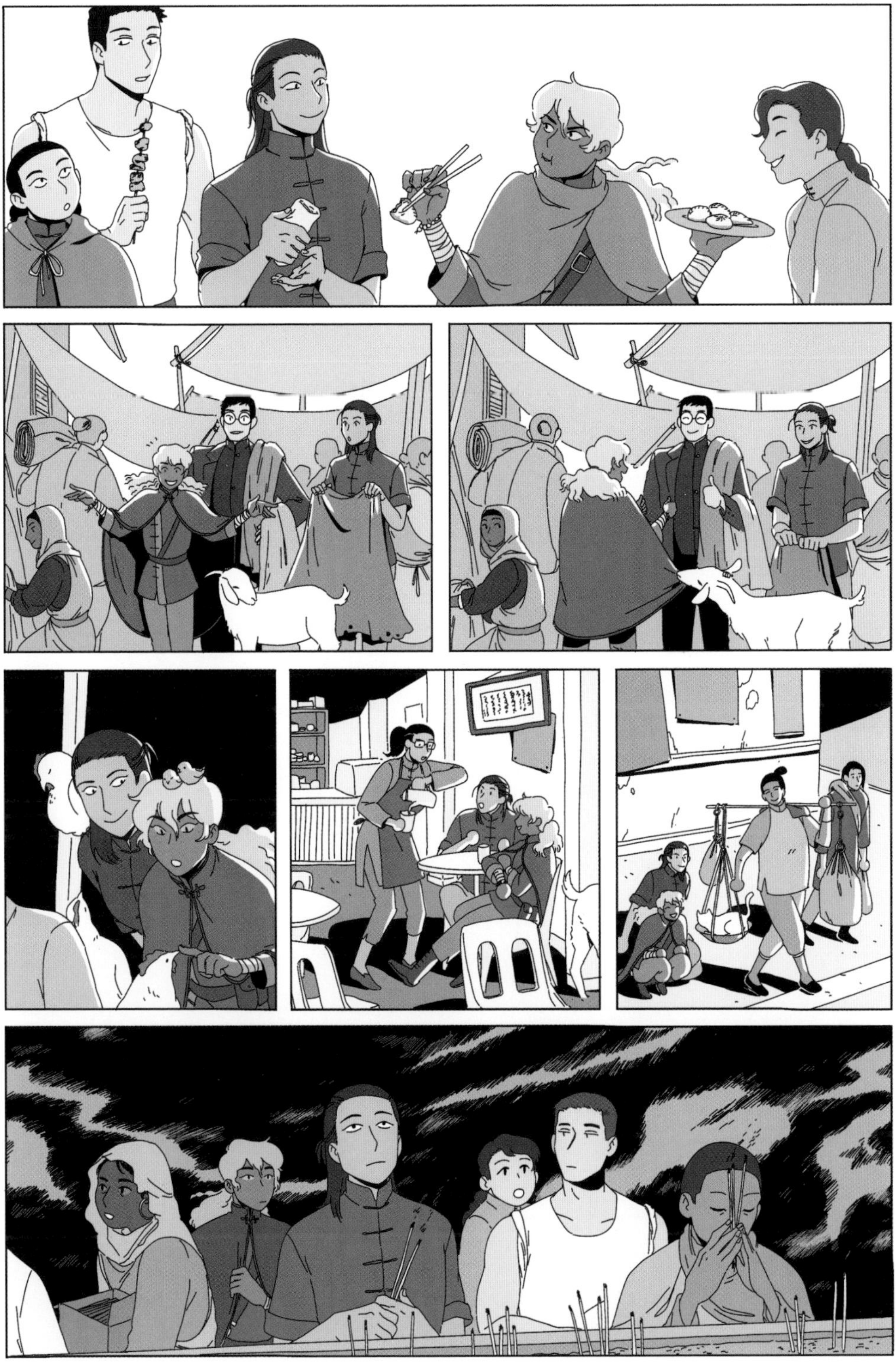

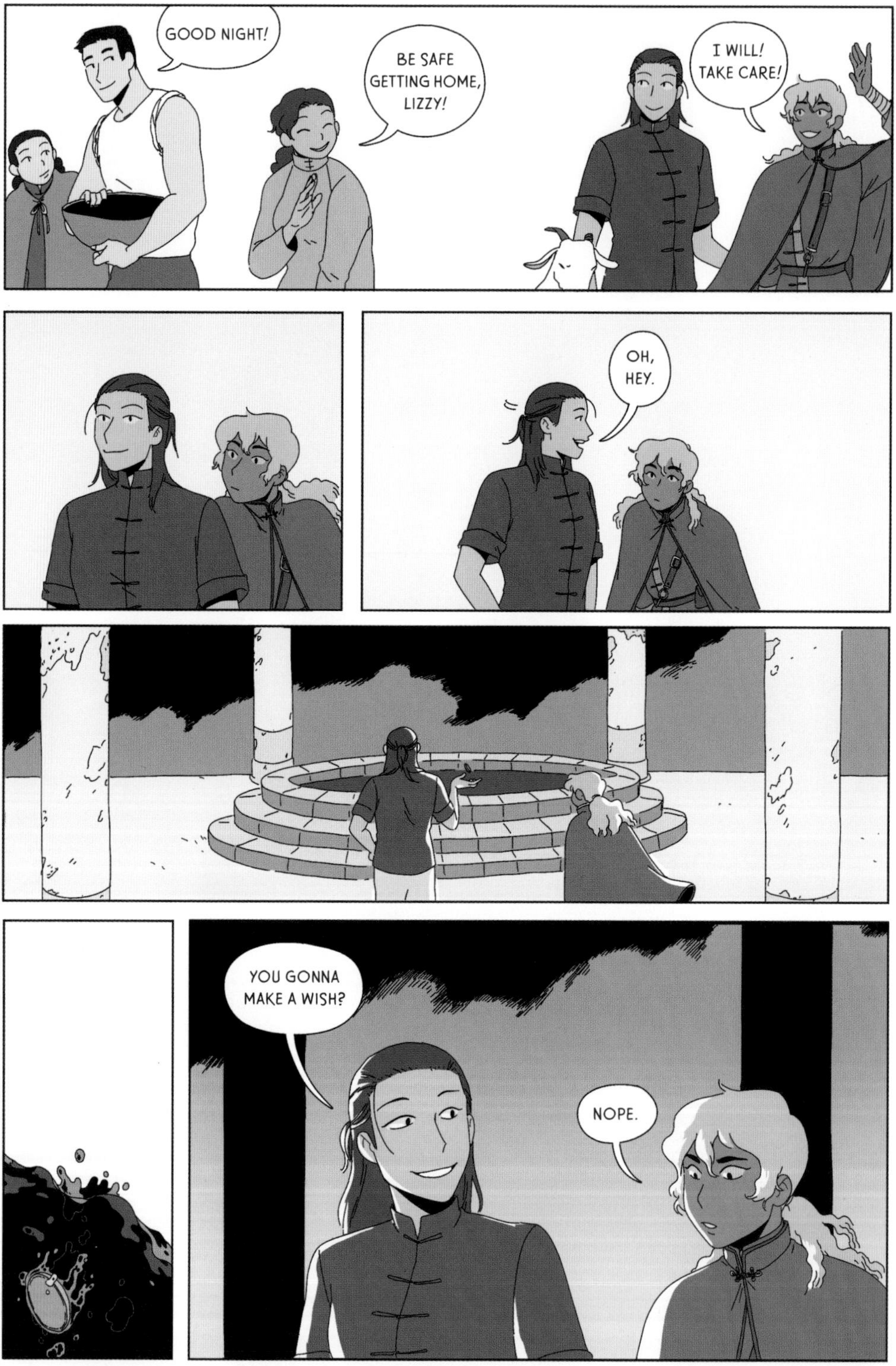
GOOD NIGHT!
BE SAFE GETTING HOME, LIZZY!
I WILL! TAKE CARE!
OH, HEY.
YOU GONNA MAKE A WISH?
NOPE.

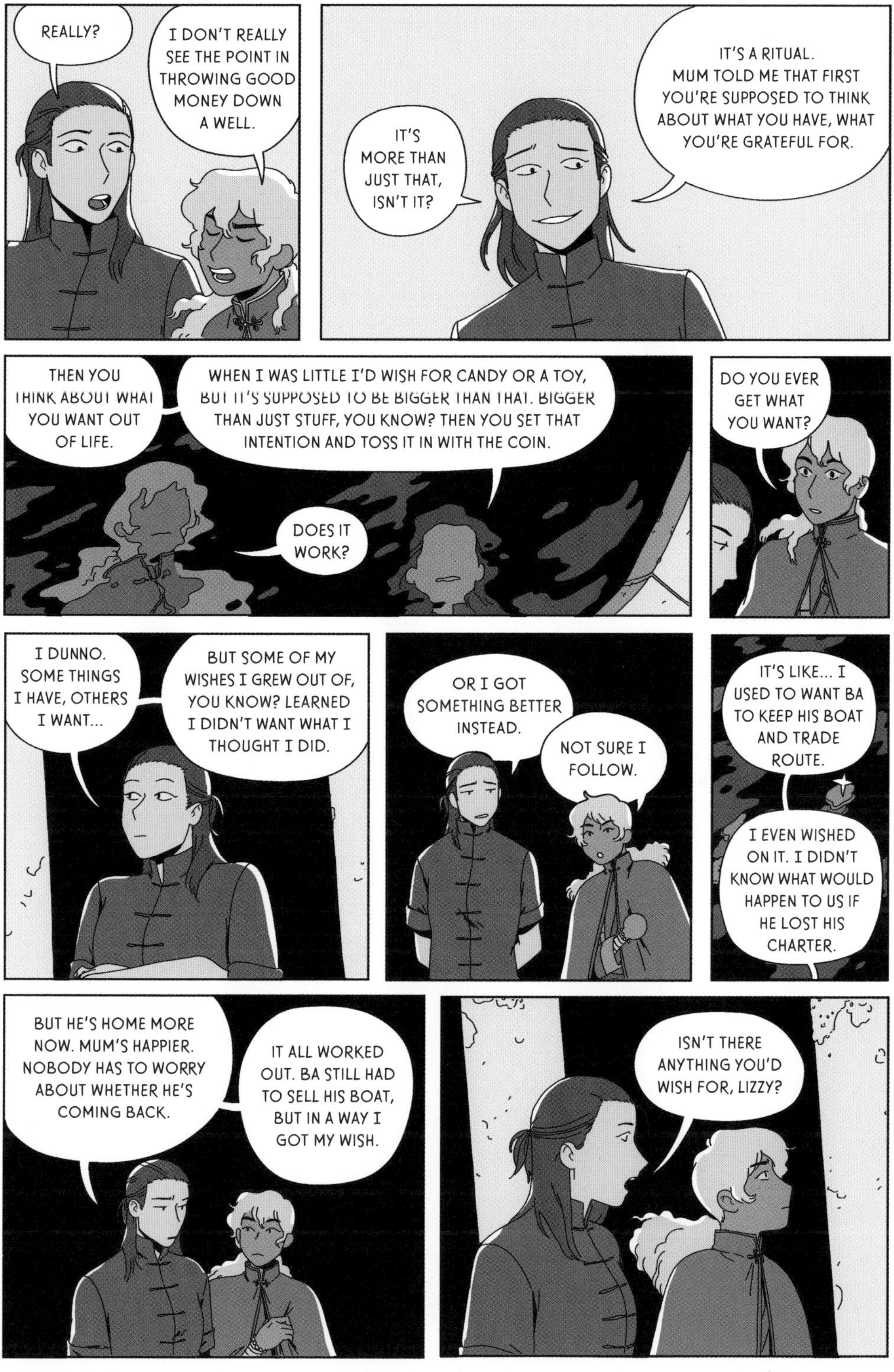
REALLY?
I DON'T REALLY SEE THE POINT IN THROWING GOOD MONEY DOWN A WELL.
IT'S MORE THAN JUST THAT, ISN'T IT?
IT'S A RITUAL. MUM TOLD ME THAT FIRST YOU'RE SUPPOSED TO THINK ABOUT WHAT YOU HAVE, WHAT YOU'RE GRATEFUL FOR.
THEN YOU THINK ABOUT WHAT YOU WANT OUT OF LIFE.
WHEN I WAS LITTLE I'D WISH FOR CANDY OR A TOY, BUT IT'S SUPPOSED TO BE BIGGER THAN THAT. BIGGER THAN JUST STUFF, YOU KNOW? THEN YOU SET THAT INTENTION AND TOSS IT IN WITH THE COIN.
DOES IT WORK?
DO YOU EVER GET WHAT YOU WANT?
I DUNNO. SOME THINGS I HAVE, OTHERS I WANT...
BUT SOME OF MY WISHES I GREW OUT OF, YOU KNOW? LEARNED I DIDN'T WANT WHAT I THOUGHT I DID.
OR I GOT SOMETHING BETTER INSTEAD.
NOT SURE I FOLLOW.
IT'S LIKE... I USED TO WANT BA TO KEEP HIS BOAT AND TRADE ROUTE.
I EVEN WISHED ON IT. I DIDN'T KNOW WHAT WOULD HAPPEN TO US IF HE LOST HIS CHARTER.
BUT HE'S HOME MORE NOW. MUM'S HAPPIER. NOBODY HAS TO WORRY ABOUT WHETHER HE'S COMING BACK.
IT ALL WORKED OUT. BA STILL HAD TO SELL HIS BOAT, BUT IN A WAY I GOT MY WISH.
ISN'T THERE ANYTHING YOU'D WISH FOR, LIZZY?

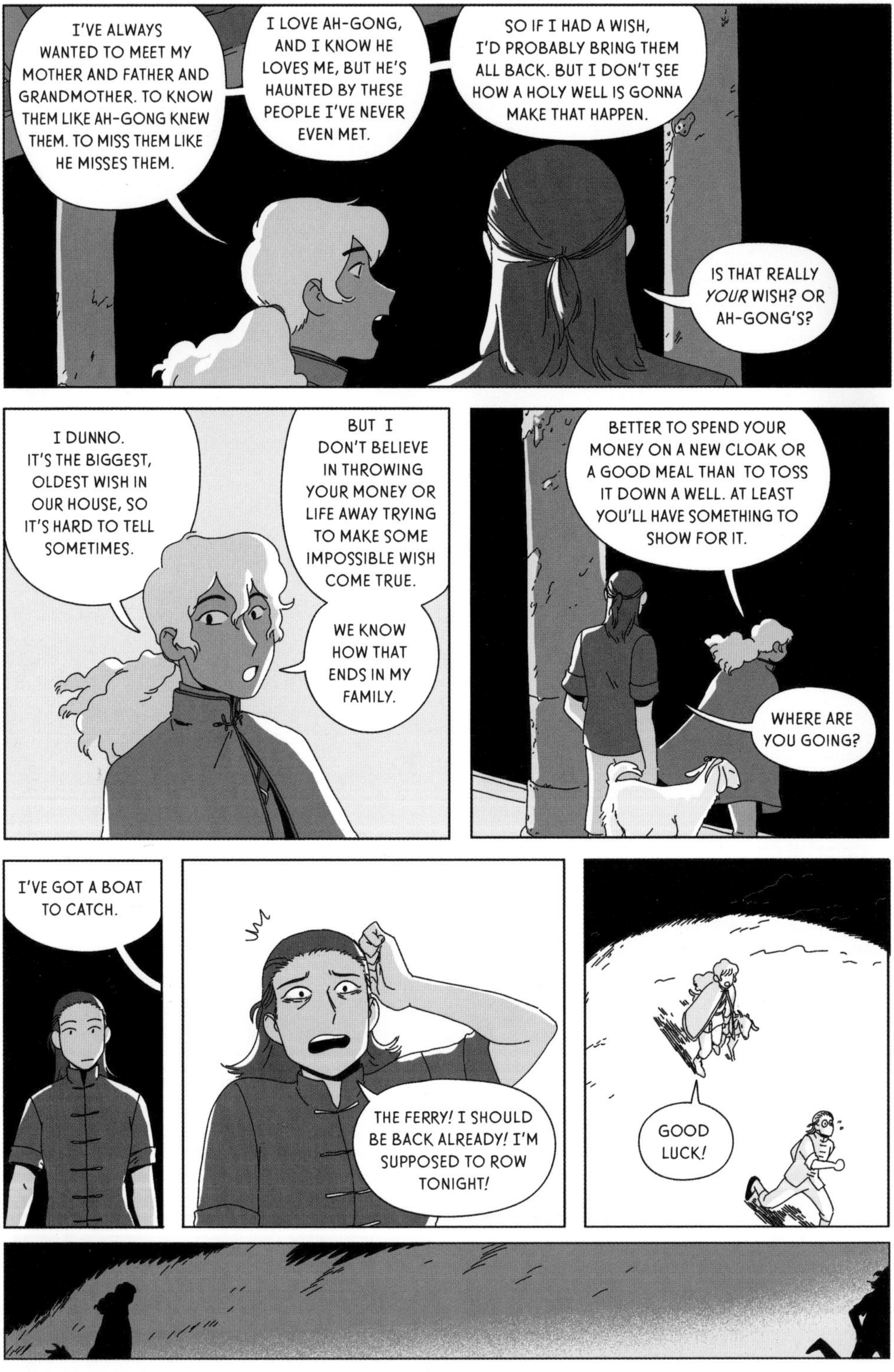
I'VE ALWAYS WANTED TO MEET MY MOTHER AND FATHER AND GRANDMOTHER. TO KNOW THEM LIKE AH-GONG KNEW THEM. TO MISS THEM LIKE HE MISSES THEM.
I LOVE AH-GONG, AND I KNOW HE LOVES ME, BUT HE'S HAUNTED BY THESE PEOPLE I'VE NEVER EVEN MET.
SO IF I HAD A WISH, I'D PROBABLY BRING THEM ALL BACK. BUT I DON'T SEE HOW A HOLY WELL IS GONNA MAKE THAT HAPPEN.
IS THAT REALLY *YOUR* WISH? OR AH-GONG'S?
I DUNNO. IT'S THE BIGGEST, OLDEST WISH IN OUR HOUSE, SO IT'S HARD TO TELL SOMETIMES.
BUT I DON'T BELIEVE IN THROWING YOUR MONEY OR LIFE AWAY TRYING TO MAKE SOME IMPOSSIBLE WISH COME TRUE.
WE KNOW HOW THAT ENDS IN MY FAMILY.
BETTER TO SPEND YOUR MONEY ON A NEW CLOAK OR A GOOD MEAL THAN TO TOSS IT DOWN A WELL. AT LEAST YOU'LL HAVE SOMETHING TO SHOW FOR IT.
WHERE ARE YOU GOING?
I'VE GOT A BOAT TO CATCH.
THE FERRY! I SHOULD BE BACK ALREADY! I'M SUPPOSED TO ROW TONIGHT!
GOOD LUCK!

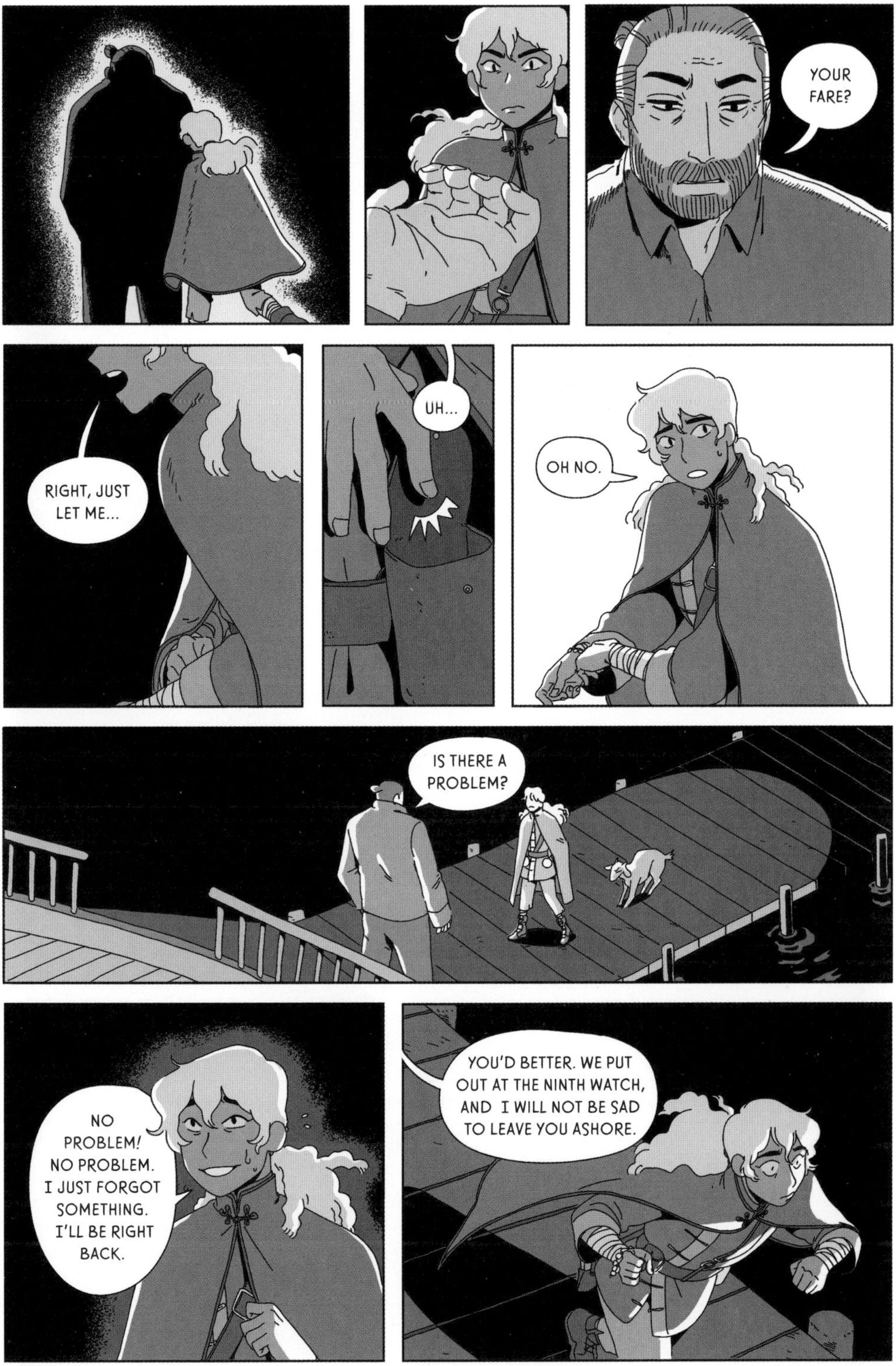
YOUR FARE?
RIGHT, JUST LET ME...
UH...
OH NO.
IS THERE A PROBLEM?
NO PROBLEM! NO PROBLEM. I JUST FORGOT SOMETHING. I'LL BE RIGHT BACK.
YOU'D BETTER. WE PUT OUT AT THE NINTH WATCH, AND I WILL NOT BE SAD TO LEAVE YOU ASHORE.

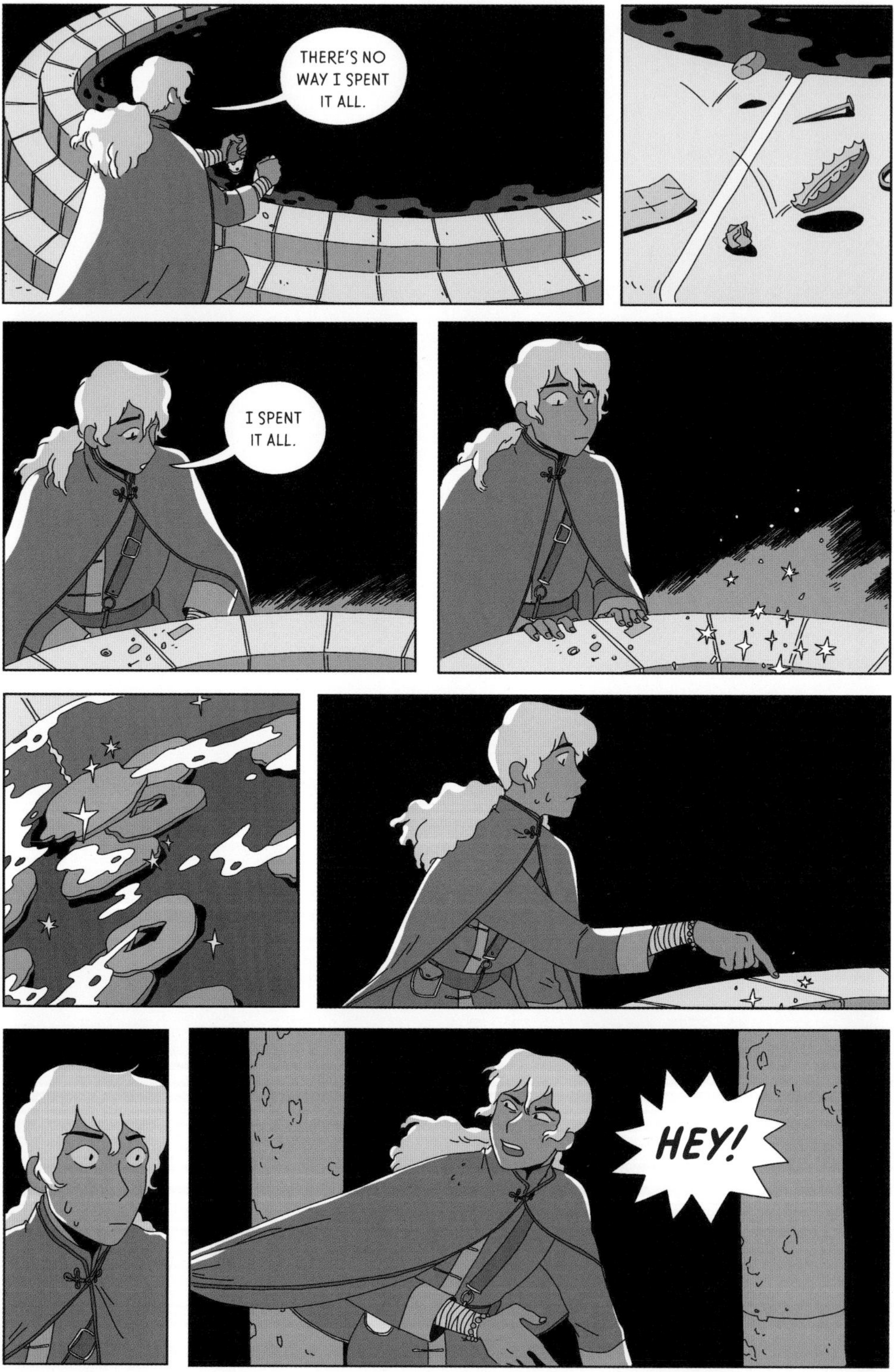
THERE'S NO WAY I SPENT IT ALL.
I SPENT IT ALL.
HEY!

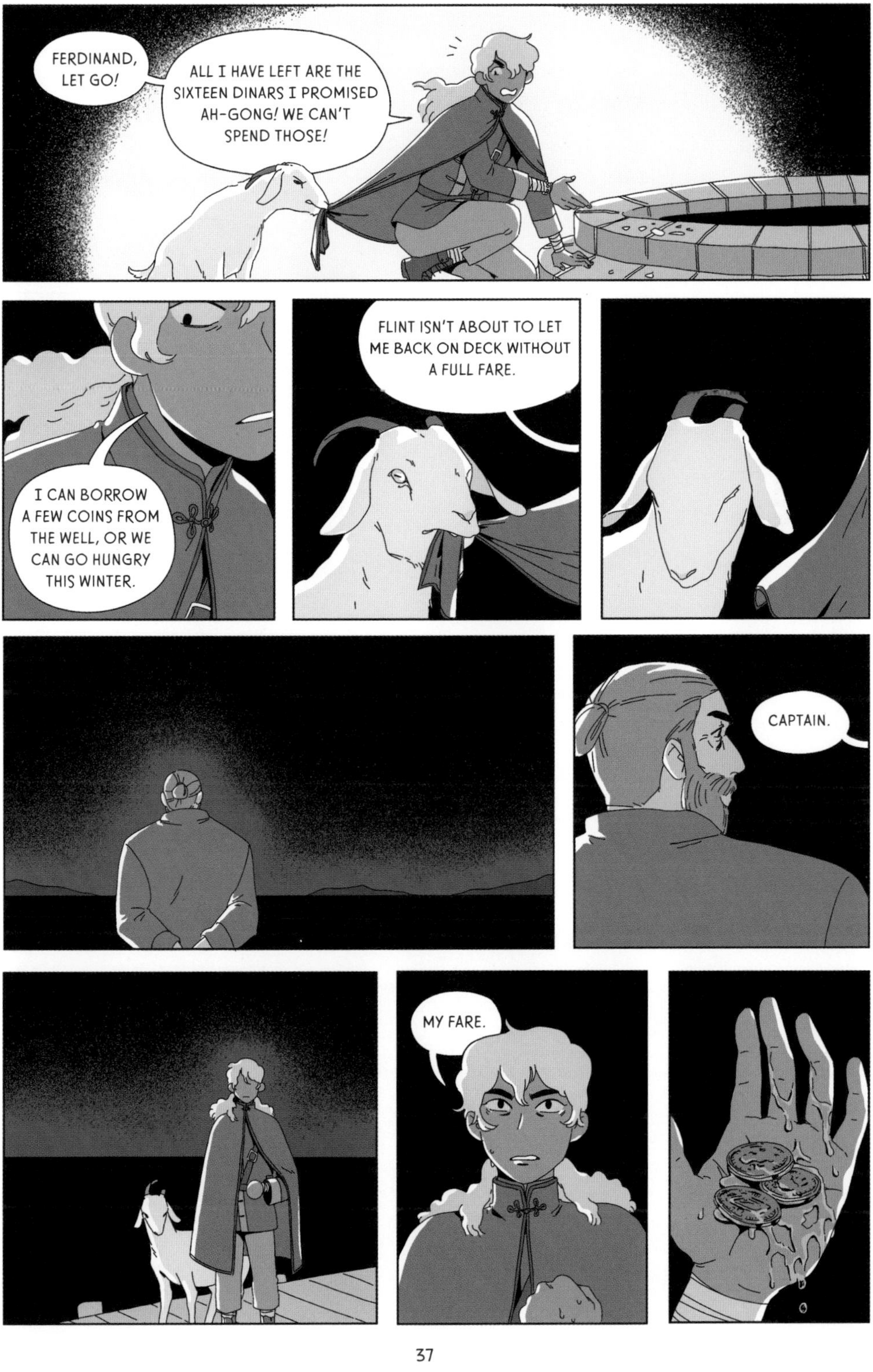
FERDINAND, LET GO!
ALL I HAVE LEFT ARE THE SIXTEEN DINARS I PROMISED AH-GONG! WE CAN'T SPEND THOSE!
I CAN BORROW A FEW COINS FROM THE WELL, OR WE CAN GO HUNGRY THIS WINTER.
FLINT ISN'T ABOUT TO LET ME BACK ON DECK WITHOUT A FULL FARE.
CAPTAIN.
MY FARE.

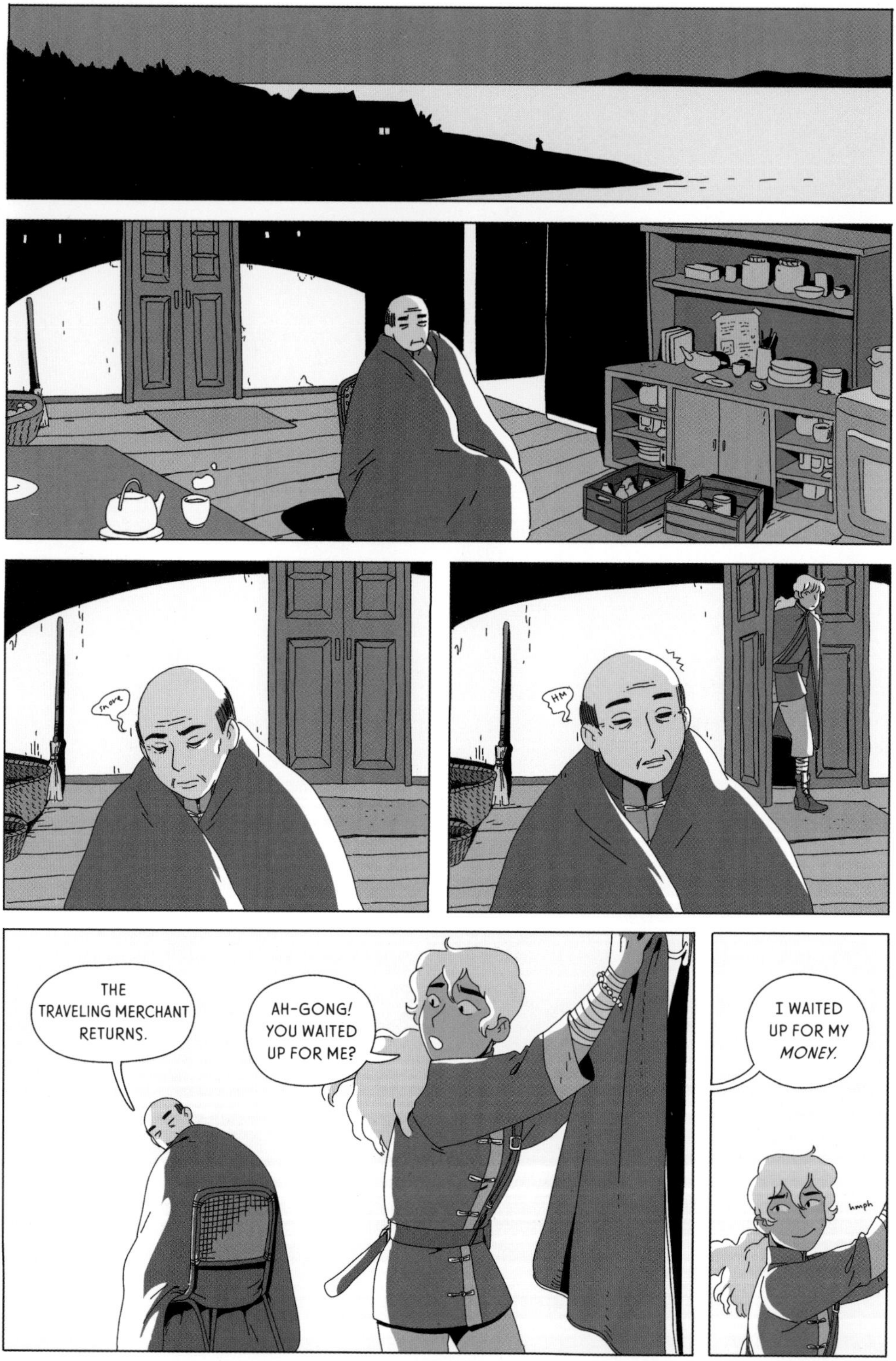
snore
HM
THE TRAVELING MERCHANT RETURNS.
AH-GONG! YOU WAITED UP FOR ME?
I WAITED UP FOR MY *MONEY.*
hmph

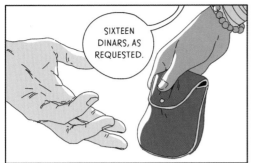

SIXTEEN DINARS, AS REQUESTED.

NICELY DONE. AND *JUST* THE SIXTEEN DINARS, HMM?

HAHA, WELL, UH, *ACTUALLY--*

IT'S FINE, LIZZY. I HOPE YOU HAD A WONDERFUL TIME.

YOU KNOW? I REALLY DID. THANK YOU, AH-GONG.

YOU EARNED IT. EVERYONE SHOULD GET TO WASTE A LITTLE MONEY AT THE FAIR WHEN THEY'RE YOUNG.

AND THAT CLOAK LOOKS NICE ON YOU.

RIGHT?! I LOOK AMAZING. AND IT'S NOT JUST THE COLOR, IT'S LIKE THEY CUT IT JUST FOR ME.

IT'S VERY FETCHING. I'M SURE YOU GOT LOTS OF COMPLIMENTS. WHAT DID YOU EAT? DID THEY HAVE THE FRIED BUNS AGAIN THIS YEAR?

THEY DID! THE ONES WITH THE PORK AND SOME NEW SWEET ONES.

WHO DID YOU EAT THEM WITH?

JUST... SOME FRIENDS. THE USUAL KIDS.

AND ELI?

MAYBE. YES.

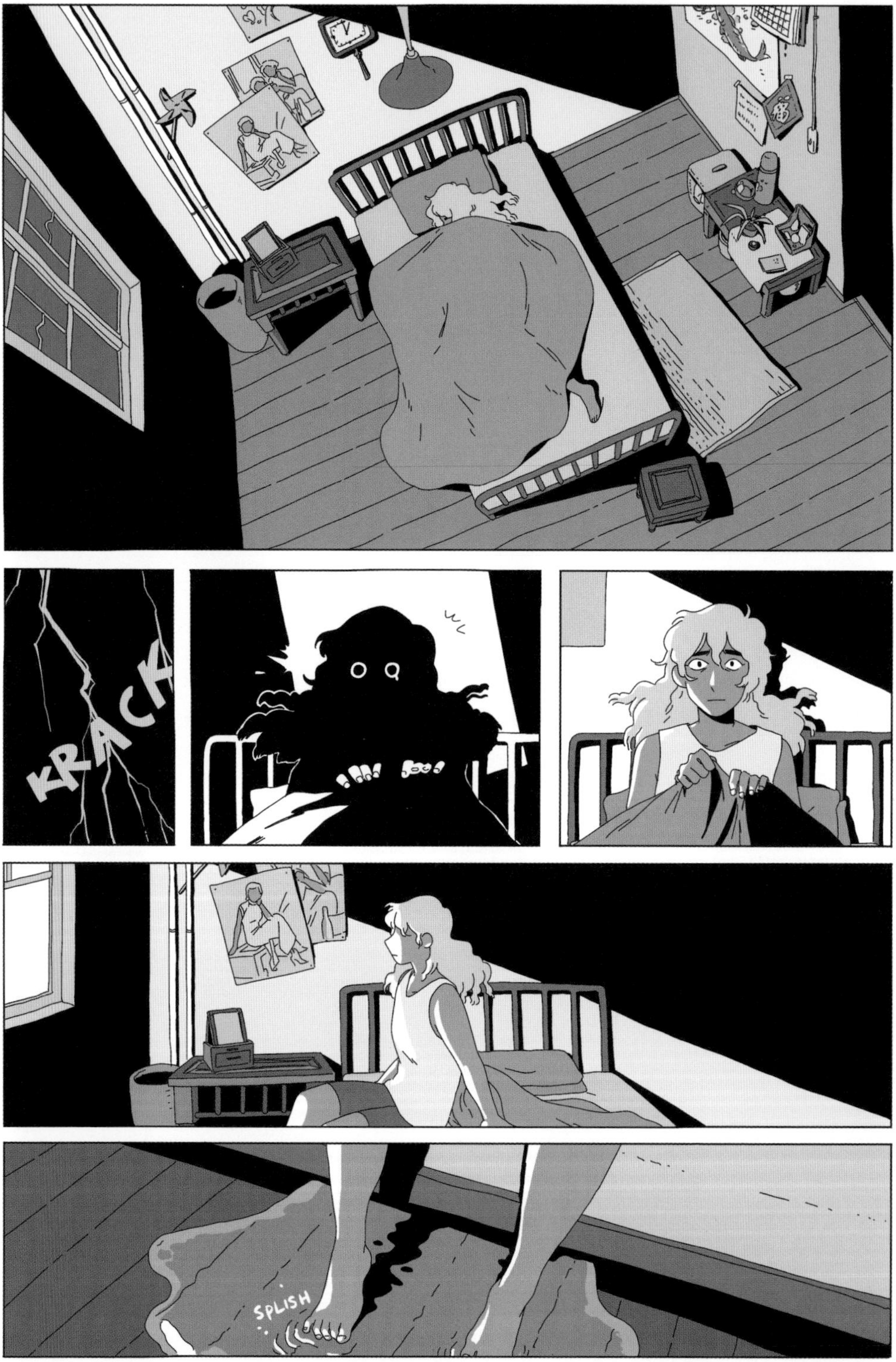
KRACK
SPLISH

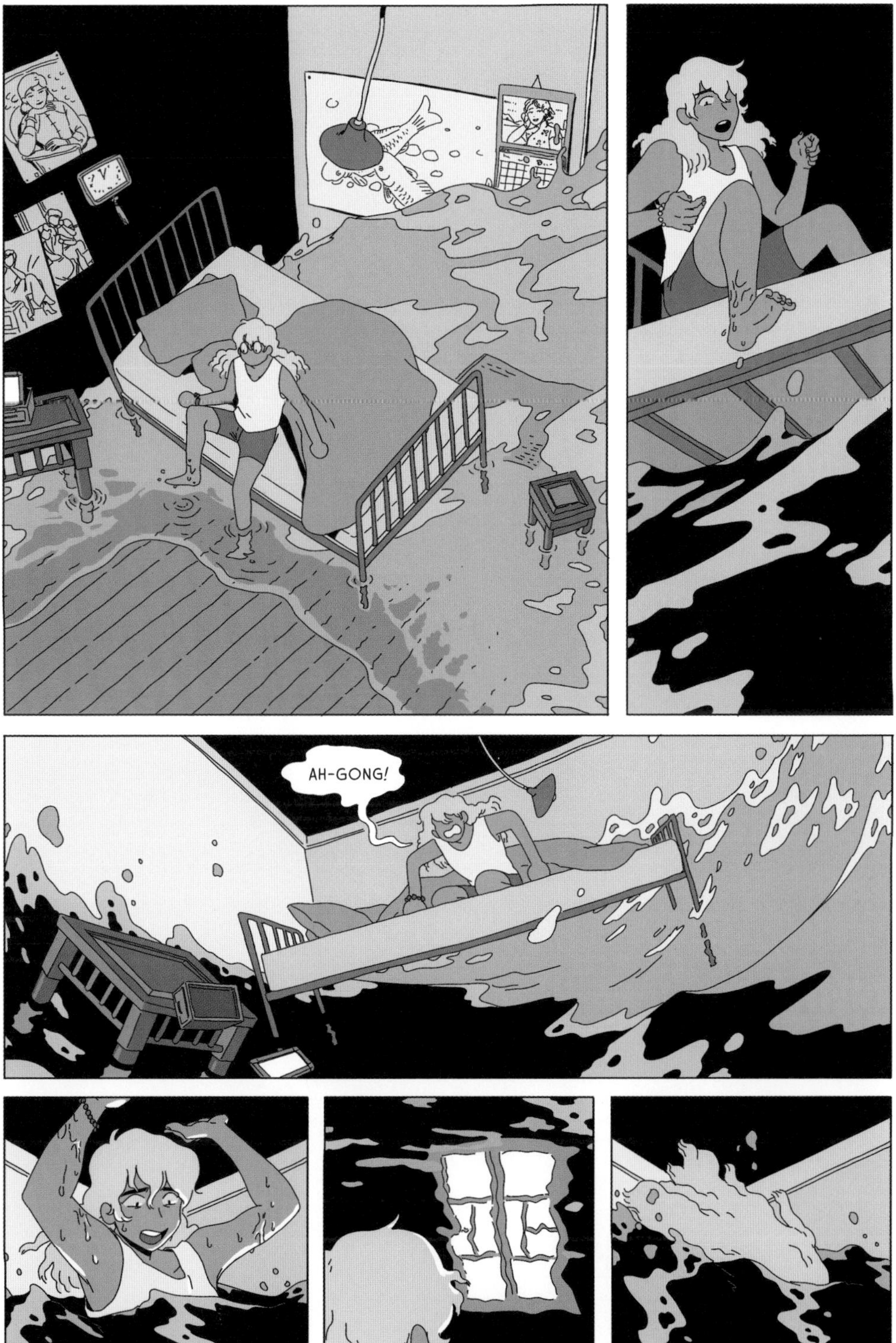
AH-GONG!

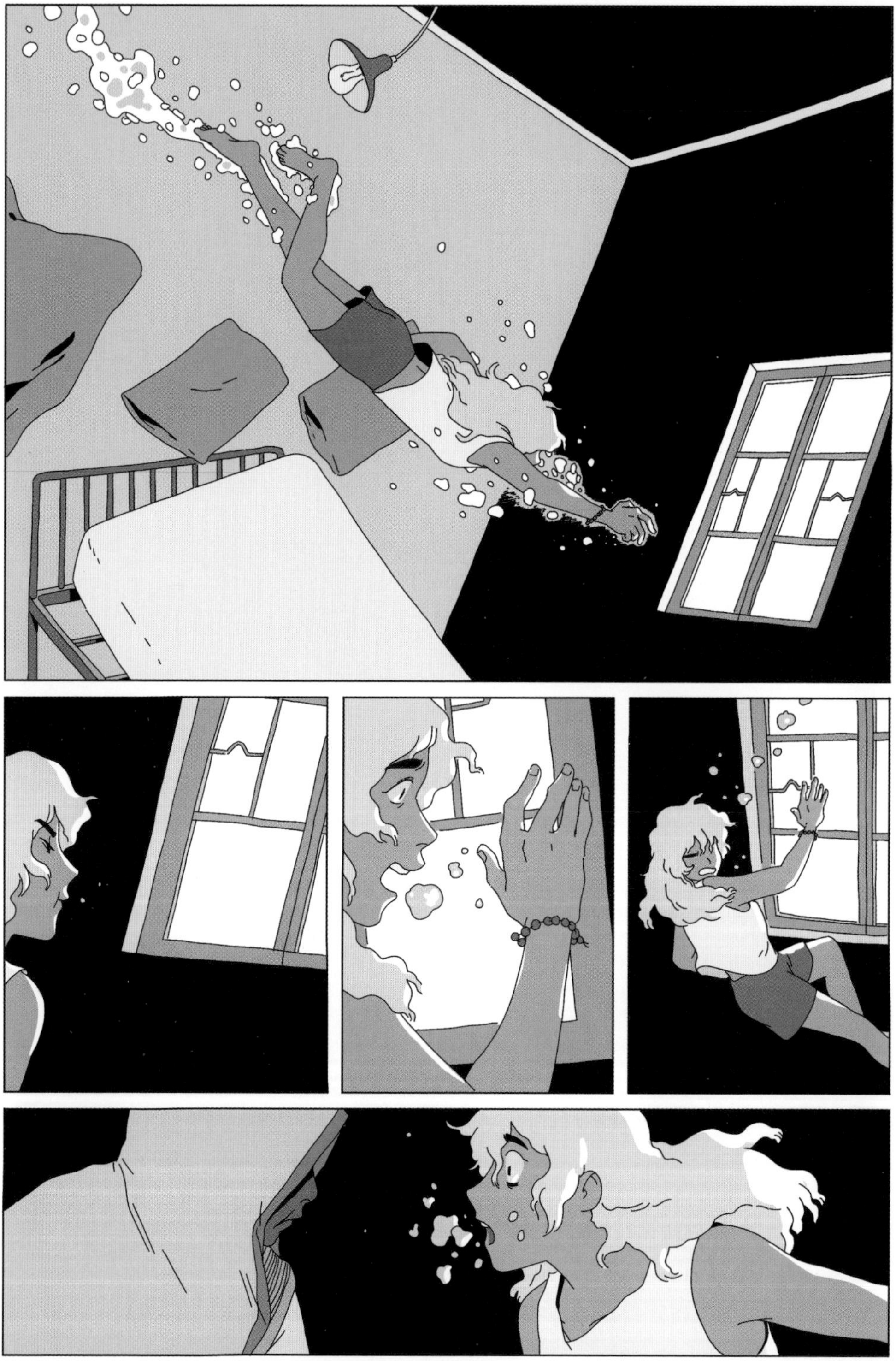

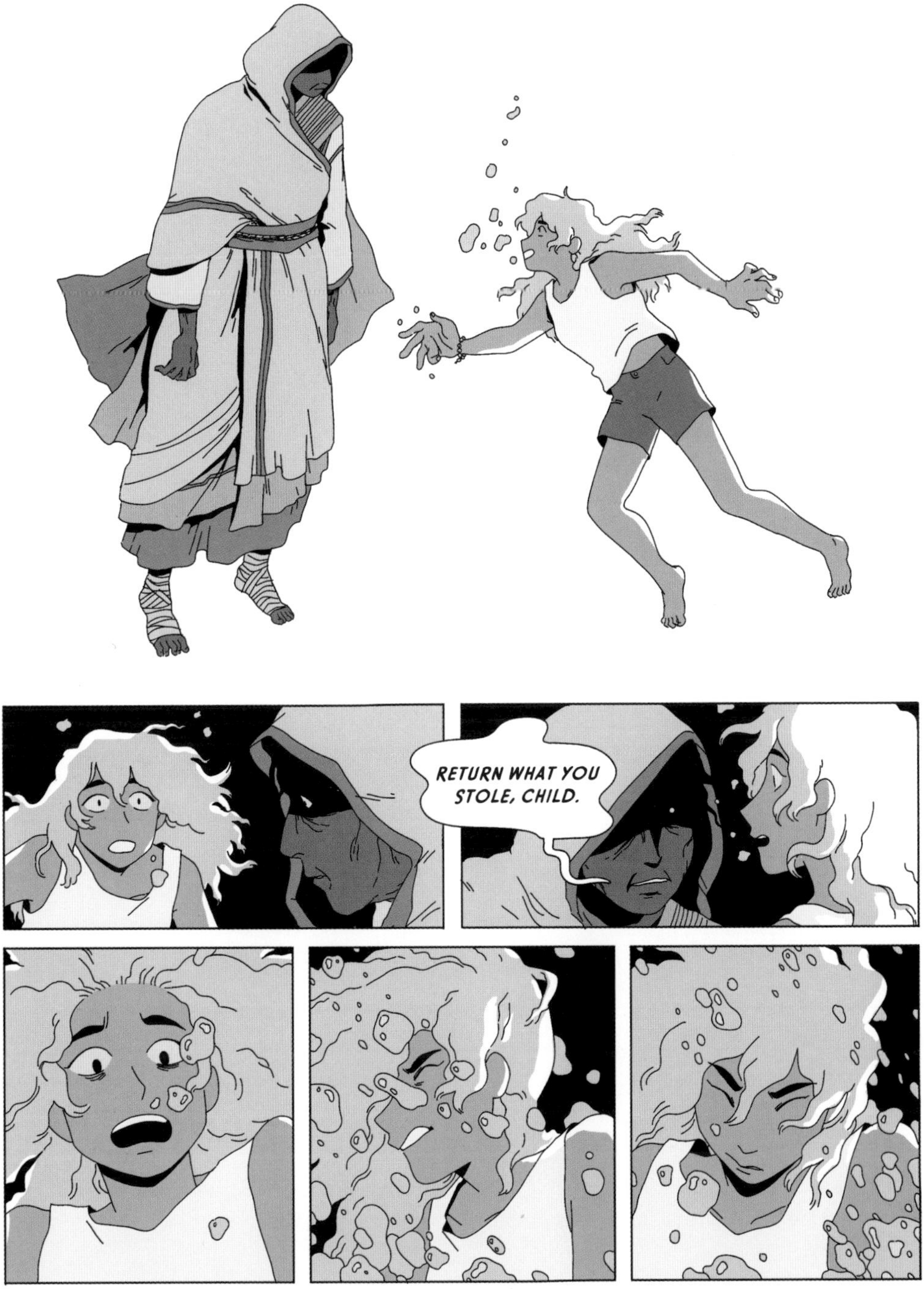
RETURN WHAT YOU STOLE, CHILD.

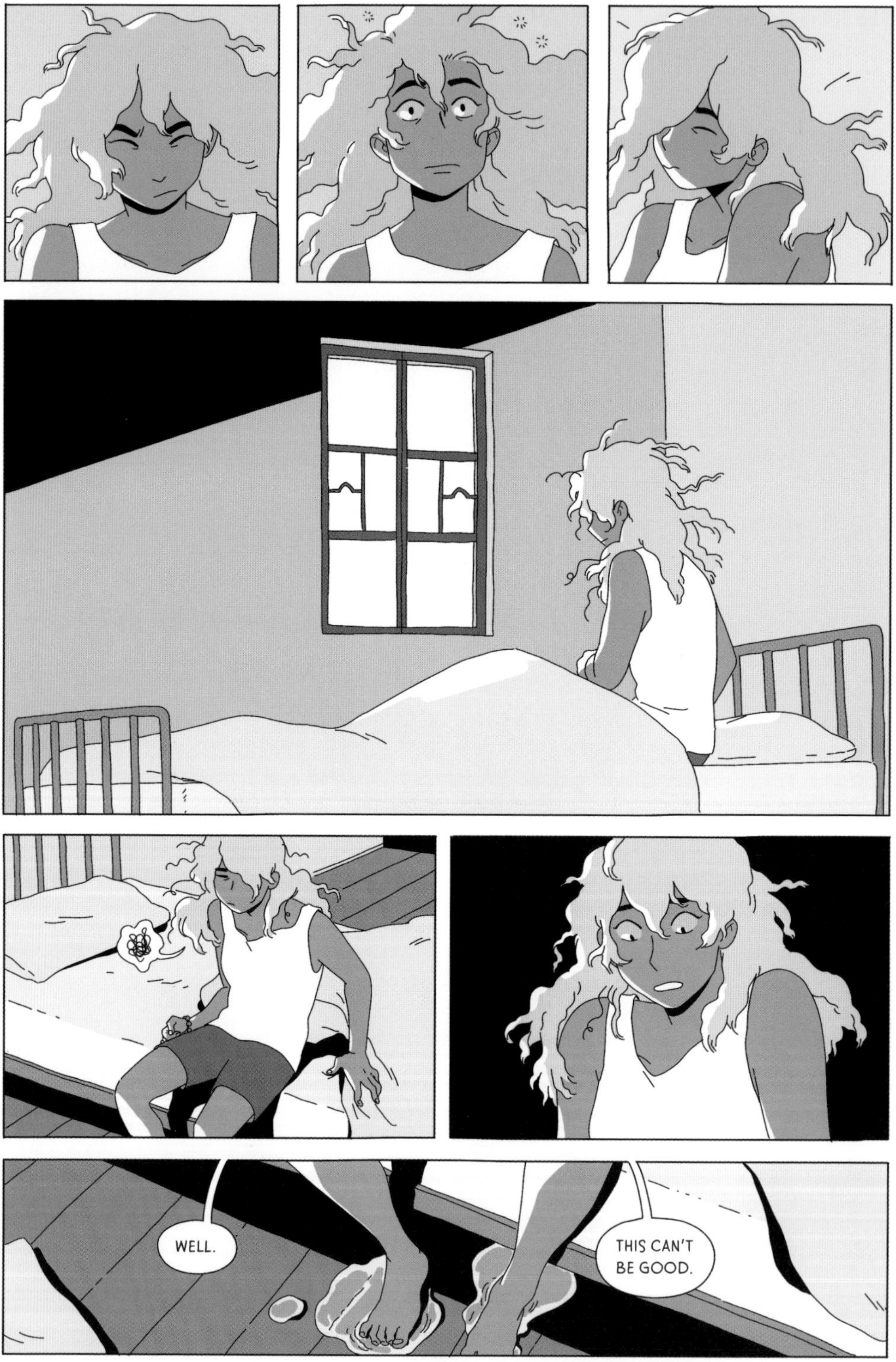
WELL.
THIS CAN'T BE GOOD.

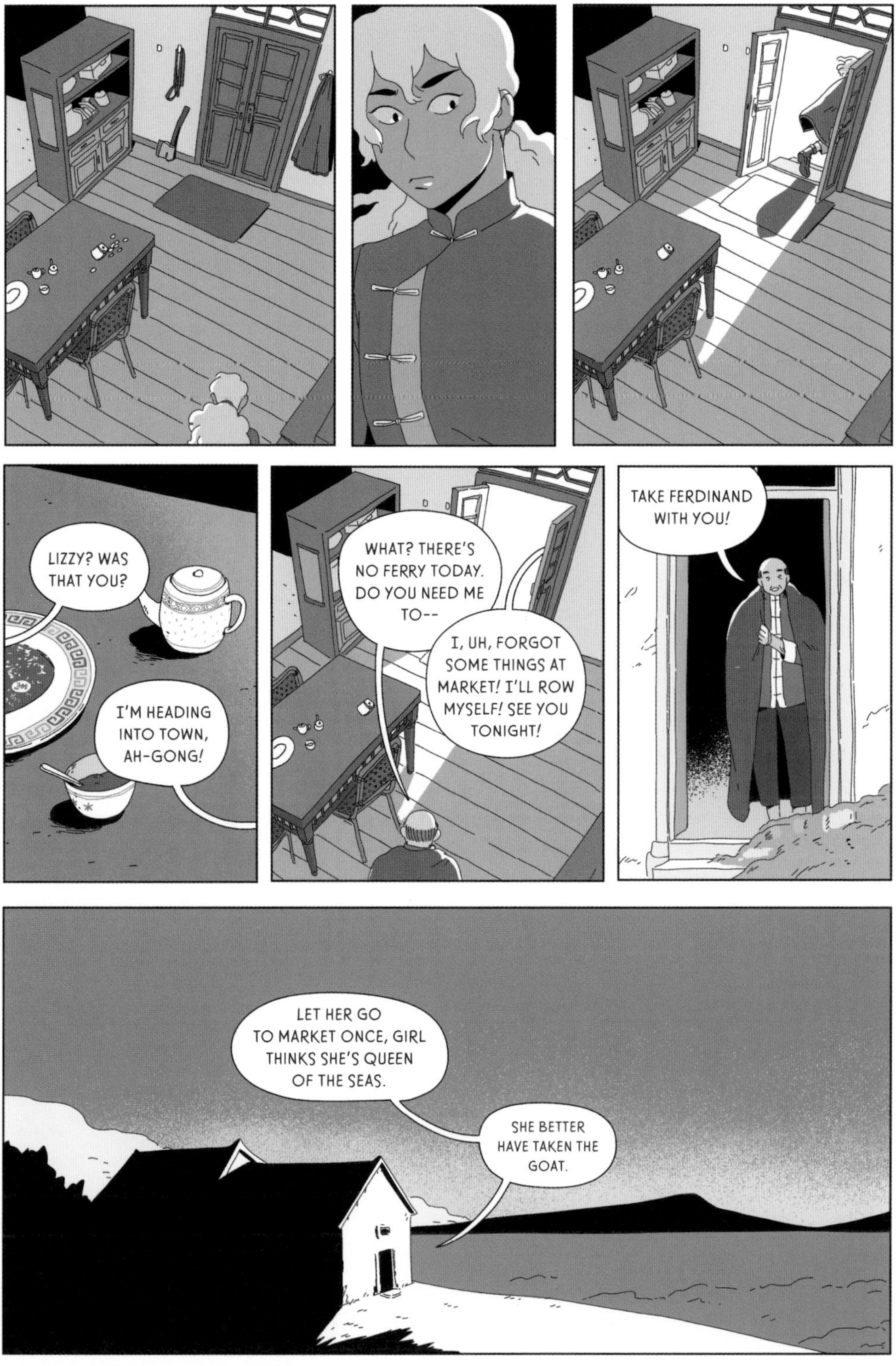

LIZZY? WAS THAT YOU?
I'M HEADING INTO TOWN, AH-GONG!
WHAT? THERE'S NO FERRY TODAY. DO YOU NEED ME TO--
I, UH, FORGOT SOME THINGS AT MARKET! I'LL ROW MYSELF! SEE YOU TONIGHT!
TAKE FERDINAND WITH YOU!
LET HER GO TO MARKET ONCE, GIRL THINKS SHE'S QUEEN OF THE SEAS.
SHE BETTER HAVE TAKEN THE GOAT.

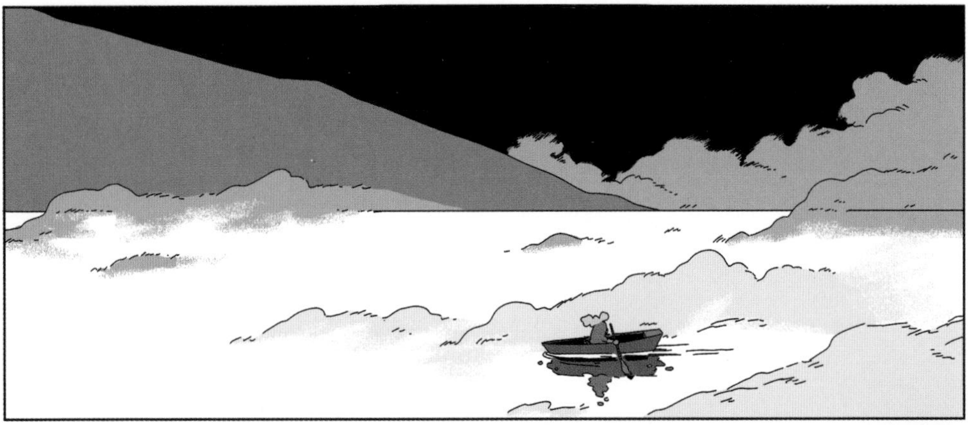

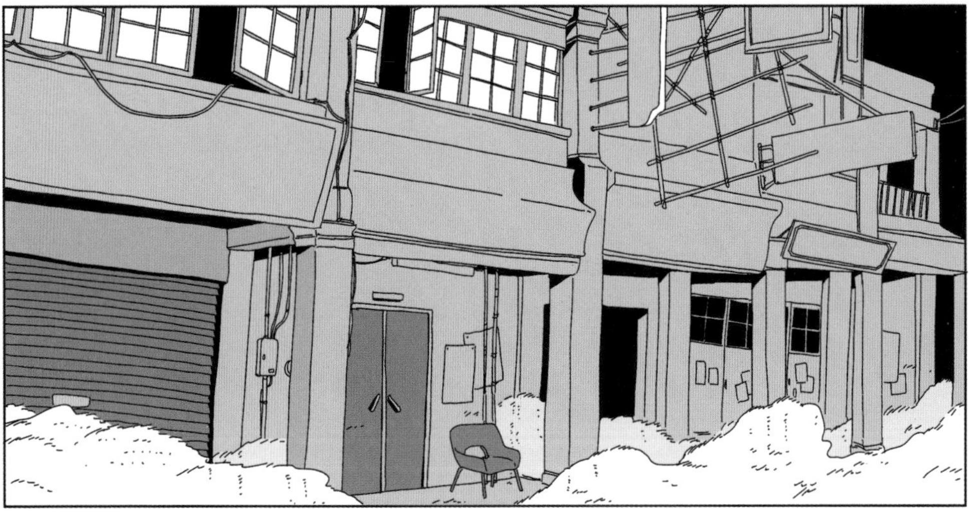

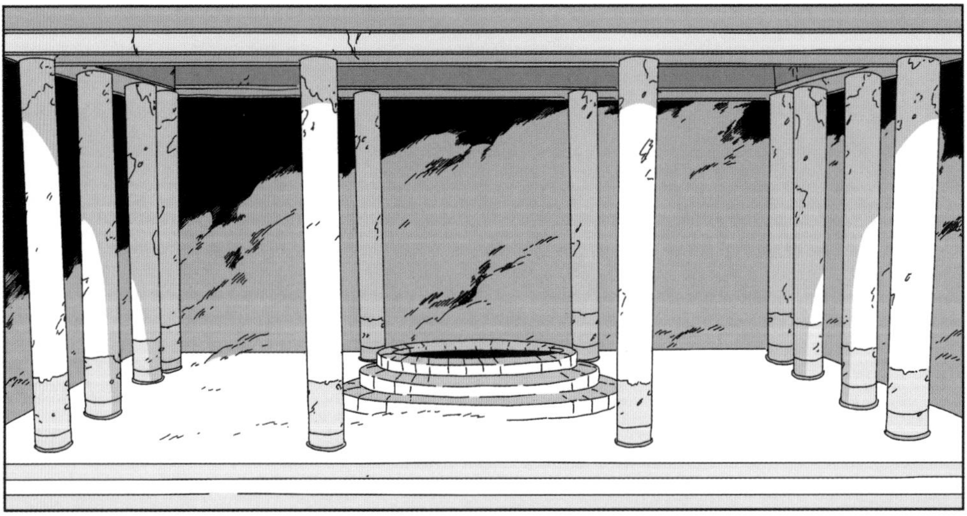

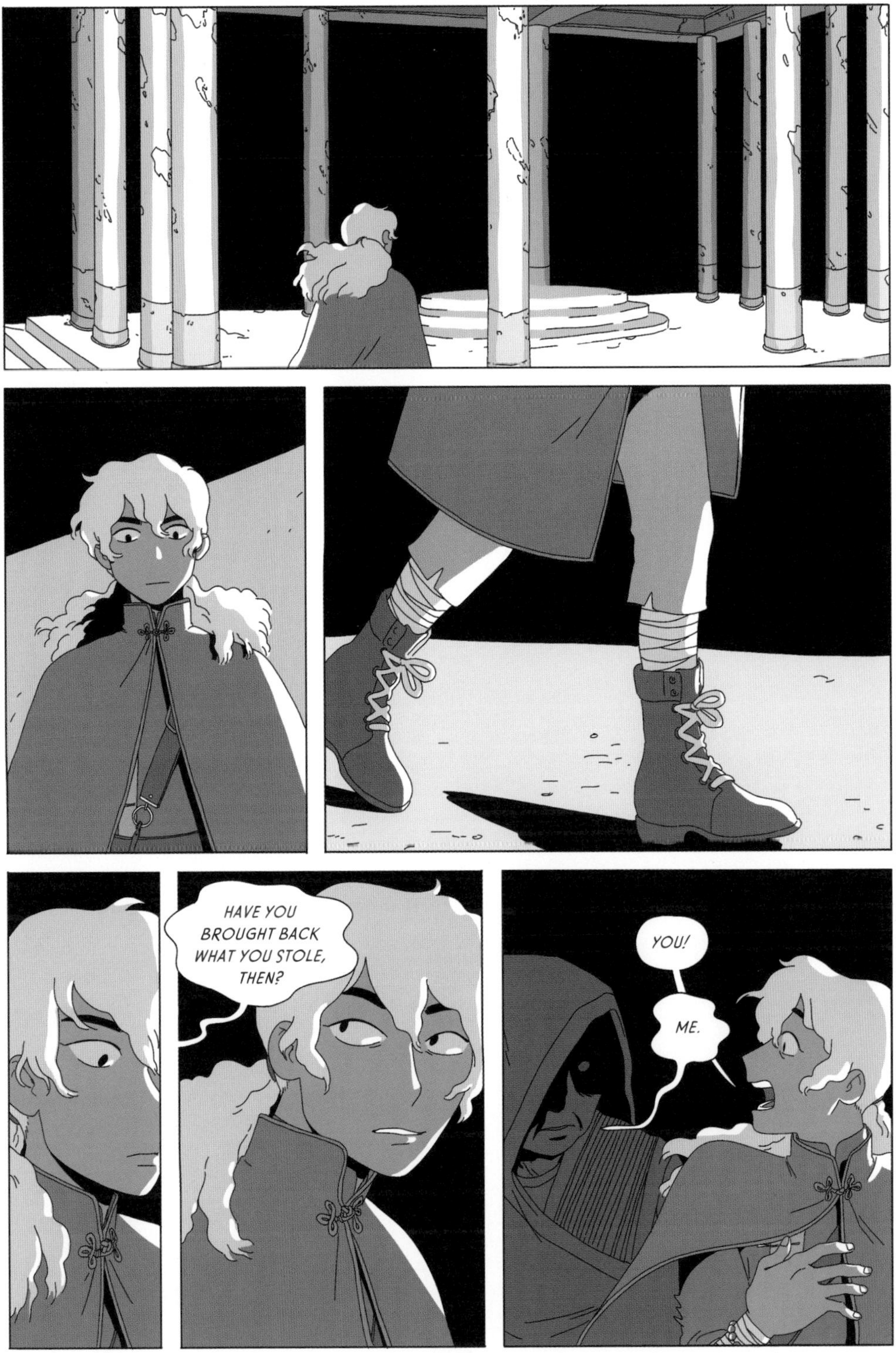
HAVE YOU BROUGHT BACK WHAT YOU STOLE, THEN?
YOU!
ME.

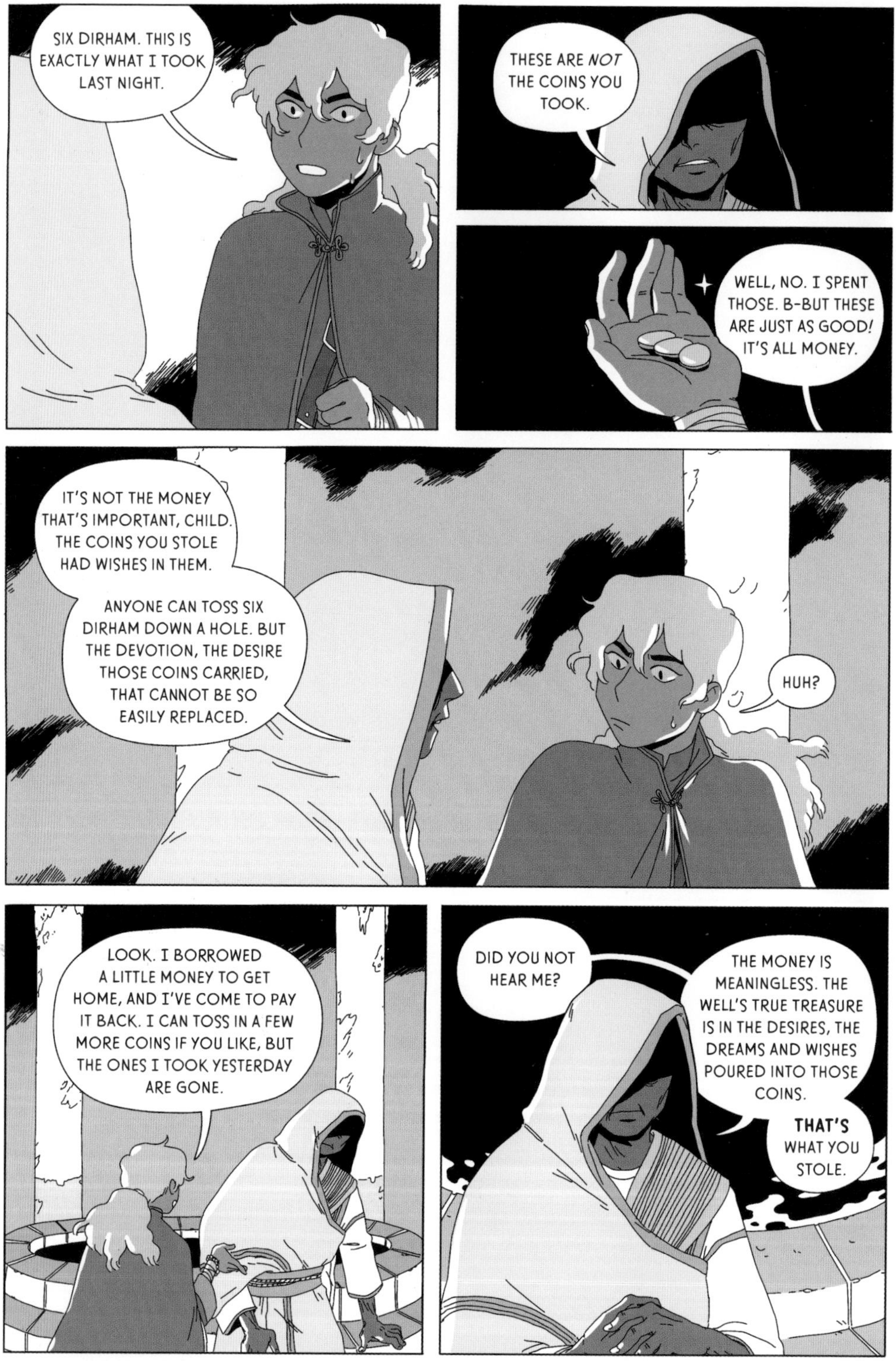
SIX DIRHAM. THIS IS EXACTLY WHAT I TOOK LAST NIGHT.
THESE ARE *NOT* THE COINS YOU TOOK.
WELL, NO. I SPENT THOSE. B-BUT THESE ARE JUST AS GOOD! IT'S ALL MONEY.
IT'S NOT THE MONEY THAT'S IMPORTANT, CHILD. THE COINS YOU STOLE HAD WISHES IN THEM.
ANYONE CAN TOSS SIX DIRHAM DOWN A HOLE. BUT THE DEVOTION, THE DESIRE THOSE COINS CARRIED, THAT CANNOT BE SO EASILY REPLACED.
HUH?
LOOK. I BORROWED A LITTLE MONEY TO GET HOME, AND I'VE COME TO PAY IT BACK. I CAN TOSS IN A FEW MORE COINS IF YOU LIKE, BUT THE ONES I TOOK YESTERDAY ARE GONE.
DID YOU NOT HEAR ME?
THE MONEY IS MEANINGLESS. THE WELL'S TRUE TREASURE IS IN THE DESIRES, THE DREAMS AND WISHES POURED INTO THOSE COINS.
**THAT'S** WHAT YOU STOLE.

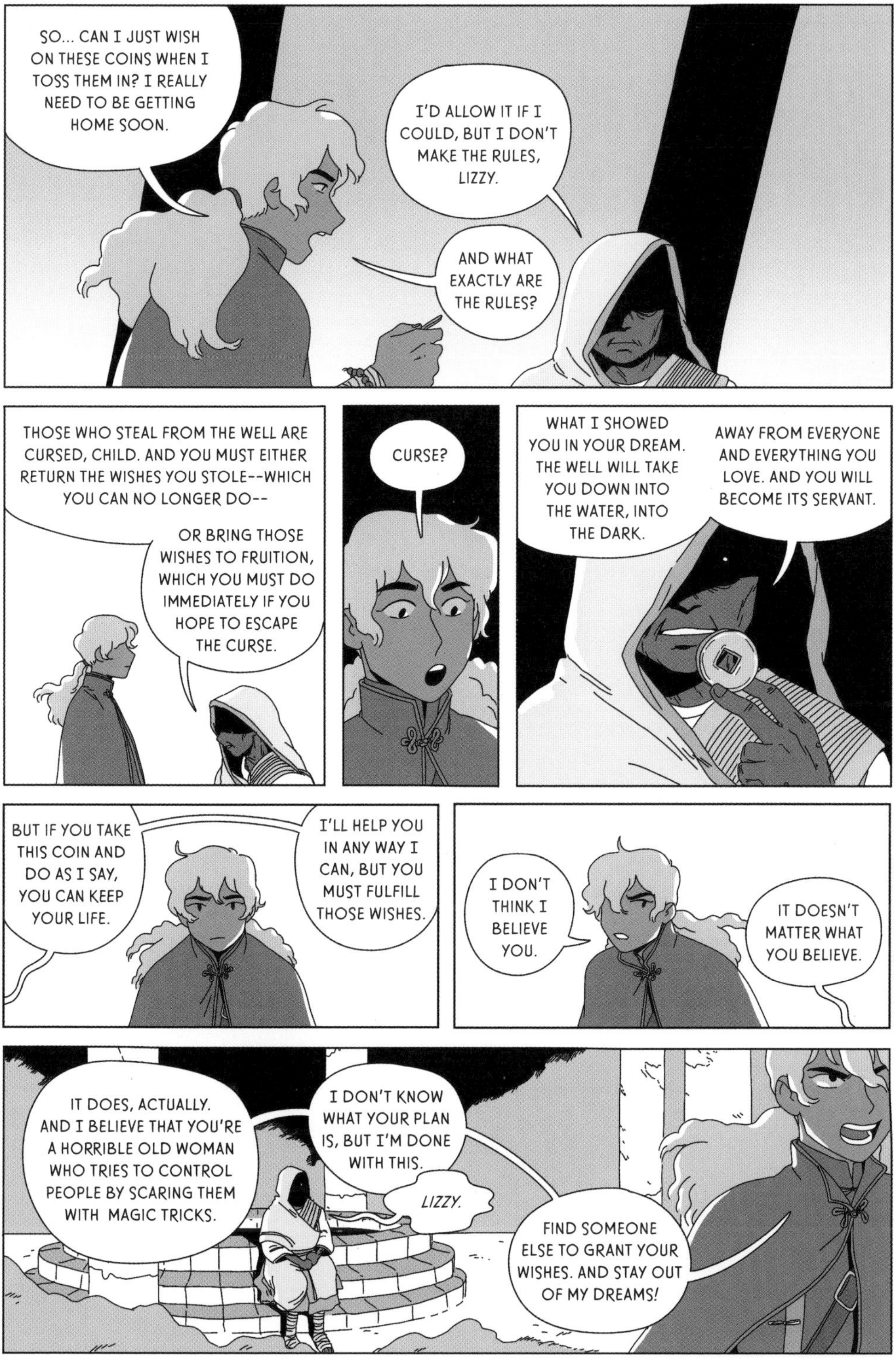
SO... CAN I JUST WISH ON THESE COINS WHEN I TOSS THEM IN? I REALLY NEED TO BE GETTING HOME SOON.
I'D ALLOW IT IF I COULD, BUT I DON'T MAKE THE RULES, LIZZY.
AND WHAT EXACTLY ARE THE RULES?
THOSE WHO STEAL FROM THE WELL ARE CURSED, CHILD. AND YOU MUST EITHER RETURN THE WISHES YOU STOLE--WHICH YOU CAN NO LONGER DO--
OR BRING THOSE WISHES TO FRUITION, WHICH YOU MUST DO IMMEDIATELY IF YOU HOPE TO ESCAPE THE CURSE.
CURSE?
WHAT I SHOWED YOU IN YOUR DREAM. THE WELL WILL TAKE YOU DOWN INTO THE WATER, INTO THE DARK.
AWAY FROM EVERYONE AND EVERYTHING YOU LOVE. AND YOU WILL BECOME ITS SERVANT.
BUT IF YOU TAKE THIS COIN AND DO AS I SAY, YOU CAN KEEP YOUR LIFE.
I'LL HELP YOU IN ANY WAY I CAN, BUT YOU MUST FULFILL THOSE WISHES.
I DON'T THINK I BELIEVE YOU.
IT DOESN'T MATTER WHAT YOU BELIEVE.
IT DOES, ACTUALLY. AND I BELIEVE THAT YOU'RE A HORRIBLE OLD WOMAN WHO TRIES TO CONTROL PEOPLE BY SCARING THEM WITH MAGIC TRICKS.
I DON'T KNOW WHAT YOUR PLAN IS, BUT I'M DONE WITH THIS.
LIZZY.
FIND SOMEONE ELSE TO GRANT YOUR WISHES. AND STAY OUT OF MY DREAMS!

...OLD BIDDY TALKING TO ME ABOUT DEBTS AND MAGIC LIKE I'M NOT THE WITCH'S OWN DAUGHTER...
...SNEAKING INTO OTHER PEOPLE'S DREAMS JUST TO SCARE THEM...
I'VE LIVED BY THAT WELL MY WHOLE LIFE, AND IT'S NOTHING TO BE AFRAID OF...
IT'S JUST A HOLE FULL OF WATER.
AND THERE'S NOTHING SCARY... ABOUT...
...WATER.

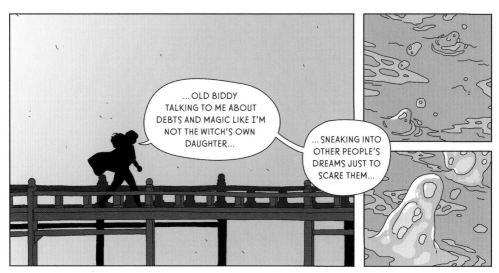

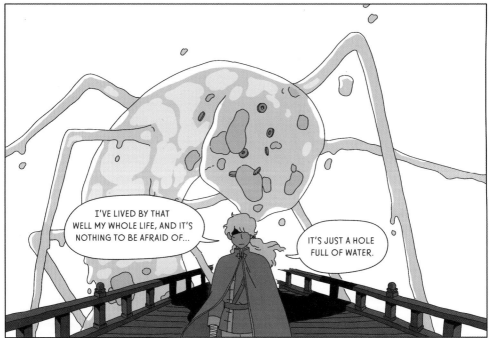

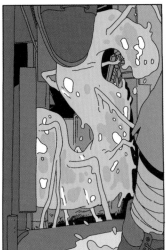

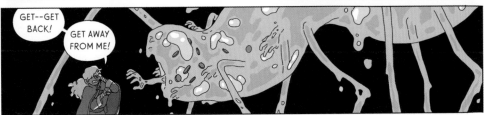

GET--GET BACK!

GET AWAY FROM ME!

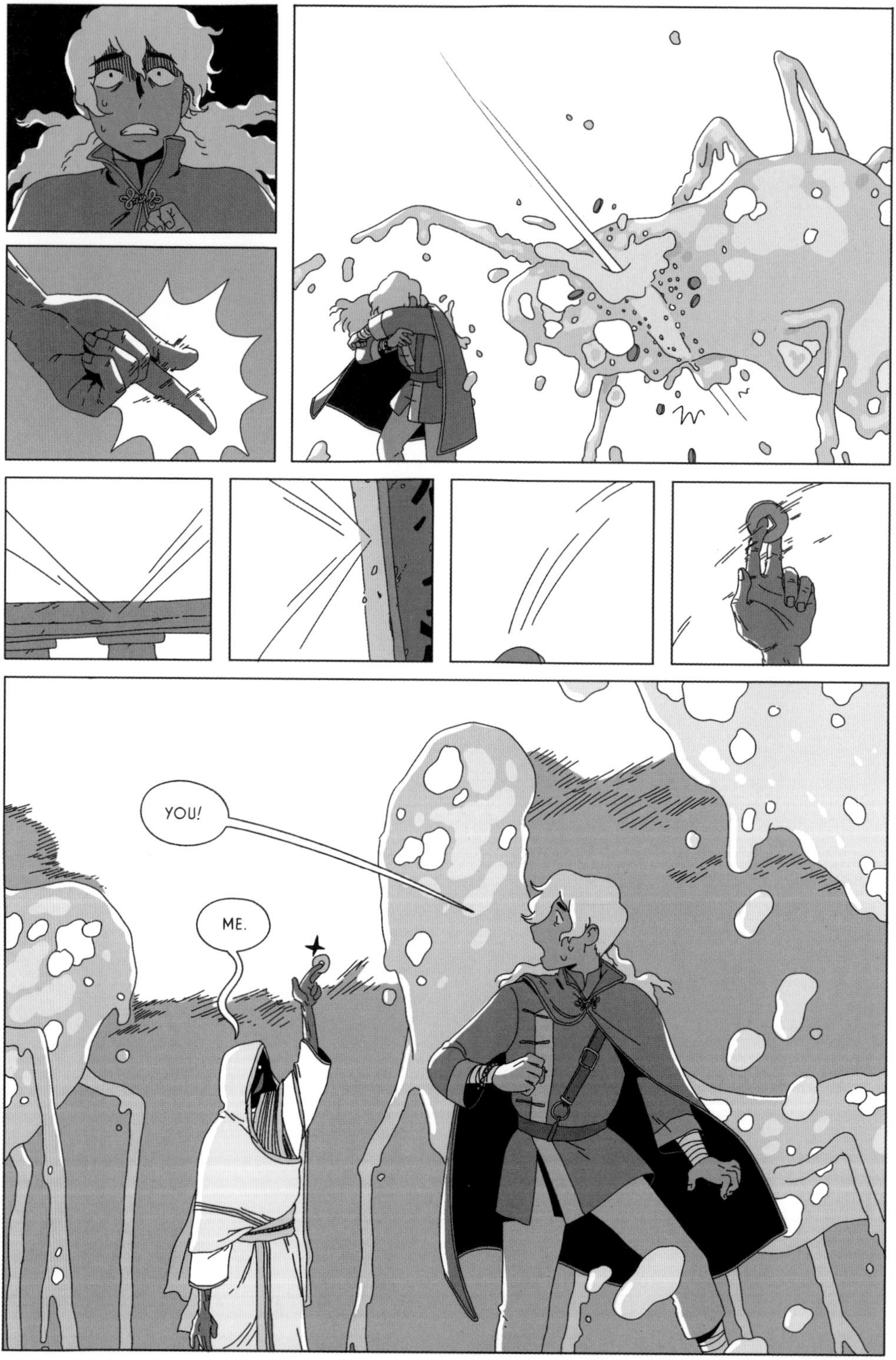
YOU!
ME.

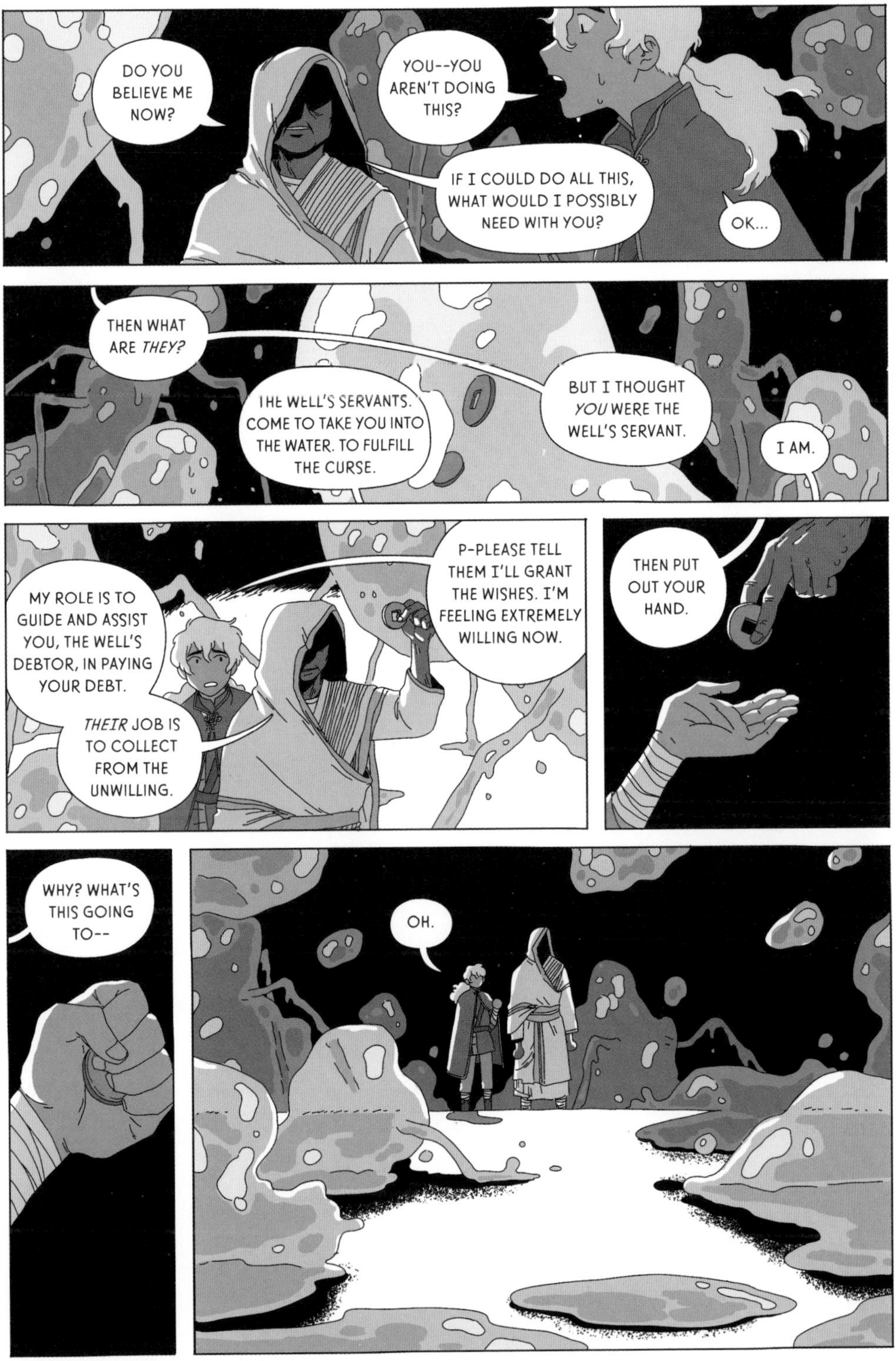
DO YOU BELIEVE ME NOW?
YOU--YOU AREN'T DOING THIS?
IF I COULD DO ALL THIS, WHAT WOULD I POSSIBLY NEED WITH YOU?
OK...
THEN WHAT ARE *THEY?*
THE WELL'S SERVANTS. COME TO TAKE YOU INTO THE WATER. TO FULFILL THE CURSE.
BUT I THOUGHT *YOU* WERE THE WELL'S SERVANT.
I AM.
MY ROLE IS TO GUIDE AND ASSIST YOU, THE WELL'S DEBTOR, IN PAYING YOUR DEBT.
*THEIR* JOB IS TO COLLECT FROM THE UNWILLING.
P-PLEASE TELL THEM I'LL GRANT THE WISHES. I'M FEELING EXTREMELY WILLING NOW.
THEN PUT OUT YOUR HAND.
WHY? WHAT'S THIS GOING TO--
OH.

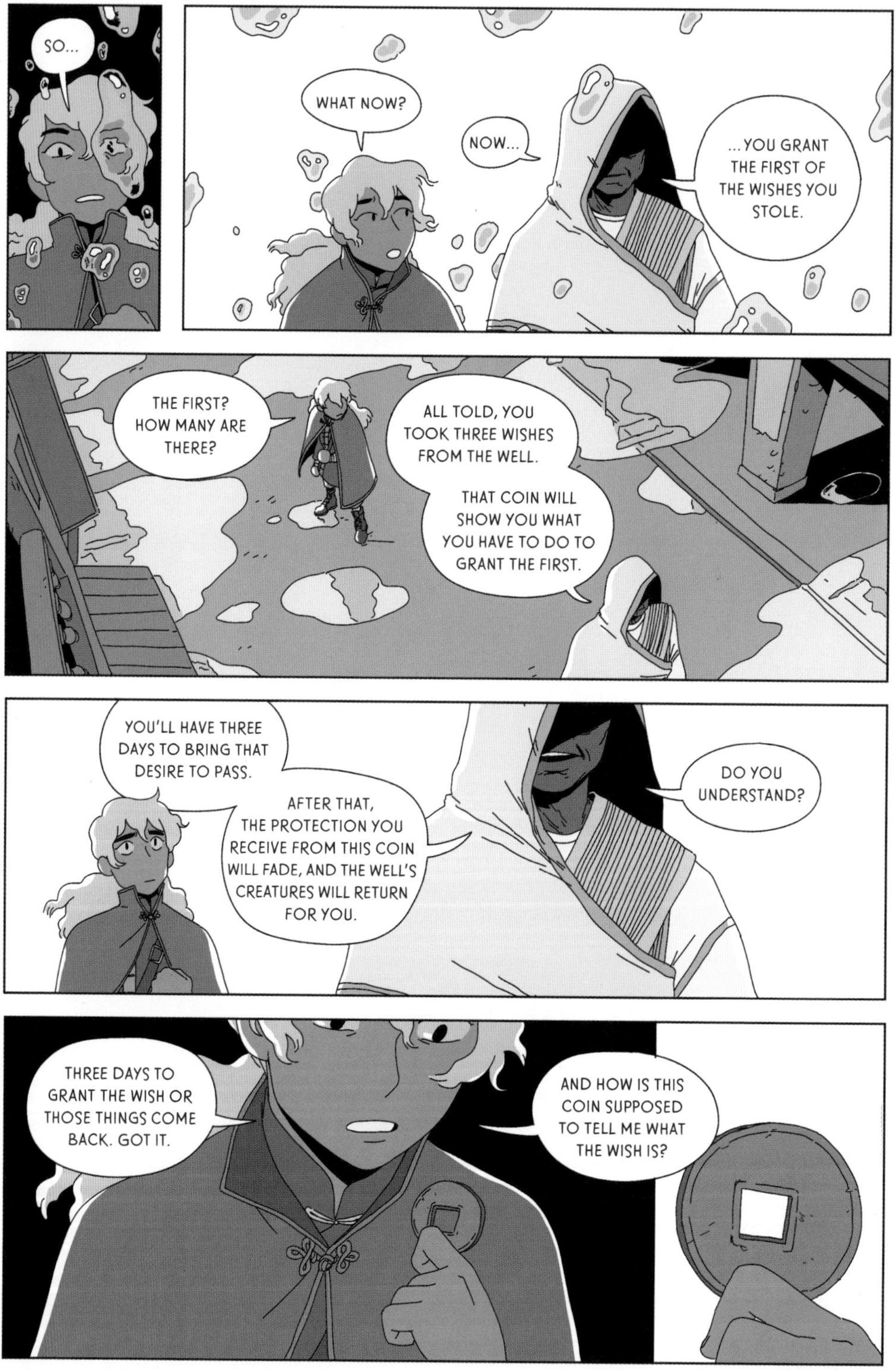
SO...
WHAT NOW?
NOW...
...YOU GRANT THE FIRST OF THE WISHES YOU STOLE.
THE FIRST? HOW MANY ARE THERE?
ALL TOLD, YOU TOOK THREE WISHES FROM THE WELL.
THAT COIN WILL SHOW YOU WHAT YOU HAVE TO DO TO GRANT THE FIRST.
YOU'LL HAVE THREE DAYS TO BRING THAT DESIRE TO PASS.
AFTER THAT, THE PROTECTION YOU RECEIVE FROM THIS COIN WILL FADE, AND THE WELL'S CREATURES WILL RETURN FOR YOU.
DO YOU UNDERSTAND?
THREE DAYS TO GRANT THE WISH OR THOSE THINGS COME BACK. GOT IT.
AND HOW IS THIS COIN SUPPOSED TO TELL ME WHAT THE WISH IS?

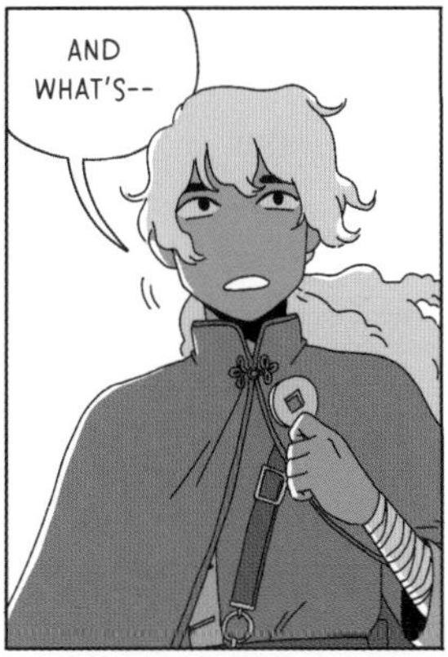
AND WHAT'S--
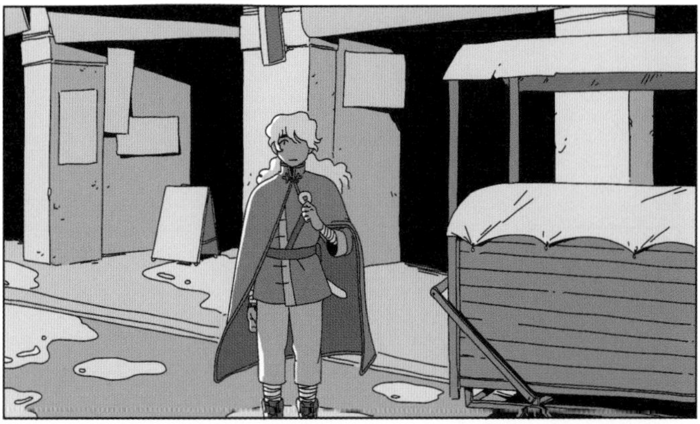
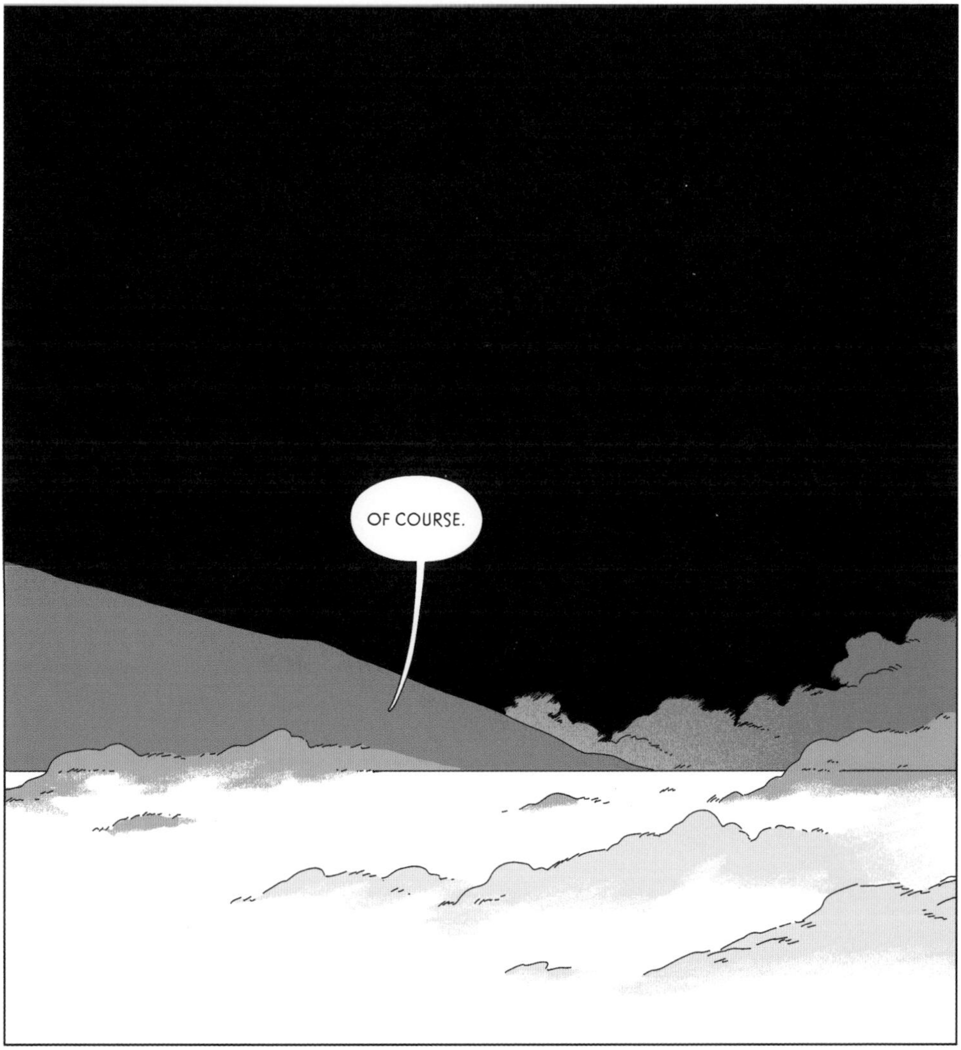
OF COURSE.

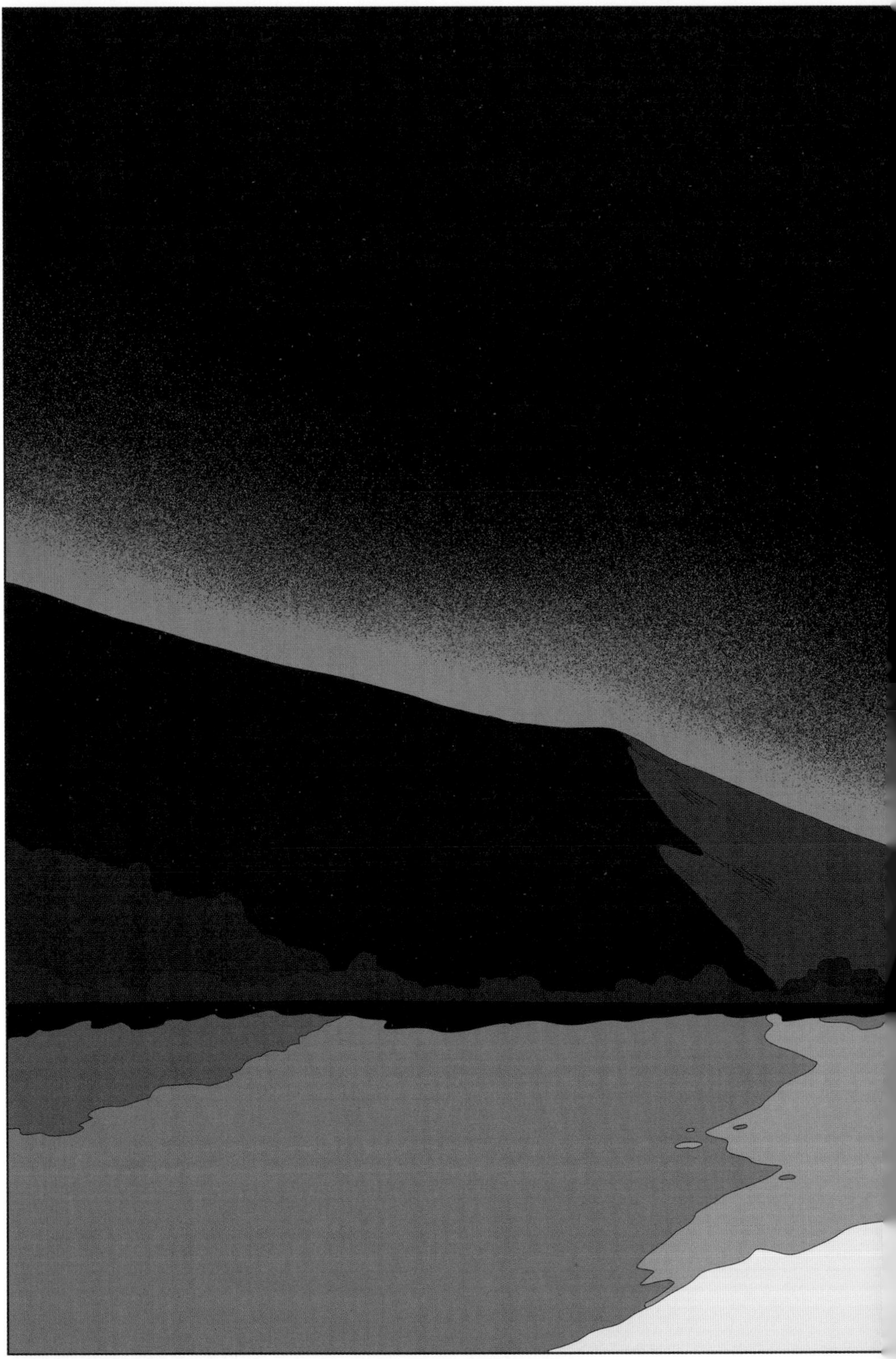

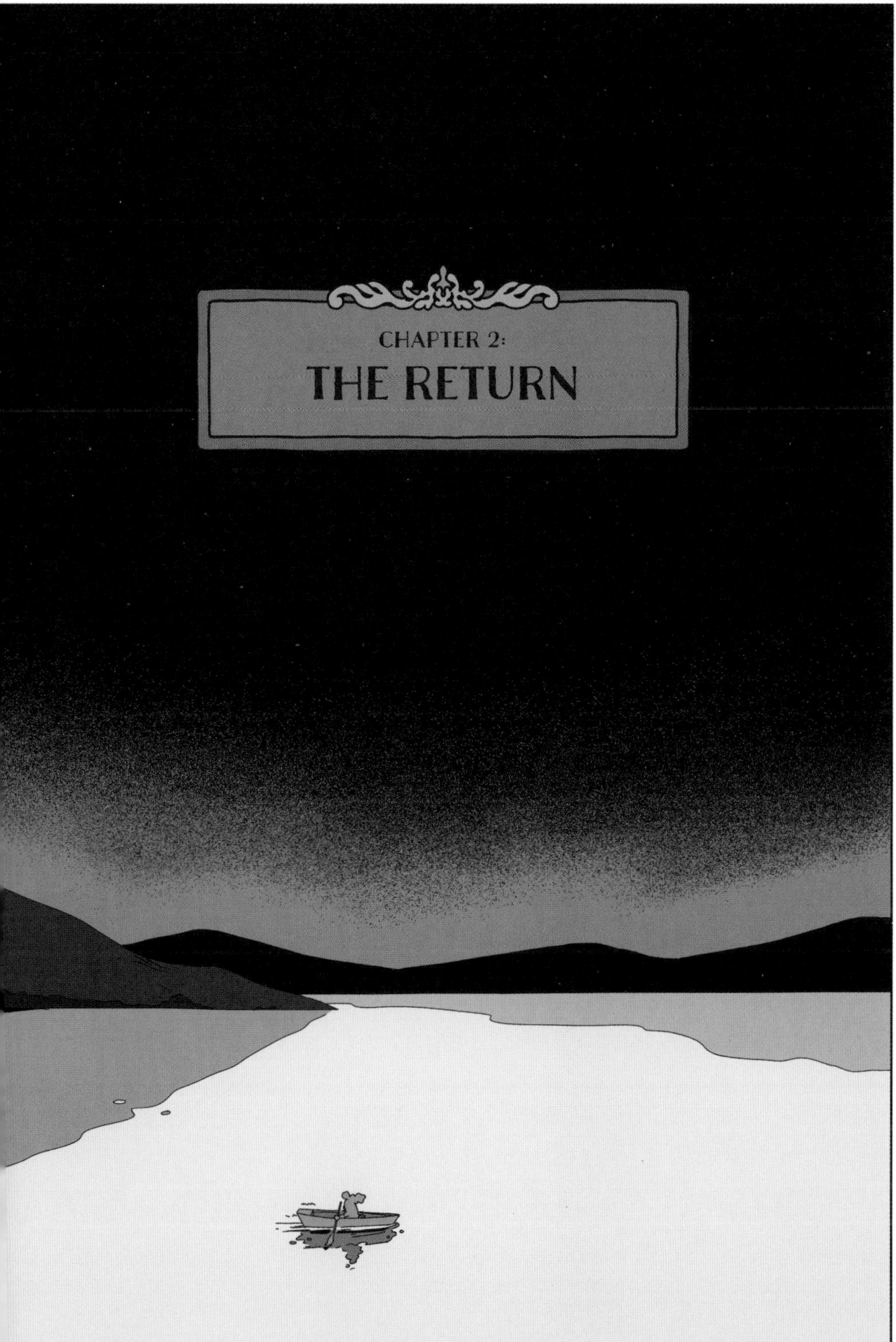
CHAPTER 2:
THE RETURN

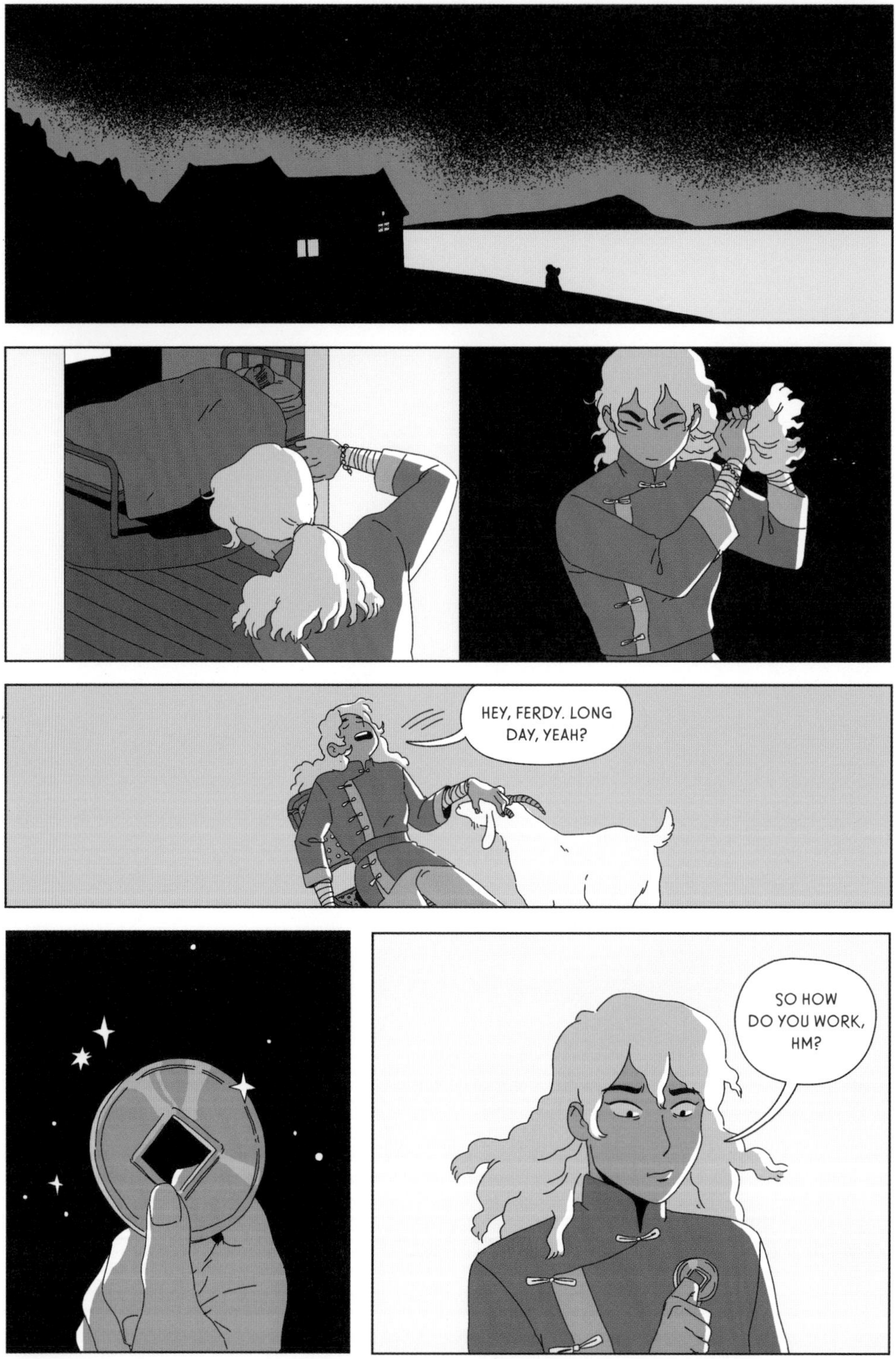
HEY, FERDY. LONG DAY, YEAH?
SO HOW DO YOU WORK, HM?

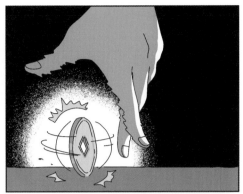

HEYYY...

I KNOW YOU CAN'T UNDO WHAT'S DONE, I JUST...

I JUST WANT TO GO BACK TO DECAO.

PLEASE. PLEASE LET ME GO HOME.

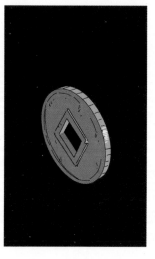

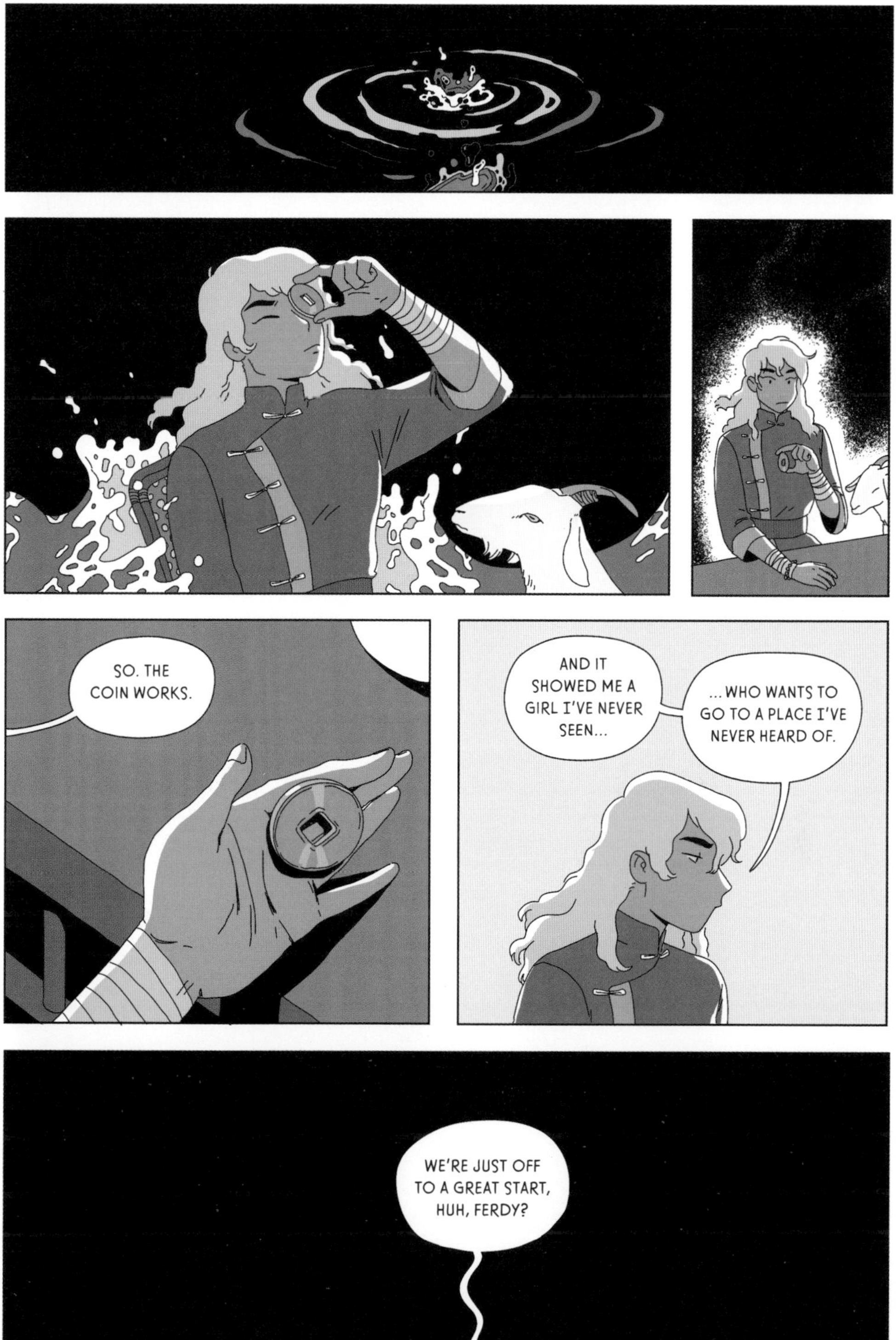
SO. THE COIN WORKS.
AND IT SHOWED ME A GIRL I'VE NEVER SEEN...
...WHO WANTS TO GO TO A PLACE I'VE NEVER HEARD OF.
WE'RE JUST OFF TO A GREAT START, HUH, FERDY?

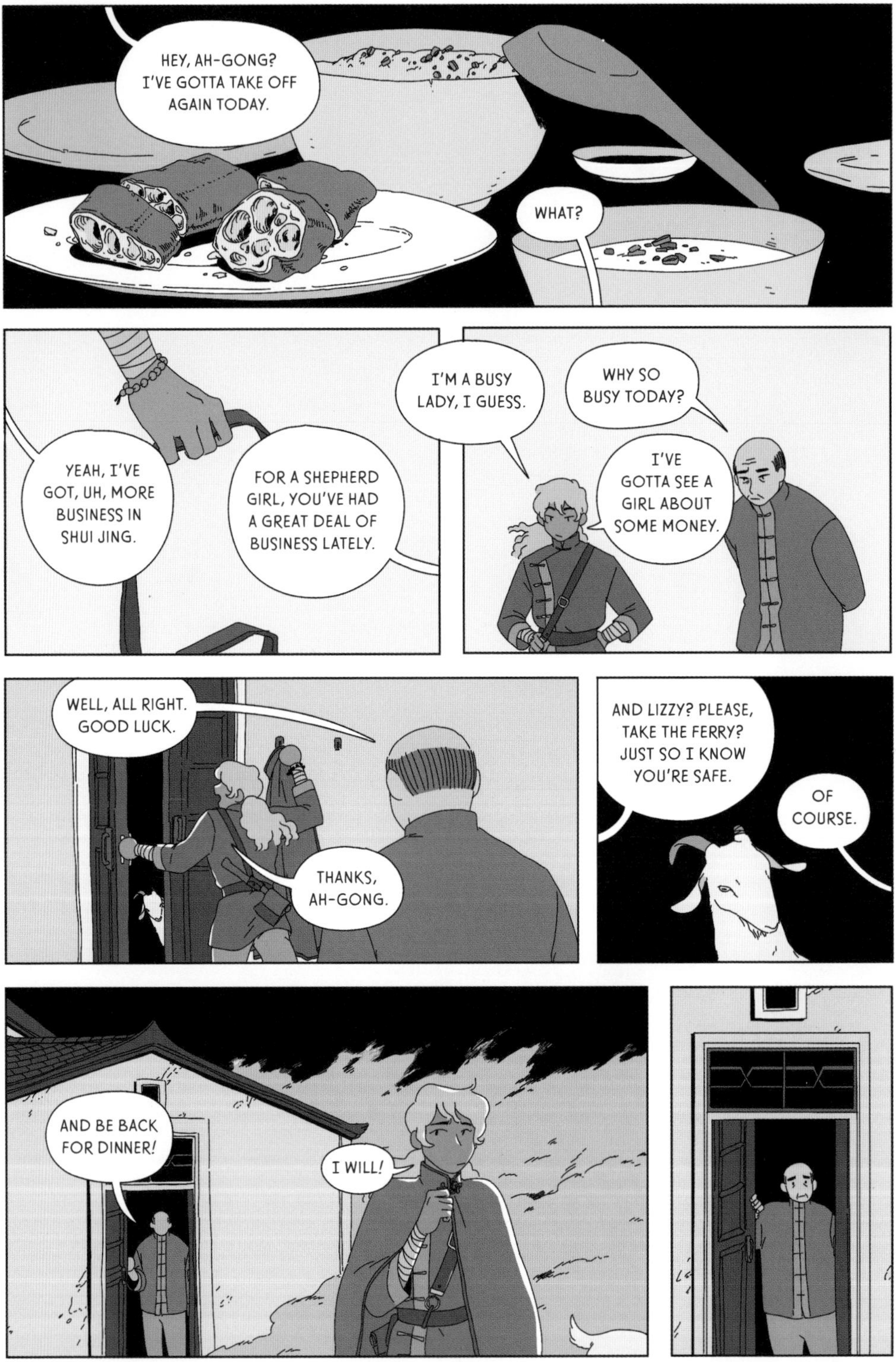
HEY, AH-GONG? I'VE GOTTA TAKE OFF AGAIN TODAY.
WHAT?
YEAH, I'VE GOT, UH, MORE BUSINESS IN SHUI JING.
FOR A SHEPHERD GIRL, YOU'VE HAD A GREAT DEAL OF BUSINESS LATELY.
WHY SO BUSY TODAY?
I'M A BUSY LADY, I GUESS.
I'VE GOTTA SEE A GIRL ABOUT SOME MONEY.
WELL, ALL RIGHT. GOOD LUCK.
THANKS, AH-GONG.
AND LIZZY? PLEASE, TAKE THE FERRY? JUST SO I KNOW YOU'RE SAFE.
OF COURSE.
AND BE BACK FOR DINNER!
I WILL!

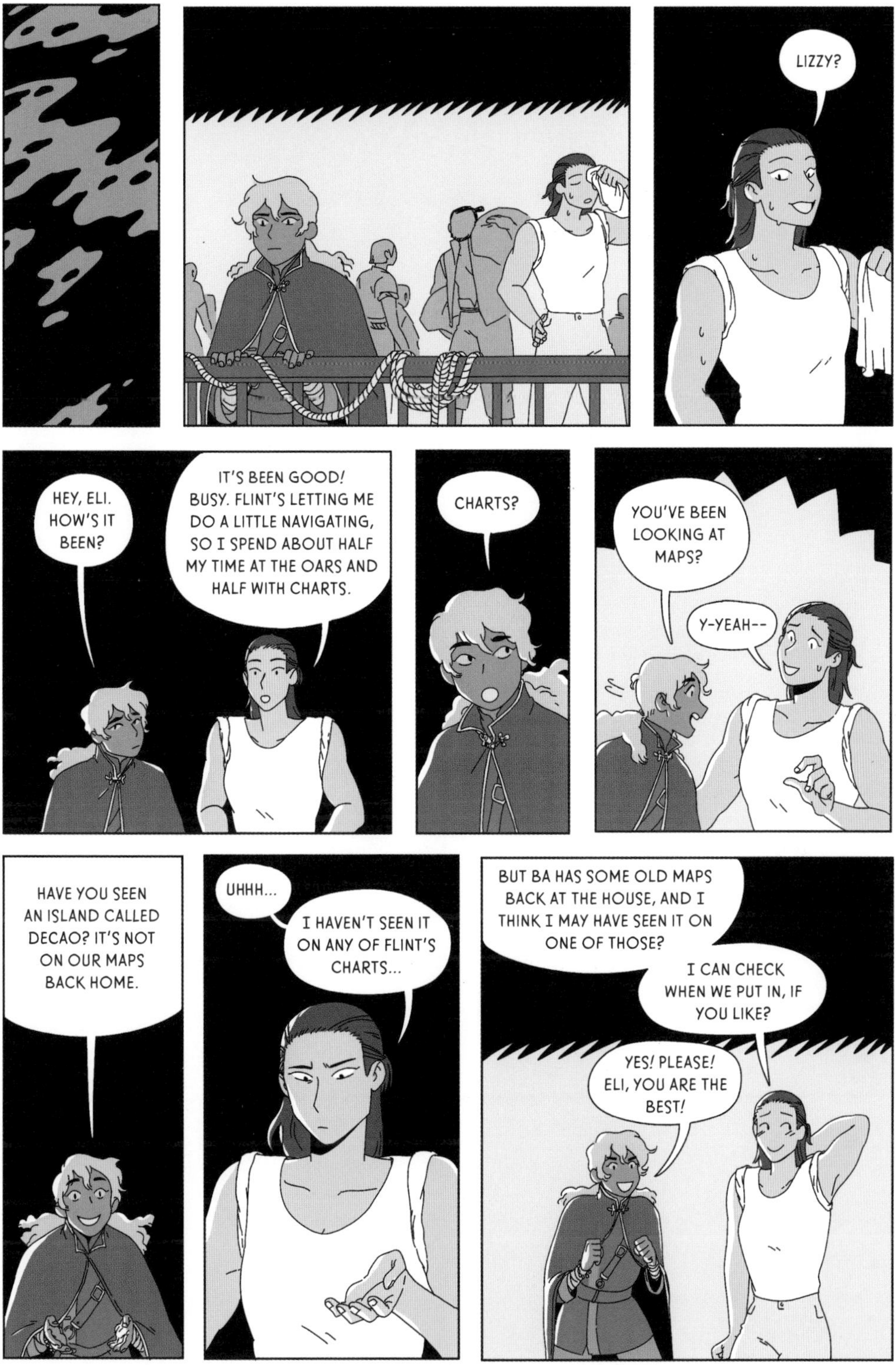
LIZZY?
HEY, ELI. HOW'S IT BEEN?
IT'S BEEN GOOD! BUSY. FLINT'S LETTING ME DO A LITTLE NAVIGATING, SO I SPEND ABOUT HALF MY TIME AT THE OARS AND HALF WITH CHARTS.
CHARTS?
YOU'VE BEEN LOOKING AT MAPS?
Y-YEAH--
HAVE YOU SEEN AN ISLAND CALLED DECAO? IT'S NOT ON OUR MAPS BACK HOME.
UHHH...
I HAVEN'T SEEN IT ON ANY OF FLINT'S CHARTS...
BUT BA HAS SOME OLD MAPS BACK AT THE HOUSE, AND I THINK I MAY HAVE SEEN IT ON ONE OF THOSE?
I CAN CHECK WHEN WE PUT IN, IF YOU LIKE?
YES! PLEASE! ELI, YOU ARE THE BEST!

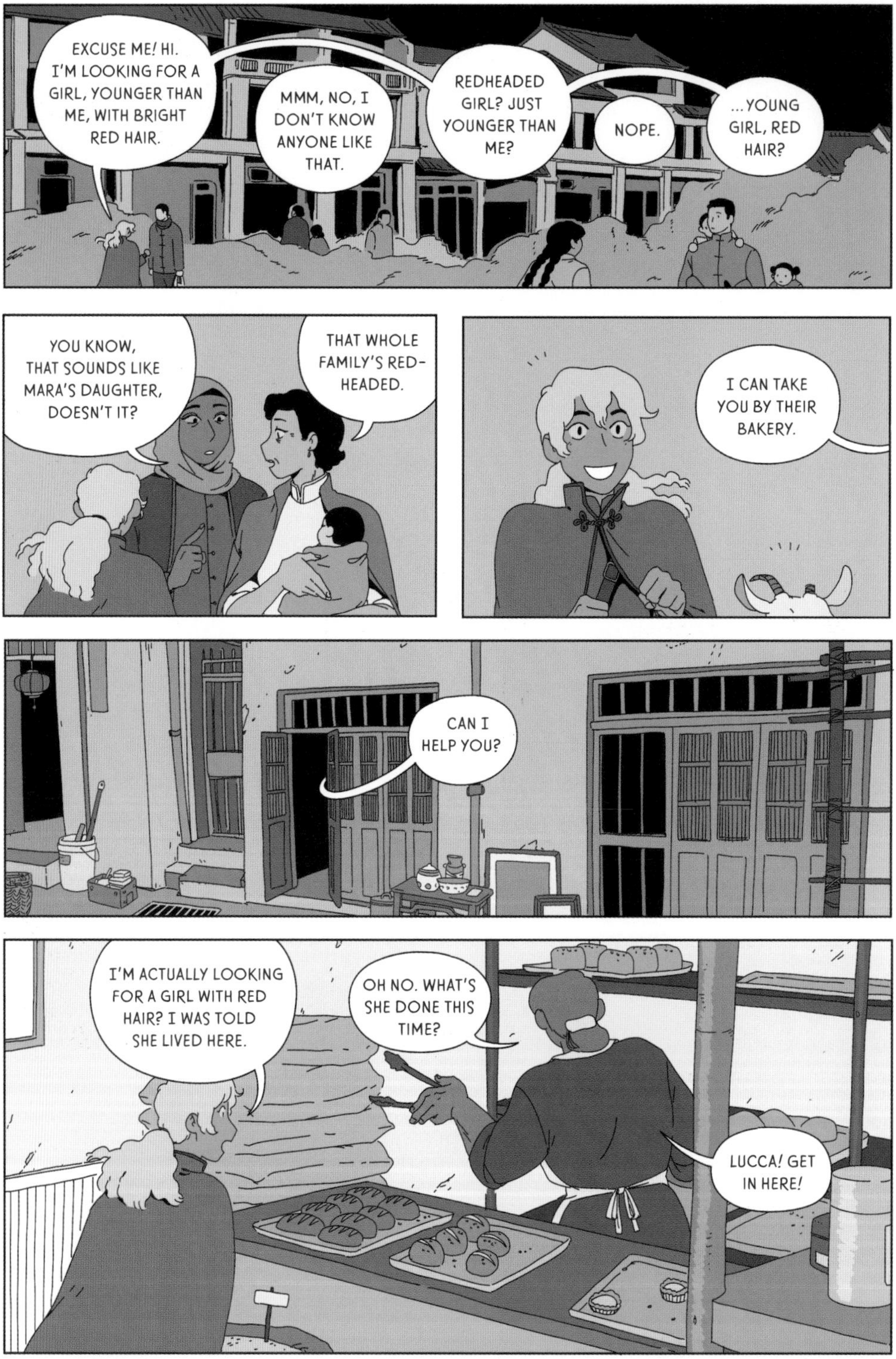

EXCUSE ME! HI. I'M LOOKING FOR A GIRL, YOUNGER THAN ME, WITH BRIGHT RED HAIR.
MMM, NO, I DON'T KNOW ANYONE LIKE THAT.
REDHEADED GIRL? JUST YOUNGER THAN ME?
NOPE.
...YOUNG GIRL, RED HAIR?
YOU KNOW, THAT SOUNDS LIKE MARA'S DAUGHTER, DOESN'T IT?
THAT WHOLE FAMILY'S RED-HEADED.
I CAN TAKE YOU BY THEIR BAKERY.
CAN I HELP YOU?
I'M ACTUALLY LOOKING FOR A GIRL WITH RED HAIR? I WAS TOLD SHE LIVED HERE.
OH NO. WHAT'S SHE DONE THIS TIME?
LUCCA! GET IN HERE!

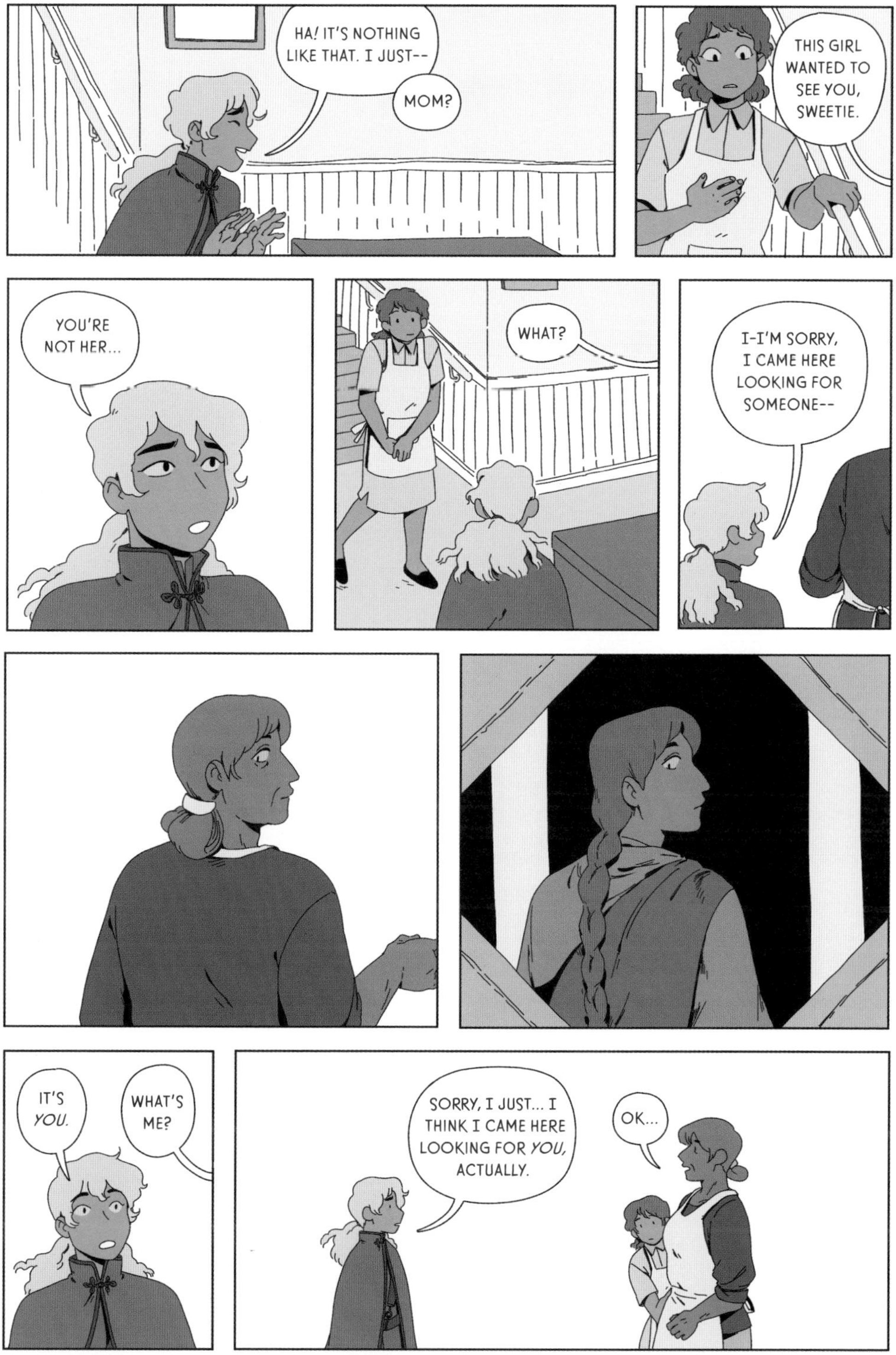
HA! IT'S NOTHING LIKE THAT. I JUST--
MOM?
THIS GIRL WANTED TO SEE YOU, SWEETIE.
YOU'RE NOT HER...
WHAT?
I-I'M SORRY, I CAME HERE LOOKING FOR SOMEONE--
IT'S *YOU.*
WHAT'S ME?
SORRY, I JUST... I THINK I CAME HERE LOOKING FOR *YOU,* ACTUALLY.
OK...

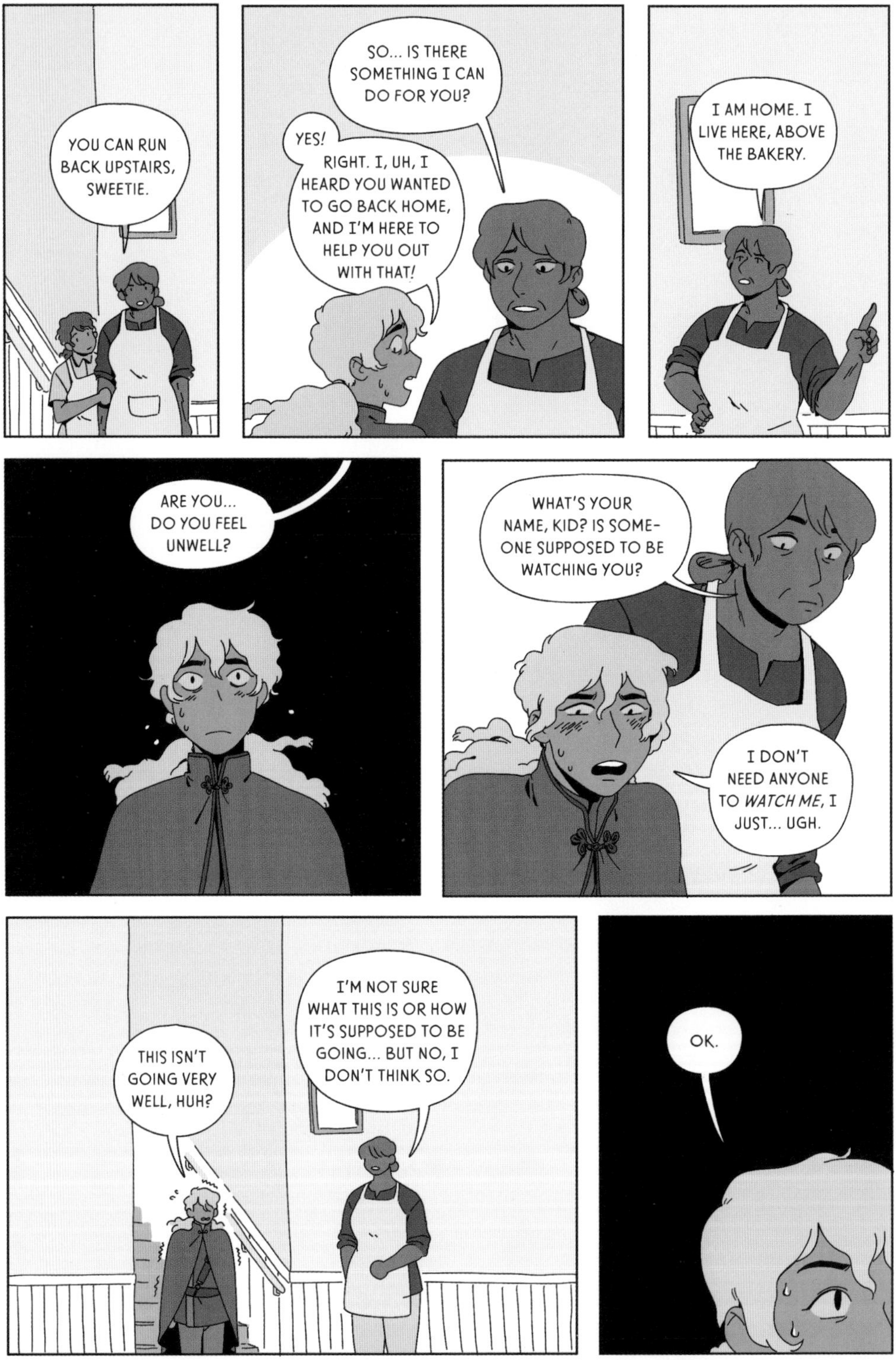
YOU CAN RUN BACK UPSTAIRS, SWEETIE.
SO... IS THERE SOMETHING I CAN DO FOR YOU?
YES!
RIGHT. I, UH, I HEARD YOU WANTED TO GO BACK HOME, AND I'M HERE TO HELP YOU OUT WITH THAT!
I AM HOME. I LIVE HERE, ABOVE THE BAKERY.
ARE YOU... DO YOU FEEL UNWELL?
WHAT'S YOUR NAME, KID? IS SOME-ONE SUPPOSED TO BE WATCHING YOU?
I DON'T NEED ANYONE TO *WATCH ME*, I JUST... UGH.
THIS ISN'T GOING VERY WELL, HUH?
I'M NOT SURE WHAT THIS IS OR HOW IT'S SUPPOSED TO BE GOING... BUT NO, I DON'T THINK SO.
OK.

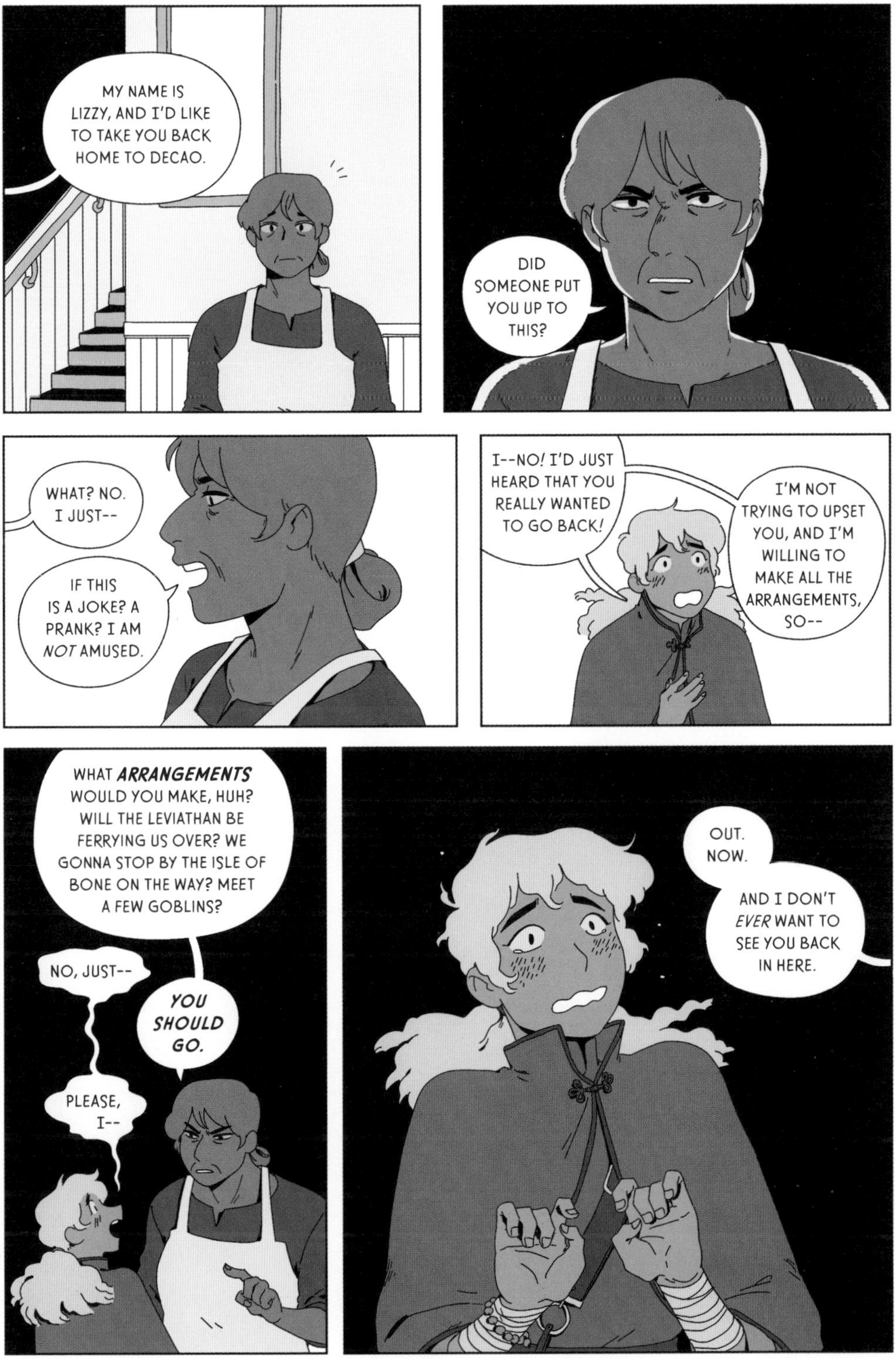
MY NAME IS LIZZY, AND I'D LIKE TO TAKE YOU BACK HOME TO DECAO.
DID SOMEONE PUT YOU UP TO THIS?
WHAT? NO. I JUST--
IF THIS IS A JOKE? A PRANK? I AM *NOT* AMUSED.
I--NO! I'D JUST HEARD THAT YOU REALLY WANTED TO GO BACK!
I'M NOT TRYING TO UPSET YOU, AND I'M WILLING TO MAKE ALL THE ARRANGEMENTS, SO--
WHAT **ARRANGEMENTS** WOULD YOU MAKE, HUH? WILL THE LEVIATHAN BE FERRYING US OVER? WE GONNA STOP BY THE ISLE OF BONE ON THE WAY? MEET A FEW GOBLINS?
NO, JUST--
***YOU SHOULD GO.***
PLEASE, I--
OUT. NOW.
AND I DON'T *EVER* WANT TO SEE YOU BACK IN HERE.

IT'S TERRIBLE. I JUST GOT MY FIRST CUSTOMER, AND SHE ALREADY HATES ME.

OH?

HOW'S THE WISH-GRANTING BUSINESS?

YEAH. SHE WISHED TO GET BACK TO SOME ISLAND CALLED DECAO? AND WHEN I OFFERED TO TAKE HER SHE *THREW ME OUT OF HER BAKERY.* YOU GOT ANY TRICKS TO SOLVE THAT?

DECAO...

YOU BEEN?

ONCE.

HOW WAS IT?

...BRIEF.

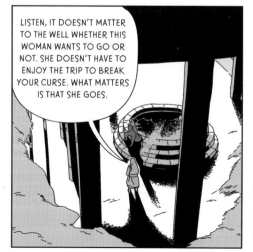

LISTEN, IT DOESN'T MATTER TO THE WELL WHETHER THIS WOMAN WANTS TO GO OR NOT. SHE DOESN'T HAVE TO ENJOY THE TRIP TO BREAK YOUR CURSE. WHAT MATTERS IS THAT SHE GOES.

SO YOU JUST GET HER TO DECAO IN THE NEXT TWO DAYS.

HOWEVER YOU HAVE TO. YOU KNOW THE CONSEQUENCES, LIZZY.

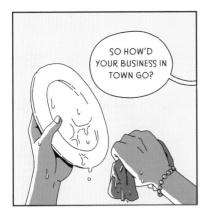

SO HOW'D YOUR BUSINESS IN TOWN GO?

BUSINESS IN TOWN WAS... DIFFICULT. HOW WERE THINGS AROUND HERE?

I TRIED PULLING WEEDS IN THE GARDEN--

AH-GONG!

THAT'S *MY* CHORE!

I KNOW, I KNOW. AND LET'S KEEP IT THAT WAY. YOU MAY FORGIVE AN OLD MAN HIS INDULGENCES, BUT MY BACK WON'T.

I'LL BE LUCKY IF IT LETS ME SLEEP AT ALL TONIGHT.

SOUNDS LIKE IT'S TRYING TO TEACH YOU A LESSON.

WELL, I'D BETTER BREW UP A SLEEPING DRAUGHT TO HELP ME FORGET.

WHERE DID YOU PUT THE VIALS, LIZZY?

IN, UH, IN THE CABINET ABOVE THE KNIVES.

AND AH-GONG?

I'LL BREW IT FOR YOU.

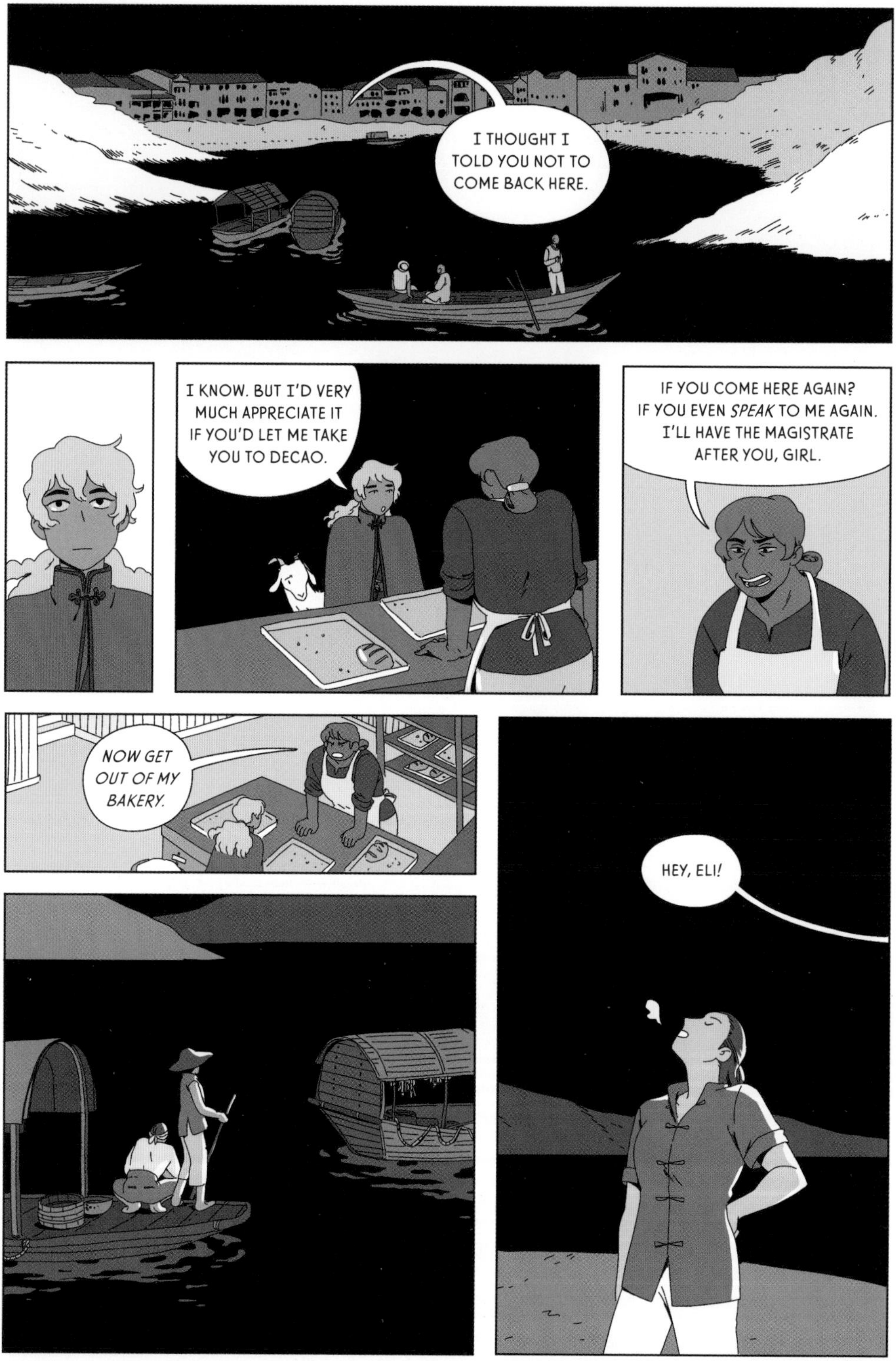
I THOUGHT I TOLD YOU NOT TO COME BACK HERE.
I KNOW. BUT I'D VERY MUCH APPRECIATE IT IF YOU'D LET ME TAKE YOU TO DECAO.
IF YOU COME HERE AGAIN? IF YOU EVEN *SPEAK* TO ME AGAIN. I'LL HAVE THE MAGISTRATE AFTER YOU, GIRL.
*NOW GET OUT OF MY BAKERY.*
HEY, ELI!

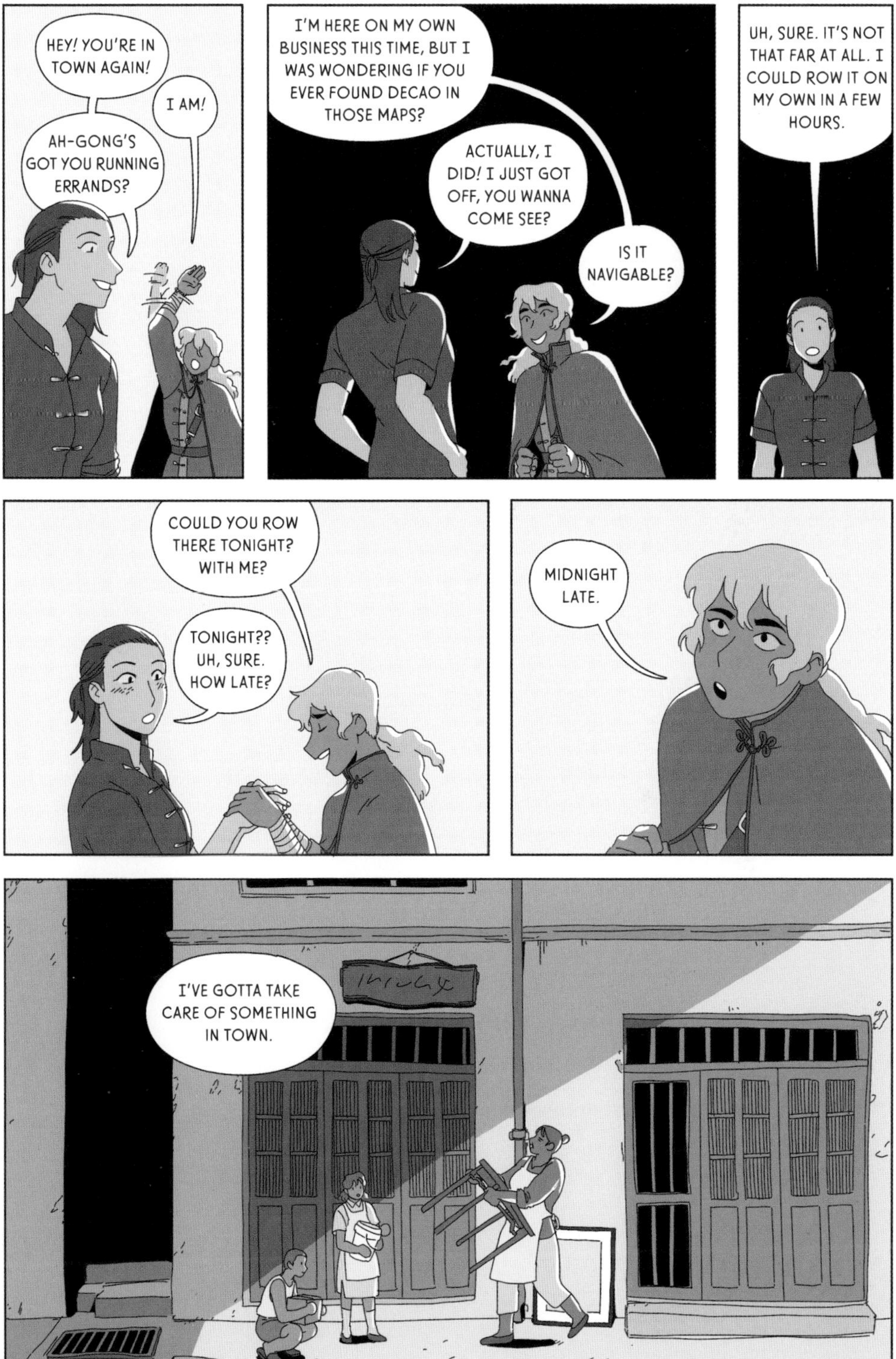
HEY! YOU'RE IN TOWN AGAIN!
I AM!
AH-GONG'S GOT YOU RUNNING ERRANDS?
I'M HERE ON MY OWN BUSINESS THIS TIME, BUT I WAS WONDERING IF YOU EVER FOUND DECAO IN THOSE MAPS?
ACTUALLY, I DID! I JUST GOT OFF, YOU WANNA COME SEE?
IS IT NAVIGABLE?
UH, SURE. IT'S NOT THAT FAR AT ALL. I COULD ROW IT ON MY OWN IN A FEW HOURS.
COULD YOU ROW THERE TONIGHT? WITH ME?
TONIGHT?? UH, SURE. HOW LATE?
MIDNIGHT LATE.
I'VE GOTTA TAKE CARE OF SOMETHING IN TOWN.

CLACK

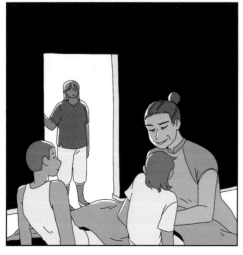

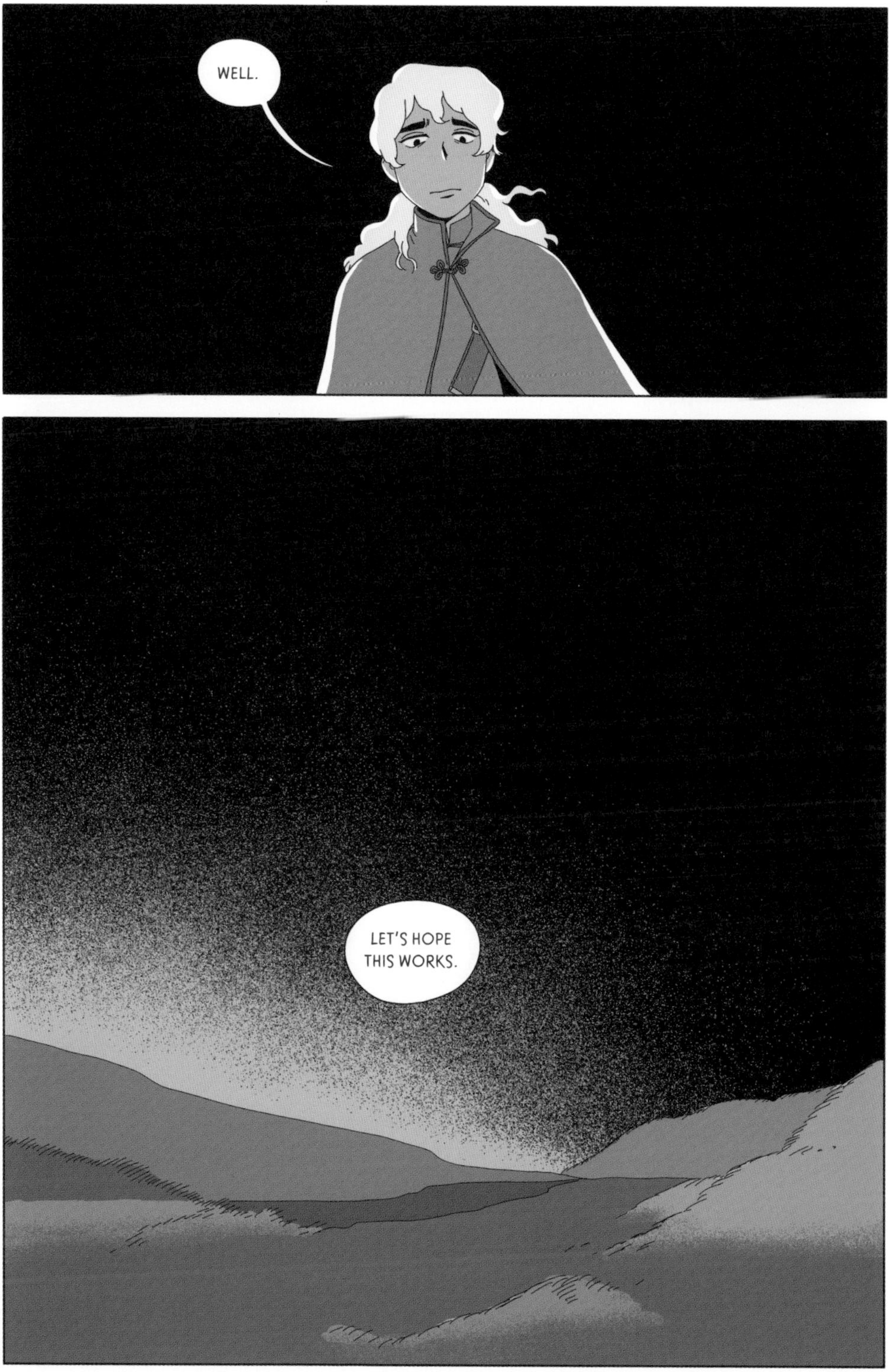
WELL.
LET'S HOPE THIS WORKS.

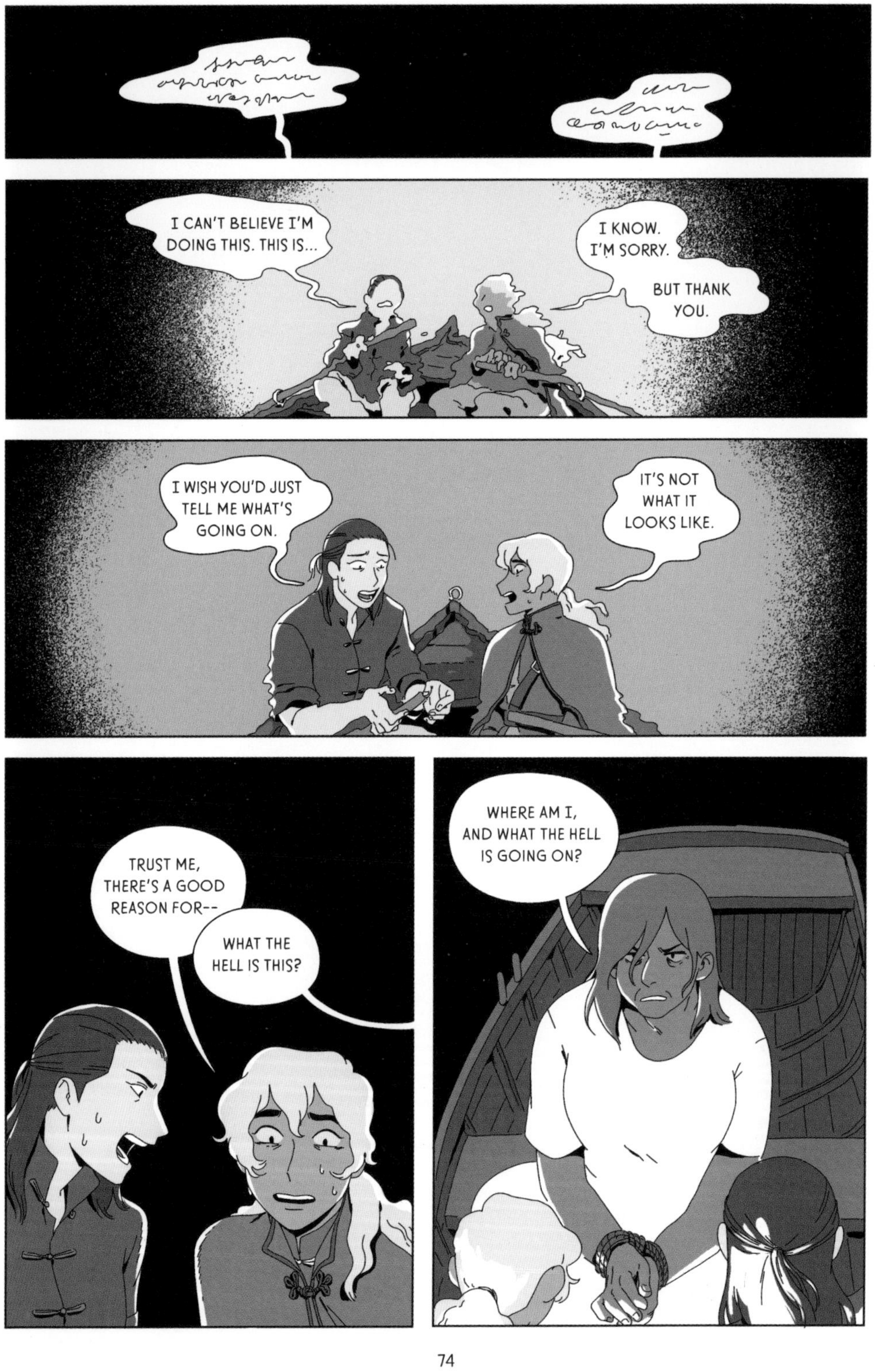
I CAN'T BELIEVE I'M DOING THIS. THIS IS...
I KNOW. I'M SORRY.
BUT THANK YOU.
I WISH YOU'D JUST TELL ME WHAT'S GOING ON.
IT'S NOT WHAT IT LOOKS LIKE.
TRUST ME, THERE'S A GOOD REASON FOR--
WHAT THE HELL IS THIS?
WHERE AM I, AND WHAT THE HELL IS GOING ON?

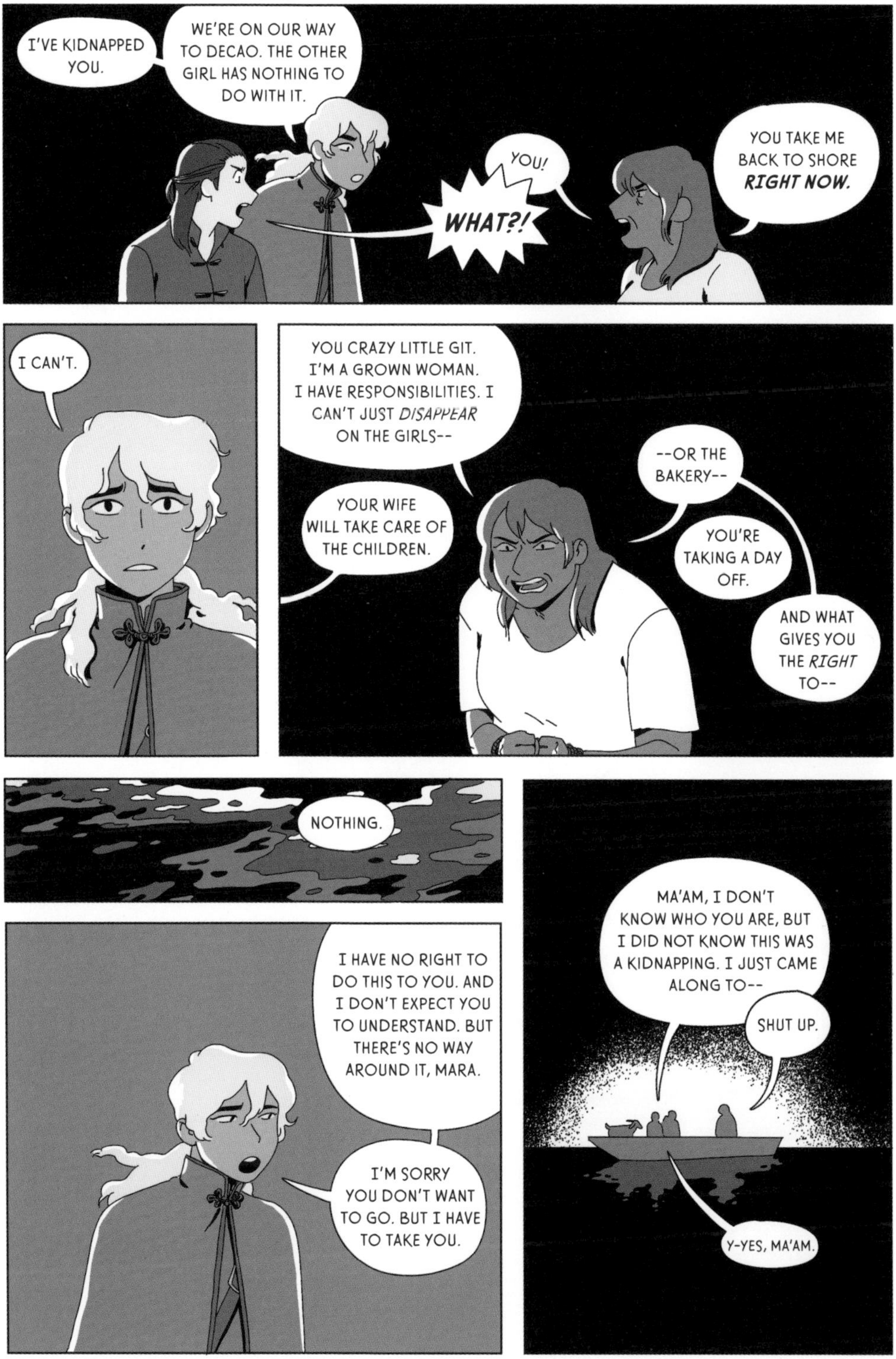
I'VE KIDNAPPED YOU.
WE'RE ON OUR WAY TO DECAO. THE OTHER GIRL HAS NOTHING TO DO WITH IT.
WHAT?!
YOU!
YOU TAKE ME BACK TO SHORE *RIGHT NOW.*
I CAN'T.
YOU CRAZY LITTLE GIT. I'M A GROWN WOMAN. I HAVE RESPONSIBILITIES. I CAN'T JUST *DISAPPEAR* ON THE GIRLS--
YOUR WIFE WILL TAKE CARE OF THE CHILDREN.
--OR THE BAKERY--
YOU'RE TAKING A DAY OFF.
AND WHAT GIVES YOU THE *RIGHT* TO--
NOTHING.
I HAVE NO RIGHT TO DO THIS TO YOU. AND I DON'T EXPECT YOU TO UNDERSTAND. BUT THERE'S NO WAY AROUND IT, MARA.
I'M SORRY YOU DON'T WANT TO GO. BUT I HAVE TO TAKE YOU.
MA'AM, I DON'T KNOW WHO YOU ARE, BUT I DID NOT KNOW THIS WAS A KIDNAPPING. I JUST CAME ALONG TO--
SHUT UP.
Y-YES, MA'AM.

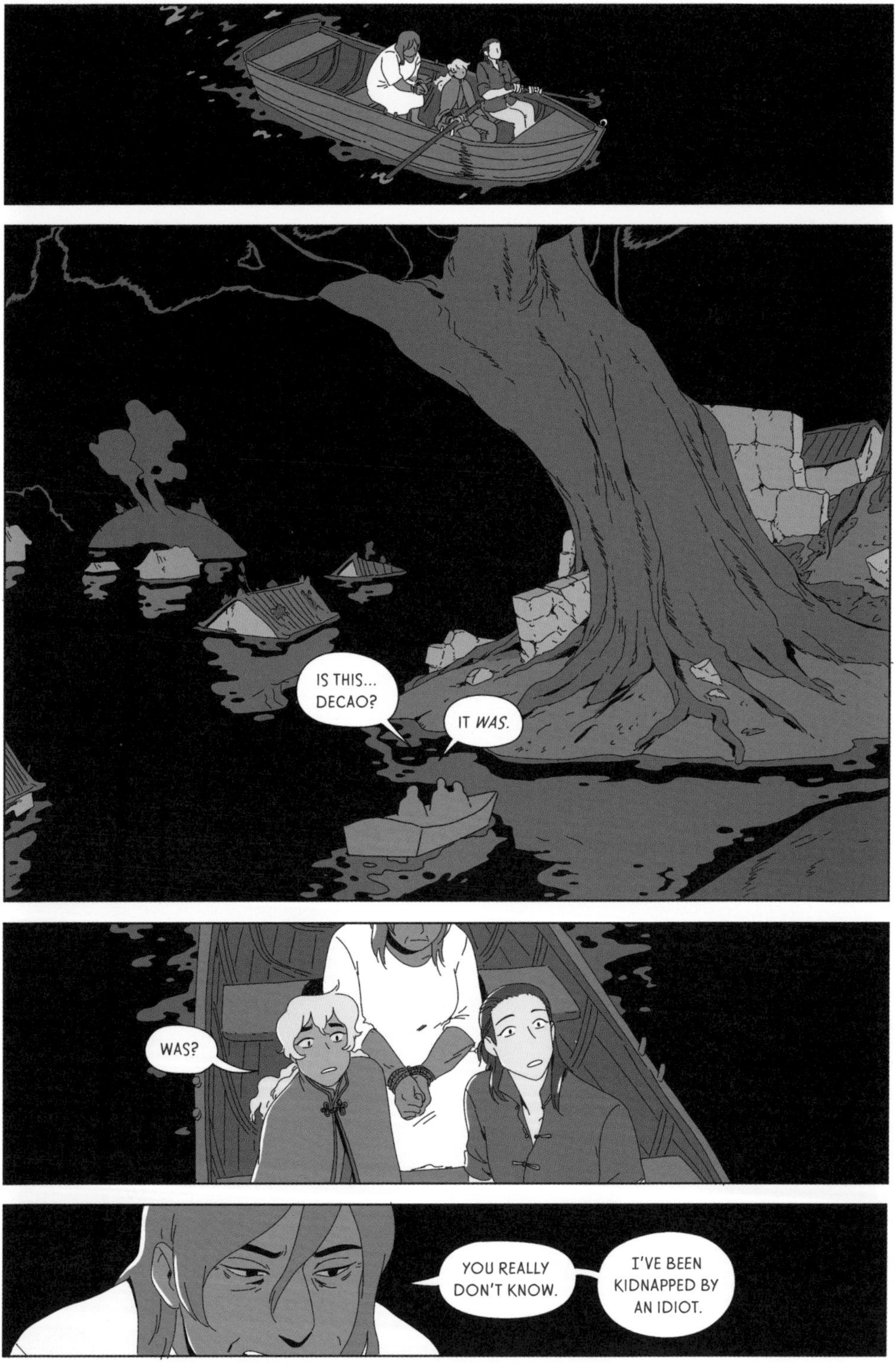
IS THIS... DECAO?
IT *WAS*.
WAS?
YOU REALLY DON'T KNOW.
I'VE BEEN KIDNAPPED BY AN IDIOT.

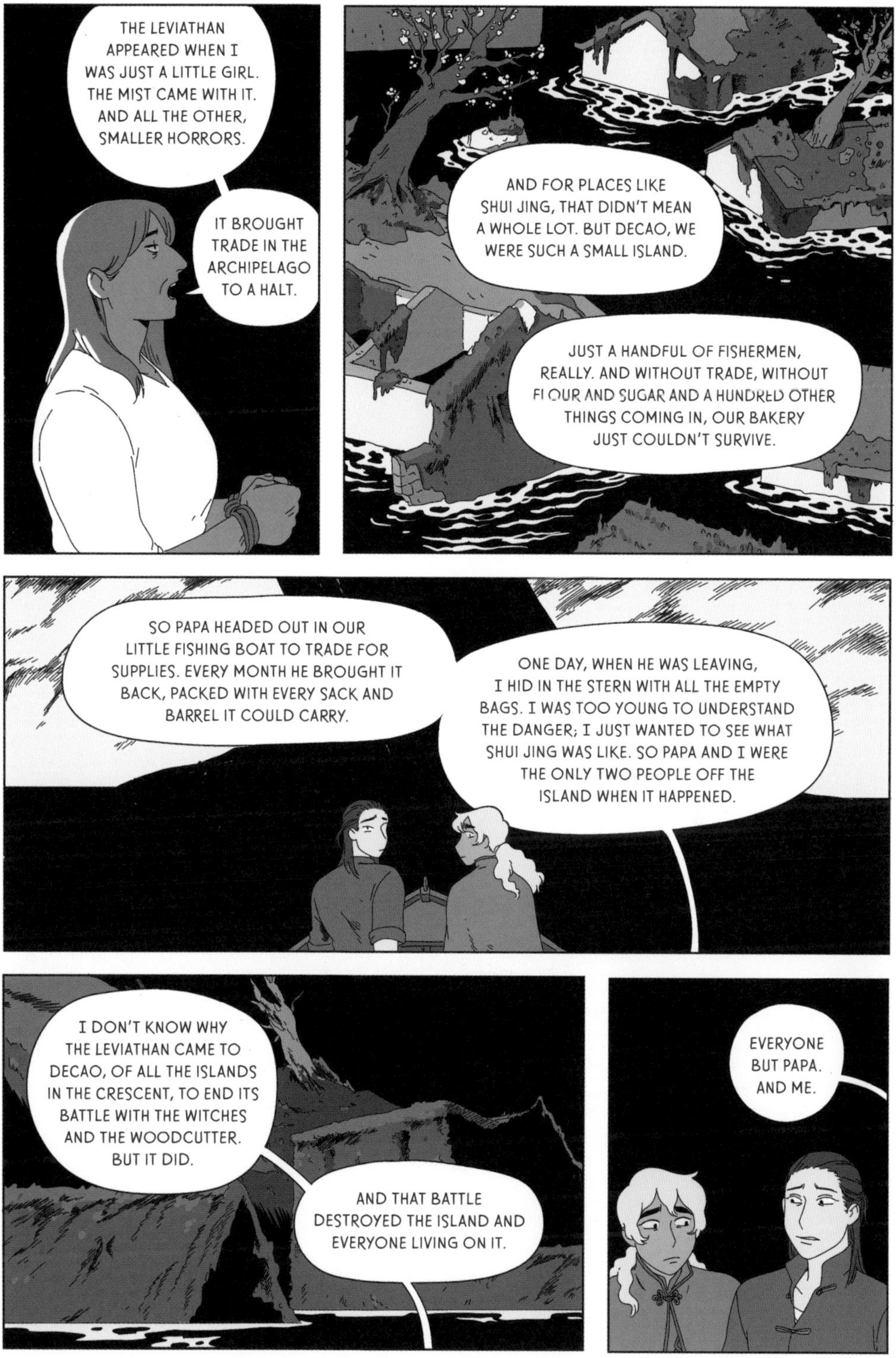
THE LEVIATHAN APPEARED WHEN I WAS JUST A LITTLE GIRL. THE MIST CAME WITH IT. AND ALL THE OTHER, SMALLER HORRORS.
IT BROUGHT TRADE IN THE ARCHIPELAGO TO A HALT.
AND FOR PLACES LIKE SHUI JING, THAT DIDN'T MEAN A WHOLE LOT. BUT DECAO, WE WERE SUCH A SMALL ISLAND.
JUST A HANDFUL OF FISHERMEN, REALLY. AND WITHOUT TRADE, WITHOUT FLOUR AND SUGAR AND A HUNDRED OTHER THINGS COMING IN, OUR BAKERY JUST COULDN'T SURVIVE.
SO PAPA HEADED OUT IN OUR LITTLE FISHING BOAT TO TRADE FOR SUPPLIES. EVERY MONTH HE BROUGHT IT BACK, PACKED WITH EVERY SACK AND BARREL IT COULD CARRY.
ONE DAY, WHEN HE WAS LEAVING, I HID IN THE STERN WITH ALL THE EMPTY BAGS. I WAS TOO YOUNG TO UNDERSTAND THE DANGER; I JUST WANTED TO SEE WHAT SHUI JING WAS LIKE. SO PAPA AND I WERE THE ONLY TWO PEOPLE OFF THE ISLAND WHEN IT HAPPENED.
I DON'T KNOW WHY THE LEVIATHAN CAME TO DECAO, OF ALL THE ISLANDS IN THE CRESCENT, TO END ITS BATTLE WITH THE WITCHES AND THE WOODCUTTER. BUT IT DID.
AND THAT BATTLE DESTROYED THE ISLAND AND EVERYONE LIVING ON IT.
EVERYONE BUT PAPA. AND ME.

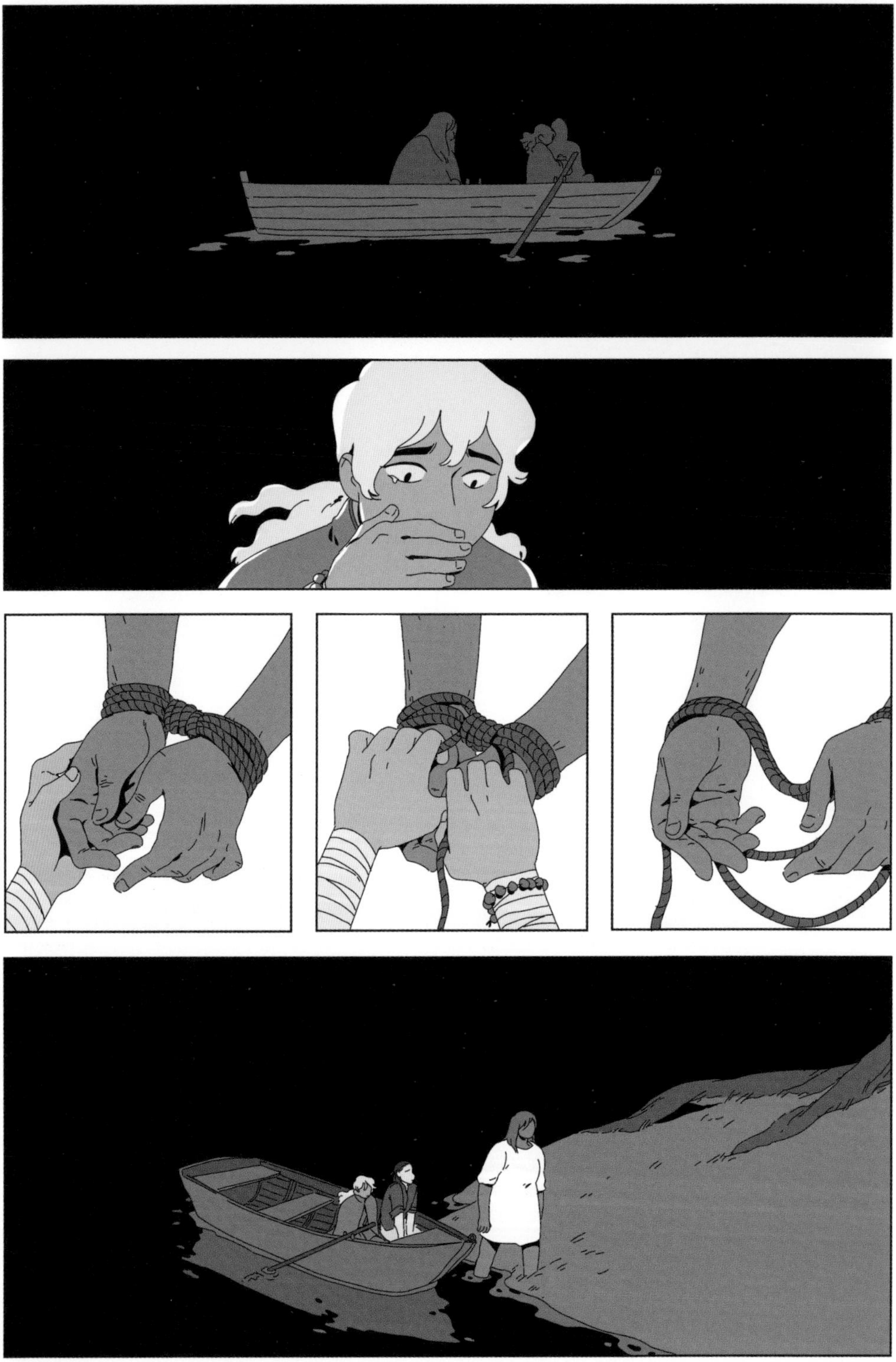

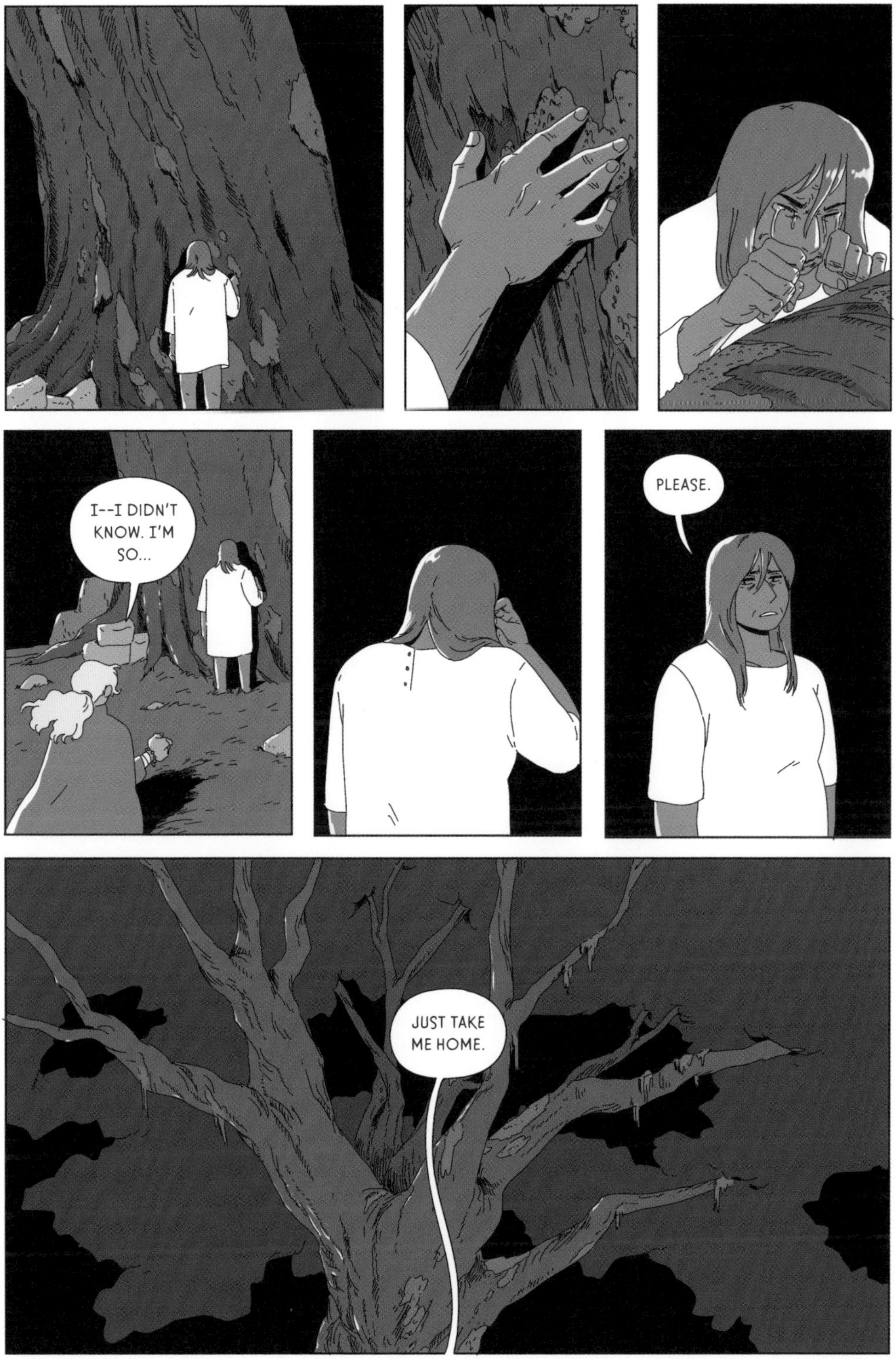
I--I DIDN'T KNOW. I'M SO...
PLEASE.
JUST TAKE ME HOME.

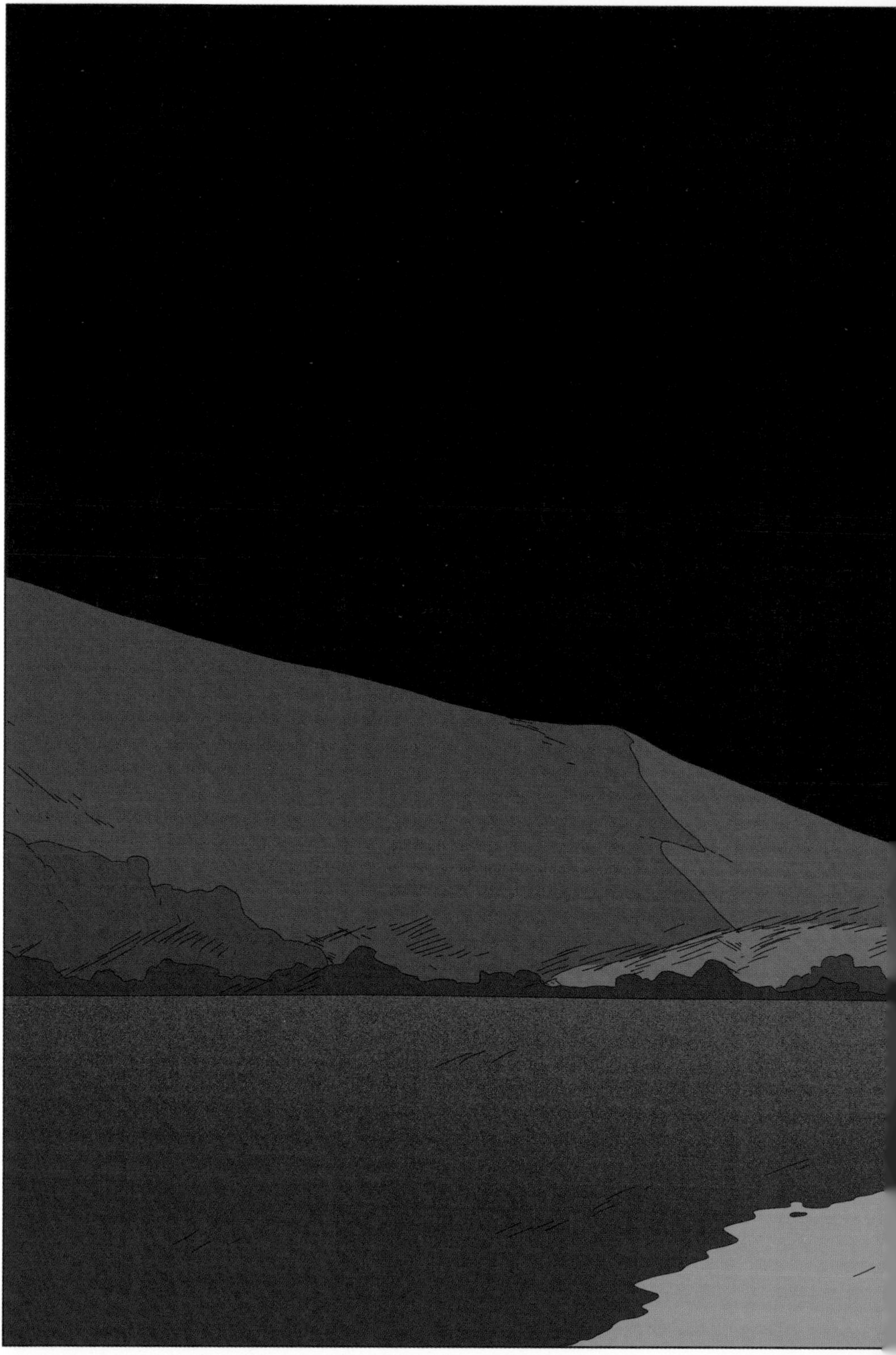

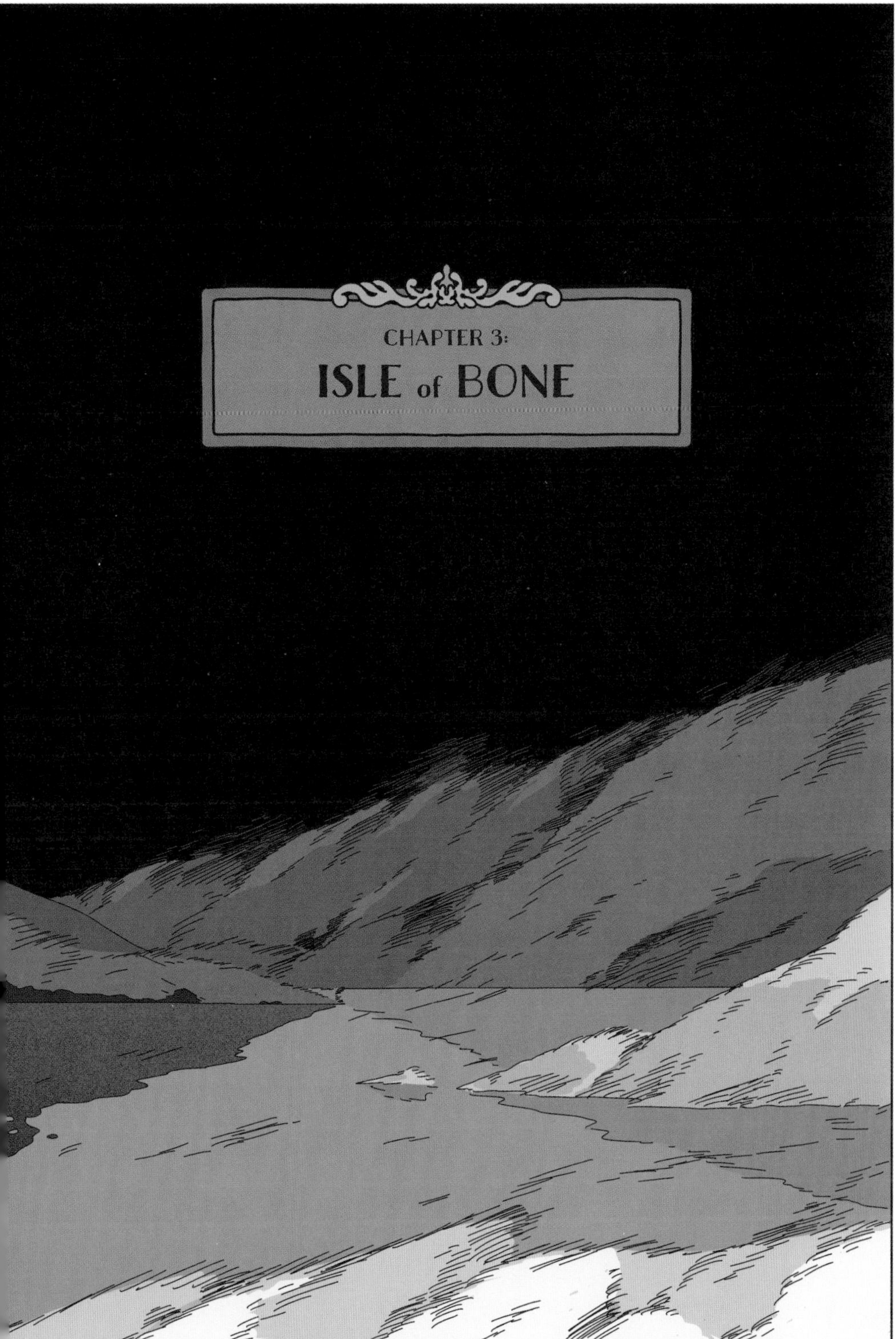
CHAPTER 3:
ISLE of BONE

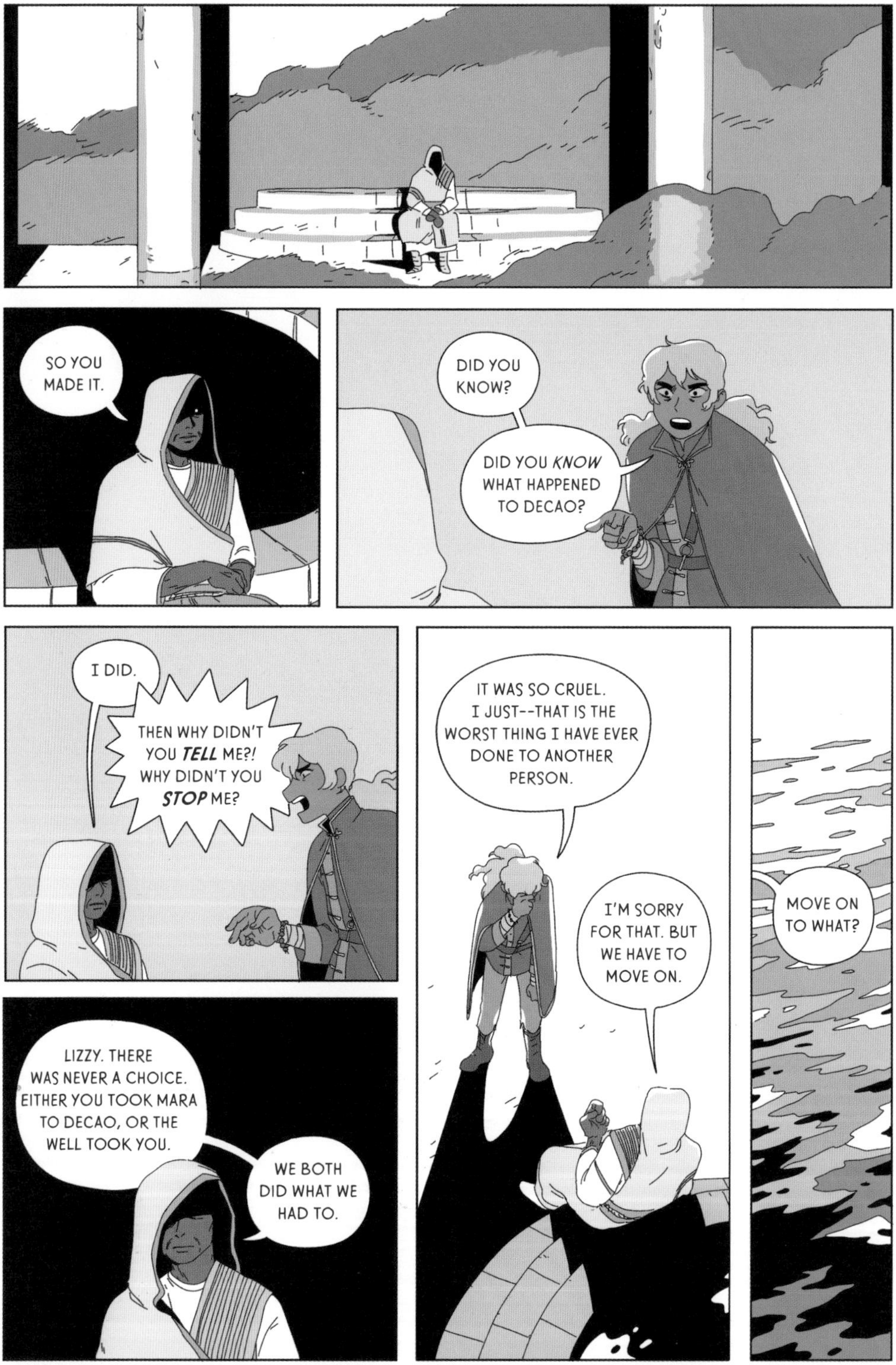

SO YOU MADE IT.
DID YOU KNOW?
DID YOU *KNOW* WHAT HAPPENED TO DECAO?
I DID.
THEN WHY DIDN'T YOU ***TELL*** ME?! WHY DIDN'T YOU ***STOP*** ME?
LIZZY. THERE WAS NEVER A CHOICE. EITHER YOU TOOK MARA TO DECAO, OR THE WELL TOOK YOU.
WE BOTH DID WHAT WE HAD TO.
IT WAS SO CRUEL. I JUST--THAT IS THE WORST THING I HAVE EVER DONE TO ANOTHER PERSON.
I'M SORRY FOR THAT. BUT WE HAVE TO MOVE ON.
MOVE ON TO WHAT?

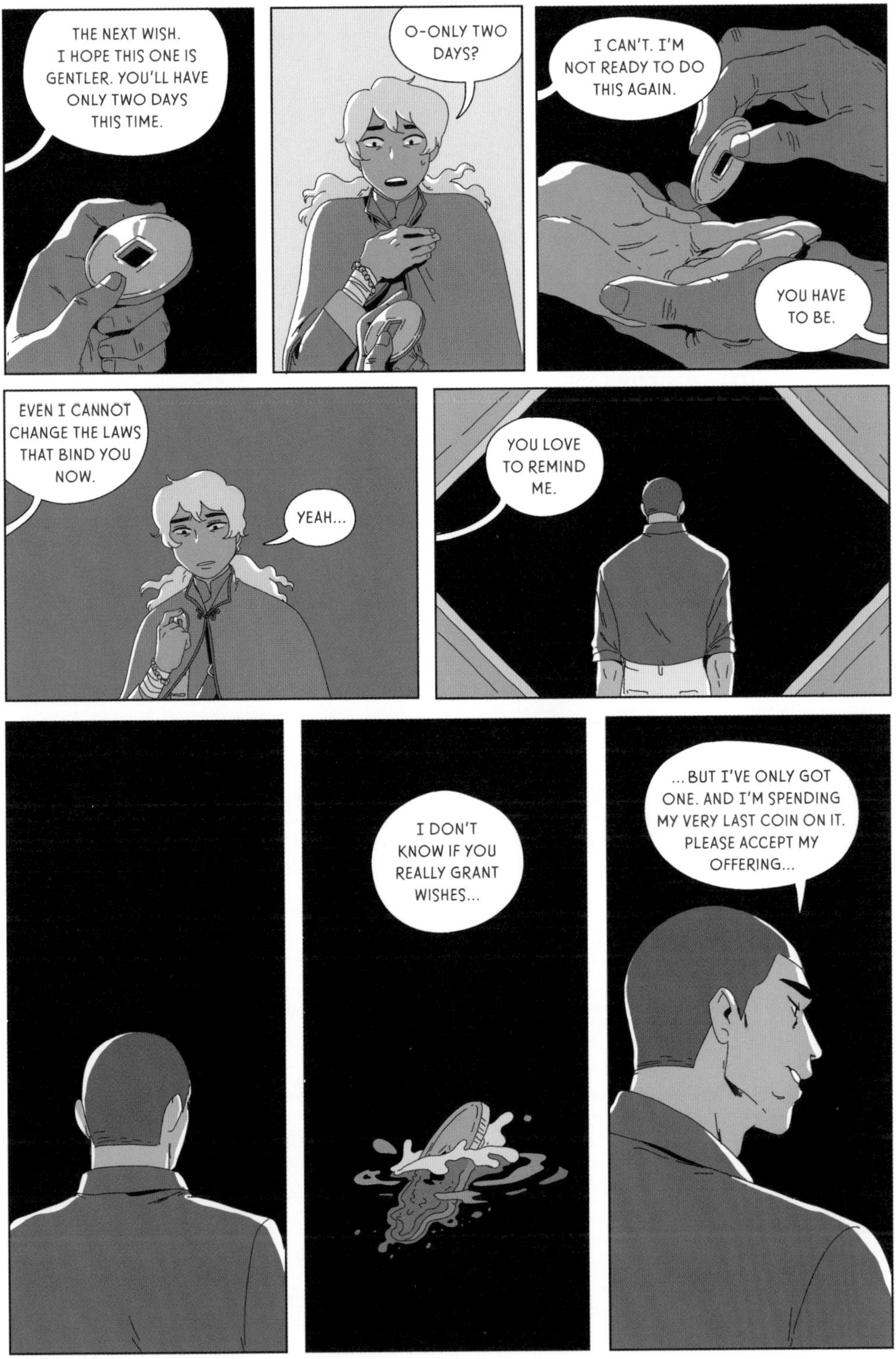
THE NEXT WISH. I HOPE THIS ONE IS GENTLER. YOU'LL HAVE ONLY TWO DAYS THIS TIME.
O-ONLY TWO DAYS?
I CAN'T. I'M NOT READY TO DO THIS AGAIN.
YOU HAVE TO BE.
EVEN I CANNOT CHANGE THE LAWS THAT BIND YOU NOW.
YEAH...
YOU LOVE TO REMIND ME.
I DON'T KNOW IF YOU REALLY GRANT WISHES...
... BUT I'VE ONLY GOT ONE. AND I'M SPENDING MY VERY LAST COIN ON IT. PLEASE ACCEPT MY OFFERING...

...AND MAKE ME THE RICHEST MAN IN THE ARCHIPELAGO.

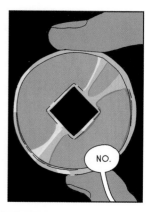

NO.

I WILL *NOT* HELP FLINT GET RICH! IT'S *HIS* FAULT THAT I'M STUCK RUNNING ERRANDS FOR A WELL IN THE FIRST PLACE!

OH? I THOUGHT IT WAS BECAUSE YOU SPENT ALL OF YOUR GRANDFATHER'S MONEY, LIED ABOUT IT, AND THEN STOLE SACRED OFFERINGS FROM A HOLY SHRINE.

IF THE WELL'S SO HOLY, SHOULDN'T THESE WISHES DO SOME GOOD?!

SHOULDN'T I BE *HELPING* PEOPLE? I JUST HURT A GOOD WOMAN FOR NO REASON, AND NOW I HAVE TO MAKE FLINT RICHER JUST BECAUSE HE'S GREEDY?

DID YOU THINK A WISHING WELL WOULD BE FULL OF NOBLE FEELINGS? A WISH IS PURE *DESIRE*, LIZZY. YOU'RE OLD ENOUGH TO KNOW THAT PEOPLE SELDOM WANT WHAT'S GOOD FOR THEM. OR ANYONE ELSE, FOR THAT MATTER.

YOU CAN CRY ABOUT IT ALL YOU LIKE. BUT IF I WERE YOU?

I'D START THINKING UP WAYS TO MAKE THE MAN RICH.

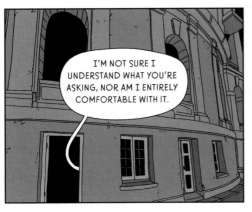

I'M NOT SURE I UNDERSTAND WHAT YOU'RE ASKING, NOR AM I ENTIRELY COMFORTABLE WITH IT.

IT IS AGAINST THE BANK'S POLICY TO REVEAL HOW MUCH MONEY IS IN A CLIENT'S ACCOUNT.

OUR PATRONS TRUST US TO BE DISCREET WITH THEIR--

I DON'T WANT TO KNOW HOW MUCH MONEY FLINT HAS, I JUST WANT TO KNOW HOW MUCH HE NEEDS TO BE THE RICHEST MAN IN SHUI JING.

WELL... THAT DOESN'T VIOLATE POLICY *PER SE...*

SEE? AND AREN'T YOU CURIOUS? DON'T YOU WANT TO KNOW?

OH, I KNOW, YOUNG LADY. HE NEEDS TWO HUNDRED THIRTY-SIX DINARS AND TWENTY-EIGHT DIRHAM TO BE THE RICHEST MAN IN THE--AH.

WELL. NOW I'VE TOLD YOU.

YOU KNEW THAT OFF THE TOP OF YOUR HEAD?

THE CAPTAIN ASKS ME ABOUT IT EVERY TIME HE MAKES A DEPOSIT. NOW, IS THERE ANYTHING ELSE I CAN DO FOR YOU?

THERE IS, ACTUALLY! I'D LIKE TO BORROW TWO HUNDRED THIRTY-SIX DINARS AND TWENTY-EIGHT DIRHAM, PLEASE.

TO WHAT PURPOSE?

TO... DEPOSIT INTO FLINT'S ACCOUNT?

NO.

WHAT? PLEASE?

NO.

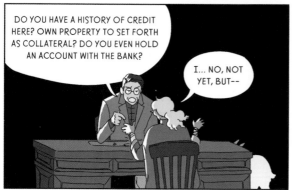

DO YOU HAVE A HISTORY OF CREDIT HERE? OWN PROPERTY TO SET FORTH AS COLLATERAL? DO YOU EVEN HOLD AN ACCOUNT WITH THE BANK?

I... NO, NOT YET, BUT--

THEN NO. I WILL NOT LEND SUCH A PREPOSTEROUS SUM OF MONEY TO A CHILD WITH NO ASSETS, NO ACCOUNTS, AND NO EXISTING CREDITORS.

SURE... OK... HOW MUCH WOULD YOU LEND ME?

IF YOU OPEN AN ACCOUNT TODAY?

FOUR DINARS. WITH HEAVY INTEREST. AND ON THE CONDITION THAT YOU NEVER BRING THIS OR ANY OTHER GOAT INTO THE BANK AGAIN.

I NEED A LOT MORE THAN THAT...

THEN YOU WILL HAVE TO GET IT ELSEWHERE.

FINE. PUT ME DOWN FOR FOUR DINARS.

AND, UH, WHAT'S "INTEREST"?

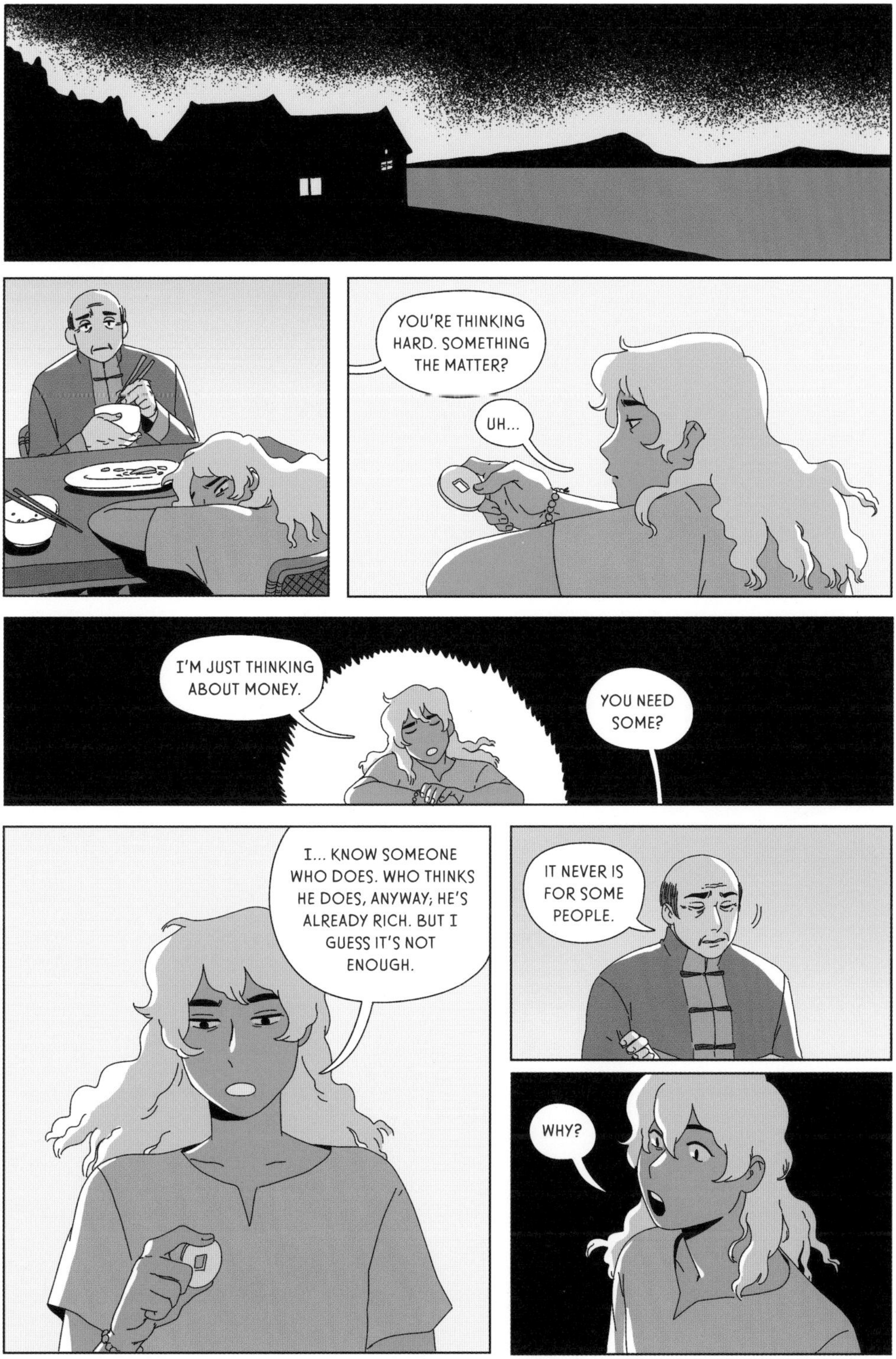
YOU'RE THINKING HARD. SOMETHING THE MATTER?
UH...
I'M JUST THINKING ABOUT MONEY.
YOU NEED SOME?
I... KNOW SOMEONE WHO DOES. WHO THINKS HE DOES, ANYWAY; HE'S ALREADY RICH. BUT I GUESS IT'S NOT ENOUGH.
IT NEVER IS FOR SOME PEOPLE.
WHY?

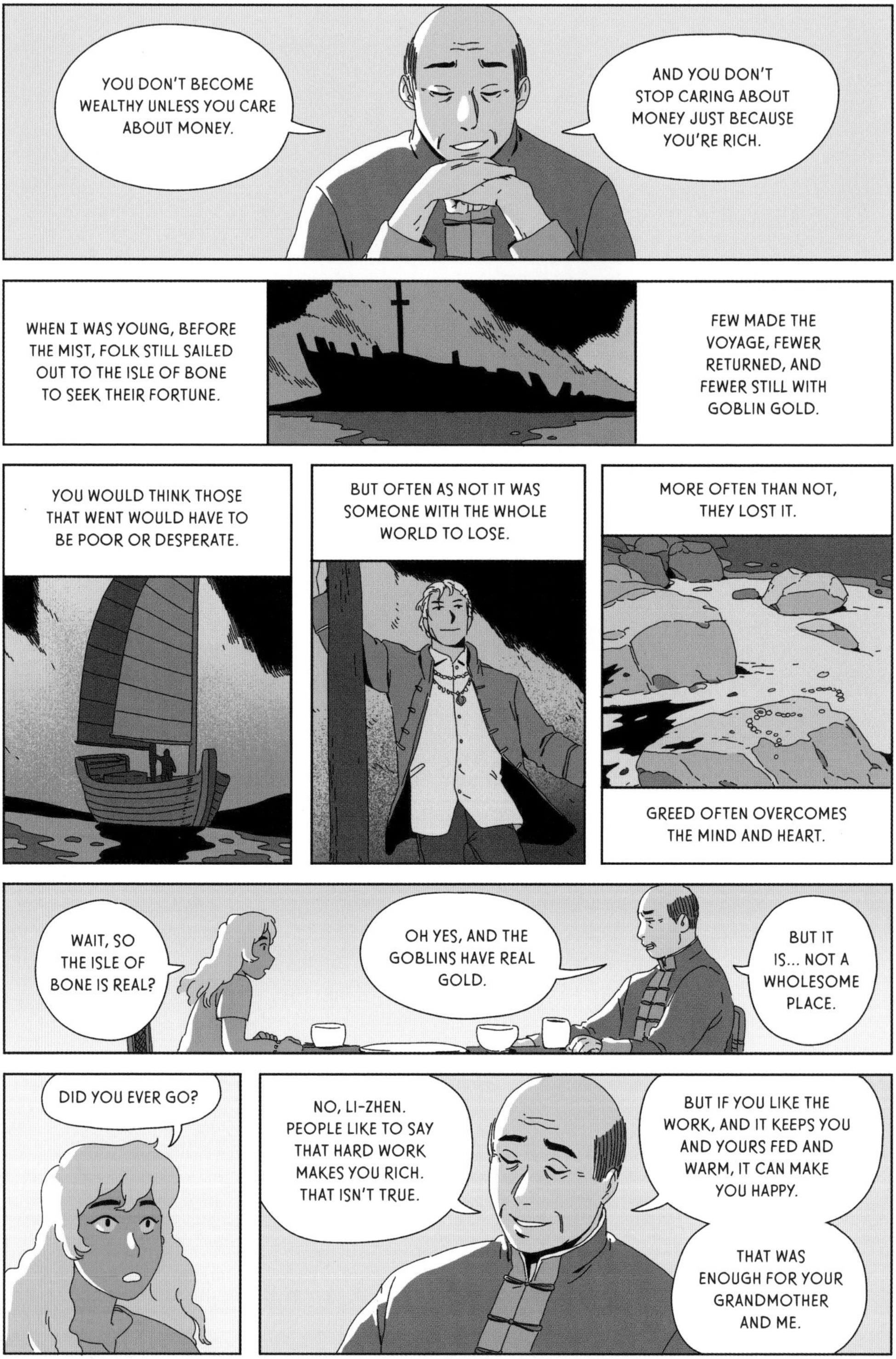
YOU DON'T BECOME WEALTHY UNLESS YOU CARE ABOUT MONEY.
AND YOU DON'T STOP CARING ABOUT MONEY JUST BECAUSE YOU'RE RICH.
WHEN I WAS YOUNG, BEFORE THE MIST, FOLK STILL SAILED OUT TO THE ISLE OF BONE TO SEEK THEIR FORTUNE.
FEW MADE THE VOYAGE, FEWER RETURNED, AND FEWER STILL WITH GOBLIN GOLD.
YOU WOULD THINK THOSE THAT WENT WOULD HAVE TO BE POOR OR DESPERATE.
BUT OFTEN AS NOT IT WAS SOMEONE WITH THE WHOLE WORLD TO LOSE.
MORE OFTEN THAN NOT, THEY LOST IT.
GREED OFTEN OVERCOMES THE MIND AND HEART.
WAIT, SO THE ISLE OF BONE IS REAL?
OH YES, AND THE GOBLINS HAVE REAL GOLD.
BUT IT IS... NOT A WHOLESOME PLACE.
DID YOU EVER GO?
NO, LI-ZHEN. PEOPLE LIKE TO SAY THAT HARD WORK MAKES YOU RICH. THAT ISN'T TRUE.
BUT IF YOU LIKE THE WORK, AND IT KEEPS YOU AND YOURS FED AND WARM, IT CAN MAKE YOU HAPPY.
THAT WAS ENOUGH FOR YOUR GRANDMOTHER AND ME.

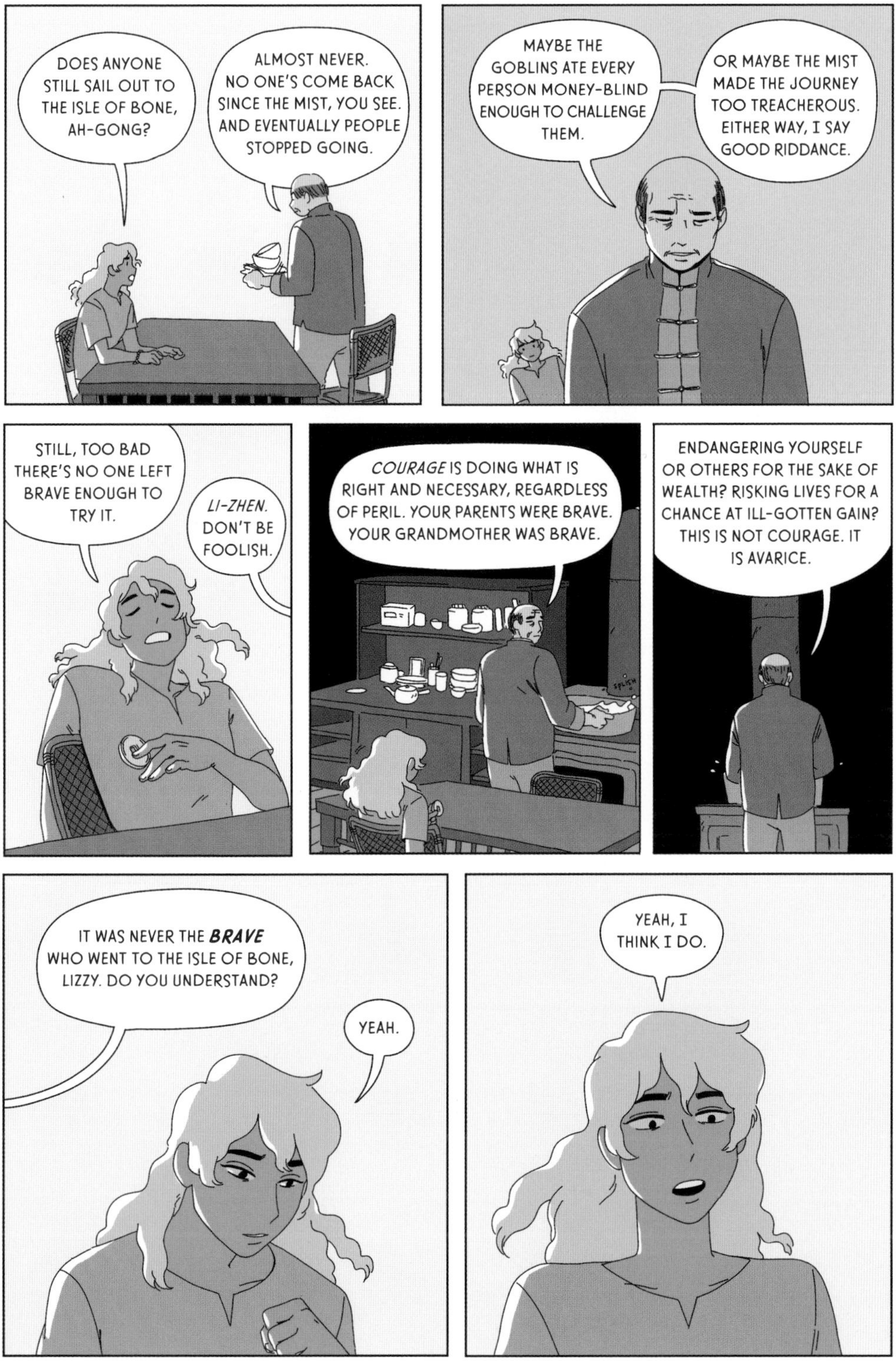
DOES ANYONE STILL SAIL OUT TO THE ISLE OF BONE, AH-GONG?
ALMOST NEVER. NO ONE'S COME BACK SINCE THE MIST, YOU SEE. AND EVENTUALLY PEOPLE STOPPED GOING.
MAYBE THE GOBLINS ATE EVERY PERSON MONEY-BLIND ENOUGH TO CHALLENGE THEM.
OR MAYBE THE MIST MADE THE JOURNEY TOO TREACHEROUS. EITHER WAY, I SAY GOOD RIDDANCE.
STILL, TOO BAD THERE'S NO ONE LEFT BRAVE ENOUGH TO TRY IT.
*LI-ZHEN.* DON'T BE FOOLISH.
*COURAGE* IS DOING WHAT IS RIGHT AND NECESSARY, REGARDLESS OF PERIL. YOUR PARENTS WERE BRAVE. YOUR GRANDMOTHER WAS BRAVE.
ENDANGERING YOURSELF OR OTHERS FOR THE SAKE OF WEALTH? RISKING LIVES FOR A CHANCE AT ILL-GOTTEN GAIN? THIS IS NOT COURAGE. IT IS AVARICE.
IT WAS NEVER THE ***BRAVE*** WHO WENT TO THE ISLE OF BONE, LIZZY. DO YOU UNDERSTAND?
YEAH.
YEAH, I THINK I DO.

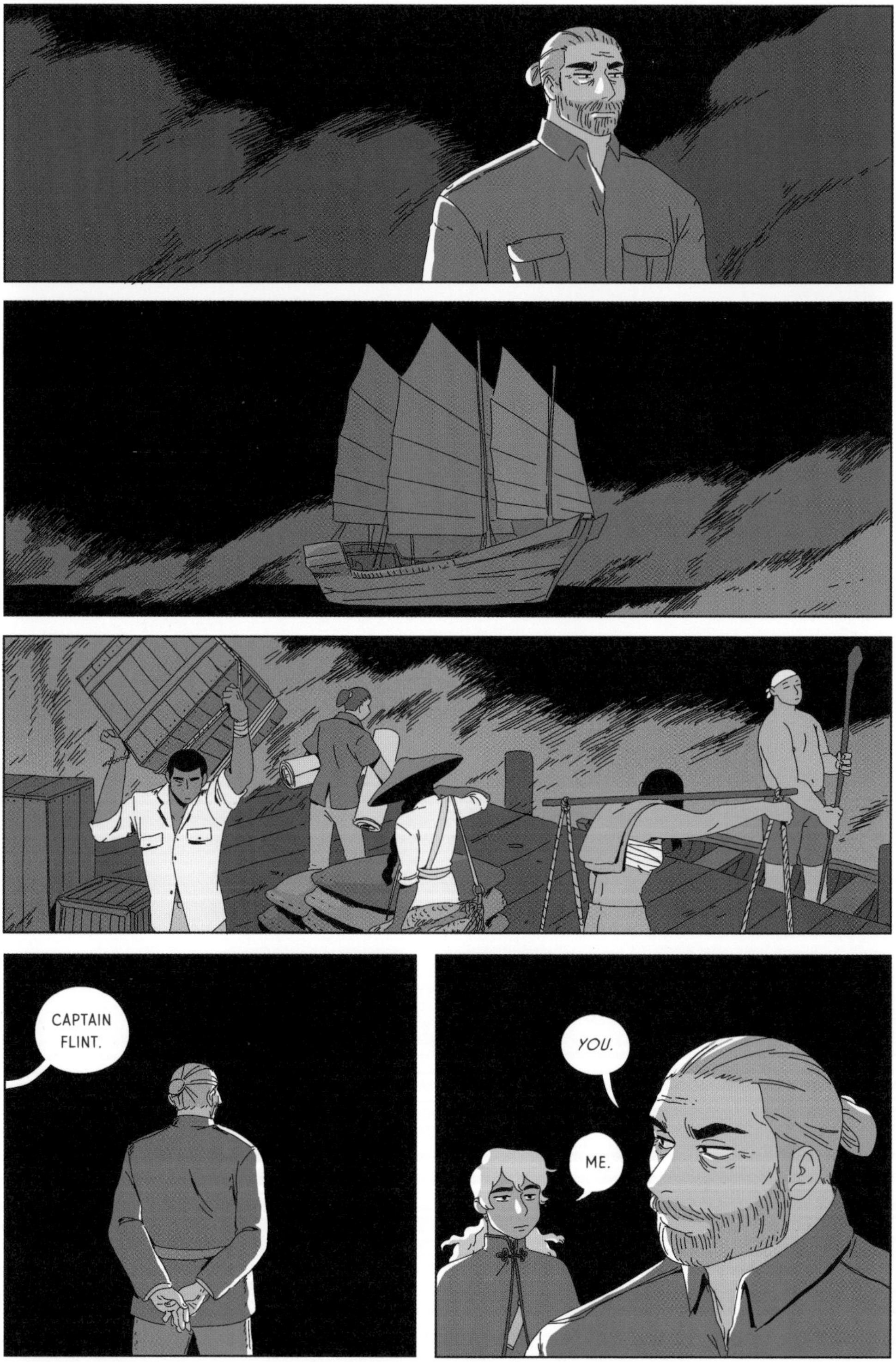
CAPTAIN FLINT.
YOU.
ME.

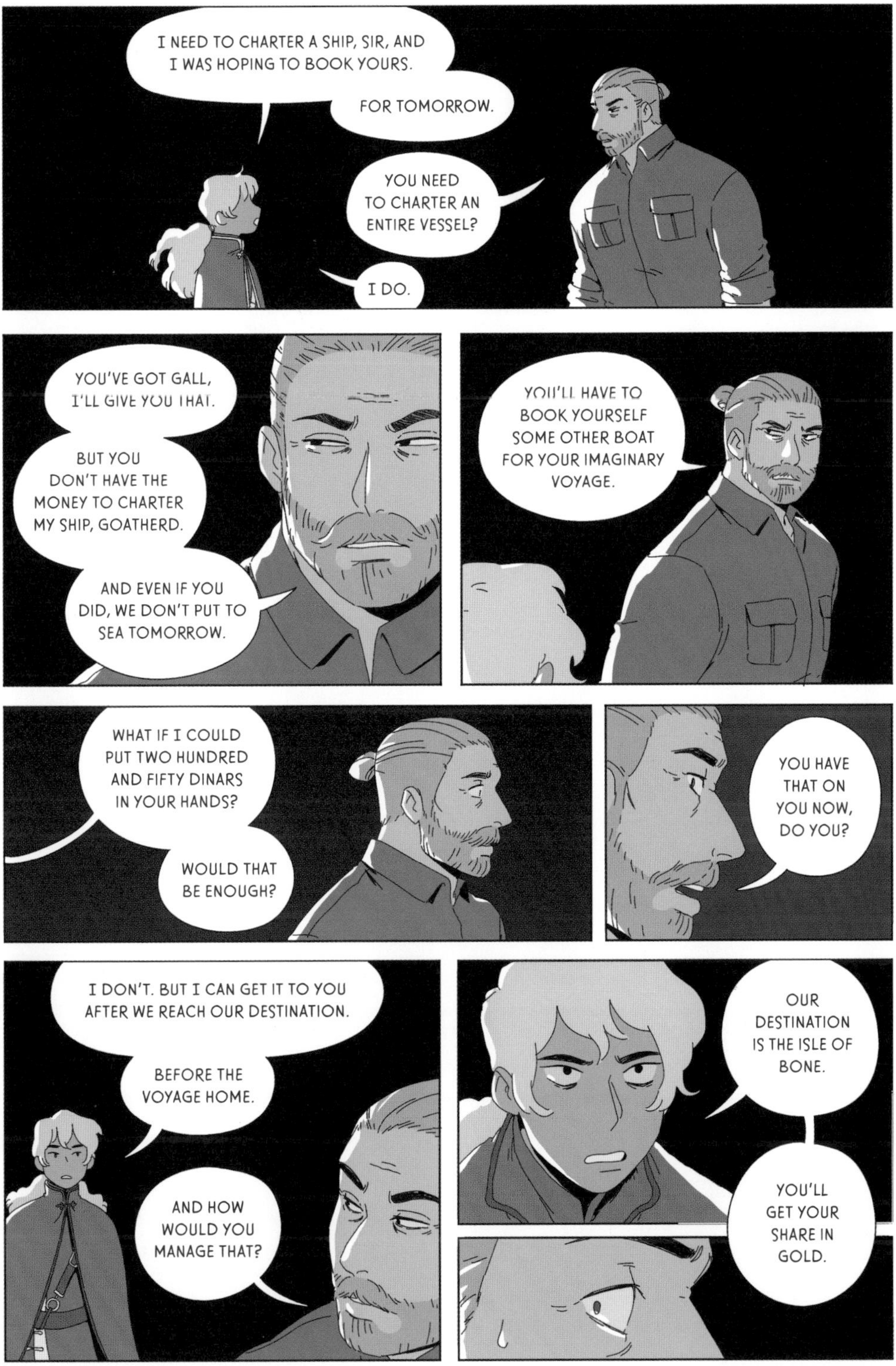
I NEED TO CHARTER A SHIP, SIR, AND I WAS HOPING TO BOOK YOURS.
FOR TOMORROW.
YOU NEED TO CHARTER AN ENTIRE VESSEL?
I DO.
YOU'VE GOT GALL, I'LL GIVE YOU THAT.
BUT YOU DON'T HAVE THE MONEY TO CHARTER MY SHIP, GOATHERD.
AND EVEN IF YOU DID, WE DON'T PUT TO SEA TOMORROW.
YOU'LL HAVE TO BOOK YOURSELF SOME OTHER BOAT FOR YOUR IMAGINARY VOYAGE.
WHAT IF I COULD PUT TWO HUNDRED AND FIFTY DINARS IN YOUR HANDS?
WOULD THAT BE ENOUGH?
YOU HAVE THAT ON YOU NOW, DO YOU?
I DON'T. BUT I CAN GET IT TO YOU AFTER WE REACH OUR DESTINATION.
BEFORE THE VOYAGE HOME.
AND HOW WOULD YOU MANAGE THAT?
OUR DESTINATION IS THE ISLE OF BONE.
YOU'LL GET YOUR SHARE IN GOLD.

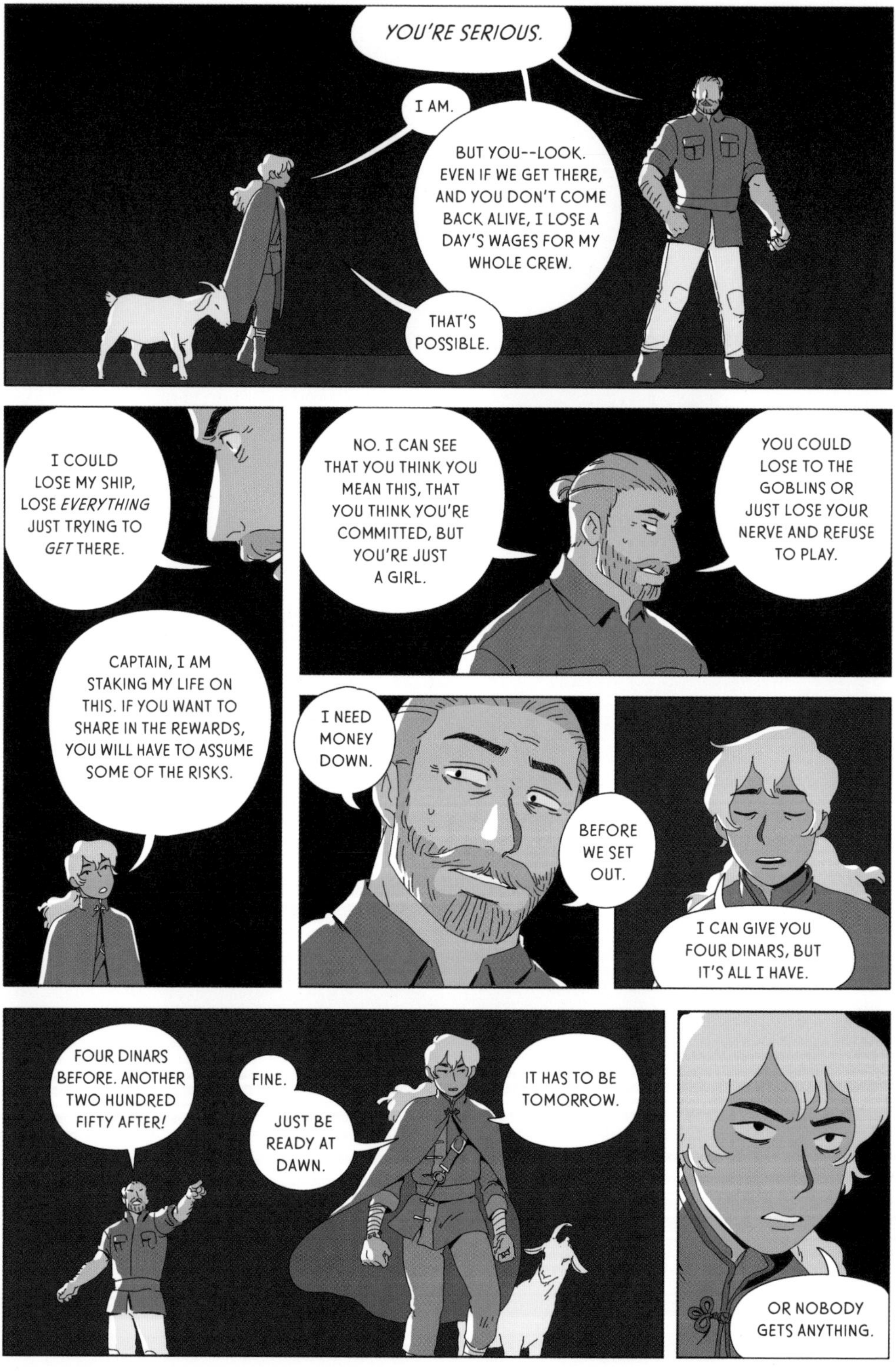
YOU'RE SERIOUS.
I AM.
BUT YOU--LOOK. EVEN IF WE GET THERE, AND YOU DON'T COME BACK ALIVE, I LOSE A DAY'S WAGES FOR MY WHOLE CREW.
THAT'S POSSIBLE.
I COULD LOSE MY SHIP, LOSE *EVERYTHING* JUST TRYING TO *GET* THERE.
NO. I CAN SEE THAT YOU THINK YOU MEAN THIS, THAT YOU THINK YOU'RE COMMITTED, BUT YOU'RE JUST A GIRL.
YOU COULD LOSE TO THE GOBLINS OR JUST LOSE YOUR NERVE AND REFUSE TO PLAY.
CAPTAIN, I AM STAKING MY LIFE ON THIS. IF YOU WANT TO SHARE IN THE REWARDS, YOU WILL HAVE TO ASSUME SOME OF THE RISKS.
I NEED MONEY DOWN.
BEFORE WE SET OUT.
I CAN GIVE YOU FOUR DINARS, BUT IT'S ALL I HAVE.
FOUR DINARS BEFORE. ANOTHER TWO HUNDRED FIFTY AFTER!
FINE.
JUST BE READY AT DAWN.
IT HAS TO BE TOMORROW.
OR NOBODY GETS ANYTHING.

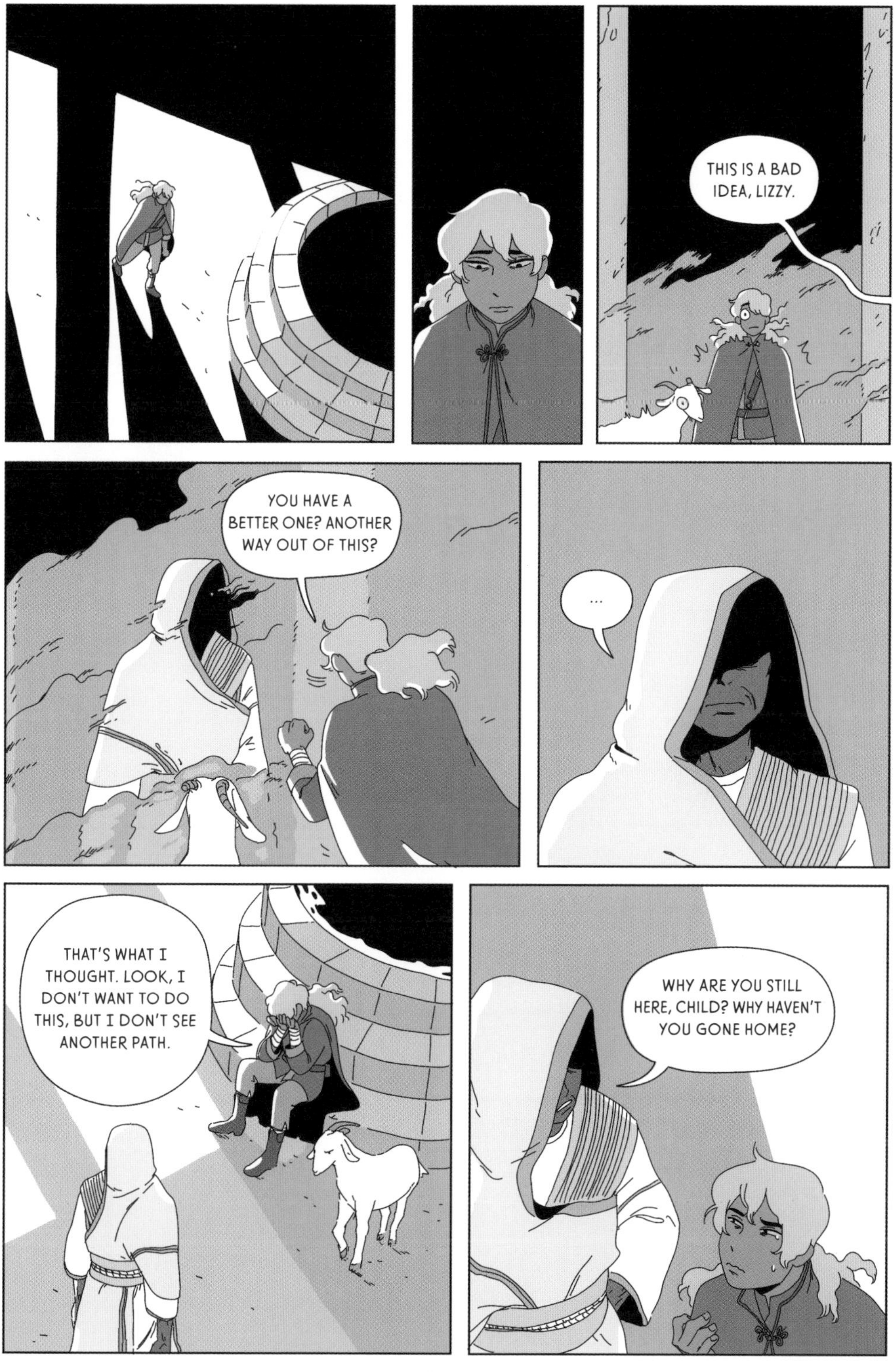
THIS IS A BAD IDEA, LIZZY.
YOU HAVE A BETTER ONE? ANOTHER WAY OUT OF THIS?
...
THAT'S WHAT I THOUGHT. LOOK, I DON'T WANT TO DO THIS, BUT I DON'T SEE ANOTHER PATH.
WHY ARE YOU STILL HERE, CHILD? WHY HAVEN'T YOU GONE HOME?

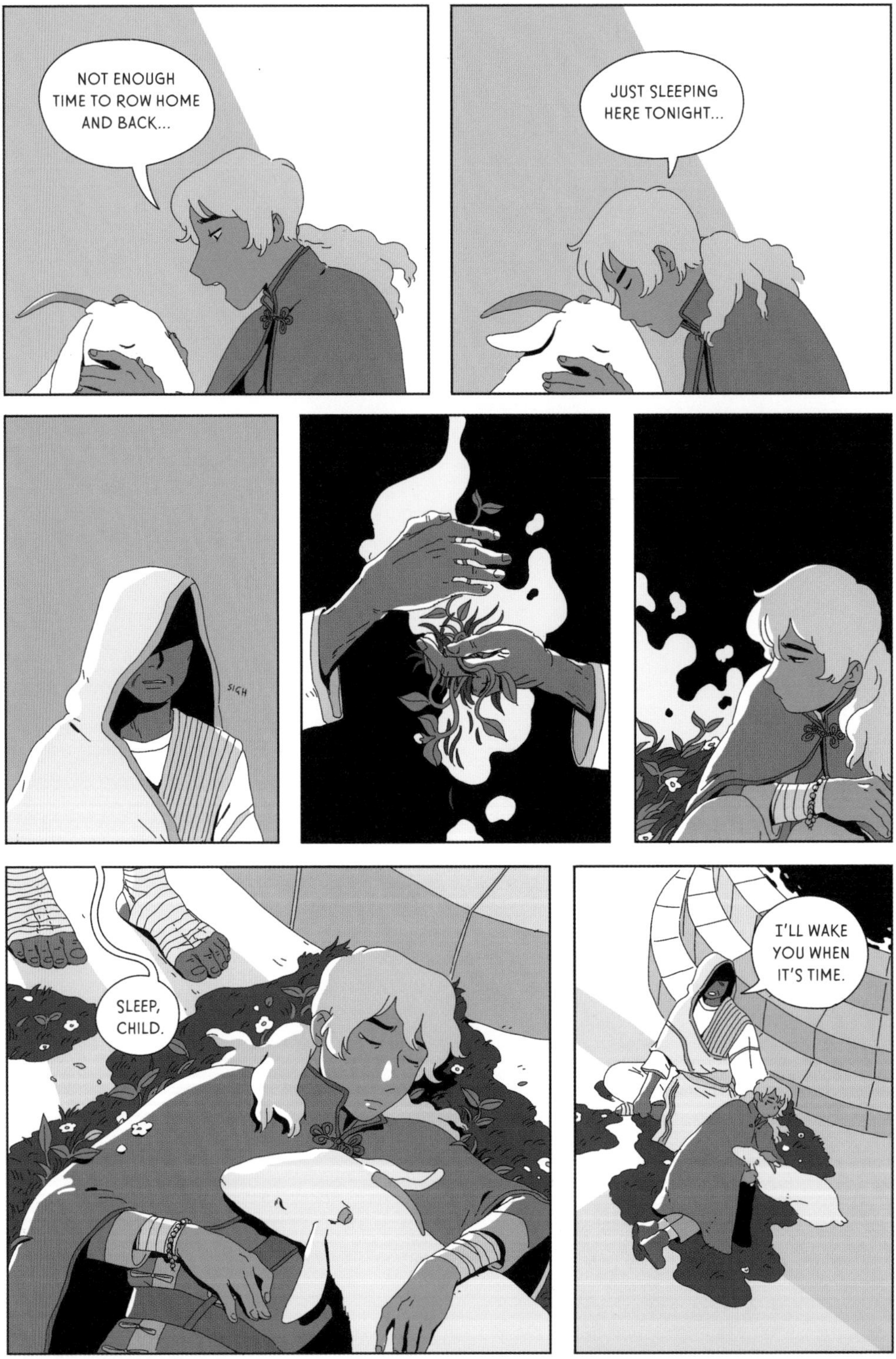
NOT ENOUGH TIME TO ROW HOME AND BACK...
JUST SLEEPING HERE TONIGHT...
SIGH
SLEEP, CHILD.
I'LL WAKE YOU WHEN IT'S TIME.

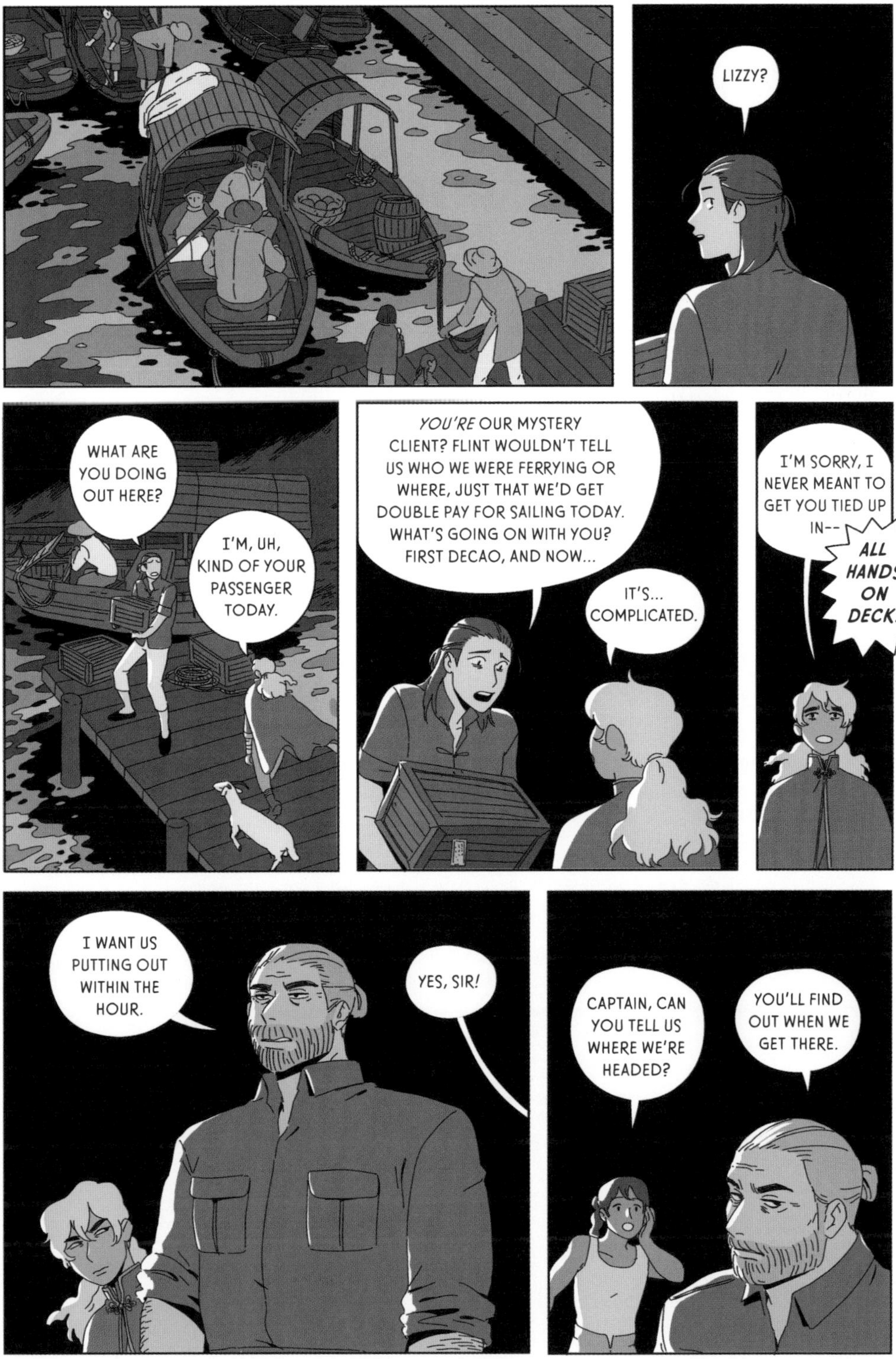
LIZZY?
WHAT ARE YOU DOING OUT HERE?
I'M, UH, KIND OF YOUR PASSENGER TODAY.
YOU'RE OUR MYSTERY CLIENT? FLINT WOULDN'T TELL US WHO WE WERE FERRYING OR WHERE, JUST THAT WE'D GET DOUBLE PAY FOR SAILING TODAY. WHAT'S GOING ON WITH YOU? FIRST DECAO, AND NOW...
IT'S... COMPLICATED.
I'M SORRY, I NEVER MEANT TO GET YOU TIED UP IN--
ALL HANDS ON DECK.
I WANT US PUTTING OUT WITHIN THE HOUR.
YES, SIR!
CAPTAIN, CAN YOU TELL US WHERE WE'RE HEADED?
YOU'LL FIND OUT WHEN WE GET THERE.

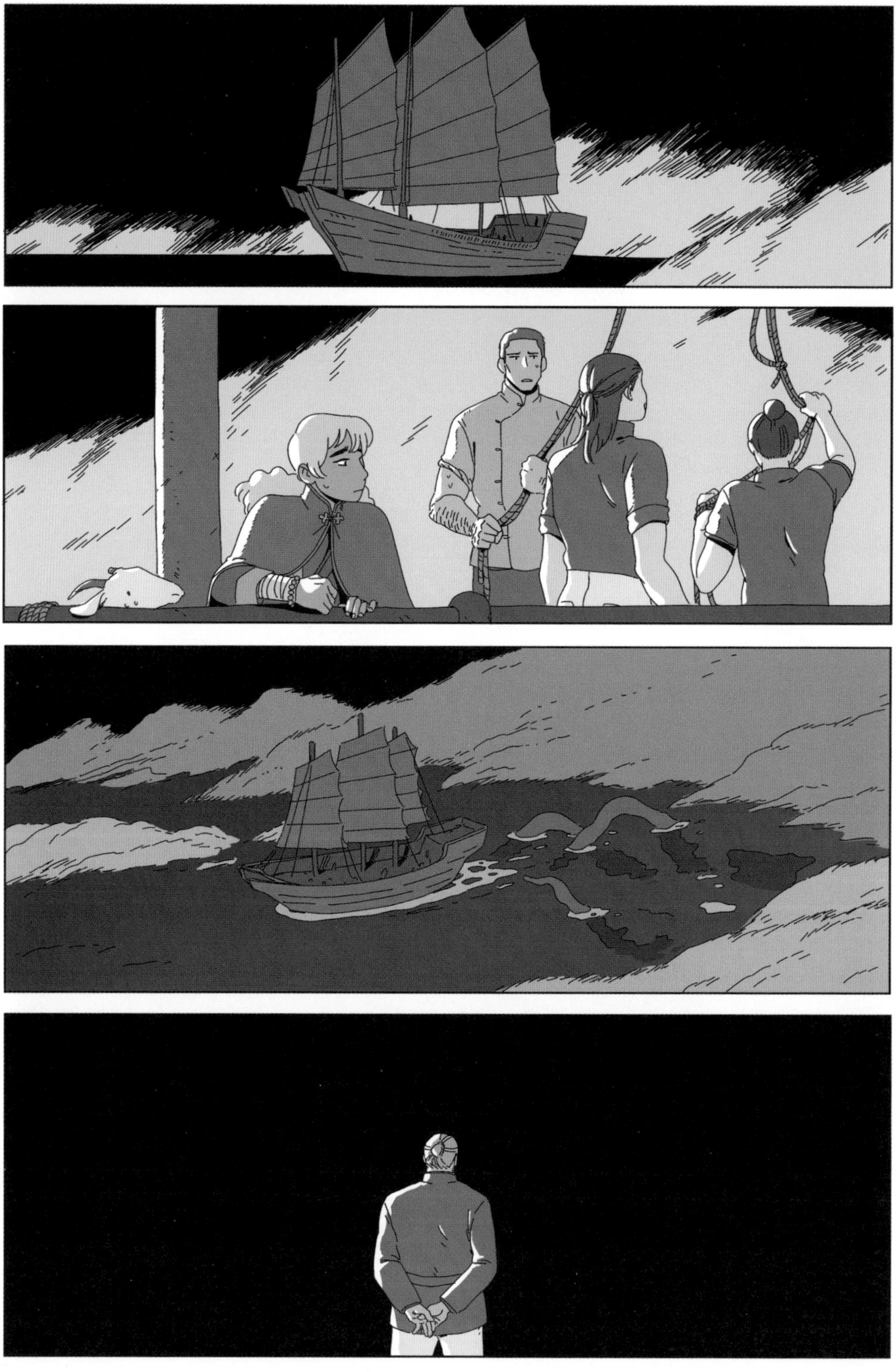

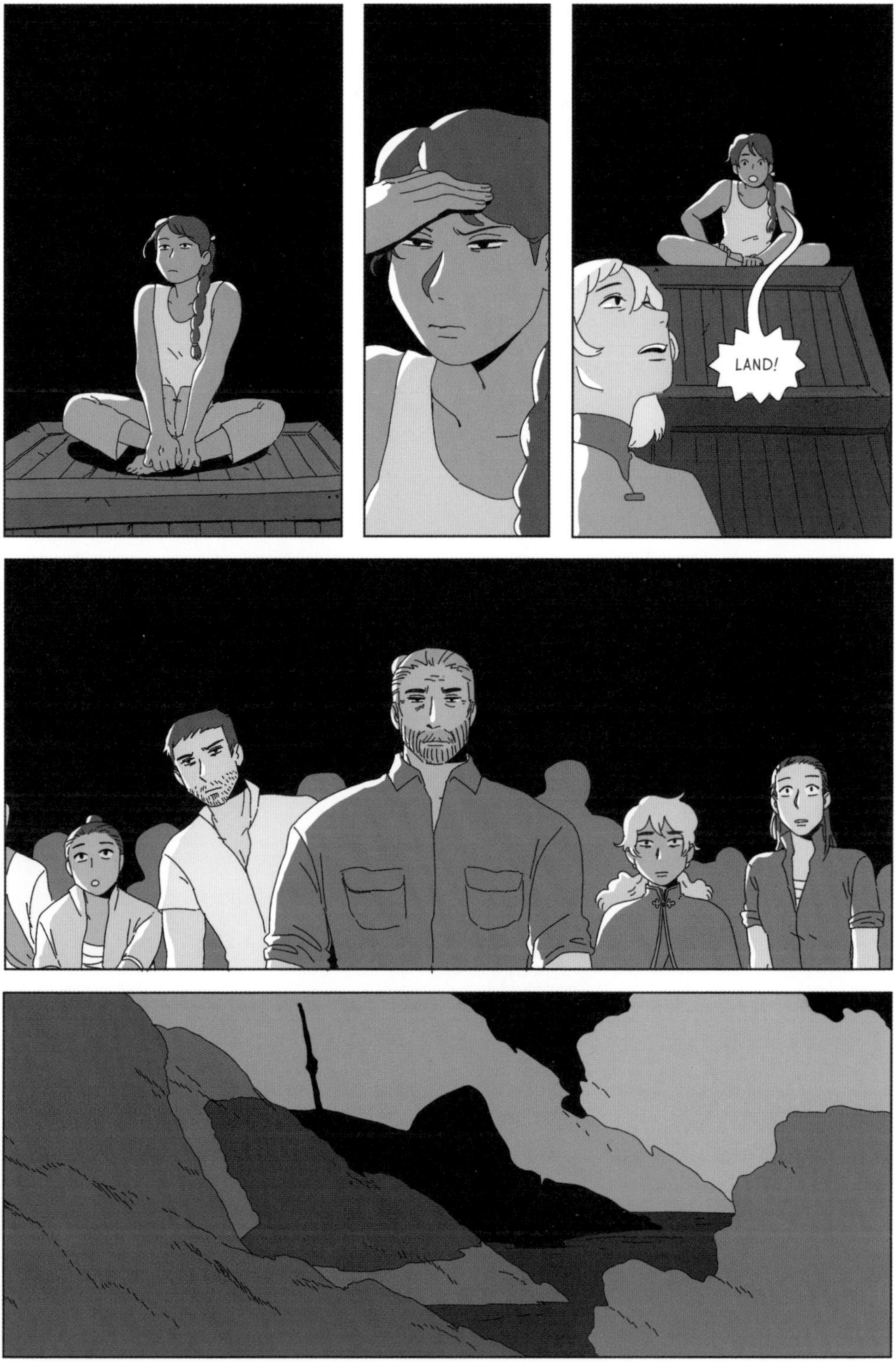
LAND!

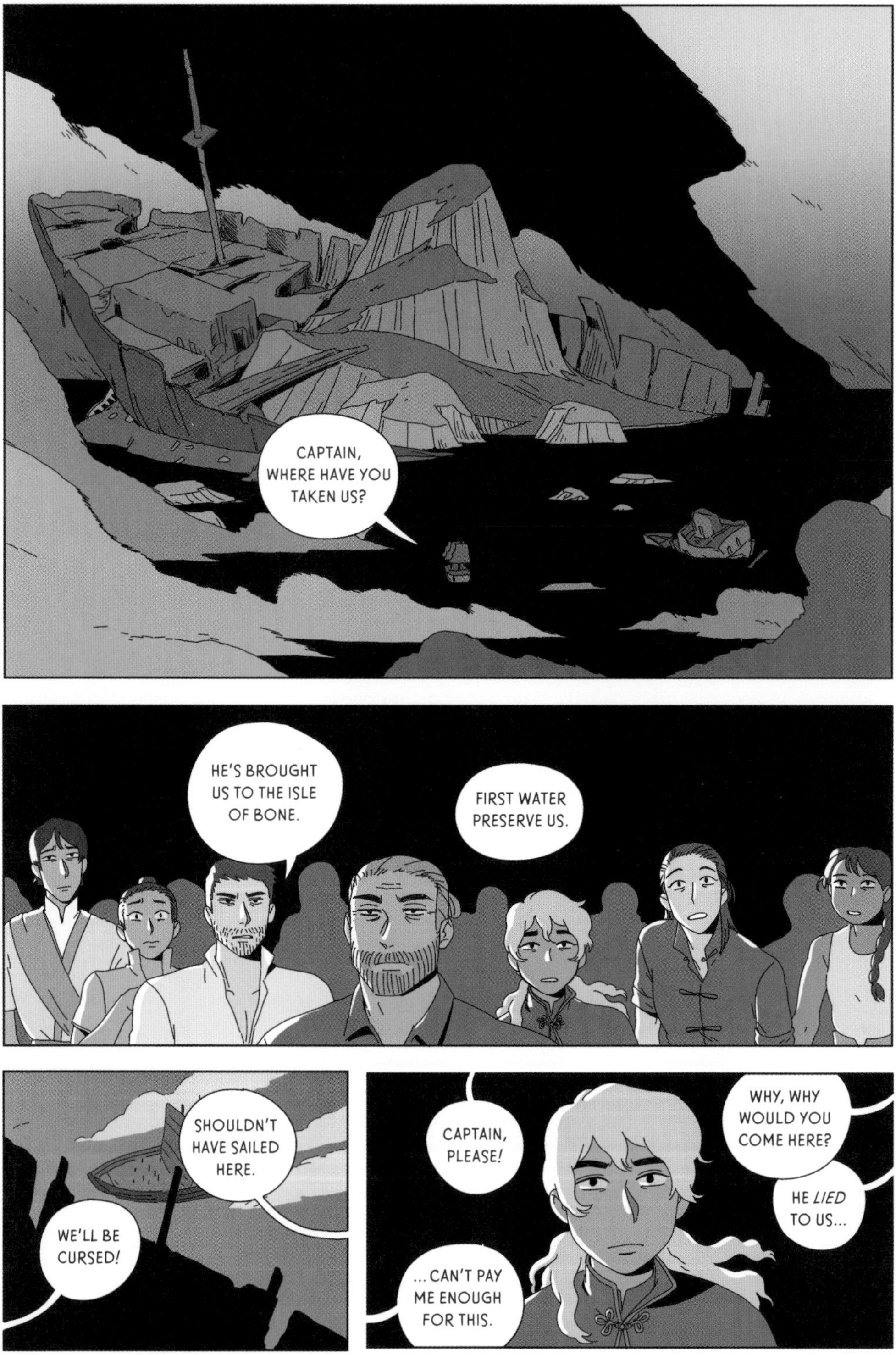
CAPTAIN, WHERE HAVE YOU TAKEN US?
HE'S BROUGHT US TO THE ISLE OF BONE.
FIRST WATER PRESERVE US.
SHOULDN'T HAVE SAILED HERE.
WE'LL BE CURSED!
CAPTAIN, PLEASE!
WHY, WHY WOULD YOU COME HERE?
HE *LIED* TO US...
...CAN'T PAY ME ENOUGH FOR THIS.

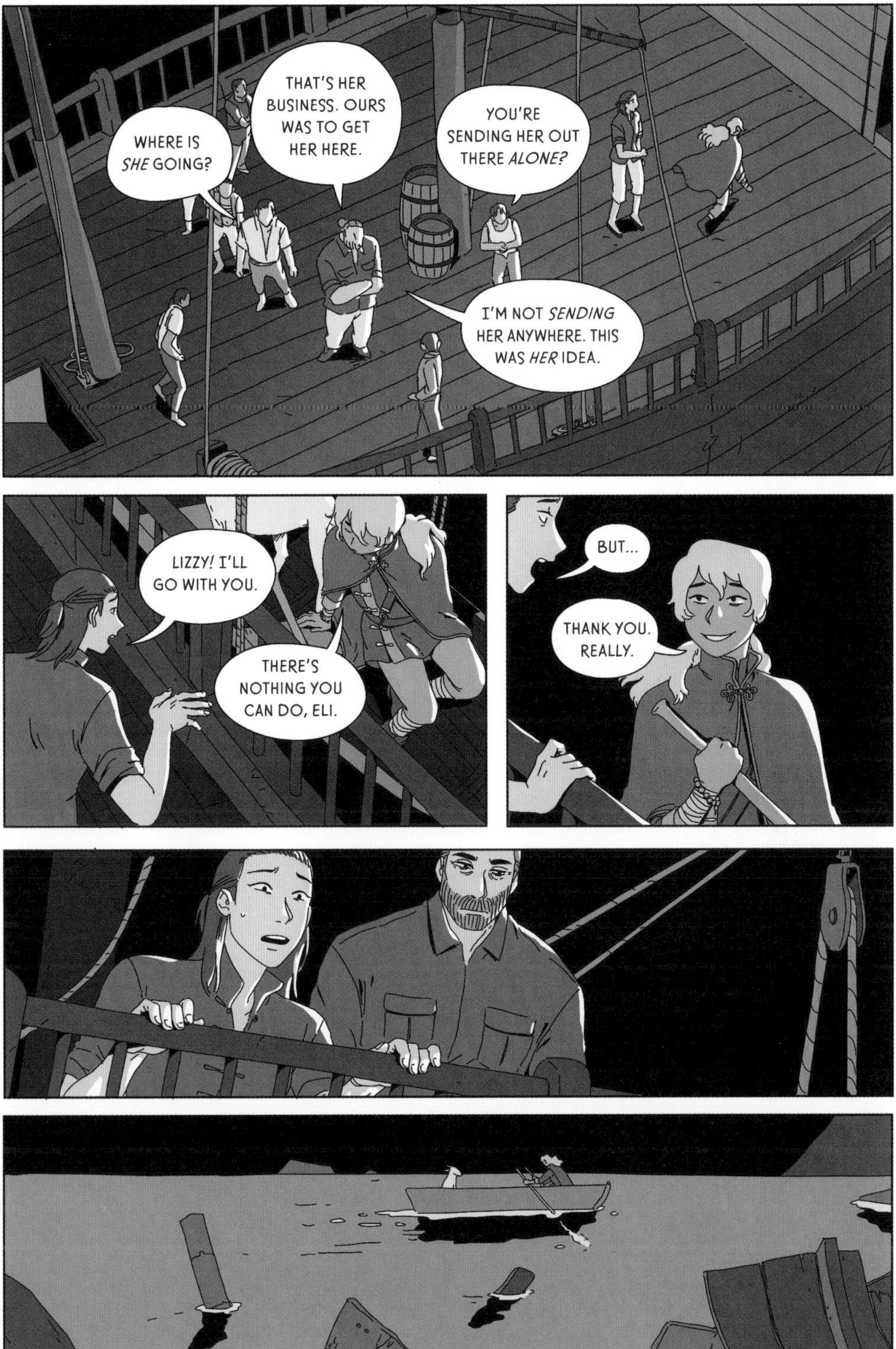
WHERE IS *SHE* GOING?
THAT'S HER BUSINESS. OURS WAS TO GET HER HERE.
YOU'RE SENDING HER OUT THERE *ALONE?*
I'M NOT *SENDING* HER ANYWHERE. THIS WAS *HER* IDEA.
LIZZY! I'LL GO WITH YOU.
THERE'S NOTHING YOU CAN DO, ELI.
BUT...
THANK YOU. REALLY.

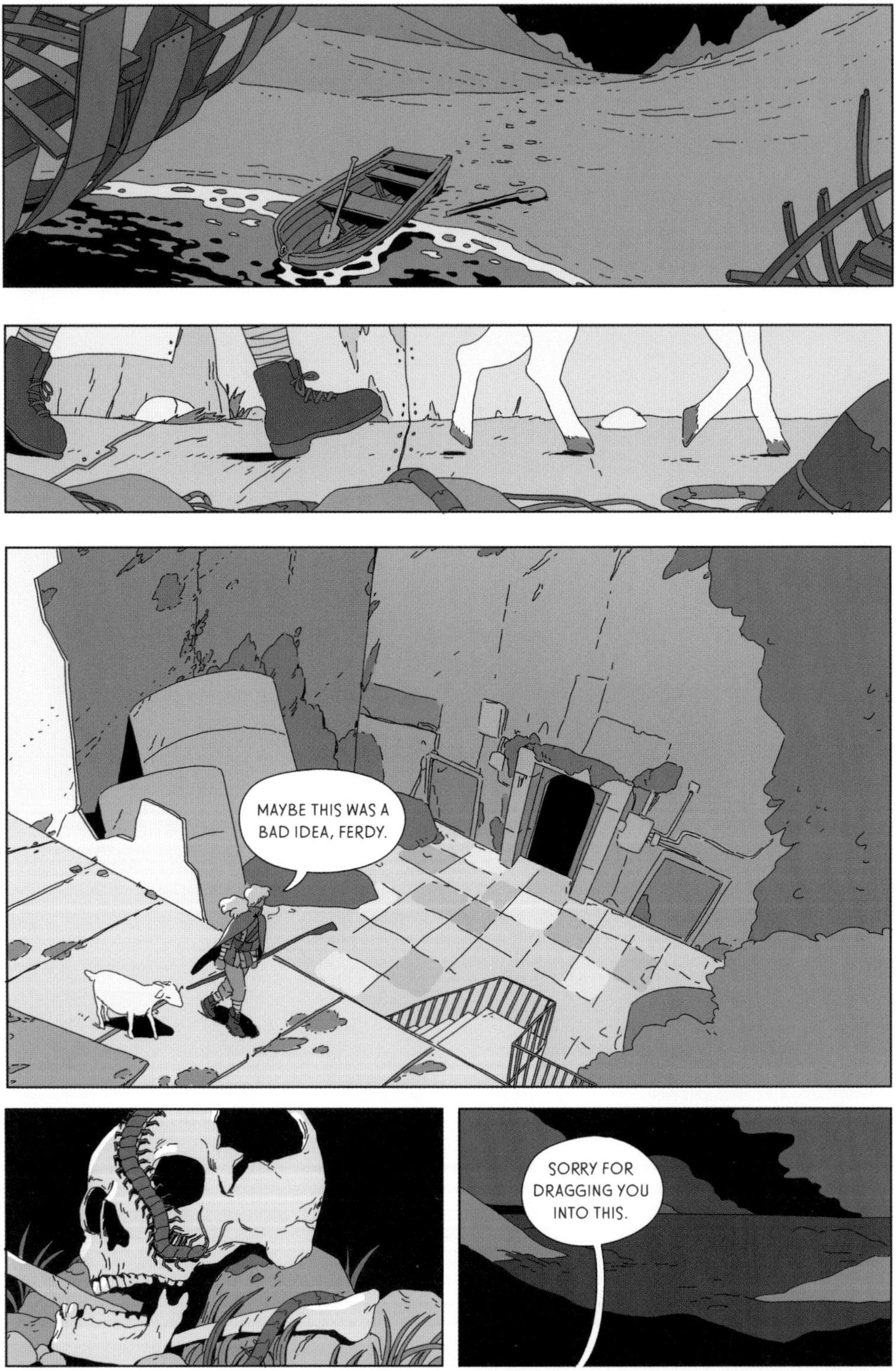
MAYBE THIS WAS A BAD IDEA, FERDY.
SORRY FOR DRAGGING YOU INTO THIS.

WELL...

THIS IS THE END OF THE PATH.

IF THERE REALLY ARE ANY GOBLINS ON THIS ROCK, I GUESS THEY'LL BE HERE?

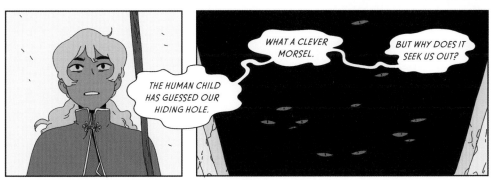

THE HUMAN CHILD HAS GUESSED OUR HIDING HOLE.

WHAT A CLEVER MORSEL.

BUT WHY DOES IT SEEK US OUT?

WHY HAS IT COME?

WHAT IS ITS BUSINESS?

I'VE COME TO PLAY FOR YOUR GOLD.

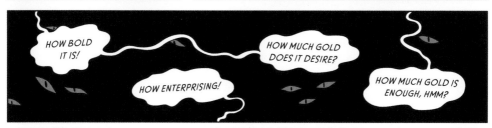

HOW BOLD IT IS!

HOW ENTERPRISING!

HOW MUCH GOLD DOES IT DESIRE?

HOW MUCH GOLD IS ENOUGH, HMM?

I NEED TWO HUND-- I NEED THREE HUNDRED DINARS. IN GOLD COIN.

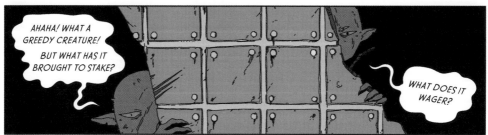

AHAHA! WHAT A GREEDY CREATURE!

BUT WHAT HAS IT BROUGHT TO STAKE?

WHAT DOES IT WAGER?

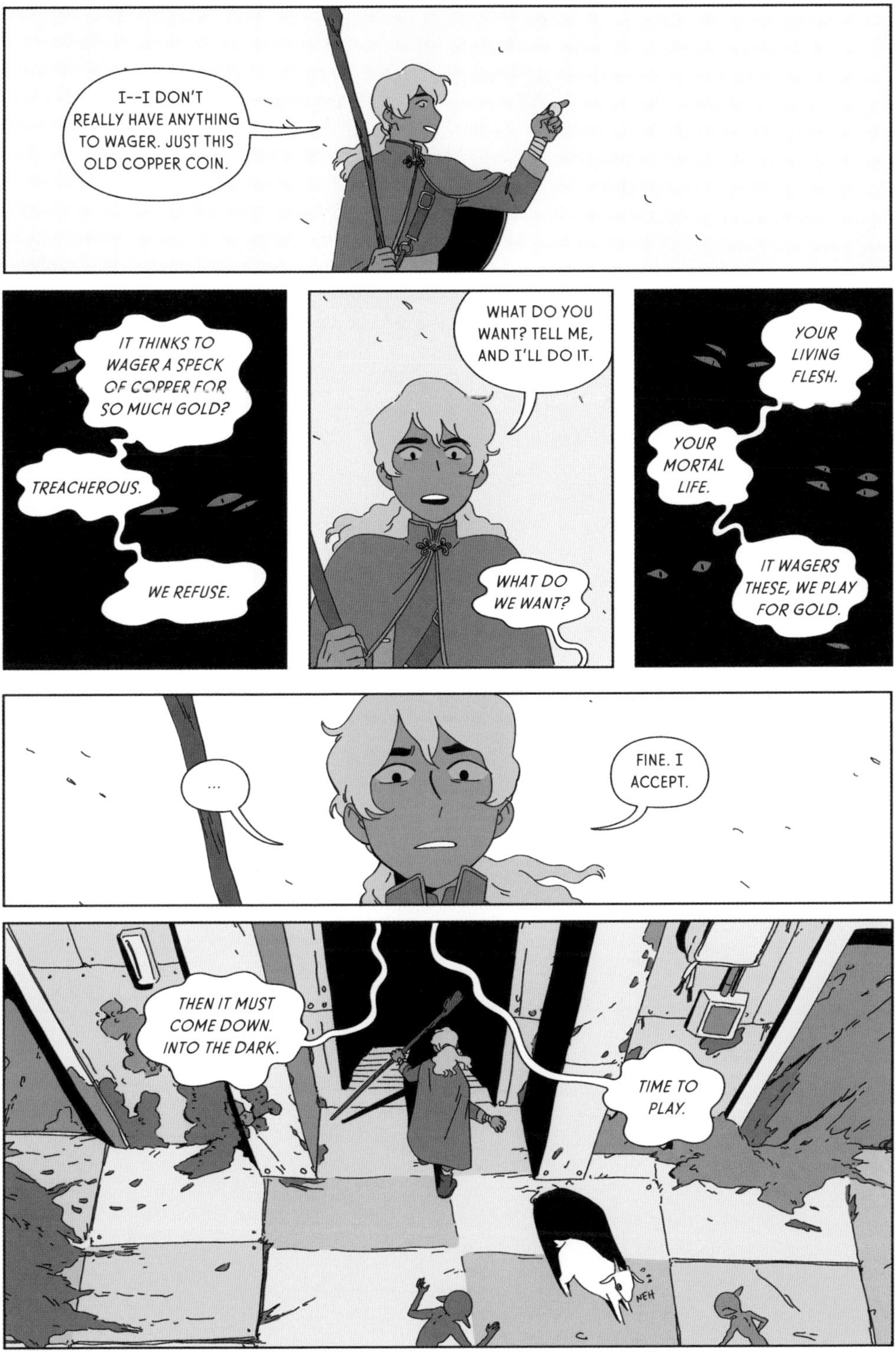
I--I DON'T REALLY HAVE ANYTHING TO WAGER. JUST THIS OLD COPPER COIN.
IT THINKS TO WAGER A SPECK OF COPPER FOR SO MUCH GOLD?
TREACHEROUS.
WE REFUSE.
WHAT DO YOU WANT? TELL ME, AND I'LL DO IT.
WHAT DO WE WANT?
YOUR LIVING FLESH.
YOUR MORTAL LIFE.
IT WAGERS THESE, WE PLAY FOR GOLD.
...
FINE. I ACCEPT.
THEN IT MUST COME DOWN. INTO THE DARK.
TIME TO PLAY.
NEH

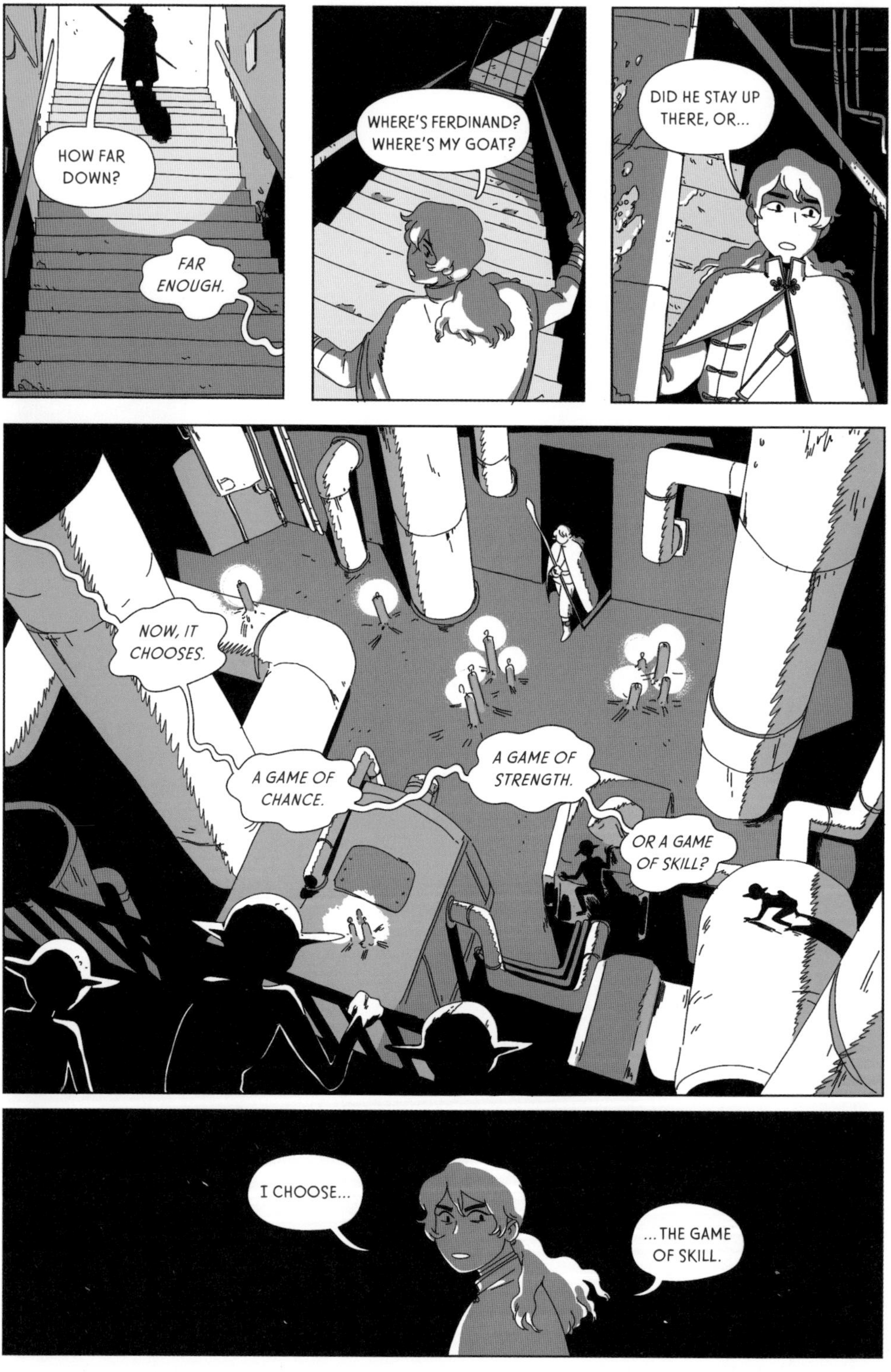
HOW FAR DOWN?
FAR ENOUGH.
WHERE'S FERDINAND? WHERE'S MY GOAT?
DID HE STAY UP THERE, OR...
NOW, IT CHOOSES.
A GAME OF CHANCE.
A GAME OF STRENGTH.
OR A GAME OF SKILL?
I CHOOSE...
...THE GAME OF SKILL.

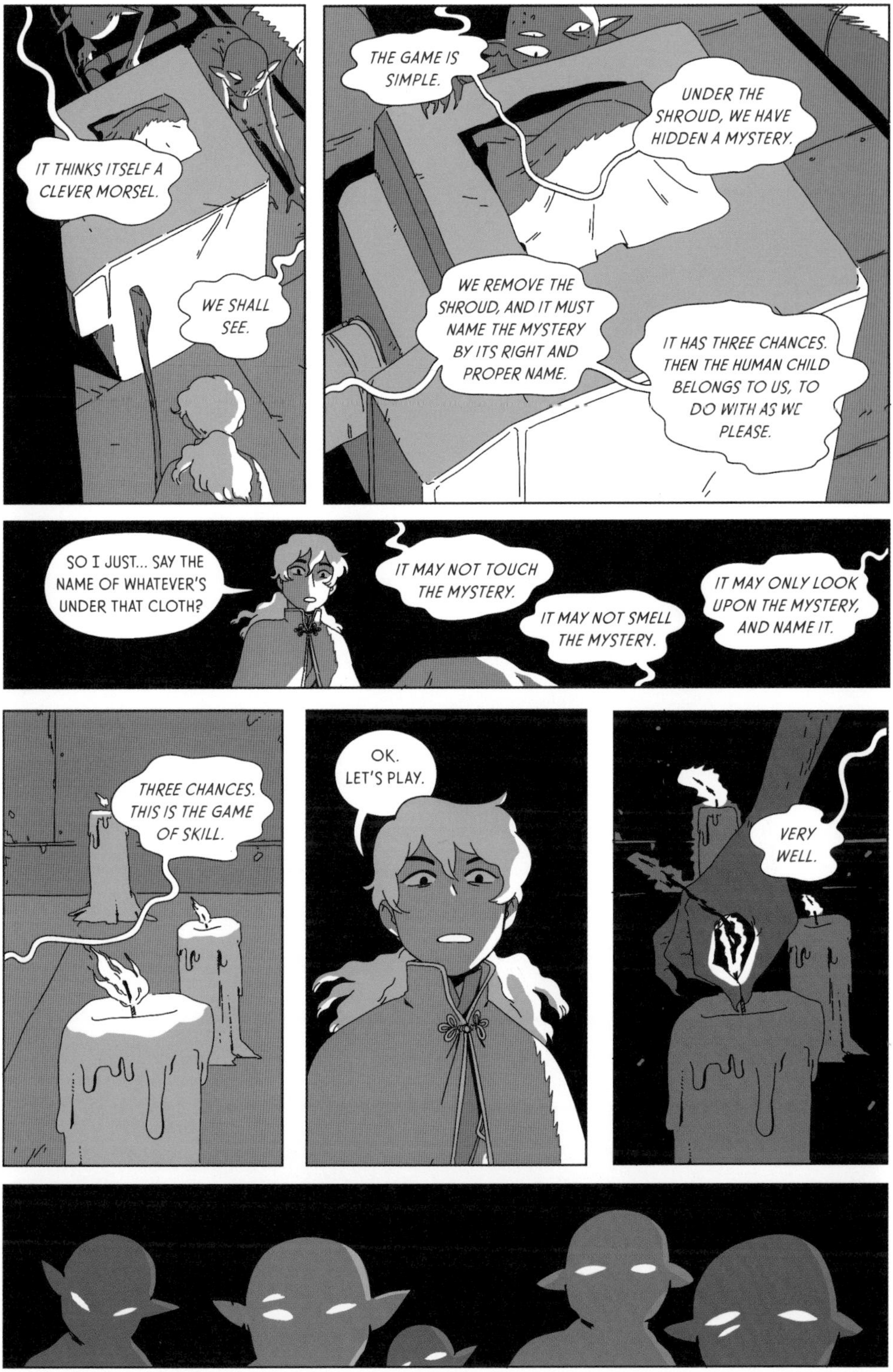
IT THINKS ITSELF A CLEVER MORSEL.
WE SHALL SEE.
THE GAME IS SIMPLE.
UNDER THE SHROUD, WE HAVE HIDDEN A MYSTERY.
WE REMOVE THE SHROUD, AND IT MUST NAME THE MYSTERY BY ITS RIGHT AND PROPER NAME.
IT HAS THREE CHANCES. THEN THE HUMAN CHILD BELONGS TO US, TO DO WITH AS WE PLEASE.
SO I JUST... SAY THE NAME OF WHATEVER'S UNDER THAT CLOTH?
IT MAY NOT TOUCH THE MYSTERY.
IT MAY NOT SMELL THE MYSTERY.
IT MAY ONLY LOOK UPON THE MYSTERY, AND NAME IT.
THREE CHANCES. THIS IS THE GAME OF SKILL.
OK. LET'S PLAY.
VERY WELL.

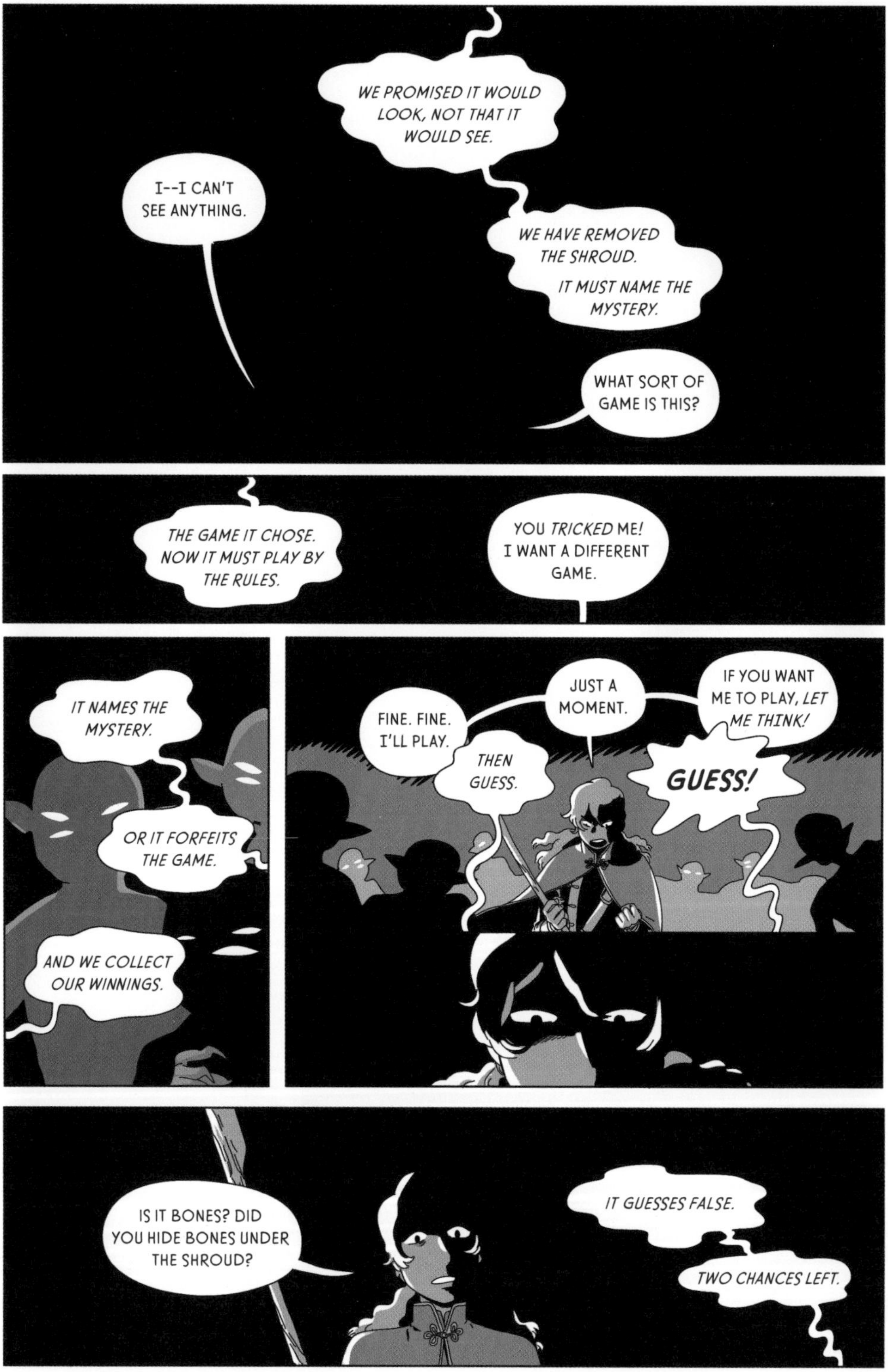
WE PROMISED IT WOULD LOOK, NOT THAT IT WOULD SEE.
I--I CAN'T SEE ANYTHING.
WE HAVE REMOVED THE SHROUD.
IT MUST NAME THE MYSTERY.
WHAT SORT OF GAME IS THIS?
THE GAME IT CHOSE. NOW IT MUST PLAY BY THE RULES.
YOU TRICKED ME! I WANT A DIFFERENT GAME.
IT NAMES THE MYSTERY.
OR IT FORFEITS THE GAME.
AND WE COLLECT OUR WINNINGS.
FINE. FINE. I'LL PLAY.
THEN GUESS.
JUST A MOMENT.
GUESS!
IF YOU WANT ME TO PLAY, LET ME THINK!
IS IT BONES? DID YOU HIDE BONES UNDER THE SHROUD?
IT GUESSES FALSE.
TWO CHANCES LEFT.

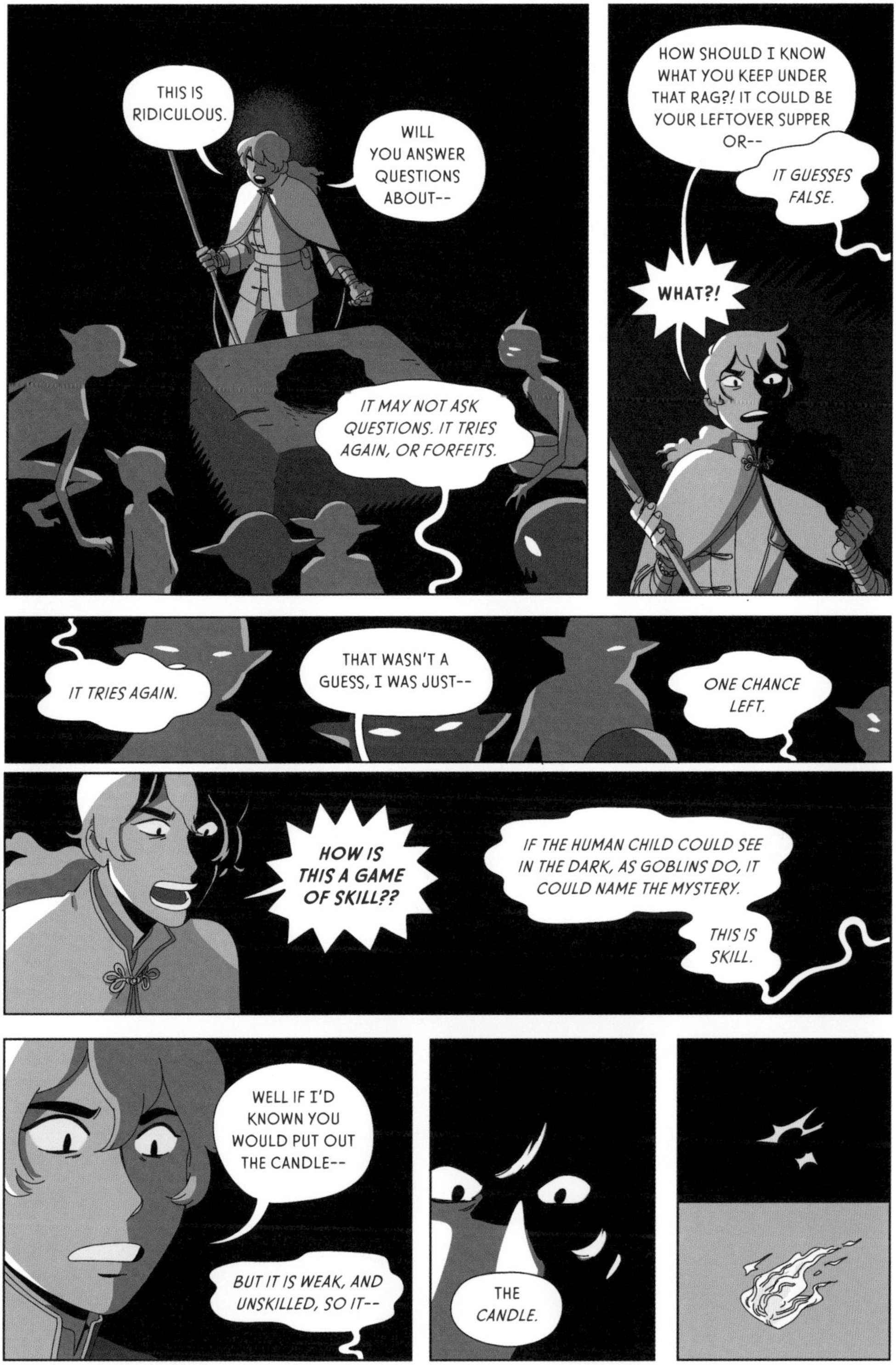

THIS IS RIDICULOUS.
WILL YOU ANSWER QUESTIONS ABOUT--
IT MAY NOT ASK QUESTIONS. IT TRIES AGAIN, OR FORFEITS.
HOW SHOULD I KNOW WHAT YOU KEEP UNDER THAT RAG?! IT COULD BE YOUR LEFTOVER SUPPER OR--
IT GUESSES FALSE.
WHAT?!
IT TRIES AGAIN.
THAT WASN'T A GUESS, I WAS JUST--
ONE CHANCE LEFT.
HOW IS THIS A GAME OF SKILL??
IF THE HUMAN CHILD COULD SEE IN THE DARK, AS GOBLINS DO, IT COULD NAME THE MYSTERY.
THIS IS SKILL.
WELL IF I'D KNOWN YOU WOULD PUT OUT THE CANDLE--
BUT IT IS WEAK, AND UNSKILLED, SO IT--
THE CANDLE.

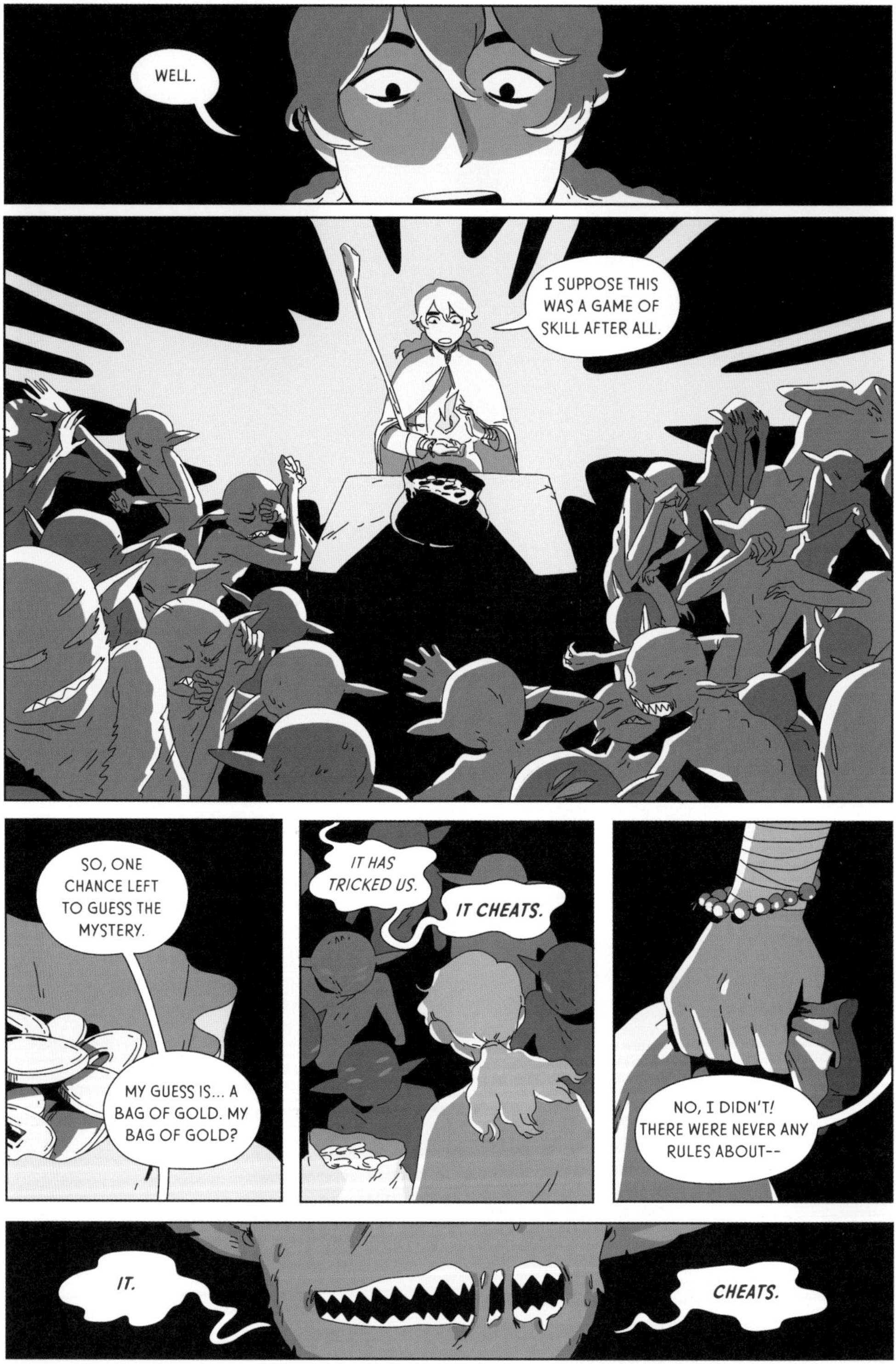
WELL.
I SUPPOSE THIS WAS A GAME OF SKILL AFTER ALL.
SO, ONE CHANCE LEFT TO GUESS THE MYSTERY.
MY GUESS IS... A BAG OF GOLD. MY BAG OF GOLD?
IT HAS TRICKED US.
IT CHEATS.
NO, I DIDN'T! THERE WERE NEVER ANY RULES ABOUT--
IT.
CHEATS.

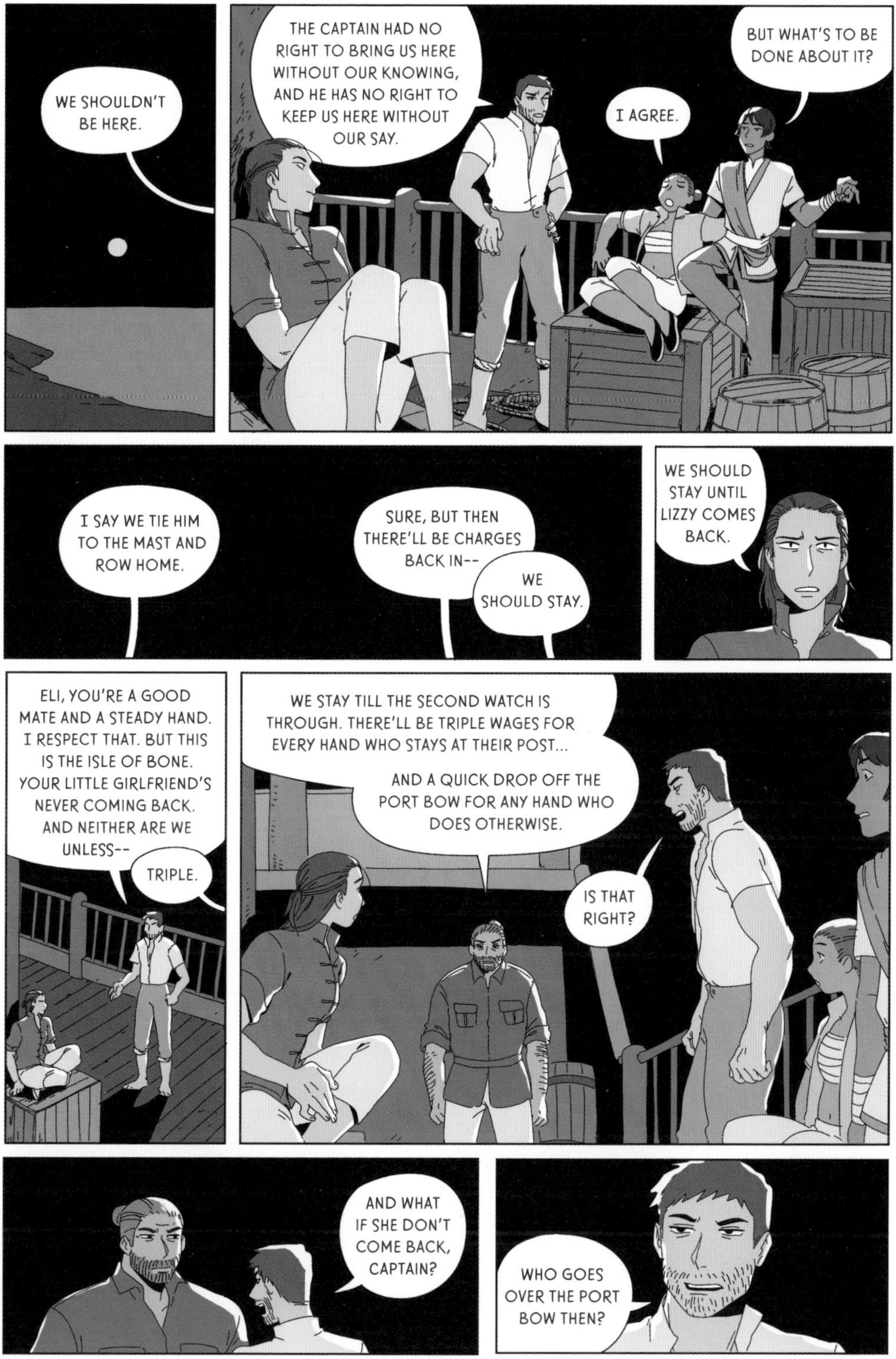
WE SHOULDN'T BE HERE.
THE CAPTAIN HAD NO RIGHT TO BRING US HERE WITHOUT OUR KNOWING, AND HE HAS NO RIGHT TO KEEP US HERE WITHOUT OUR SAY.
I AGREE.
BUT WHAT'S TO BE DONE ABOUT IT?
I SAY WE TIE HIM TO THE MAST AND ROW HOME.
SURE, BUT THEN THERE'LL BE CHARGES BACK IN--
WE SHOULD STAY.
WE SHOULD STAY UNTIL LIZZY COMES BACK.
ELI, YOU'RE A GOOD MATE AND A STEADY HAND. I RESPECT THAT. BUT THIS IS THE ISLE OF BONE. YOUR LITTLE GIRLFRIEND'S NEVER COMING BACK. AND NEITHER ARE WE UNLESS--
TRIPLE.
WE STAY TILL THE SECOND WATCH IS THROUGH. THERE'LL BE TRIPLE WAGES FOR EVERY HAND WHO STAYS AT THEIR POST...
AND A QUICK DROP OFF THE PORT BOW FOR ANY HAND WHO DOES OTHERWISE.
IS THAT RIGHT?
AND WHAT IF SHE DON'T COME BACK, CAPTAIN?
WHO GOES OVER THE PORT BOW THEN?

CHEATERS FORFEIT THEIR PRIZES.

I DIDN'T CHEAT ANY MORE THAN YOU DID.

TRICKSTERS FORFEIT THEIR RIGHTS.

LOOK. I HAVE TO BE OUT OF HERE BY SUNDOWN, BEFORE A DIFFERENT SET OF MAGICAL CREATURES TRIES TO CLAIM MY LIFE.

SO IF WE COULD JUST--

IT ESCAPES!

CAREFUL, BROTHERS!

BANG!

THE GOAT CREATURE HAS ESCAPED!!

FERDINAND! I GOT THE MONEY! LET'S GO!

NEH

NEEEHHHH

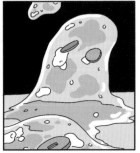

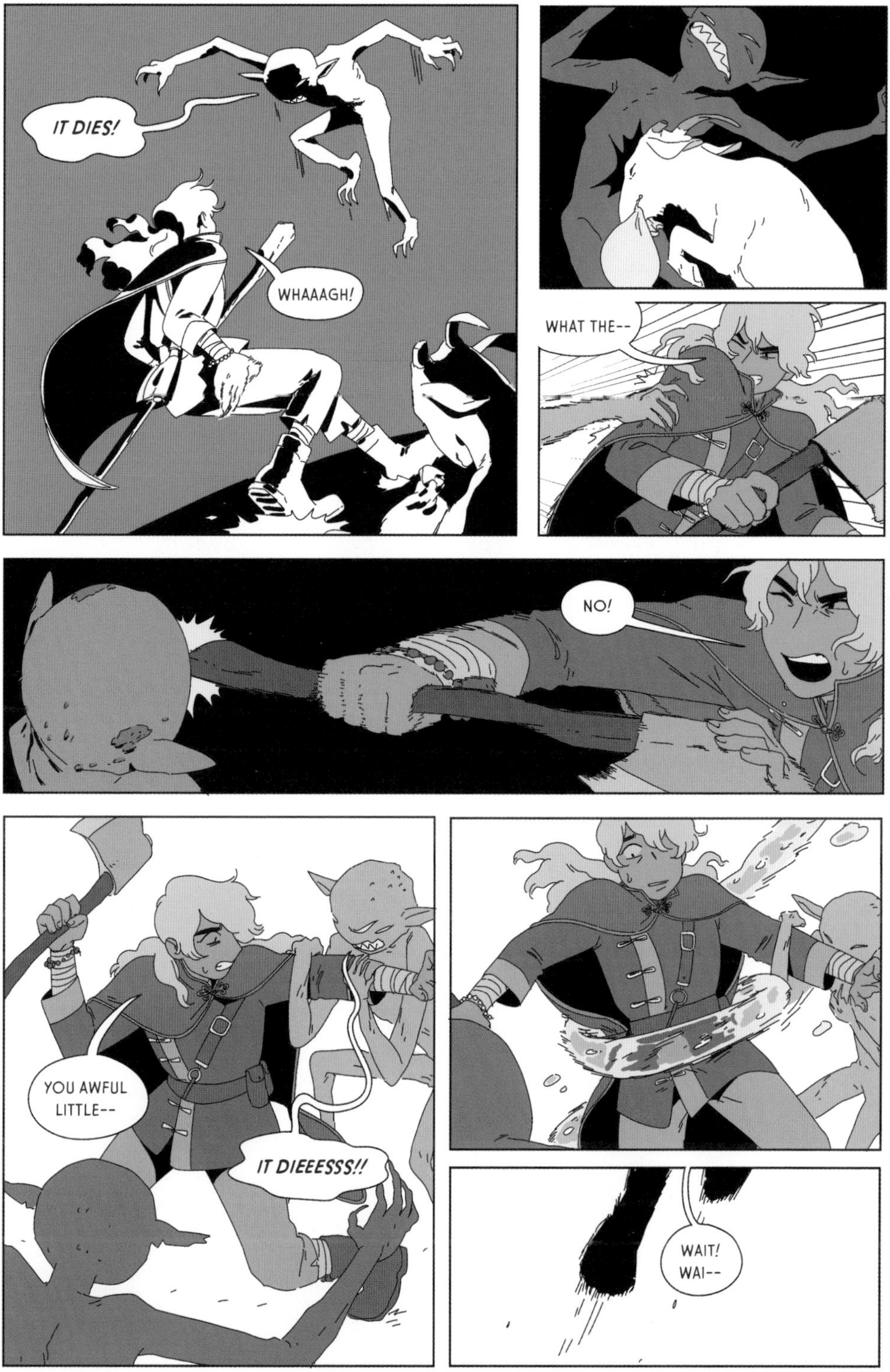

IT DIES!
WHAAAGH!
WHAT THE--
NO!
YOU AWFUL LITTLE--
IT DIEEESSS!!
WAIT! WAI--

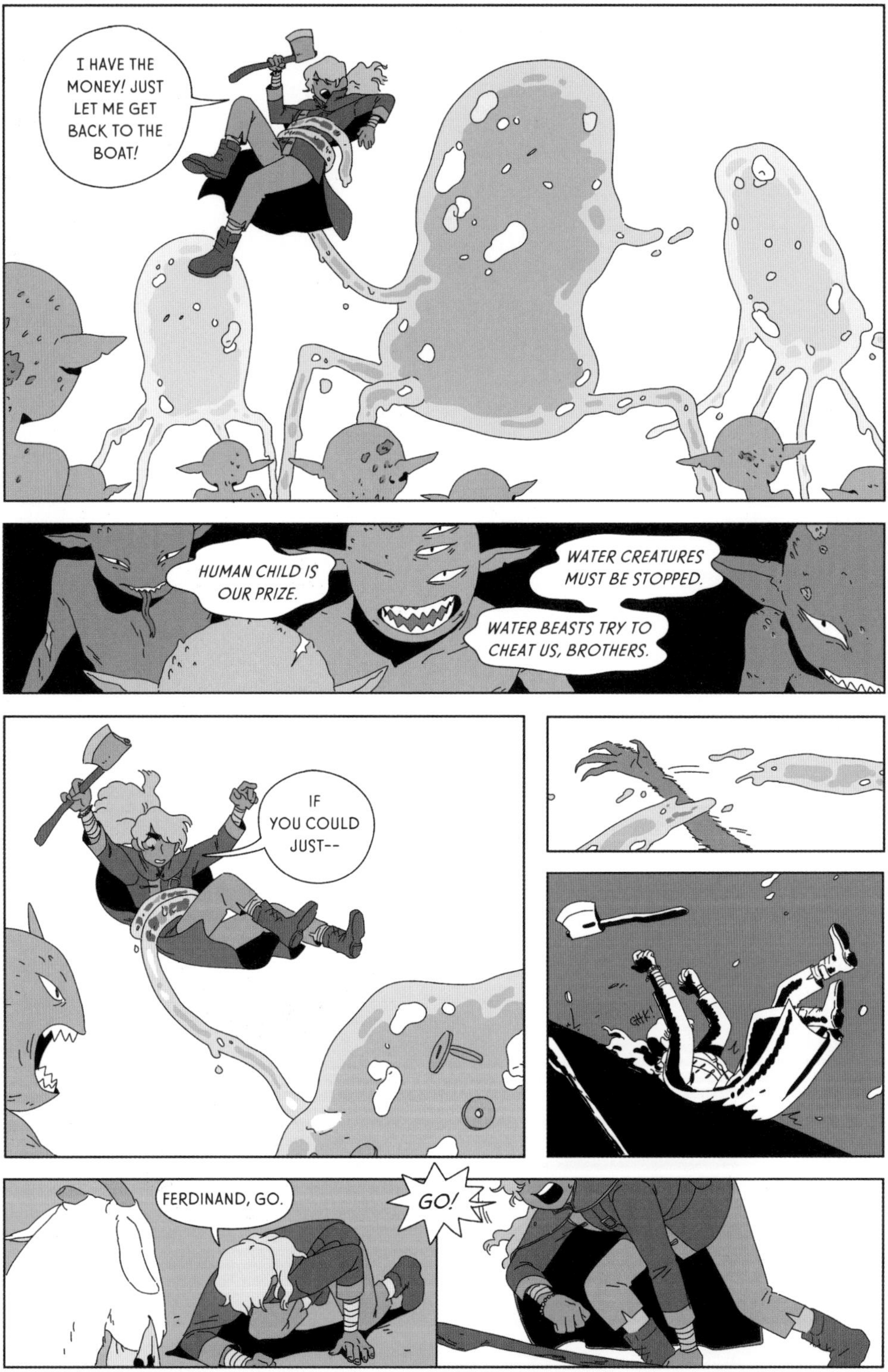
I HAVE THE MONEY! JUST LET ME GET BACK TO THE BOAT!
HUMAN CHILD IS OUR PRIZE.
WATER CREATURES MUST BE STOPPED.
WATER BEASTS TRY TO CHEAT US, BROTHERS.
IF YOU COULD JUST--
GHK!
FERDINAND, GO.
GO!

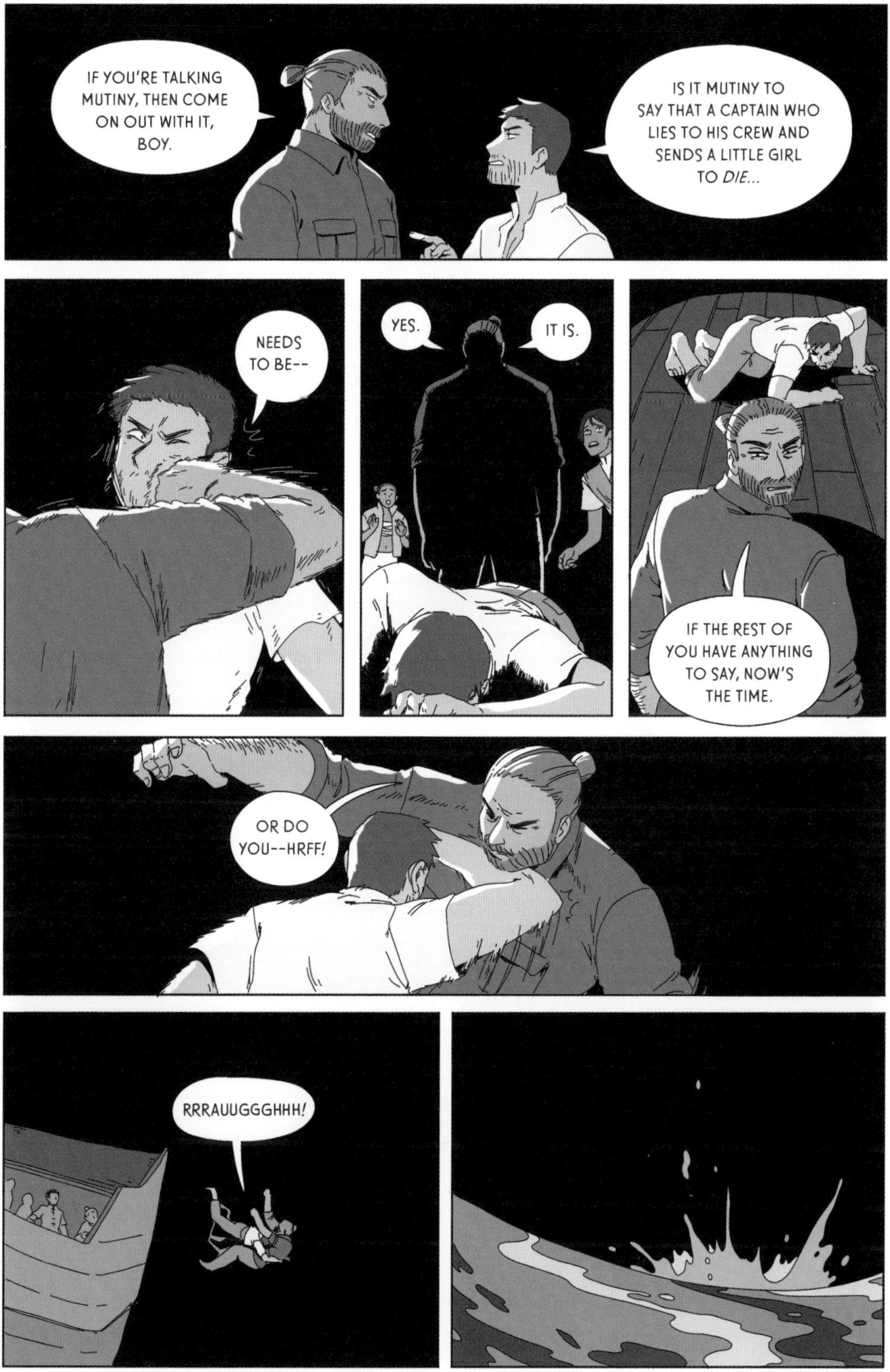
IF YOU'RE TALKING MUTINY, THEN COME ON OUT WITH IT, BOY.
IS IT MUTINY TO SAY THAT A CAPTAIN WHO LIES TO HIS CREW AND SENDS A LITTLE GIRL TO *DIE*...
NEEDS TO BE--
YES.
IT IS.
IF THE REST OF YOU HAVE ANYTHING TO SAY, NOW'S THE TIME.
OR DO YOU--HRFF!
RRRAUUGGGHHH!

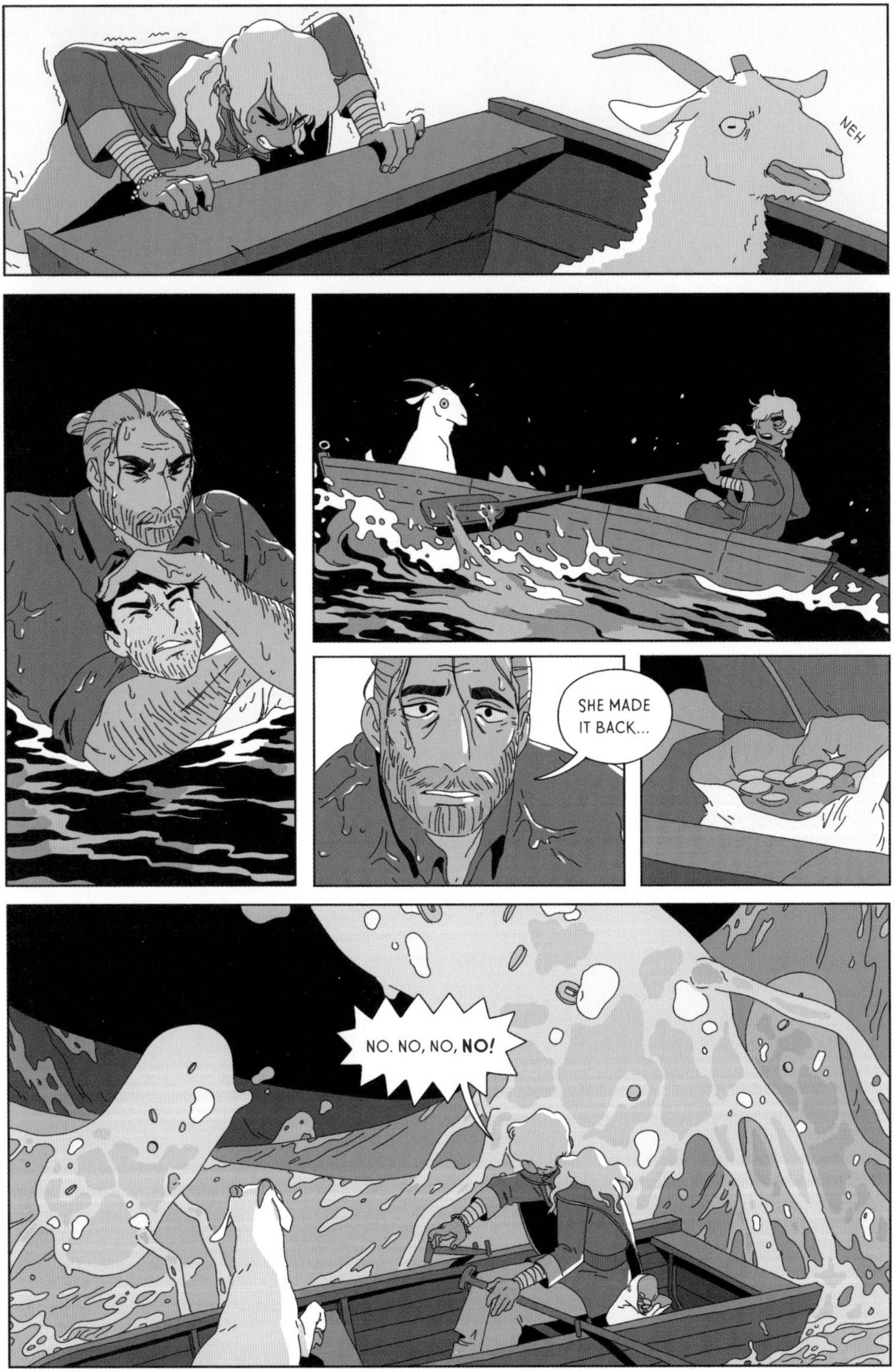
NEH
SHE MADE IT BACK...
NO. NO, NO, NO!

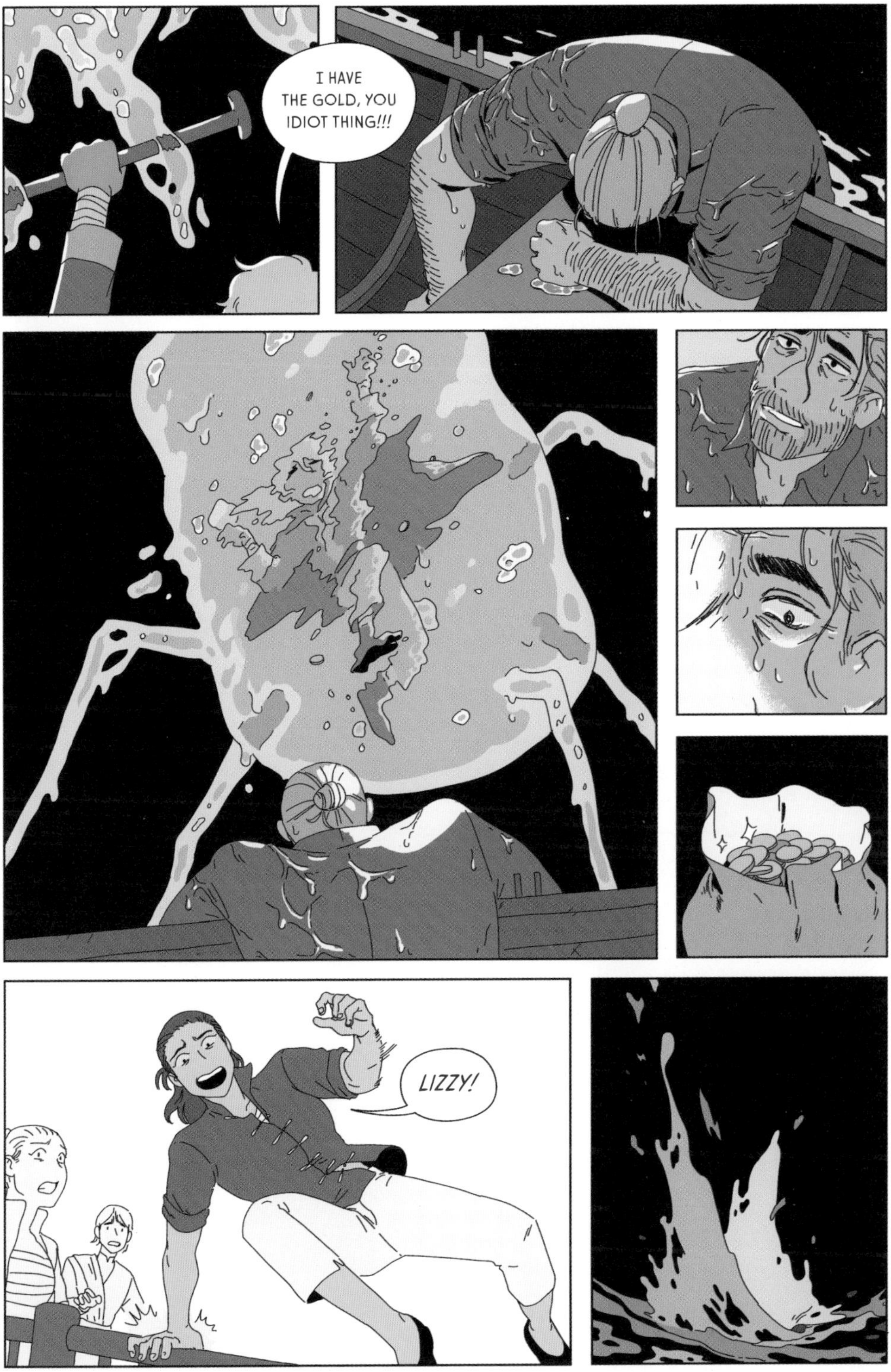
I HAVE THE GOLD, YOU IDIOT THING!!!
LIZZY!

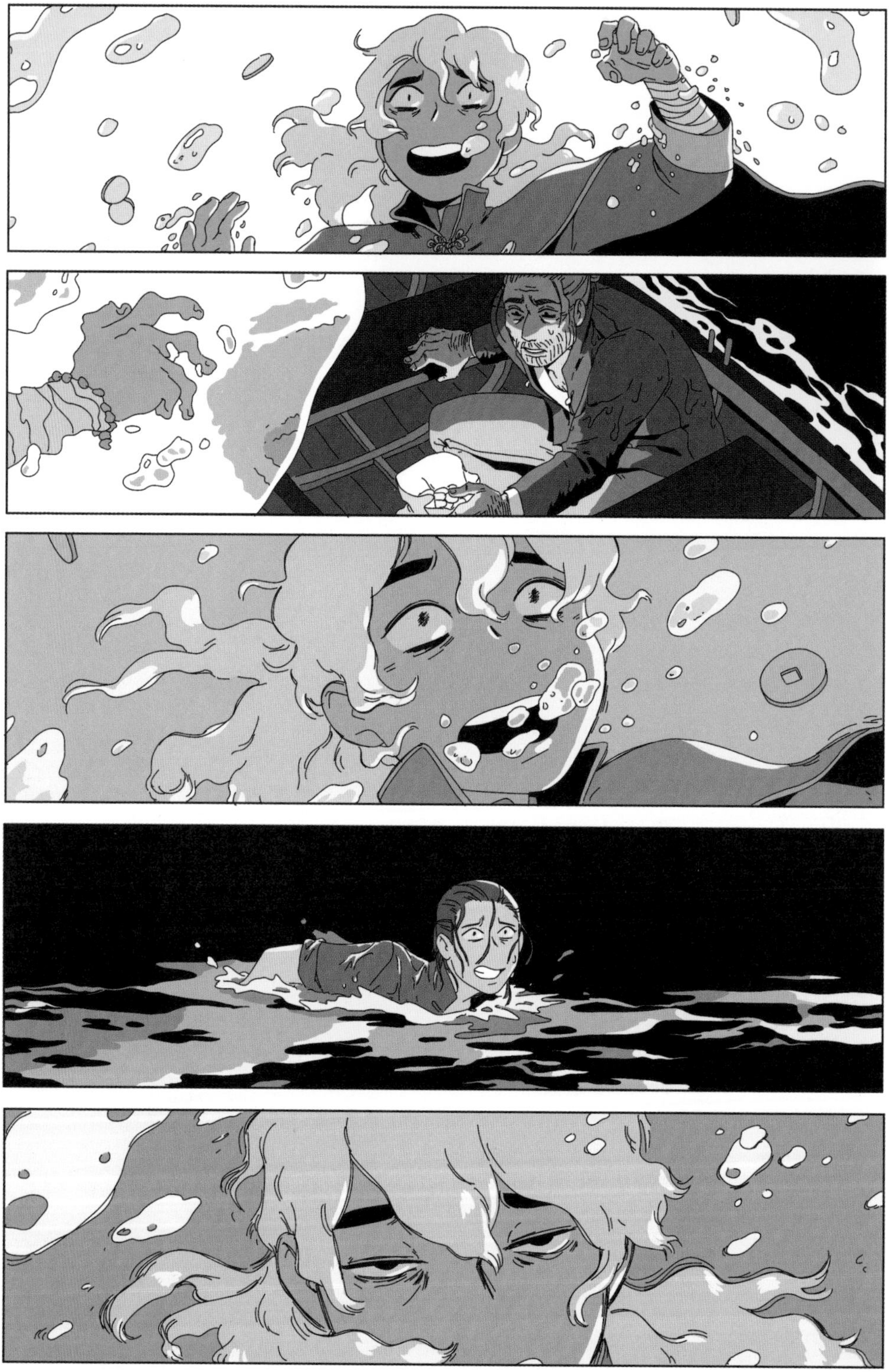

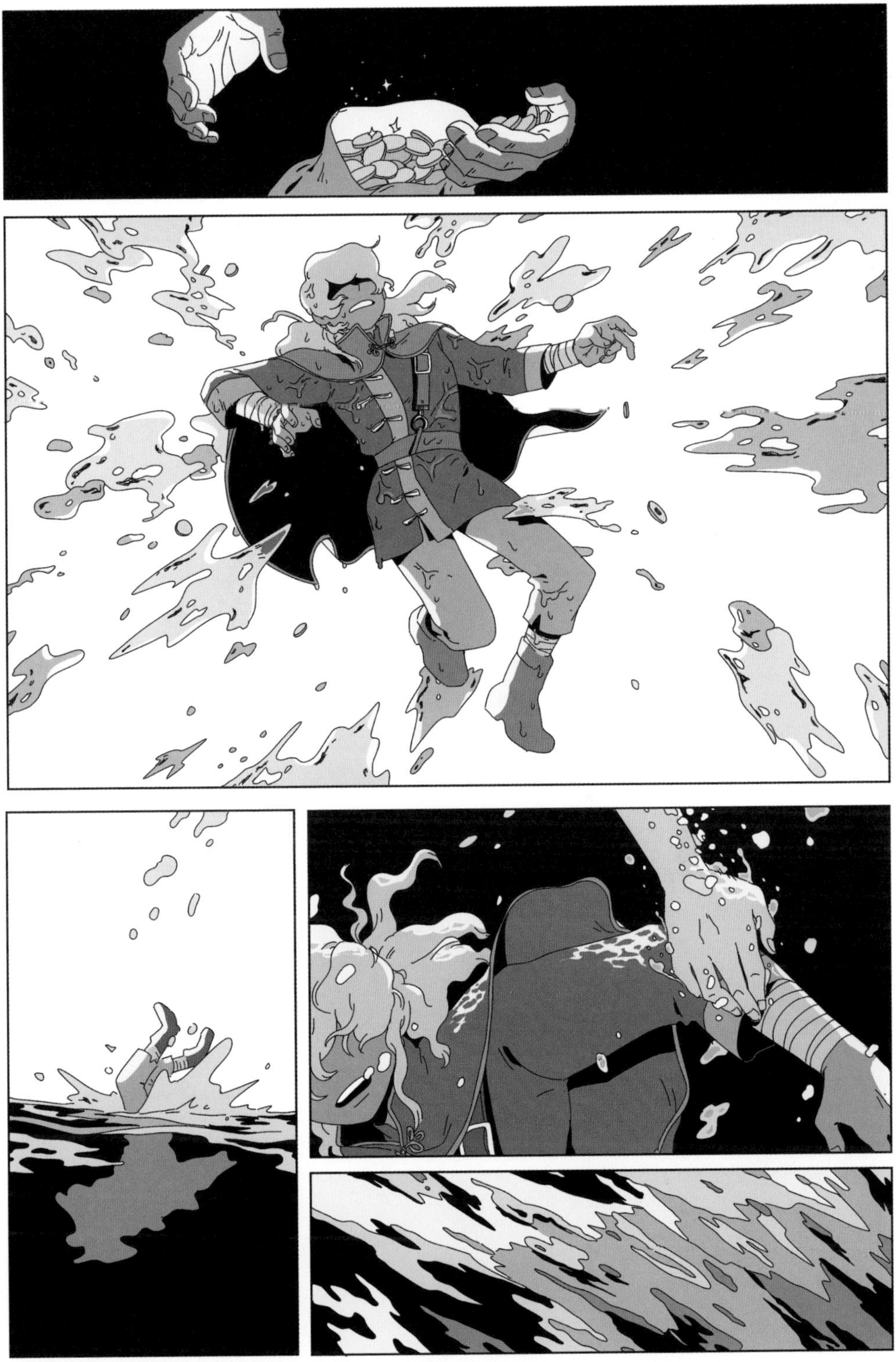

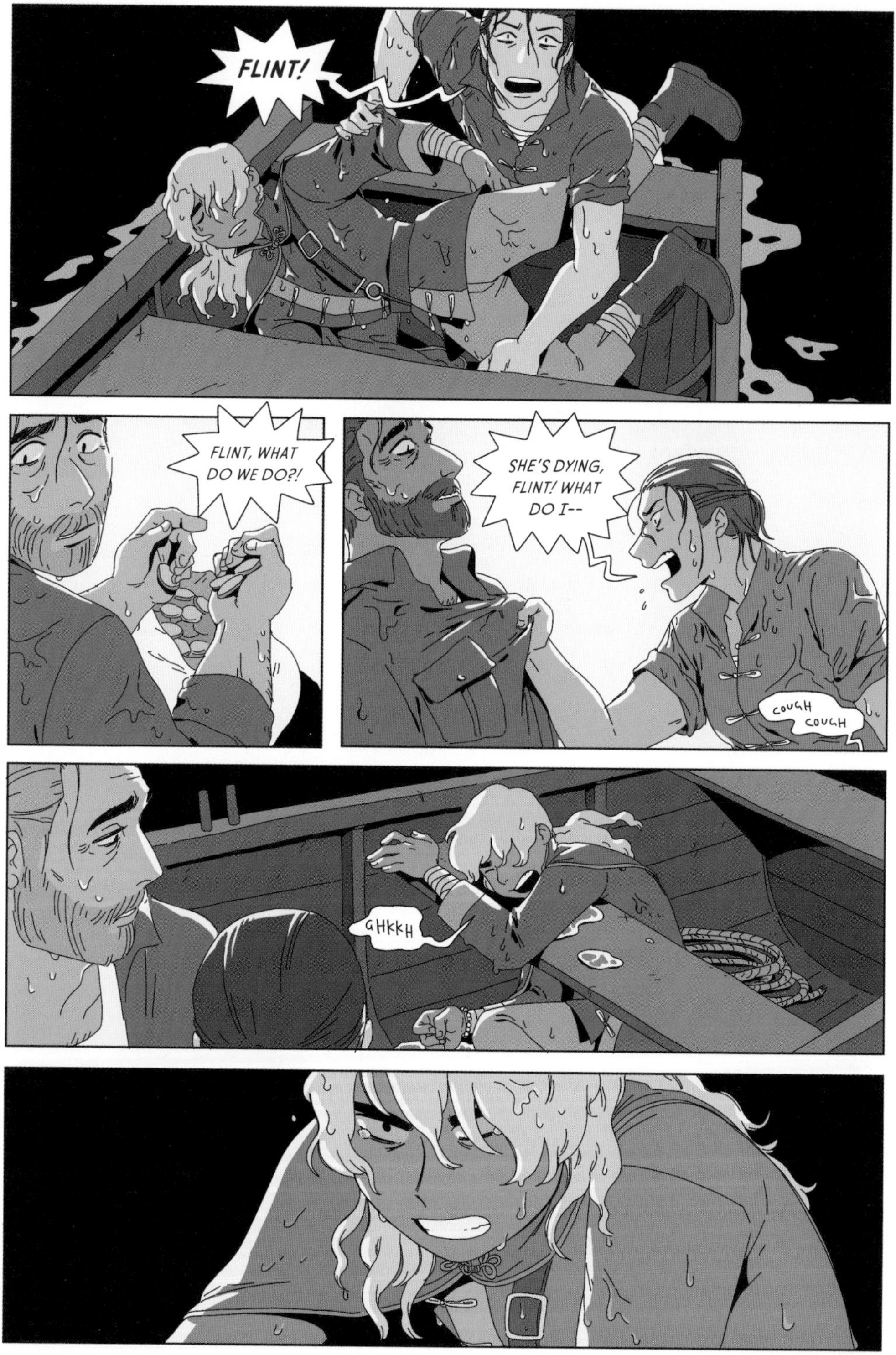
FLINT!
FLINT, WHAT DO WE DO?!
SHE'S DYING, FLINT! WHAT DO I--
COUGH COUGH
GHKKH

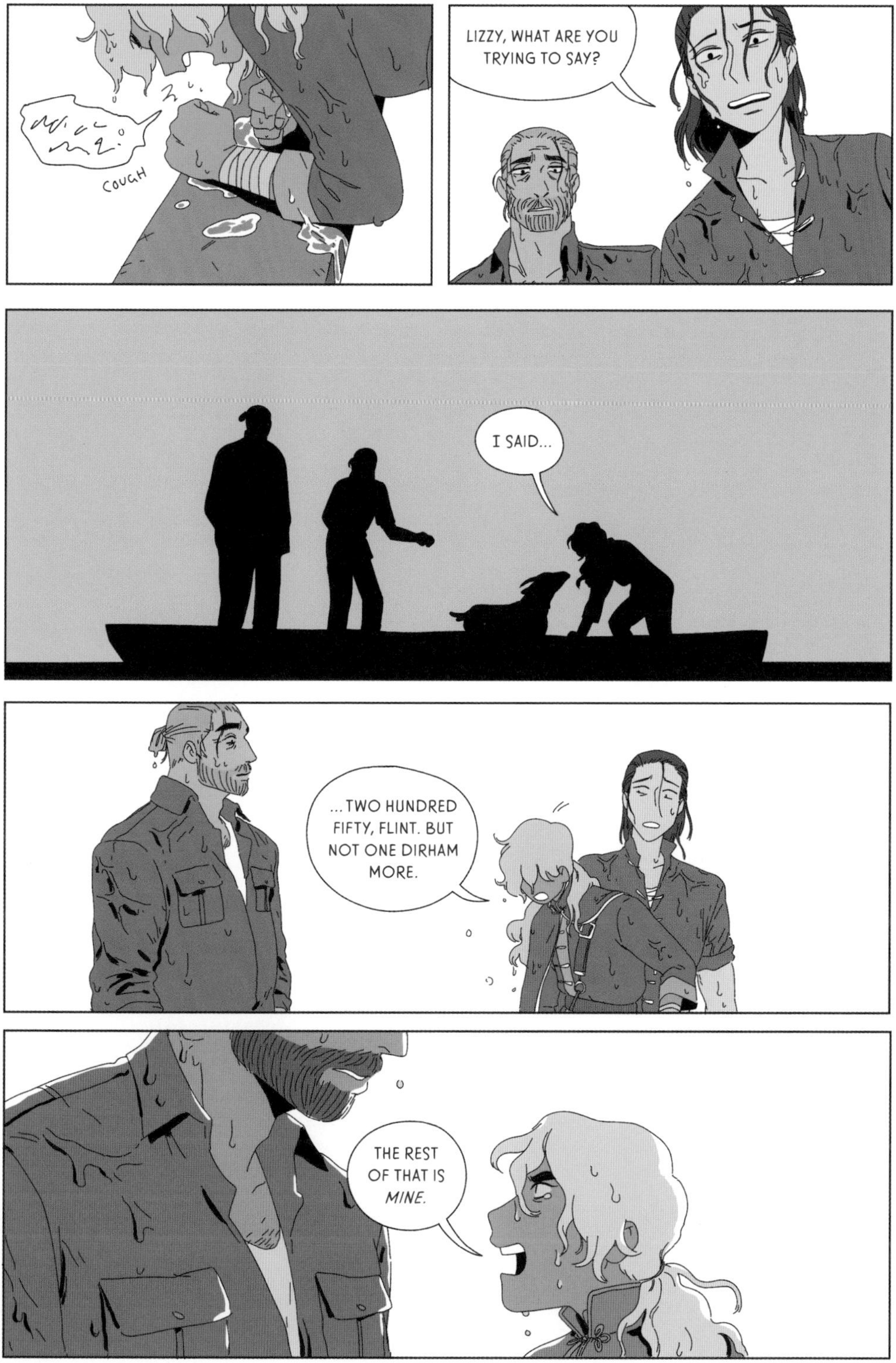
COUGH
LIZZY, WHAT ARE YOU TRYING TO SAY?
I SAID...
...TWO HUNDRED FIFTY, FLINT. BUT NOT ONE DIRHAM MORE.
THE REST OF THAT IS *MINE.*

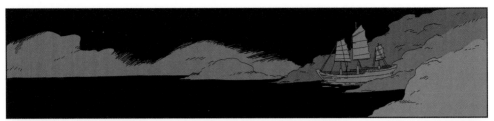

LIZZY, YOU'RE NOT ROWING BACK TO AH-GONG'S THIS LATE, ARE YOU? DO YOU NEED A PLACE TO STAY?

OH, NO. I HAVE A PLACE.

THANKS, ELI.

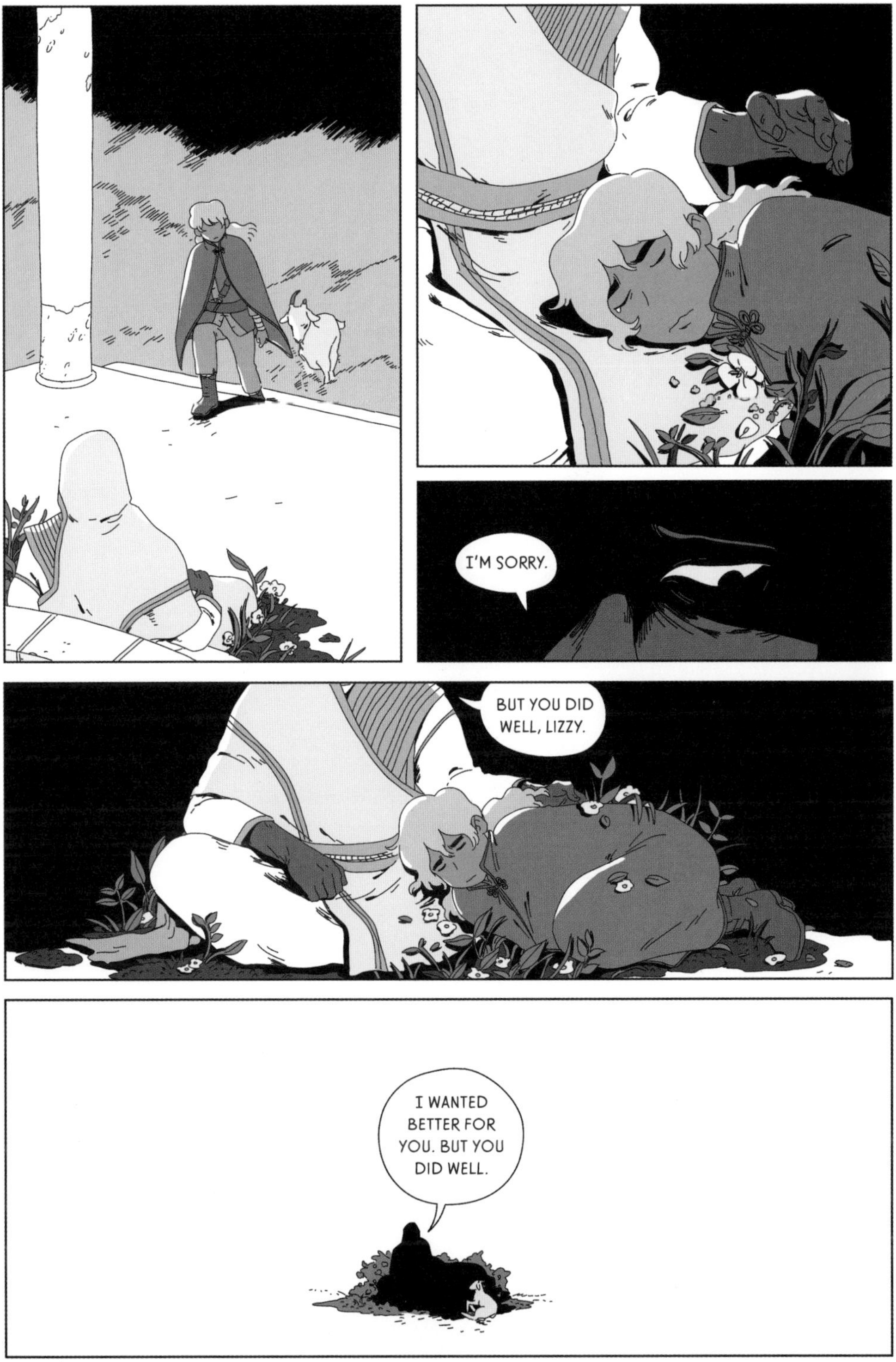
I'M SORRY.
BUT YOU DID WELL, LIZZY.
I WANTED BETTER FOR YOU. BUT YOU DID WELL.

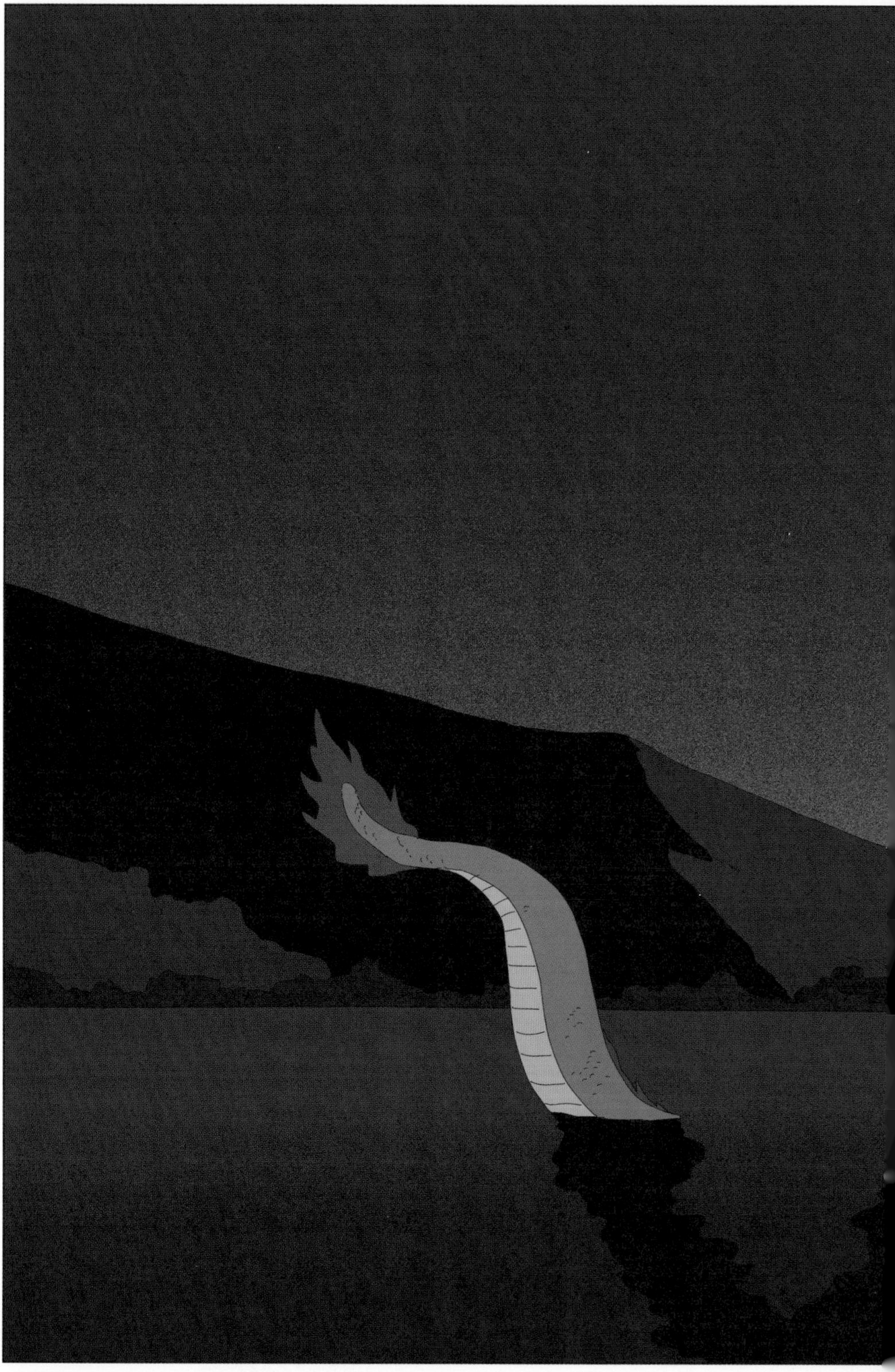

# CHAPTER 4:
# LEVIATHAN

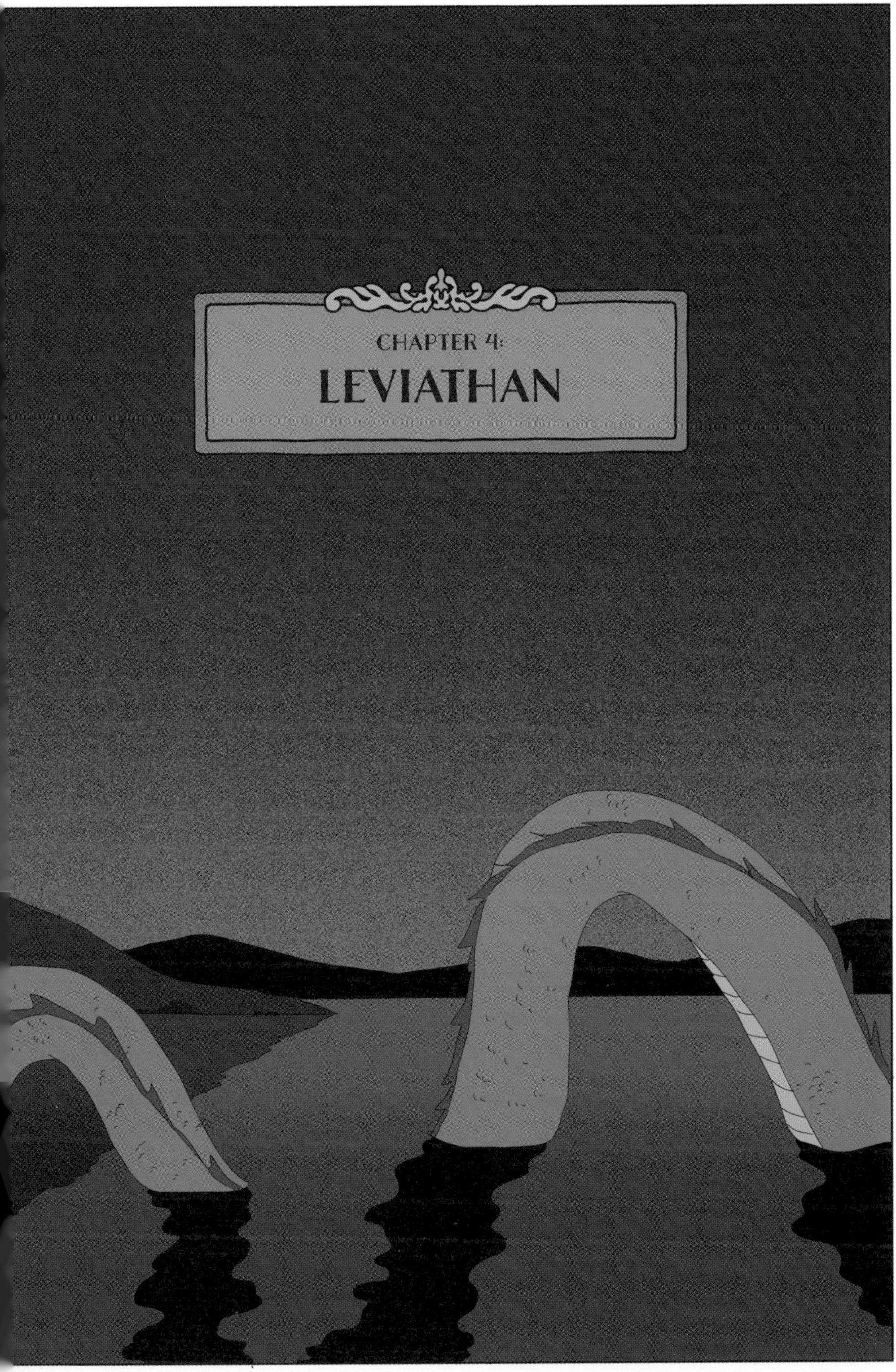

I DON'T KNOW HOW THIS WILL TURN OUT.

IF WE'LL BE ABLE TO SET THE ARCHIPELAGO BACK TO RIGHTS. OR, EVEN IF WE DO, IF I'LL BE ABLE TO COME BACK. TO SHARE A LIFE WITH MY FAMILY, FREE OF MIST AND MONSTERS.

BUT PLEASE. WHATEVER HAPPENS TO ME, LET LI-ZHEN ENJOY THAT WORLD. NOT SEEN THROUGH A FOG, NOT SHROUDED IN FEAR.

LET MY DAUGHTER LIVE IN A WORLD WITHOUT THE MIST...

WITHOUT THE LEVIATHAN, WITHOUT THE CREATURES THAT ATTEND IT.

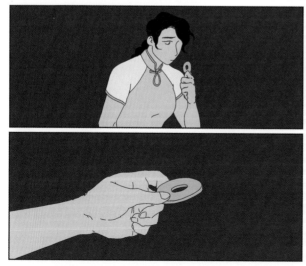

THIS IS MY WISH.

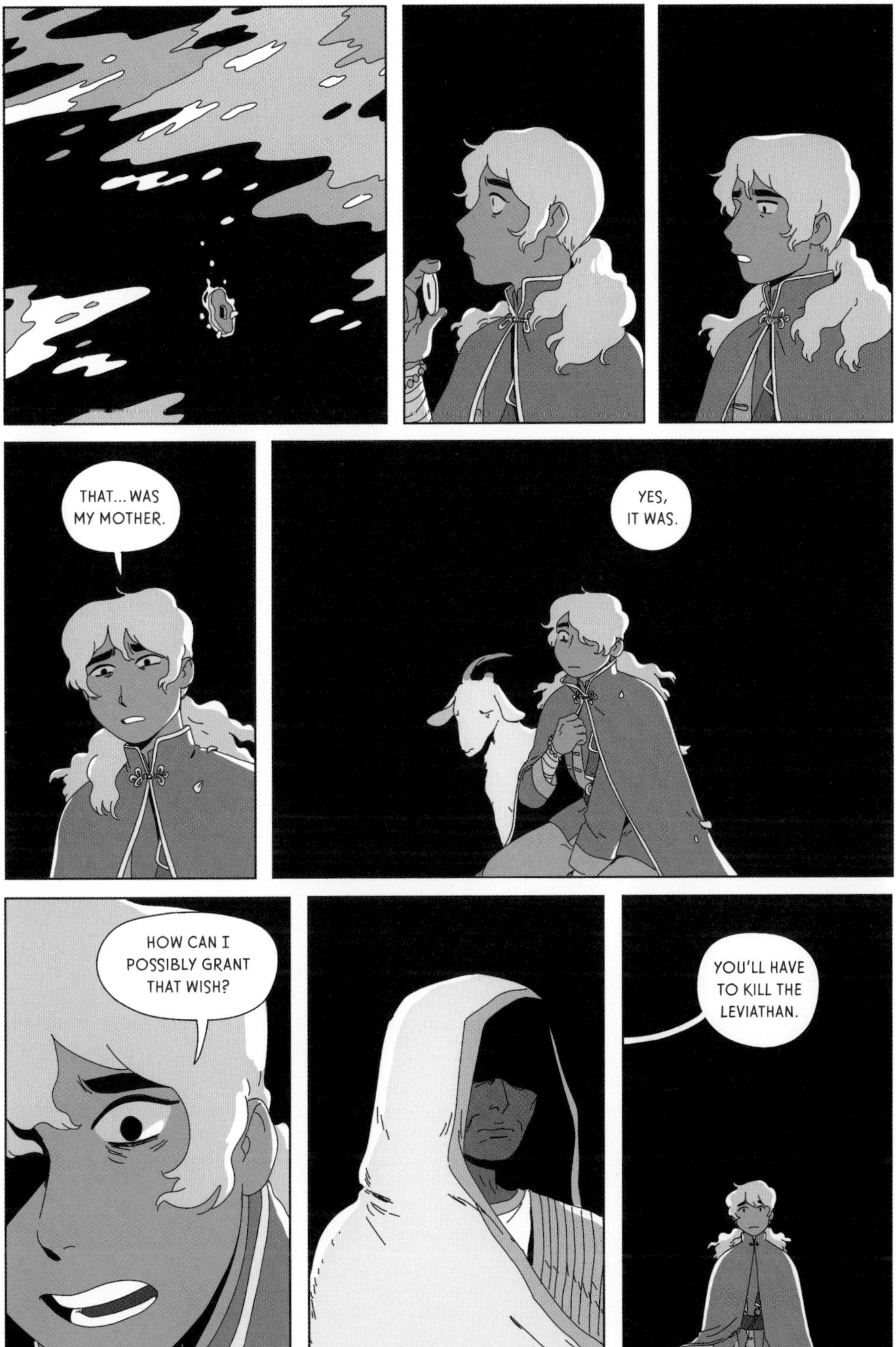
THAT... WAS MY MOTHER.
YES, IT WAS.
HOW CAN I POSSIBLY GRANT THAT WISH?
YOU'LL HAVE TO KILL THE LEVIATHAN.

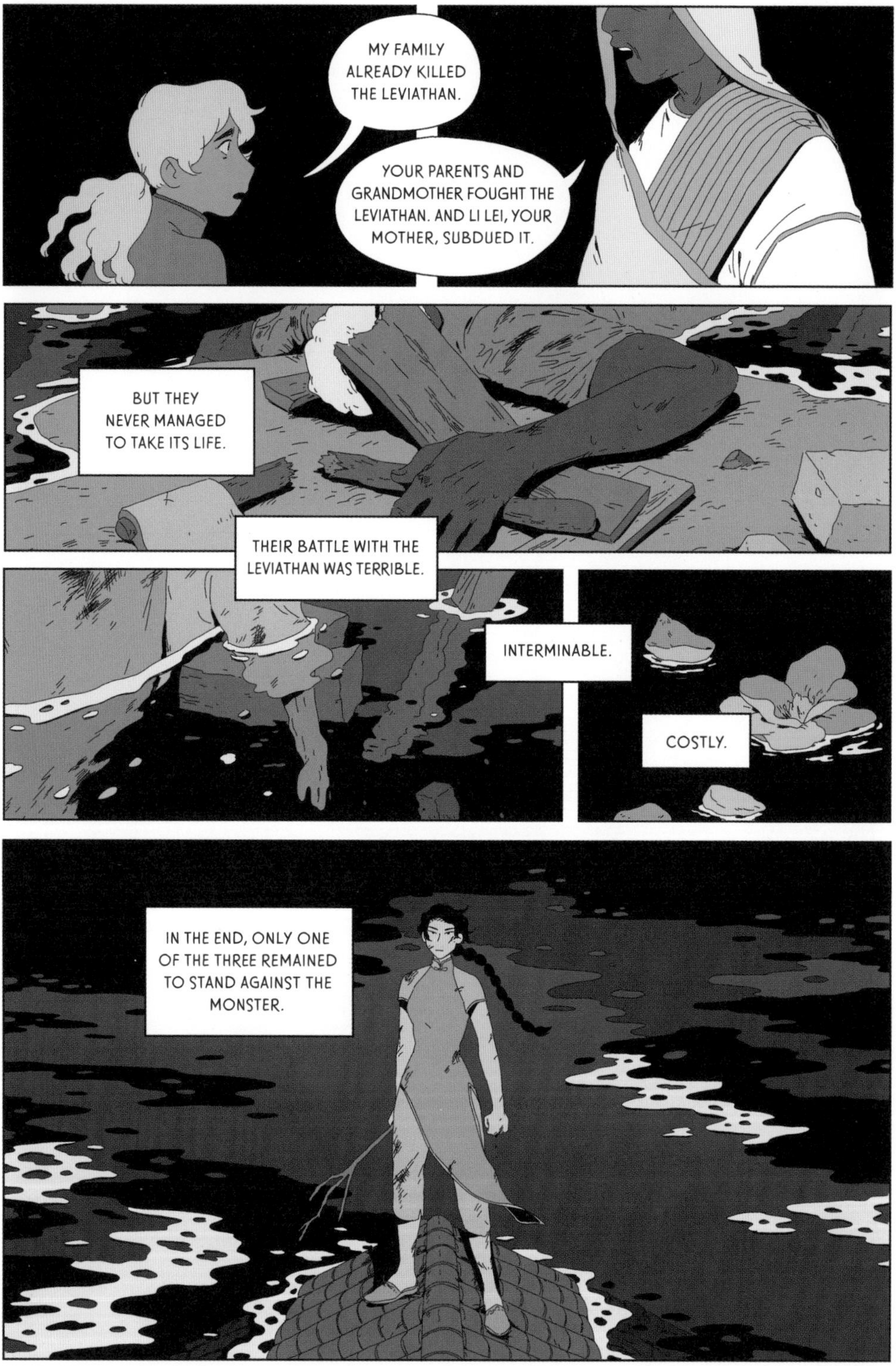
MY FAMILY ALREADY KILLED THE LEVIATHAN.
YOUR PARENTS AND GRANDMOTHER FOUGHT THE LEVIATHAN. AND LI LEI, YOUR MOTHER, SUBDUED IT.
BUT THEY NEVER MANAGED TO TAKE ITS LIFE.
THEIR BATTLE WITH THE LEVIATHAN WAS TERRIBLE.
INTERMINABLE.
COSTLY.
IN THE END, ONLY ONE OF THE THREE REMAINED TO STAND AGAINST THE MONSTER.

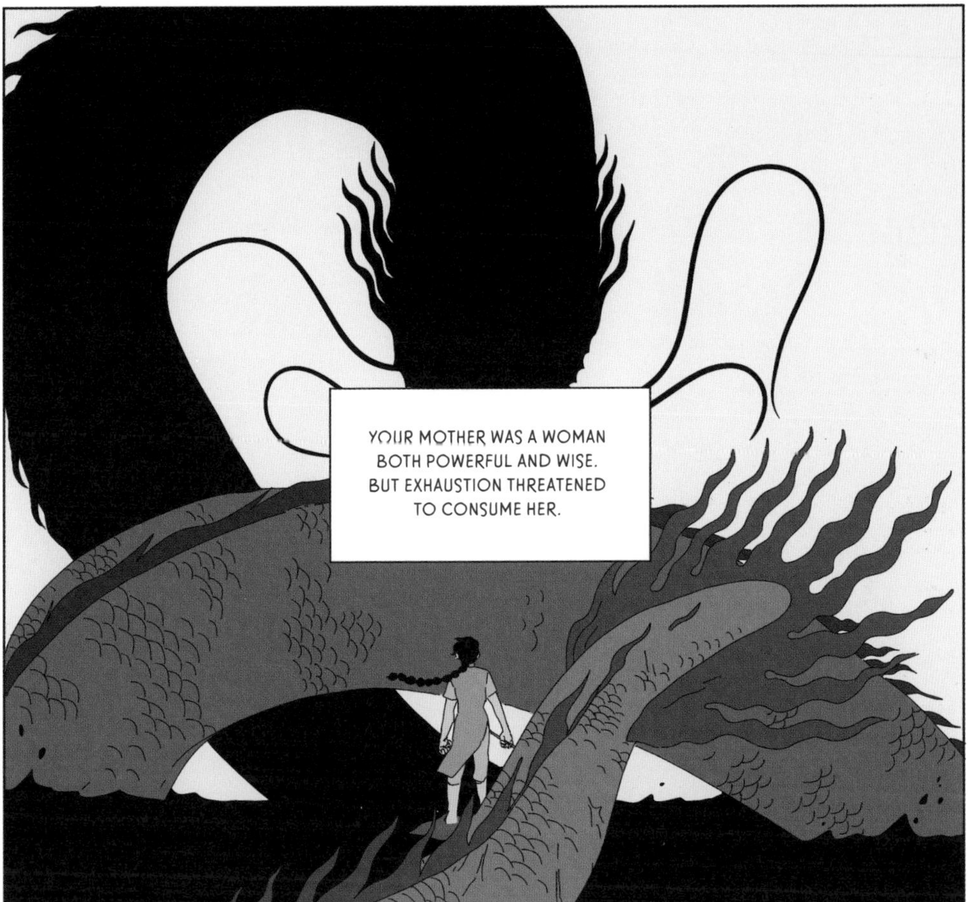
YOUR MOTHER WAS A WOMAN BOTH POWERFUL AND WISE. BUT EXHAUSTION THREATENED TO CONSUME HER.

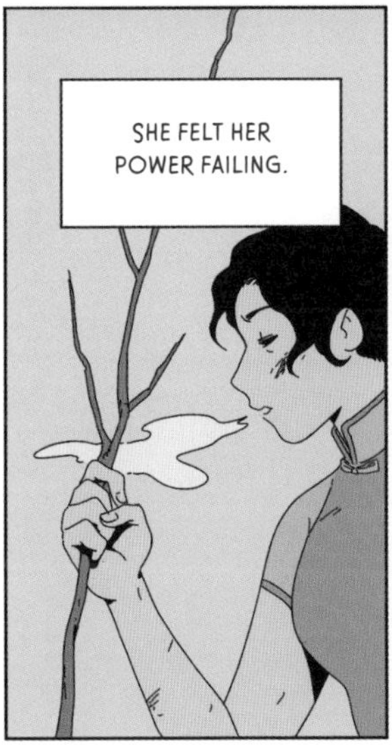
SHE FELT HER POWER FAILING.

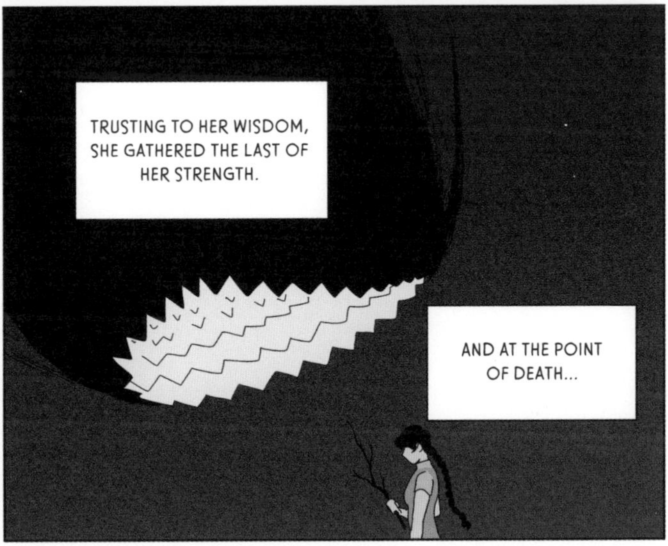
TRUSTING TO HER WISDOM, SHE GATHERED THE LAST OF HER STRENGTH.
AND AT THE POINT OF DEATH...

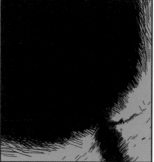

SHE CAST HER FINAL SPELL.

AND WITH THE LAST OF HER POWER,
SHE BOUND THE LEVIATHAN.

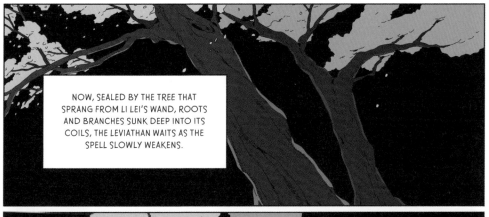

NOW, SEALED BY THE TREE THAT SPRANG FROM LI LEI'S WAND, ROOTS AND BRANCHES SUNK DEEP INTO ITS COILS, THE LEVIATHAN WAITS AS THE SPELL SLOWLY WEAKENS.

IT WATCHES FOR THE DAY THE BINDING WILL FINALLY FAIL.

FOR THE MONSTER IS BOUND, BUT NOT DEFEATED.

AND THE ONLY WAY TO STOP THE MIST, TO DRIVE AWAY THE CREATURES IT PROTECTS...

...IS TO BREAK THE BINDING THAT HOLDS THE LEVIATHAN IN STASIS. TO BREAK THE SEAL, AND KILL IT.

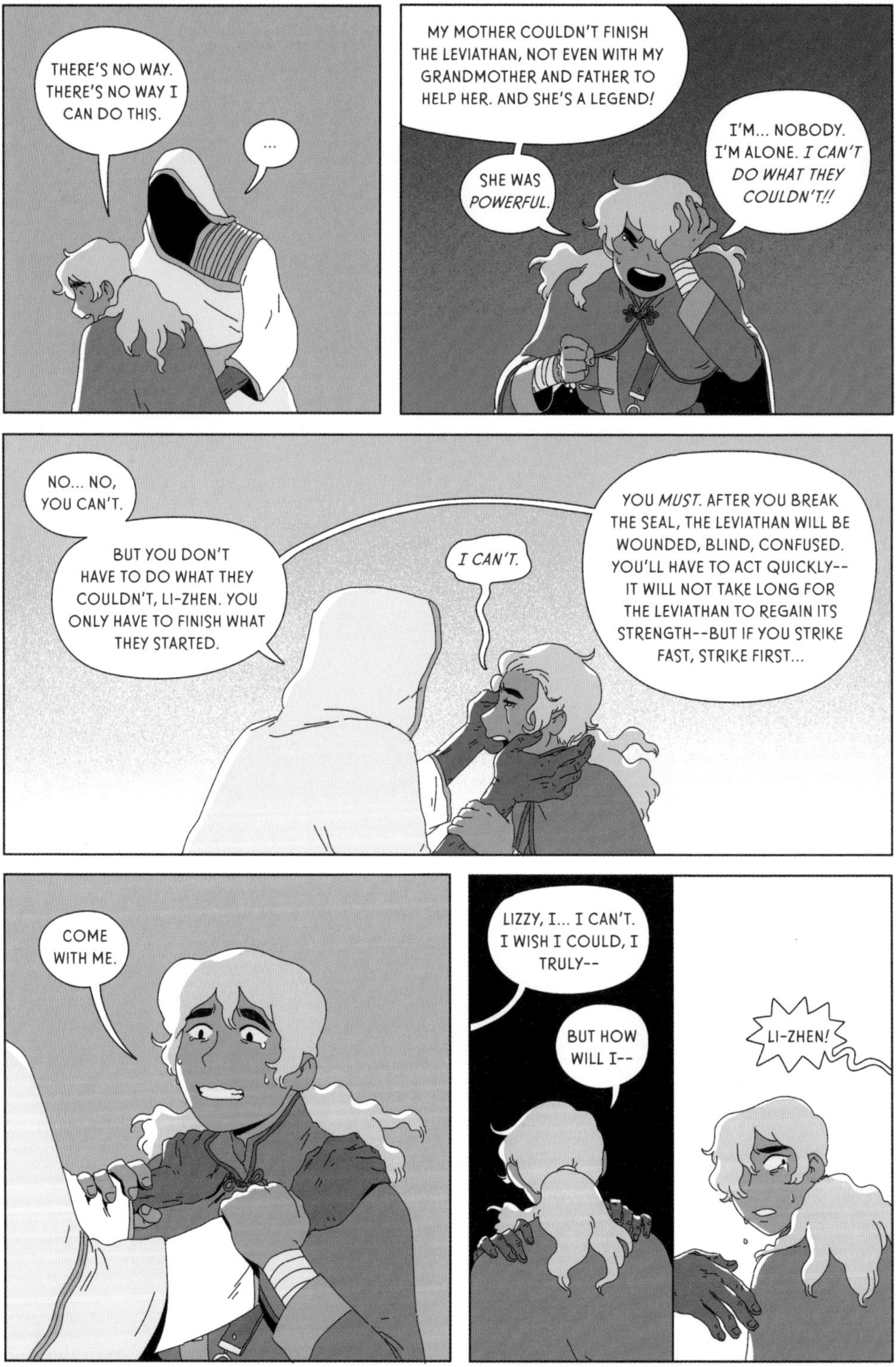
THERE'S NO WAY. THERE'S NO WAY I CAN DO THIS.
...
MY MOTHER COULDN'T FINISH THE LEVIATHAN, NOT EVEN WITH MY GRANDMOTHER AND FATHER TO HELP HER. AND SHE'S A LEGEND!
SHE WAS *POWERFUL.*
I'M... NOBODY. I'M ALONE. *I CAN'T DO WHAT THEY COULDN'T!!*
NO... NO, YOU CAN'T.
BUT YOU DON'T HAVE TO DO WHAT THEY COULDN'T, LI-ZHEN. YOU ONLY HAVE TO FINISH WHAT THEY STARTED.
*I CAN'T.*
YOU *MUST.* AFTER YOU BREAK THE SEAL, THE LEVIATHAN WILL BE WOUNDED, BLIND, CONFUSED. YOU'LL HAVE TO ACT QUICKLY-- IT WILL NOT TAKE LONG FOR THE LEVIATHAN TO REGAIN ITS STRENGTH--BUT IF YOU STRIKE FAST, STRIKE FIRST...
COME WITH ME.
LIZZY, I... I CAN'T. I WISH I COULD, I TRULY--
BUT HOW WILL I--
LI-ZHEN!

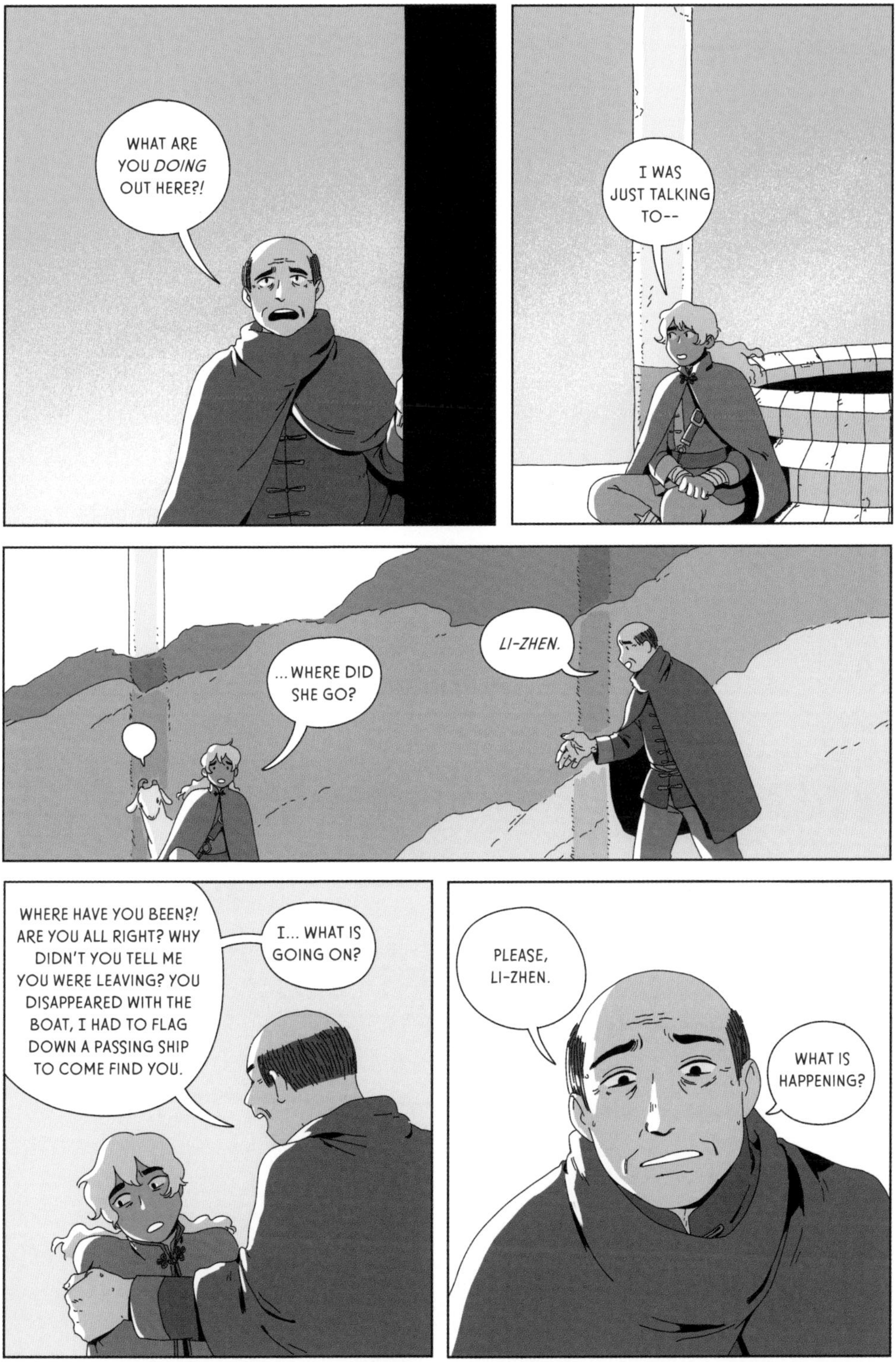
WHAT ARE YOU *DOING* OUT HERE?!
I WAS JUST TALKING TO--
...WHERE DID SHE GO?
*LI-ZHEN.*
WHERE HAVE YOU BEEN?! ARE YOU ALL RIGHT? WHY DIDN'T YOU TELL ME YOU WERE LEAVING? YOU DISAPPEARED WITH THE BOAT, I HAD TO FLAG DOWN A PASSING SHIP TO COME FIND YOU.
I... WHAT IS GOING ON?
PLEASE, LI-ZHEN.
WHAT IS HAPPENING?

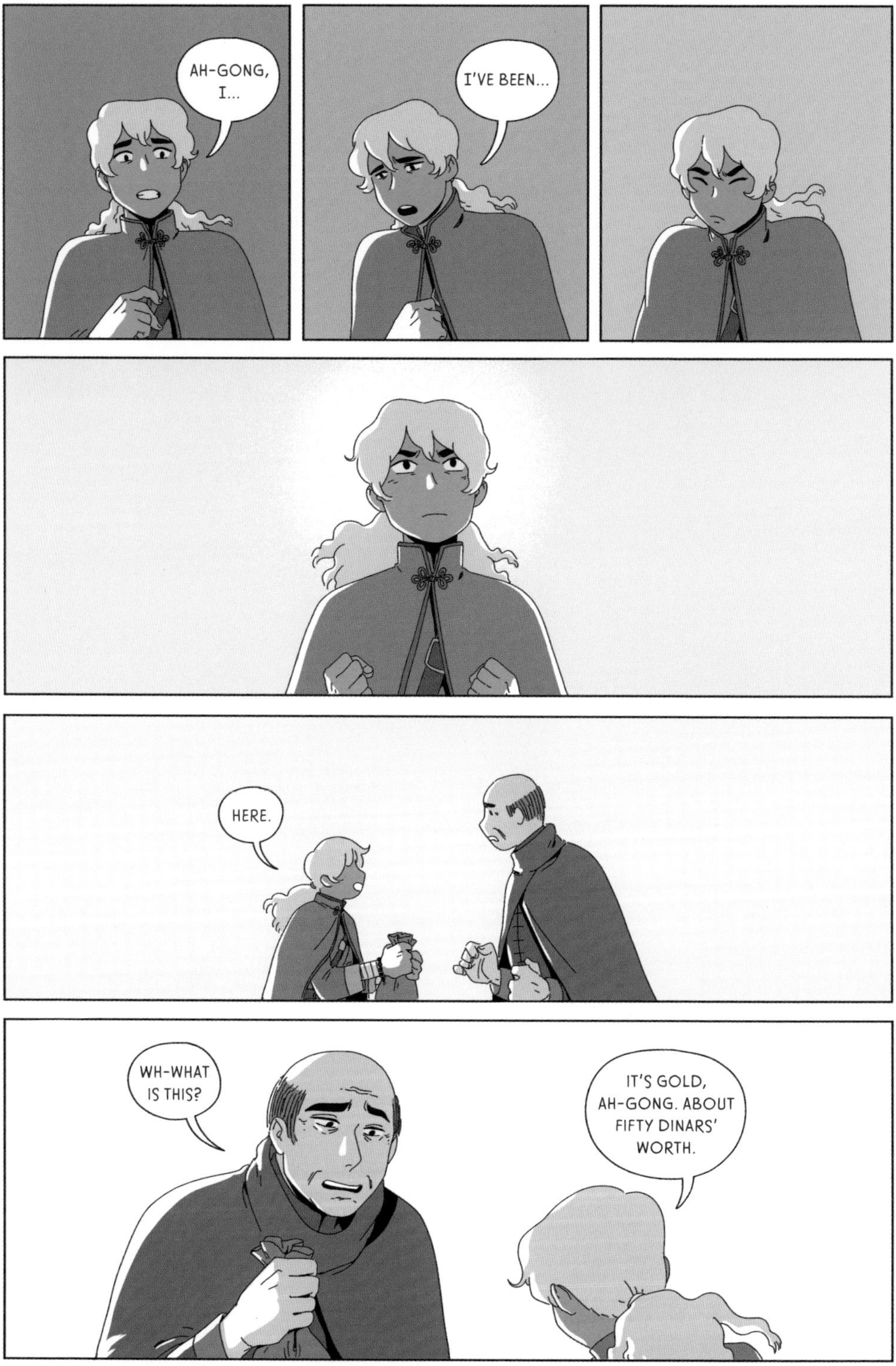
AH-GONG, I...
I'VE BEEN...
HERE.
WH-WHAT IS THIS?
IT'S GOLD, AH-GONG. ABOUT FIFTY DINARS' WORTH.

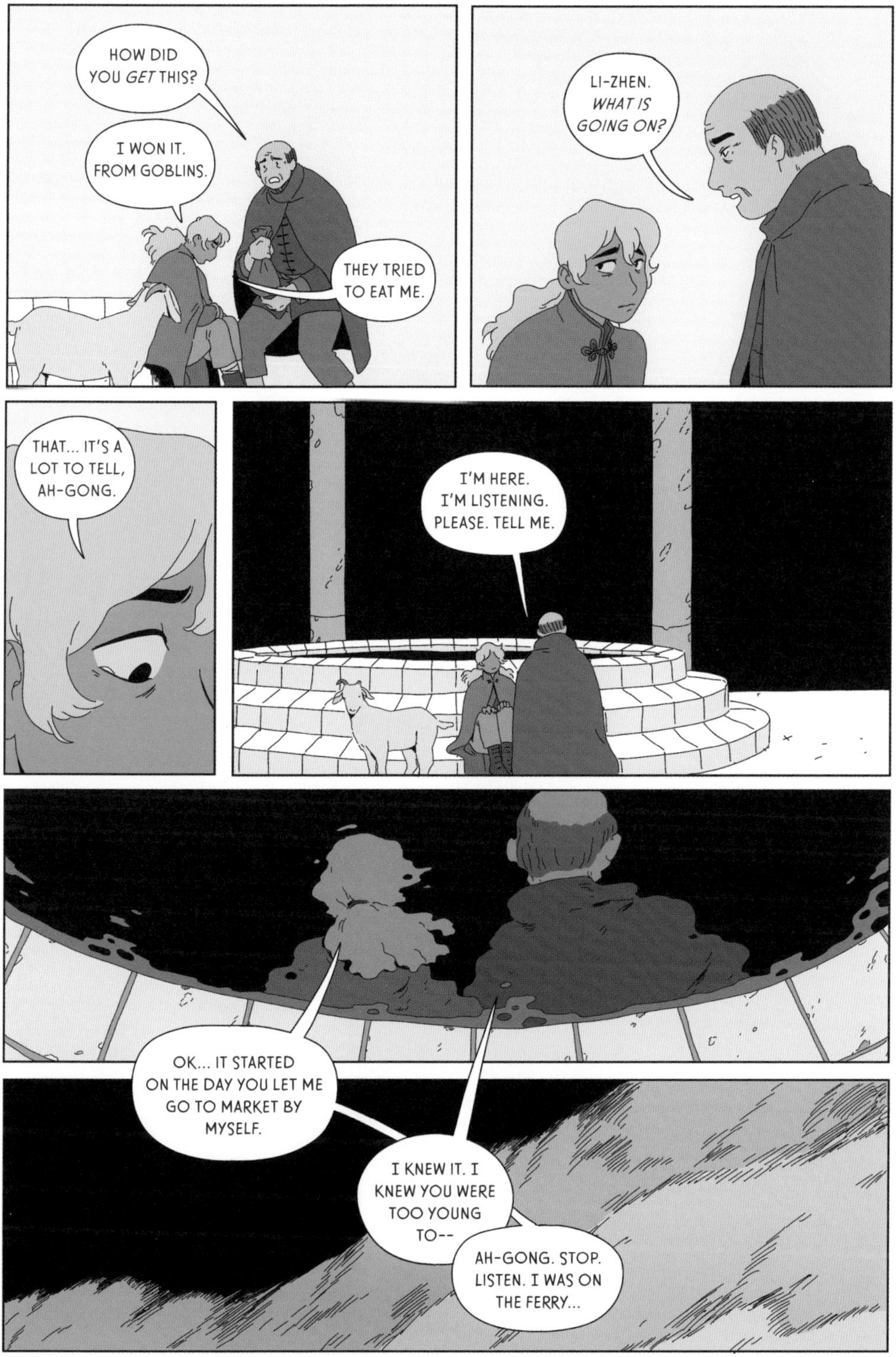
HOW DID YOU *GET* THIS?
I WON IT. FROM GOBLINS.
THEY TRIED TO EAT ME.
LI-ZHEN. *WHAT IS GOING ON?*
THAT... IT'S A LOT TO TELL, AH-GONG.
I'M HERE. I'M LISTENING. PLEASE. TELL ME.
OK... IT STARTED ON THE DAY YOU LET ME GO TO MARKET BY MYSELF.
I KNEW IT. I KNEW YOU WERE TOO YOUNG TO--
AH-GONG. STOP. LISTEN. I WAS ON THE FERRY...

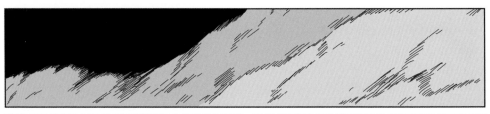

...AND NOW I HAVE JUST ONE WISH LEFT TO GRANT.

I HAVE TO KILL THE LEVIATHAN.

THE LEVIATHAN IS ALIVE?

JUST BARELY. BUT YES. AND I KNOW WHERE IT IS.

AND YOU'RE GOING THERE? TO KILL IT?

I HAVE TO DO IT BEFORE SUNDOWN TODAY, OR I LOSE MYSELF TO THE WELL. I JUST NEED TO BORROW ELI'S SKIFF FOR THE JOURNEY.

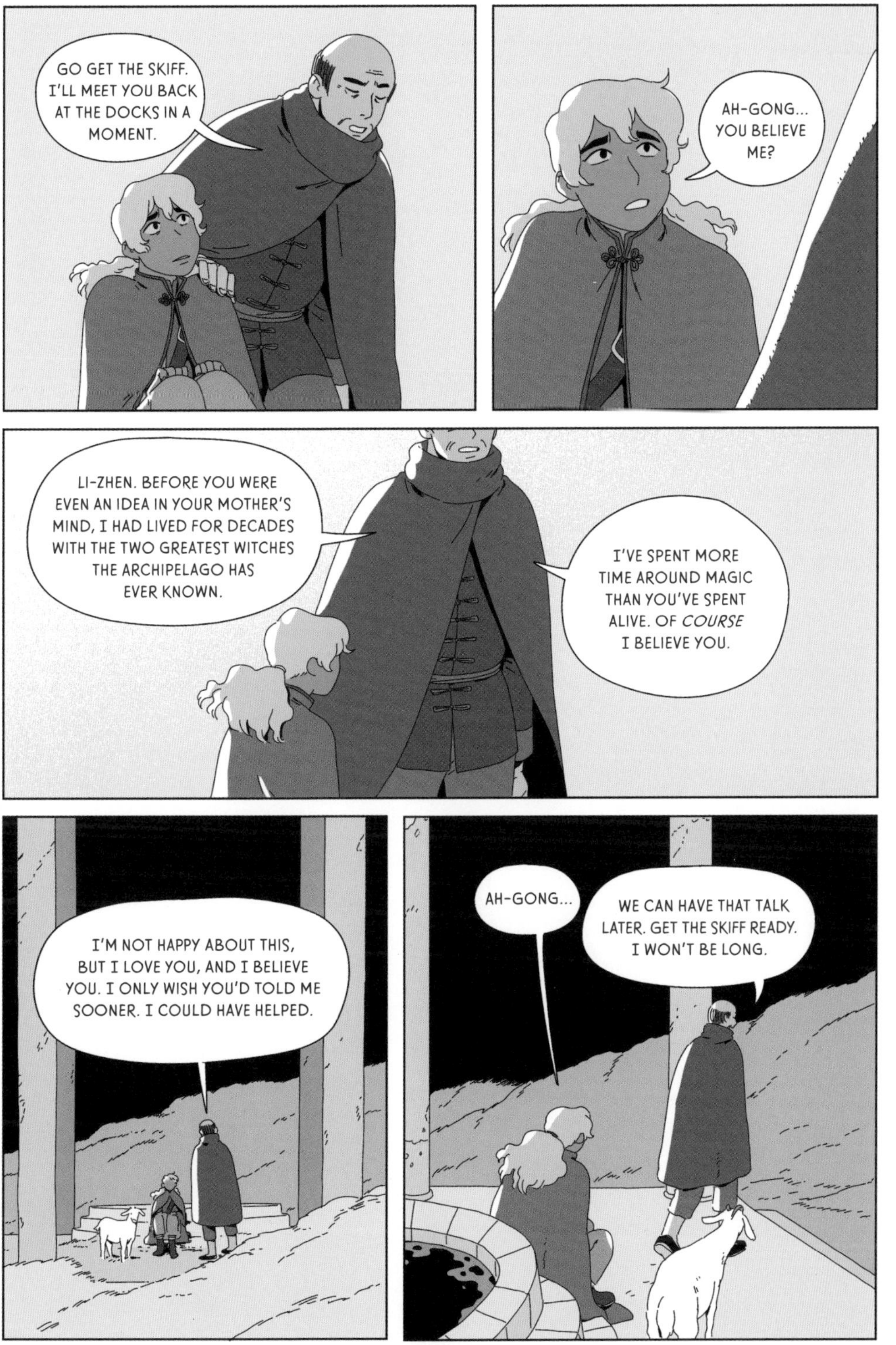
GO GET THE SKIFF. I'LL MEET YOU BACK AT THE DOCKS IN A MOMENT.
AH-GONG... YOU BELIEVE ME?
LI-ZHEN. BEFORE YOU WERE EVEN AN IDEA IN YOUR MOTHER'S MIND, I HAD LIVED FOR DECADES WITH THE TWO GREATEST WITCHES THE ARCHIPELAGO HAS EVER KNOWN.
I'VE SPENT MORE TIME AROUND MAGIC THAN YOU'VE SPENT ALIVE. OF *COURSE* I BELIEVE YOU.
I'M NOT HAPPY ABOUT THIS, BUT I LOVE YOU, AND I BELIEVE YOU. I ONLY WISH YOU'D TOLD ME SOONER. I COULD HAVE HELPED.
AH-GONG...
WE CAN HAVE THAT TALK LATER. GET THE SKIFF READY. I WON'T BE LONG.

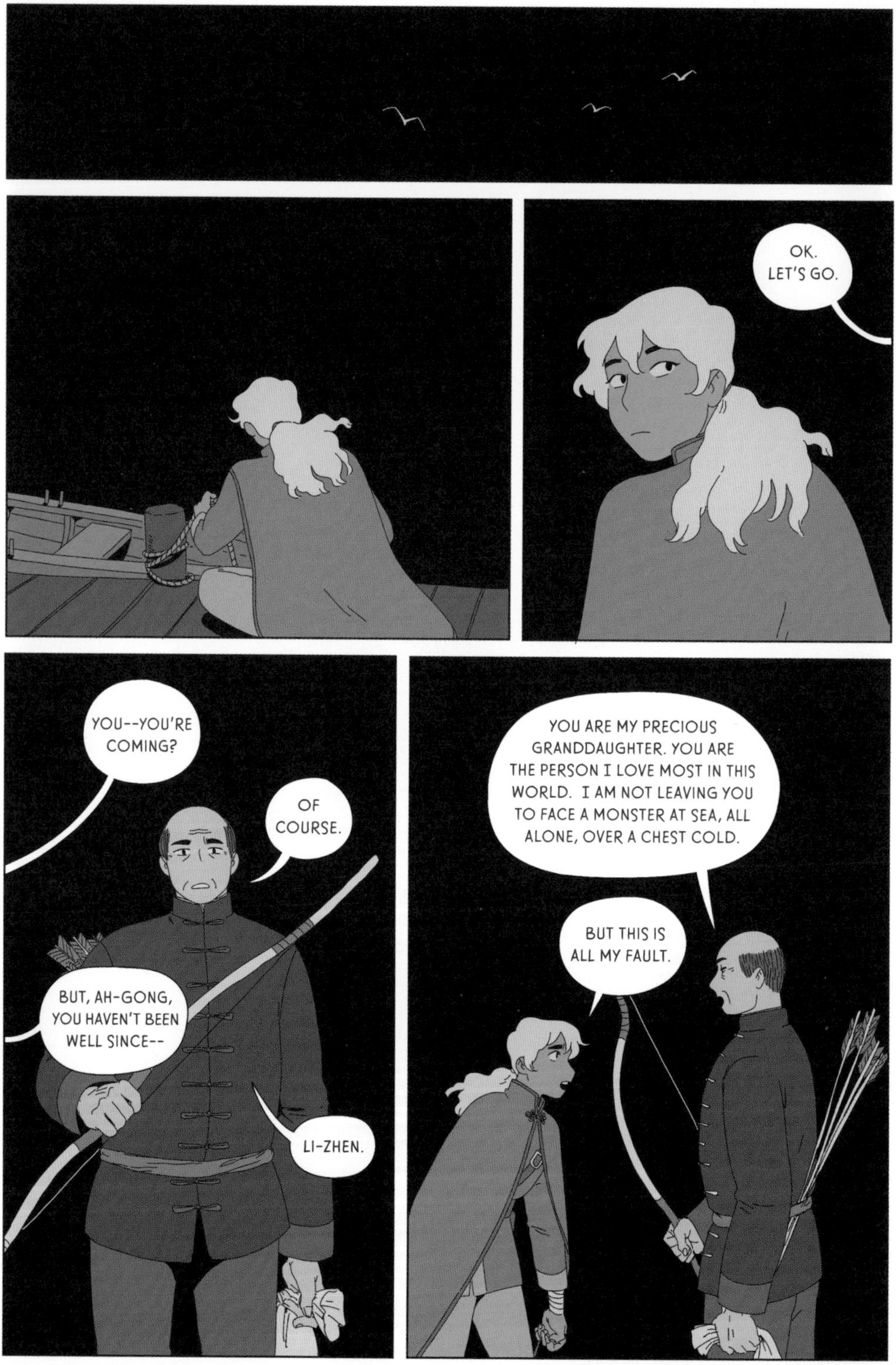
OK. LET'S GO.
YOU--YOU'RE COMING?
OF COURSE.
BUT, AH-GONG, YOU HAVEN'T BEEN WELL SINCE--
LI-ZHEN.
YOU ARE MY PRECIOUS GRANDDAUGHTER. YOU ARE THE PERSON I LOVE MOST IN THIS WORLD. I AM NOT LEAVING YOU TO FACE A MONSTER AT SEA, ALL ALONE, OVER A CHEST COLD.
BUT THIS IS ALL MY FAULT.

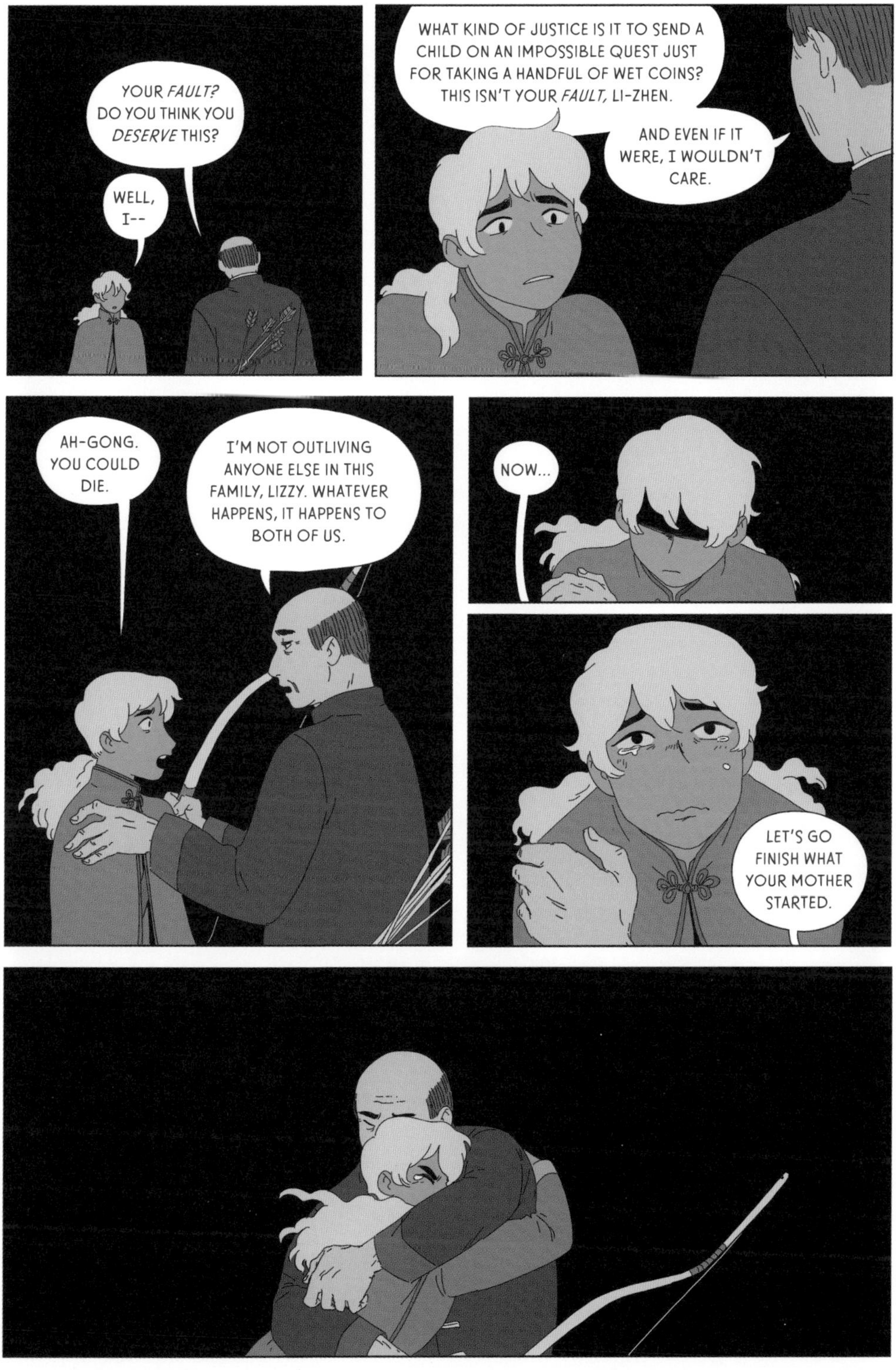
YOUR *FAULT?* DO YOU THINK YOU *DESERVE* THIS?
WELL, I--
WHAT KIND OF JUSTICE IS IT TO SEND A CHILD ON AN IMPOSSIBLE QUEST JUST FOR TAKING A HANDFUL OF WET COINS? THIS ISN'T YOUR *FAULT,* LI-ZHEN.
AND EVEN IF IT WERE, I WOULDN'T CARE.
AH-GONG. YOU COULD DIE.
I'M NOT OUTLIVING ANYONE ELSE IN THIS FAMILY, LIZZY. WHATEVER HAPPENS, IT HAPPENS TO BOTH OF US.
NOW...
LET'S GO FINISH WHAT YOUR MOTHER STARTED.

UH...

ELI

?

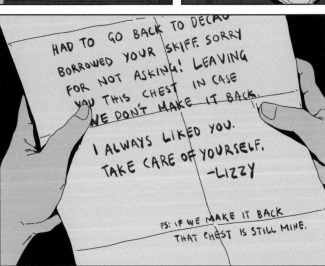

HAD TO GO BACK TO DECAU
BORROWED YOUR SKIFF. SORRY
FOR NOT ASKING! LEAVING
YOU THIS CHEST IN CASE
WE DON'T MAKE IT BACK.

I ALWAYS LIKED YOU.
TAKE CARE OF YOURSELF.
—LIZZY

PS: IF WE MAKE IT BACK
THAT CHEST IS STILL MINE.

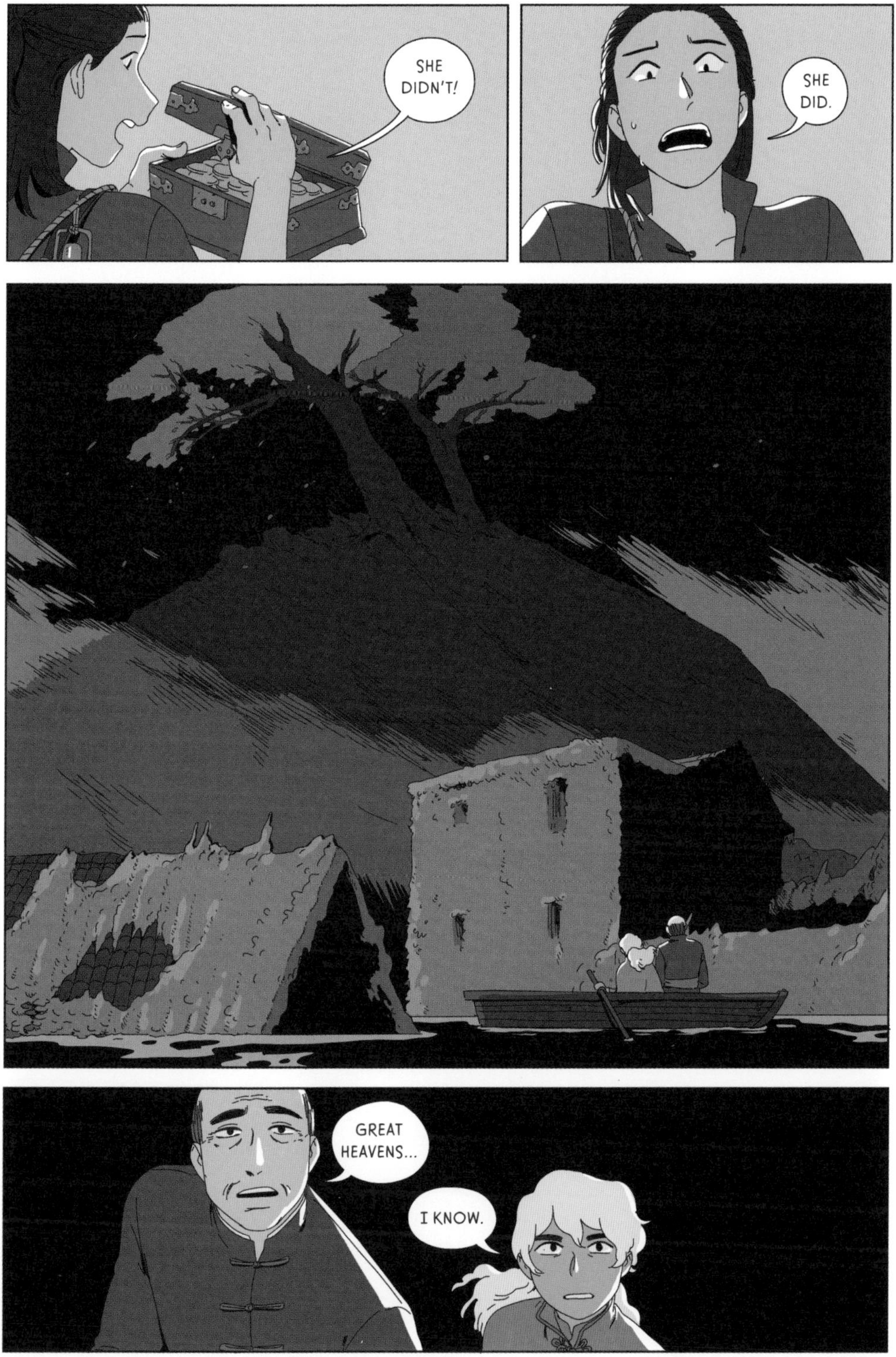
SHE DIDN'T!
SHE DID.
GREAT HEAVENS...
I KNOW.

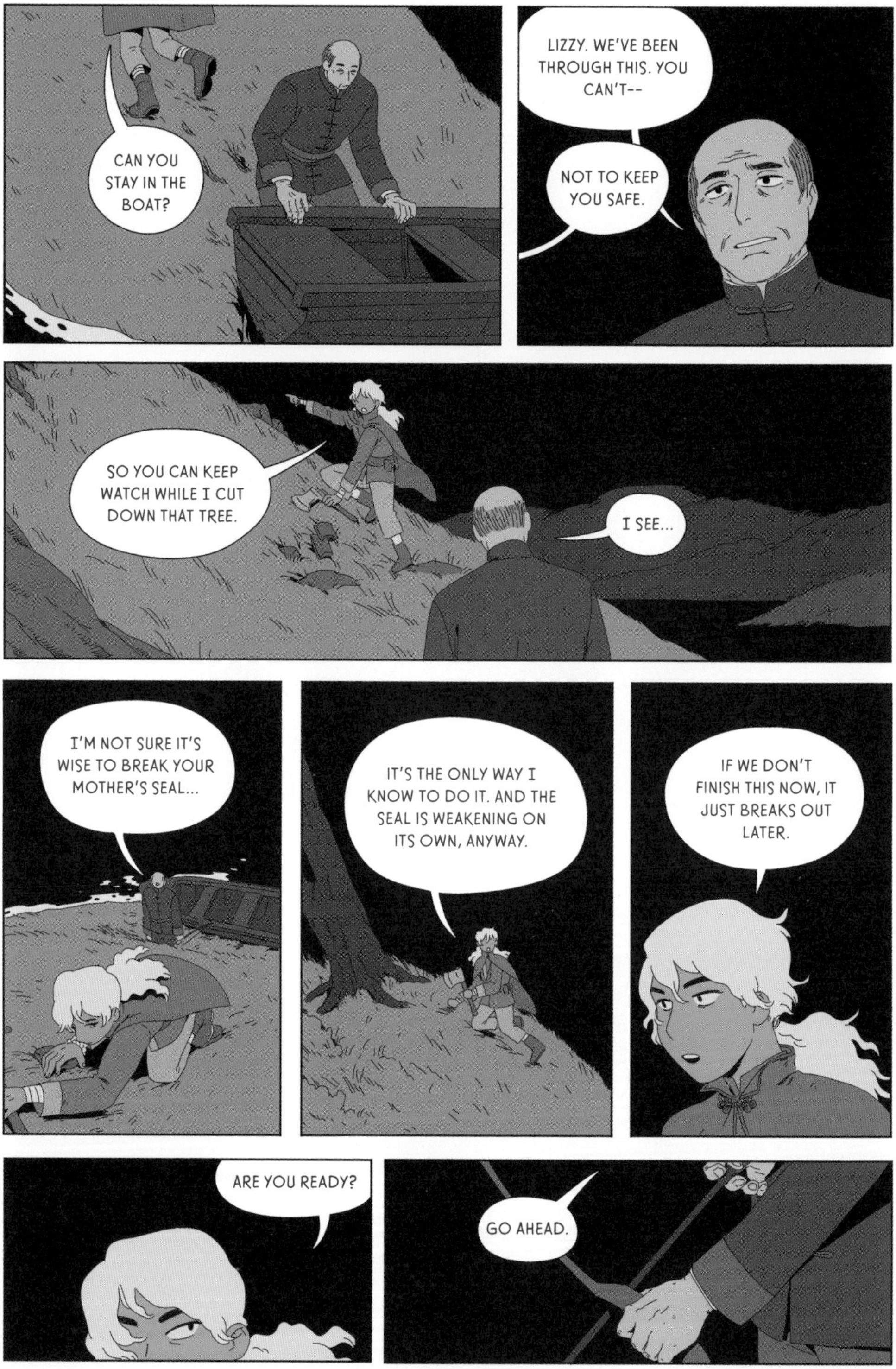
CAN YOU STAY IN THE BOAT?
LIZZY. WE'VE BEEN THROUGH THIS. YOU CAN'T--
NOT TO KEEP YOU SAFE.
SO YOU CAN KEEP WATCH WHILE I CUT DOWN THAT TREE.
I SEE...
I'M NOT SURE IT'S WISE TO BREAK YOUR MOTHER'S SEAL...
IT'S THE ONLY WAY I KNOW TO DO IT. AND THE SEAL IS WEAKENING ON ITS OWN, ANYWAY.
IF WE DON'T FINISH THIS NOW, IT JUST BREAKS OUT LATER.
ARE YOU READY?
GO AHEAD.

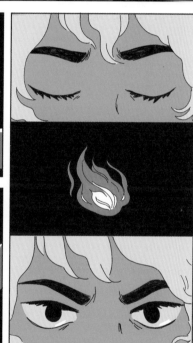

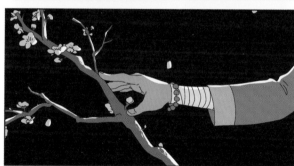

THOK!

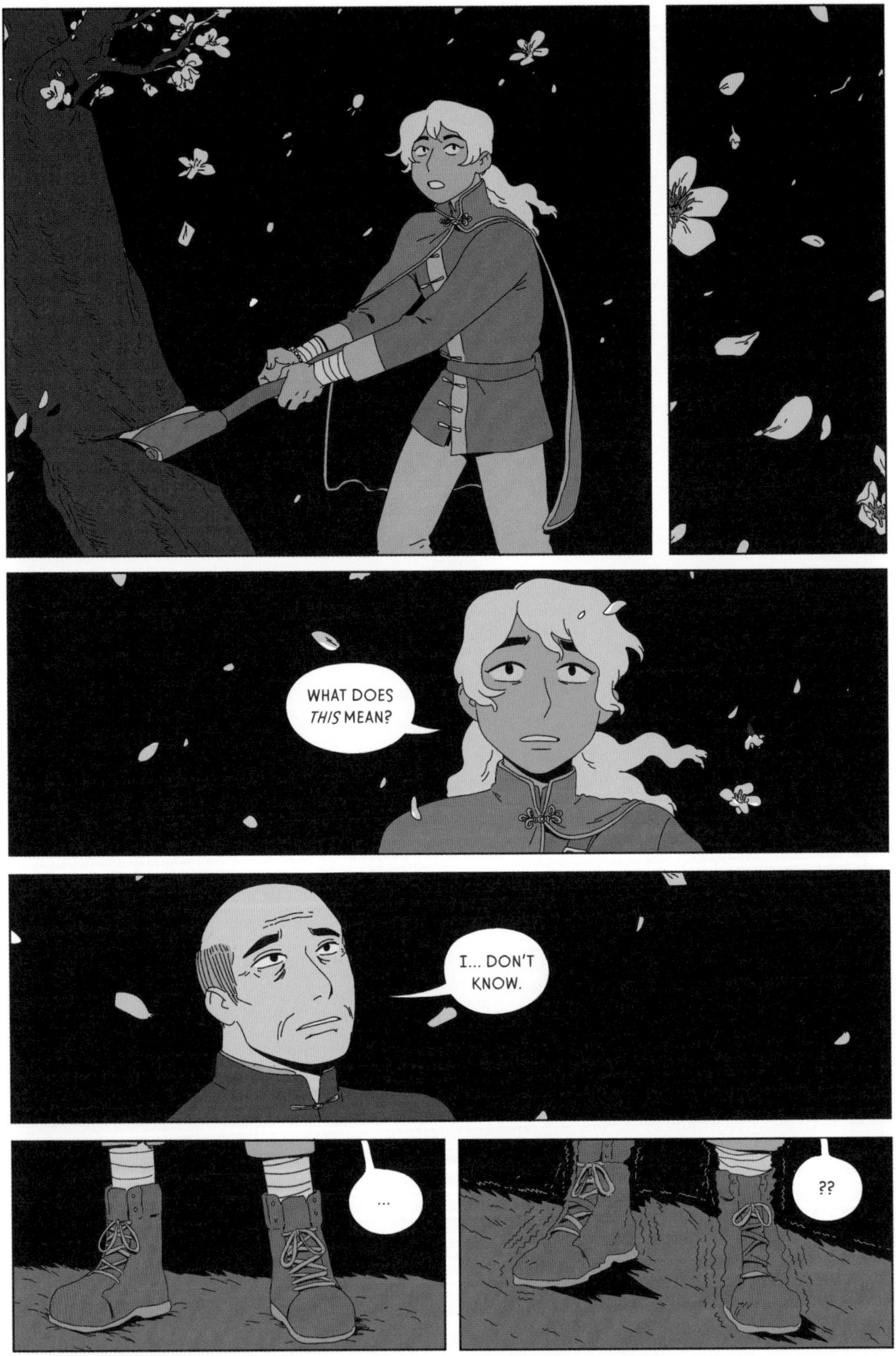
WHAT DOES *THIS* MEAN?
I... DON'T KNOW.
...
??

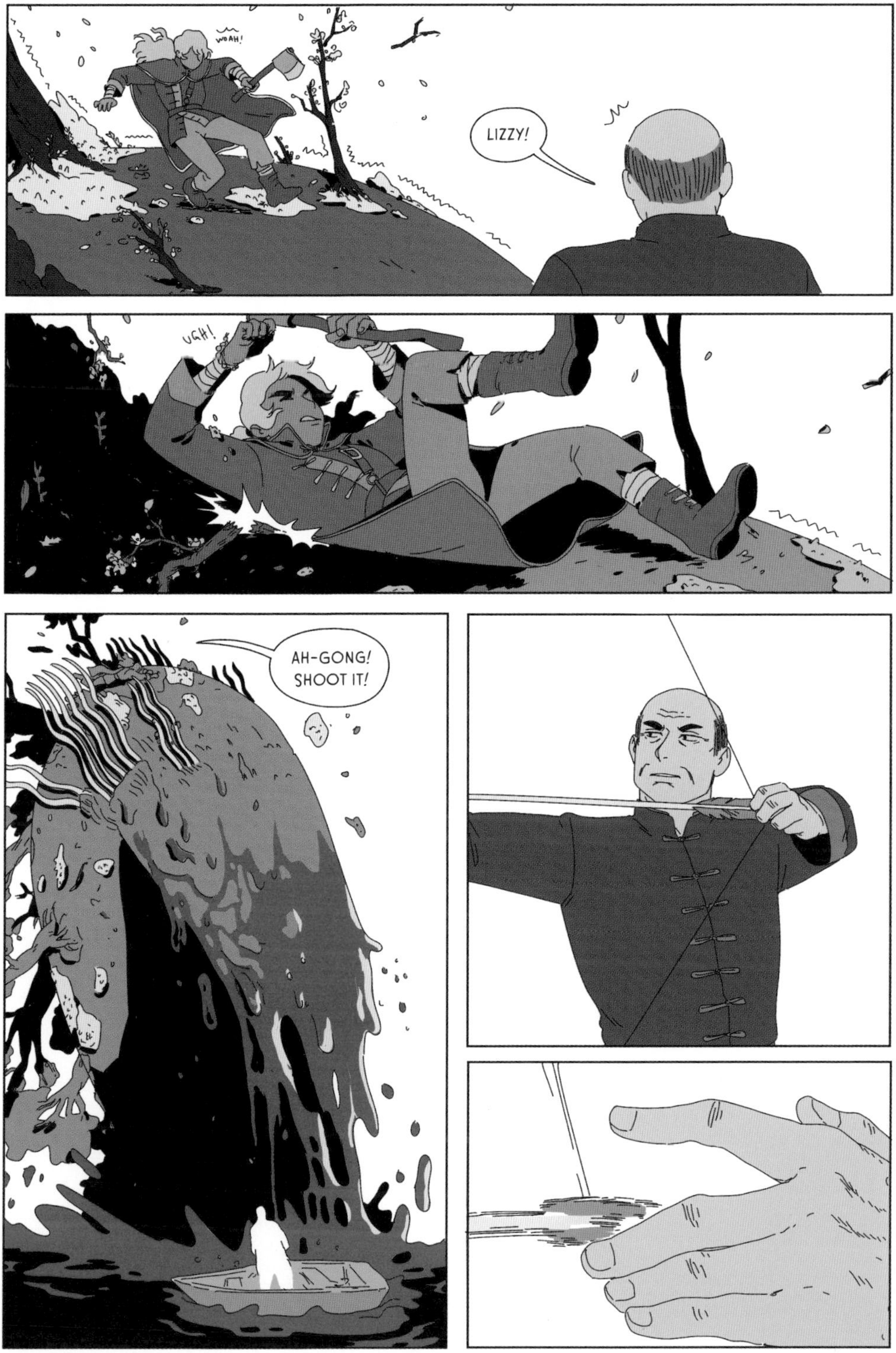
WOAH!
LIZZY!
UGH!
AH-GONG! SHOOT IT!

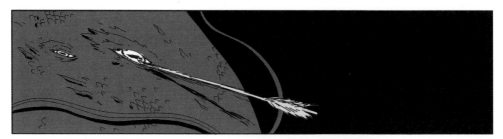

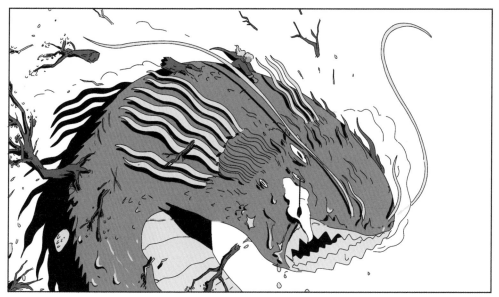

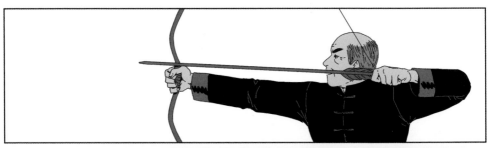

GODS.

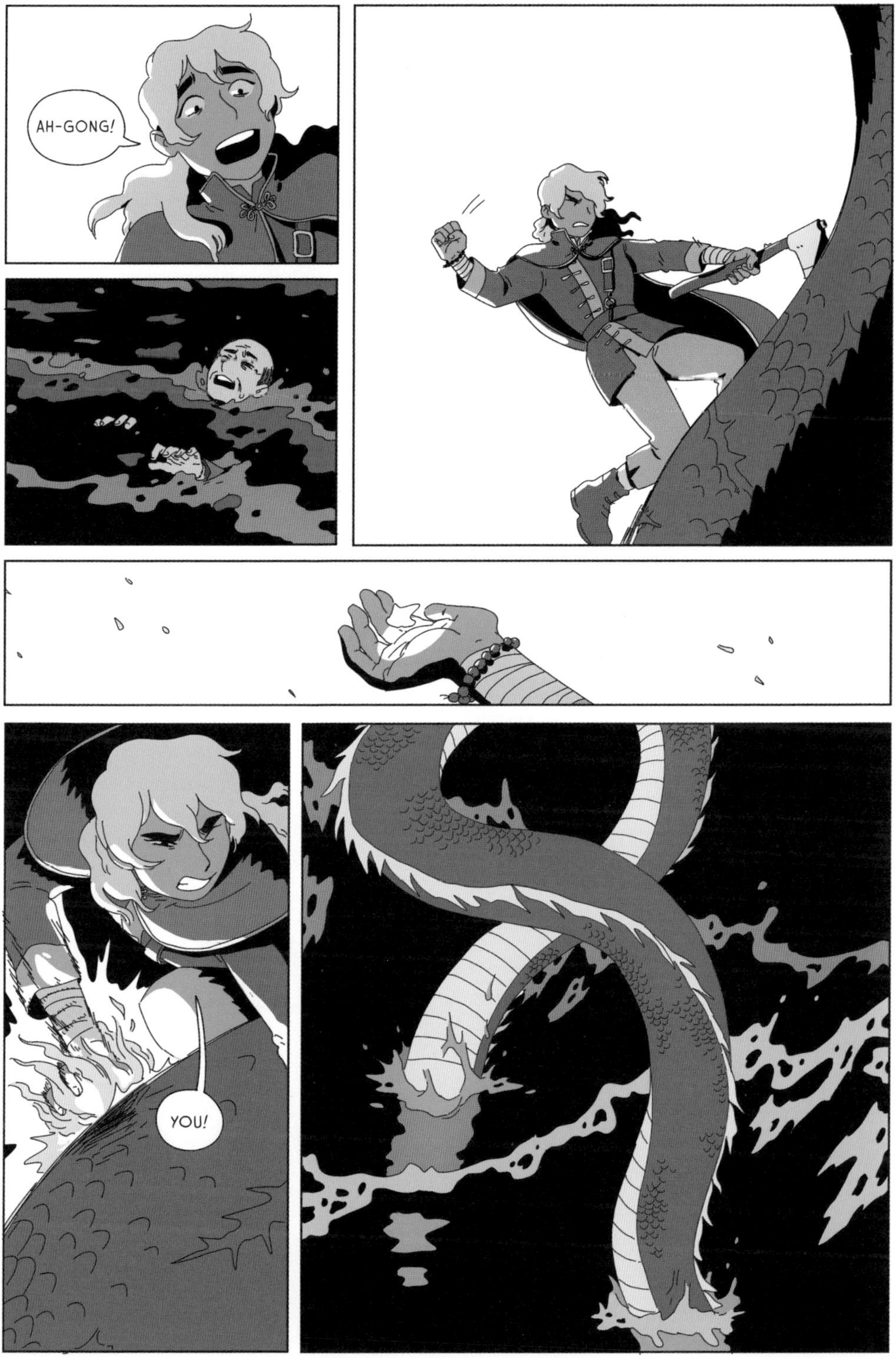
AH-GONG!
YOU!

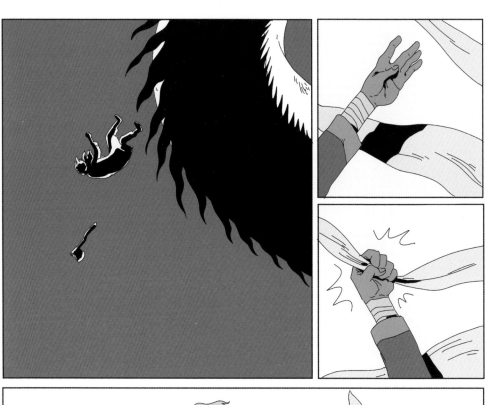

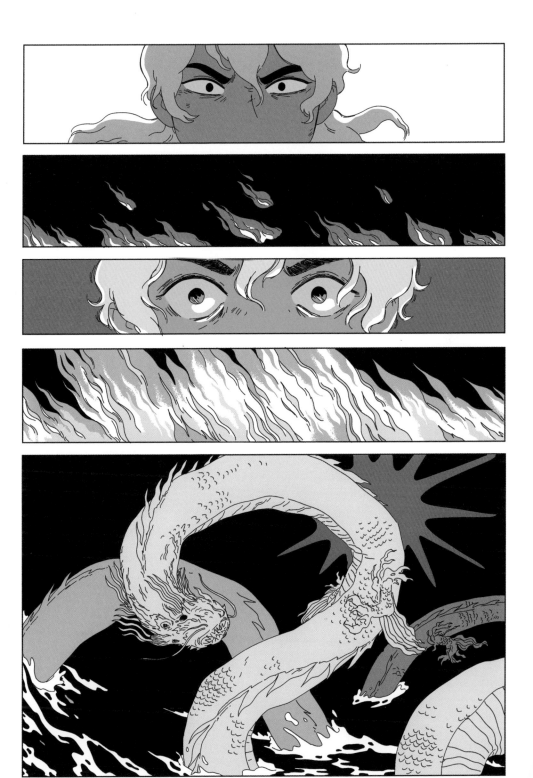

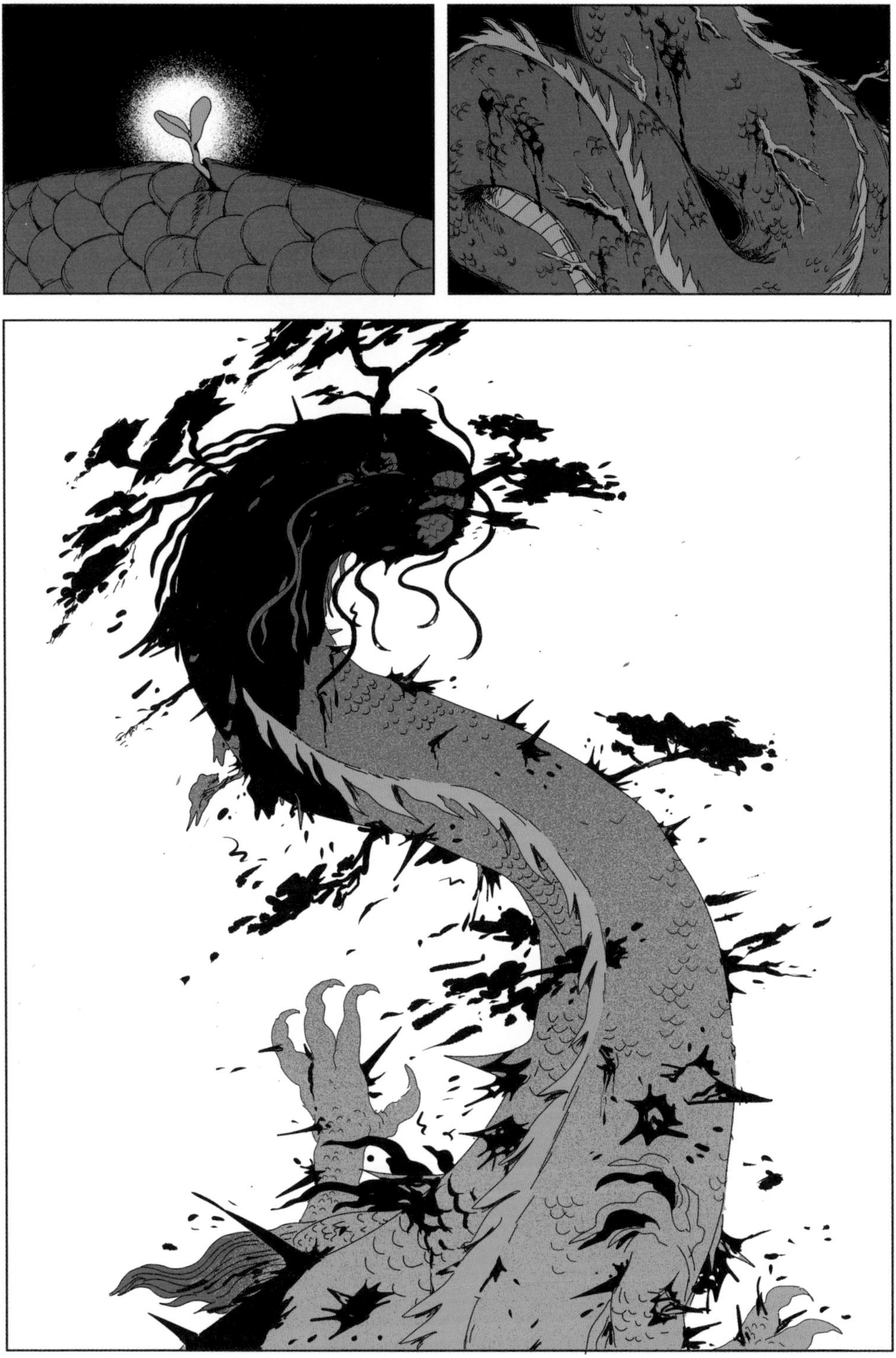

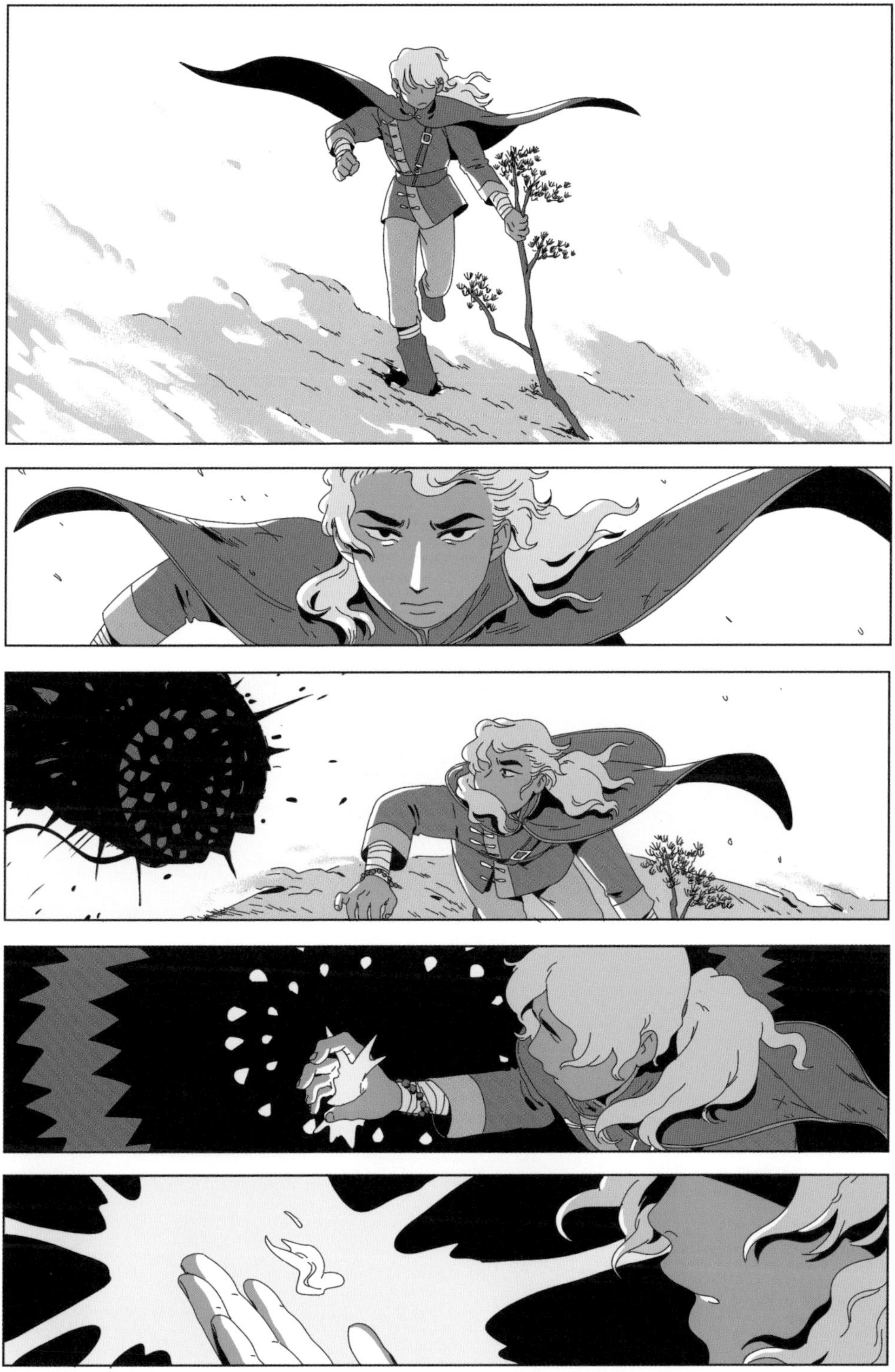

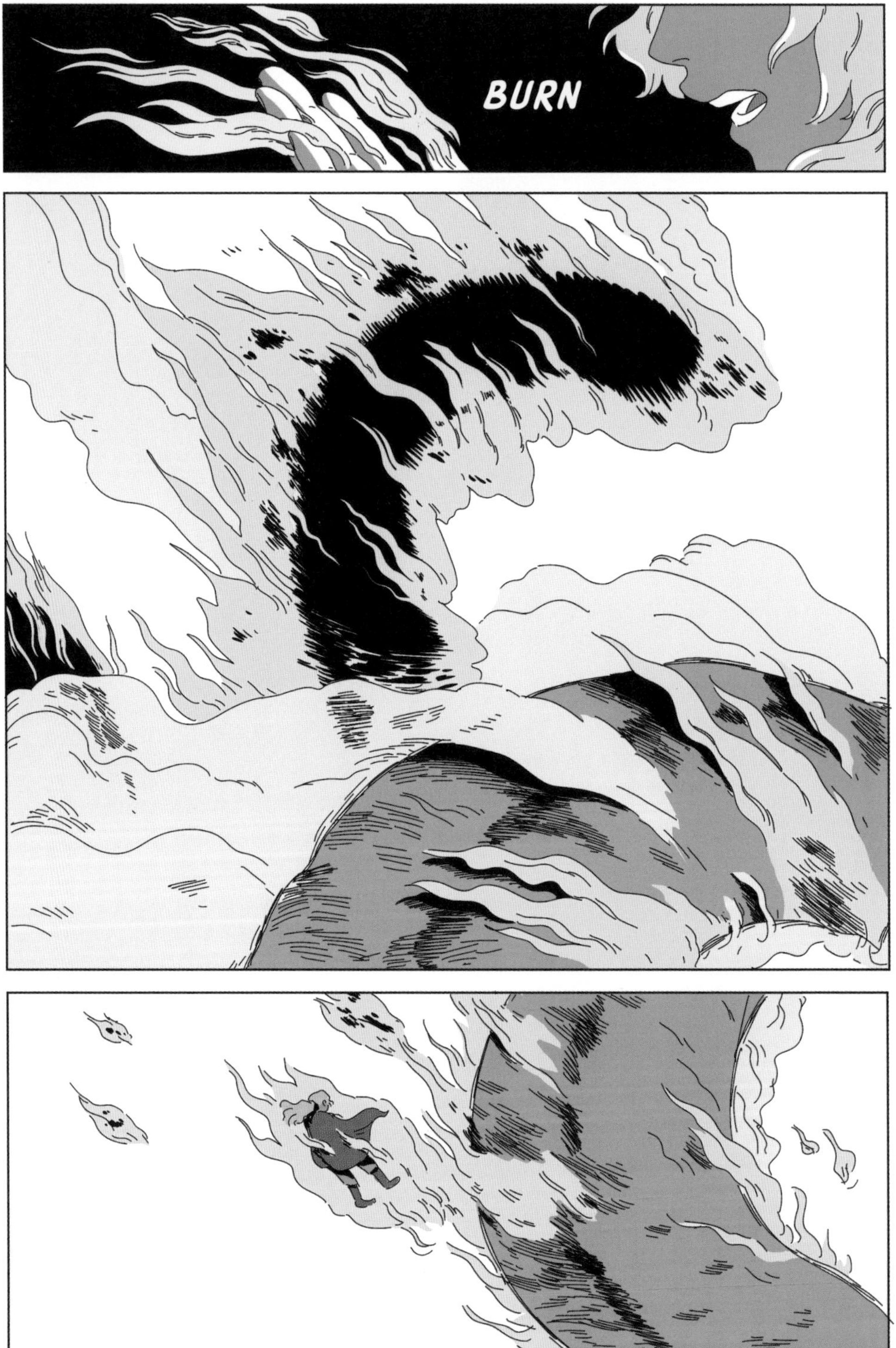
BURN

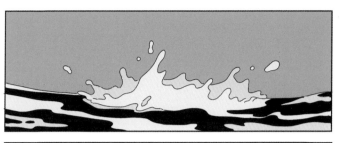
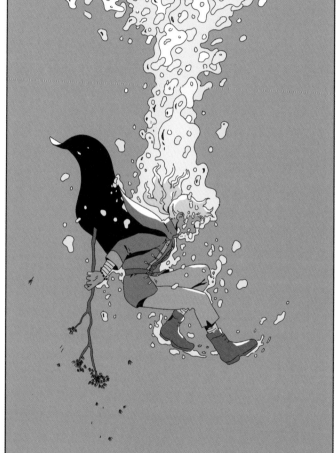

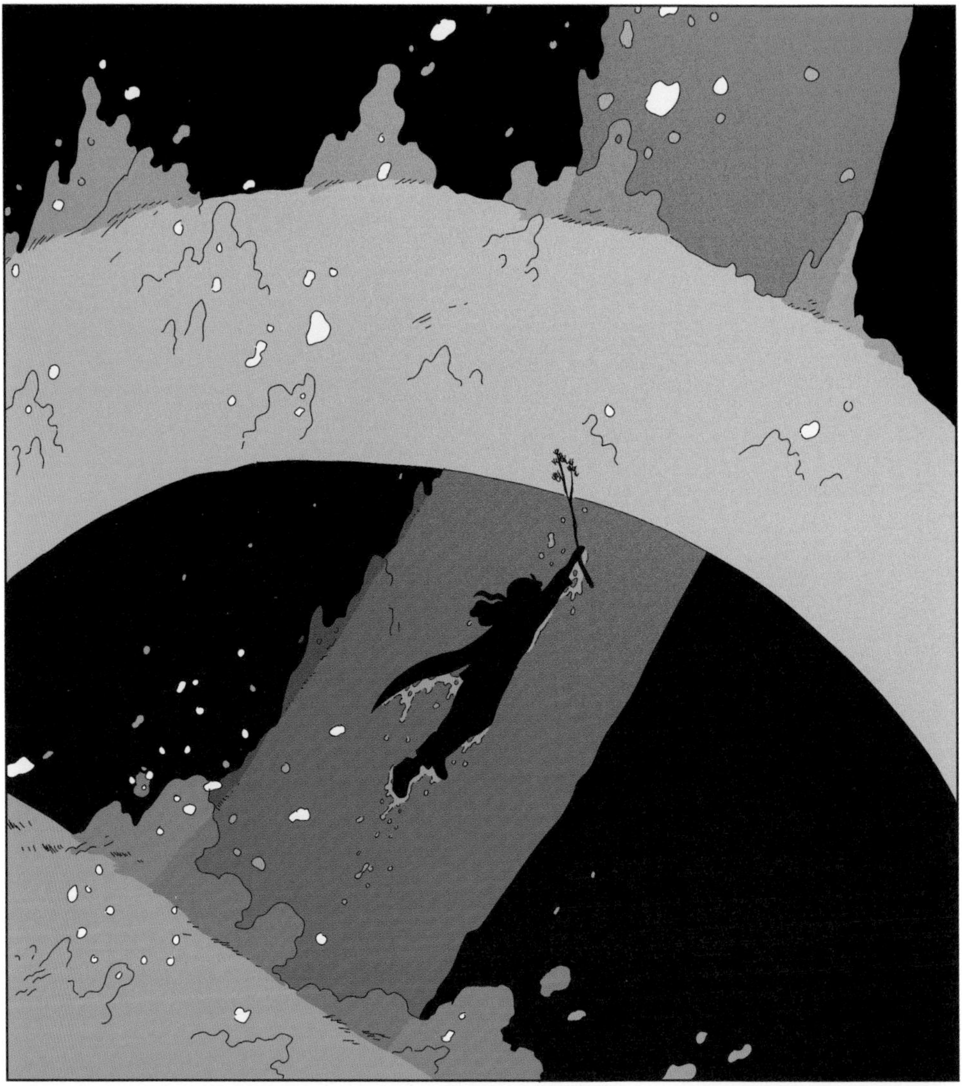

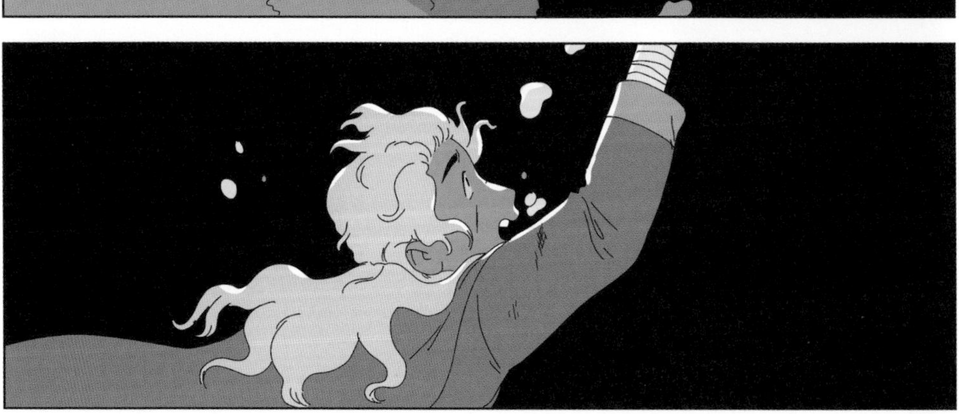

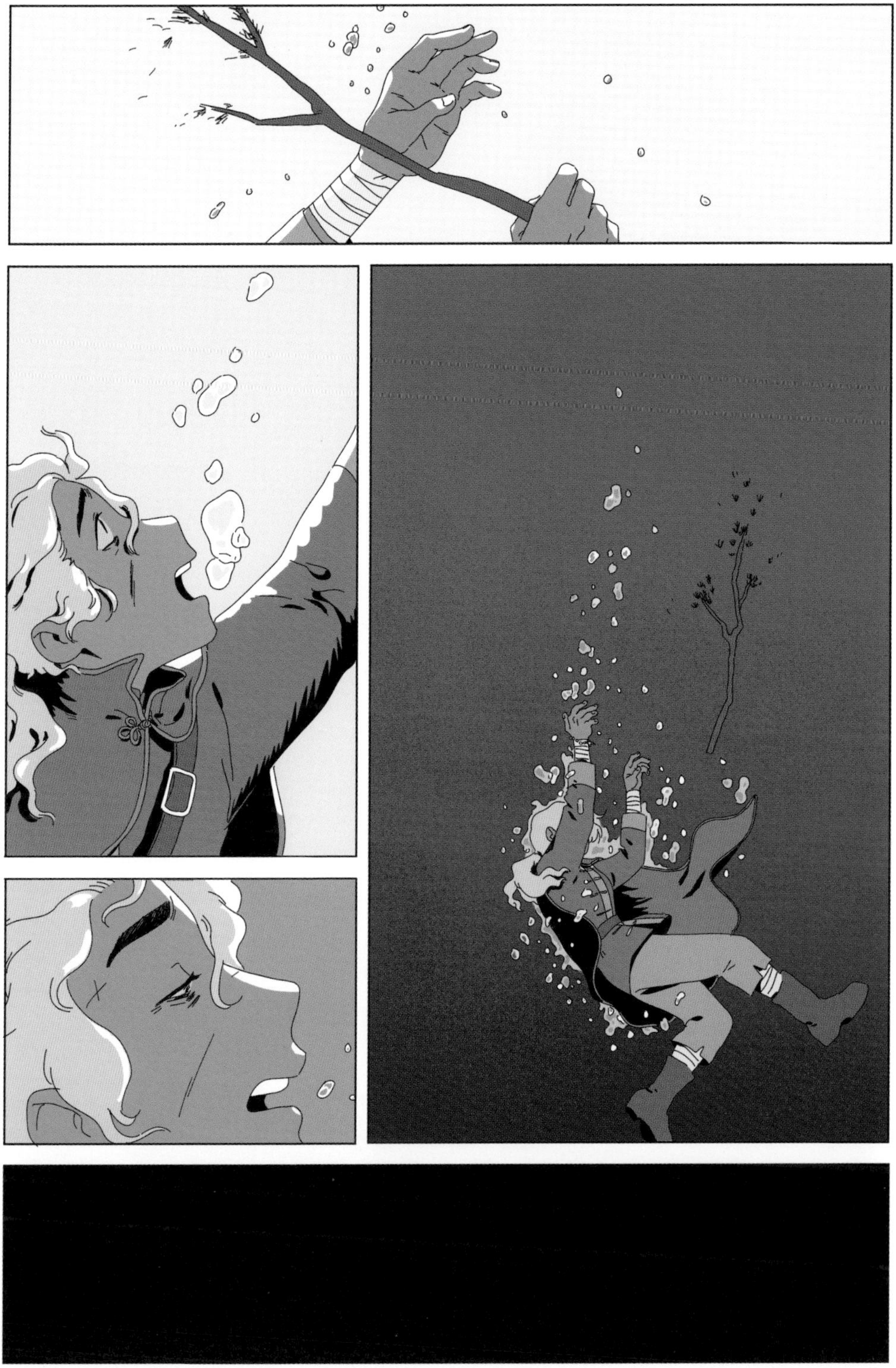

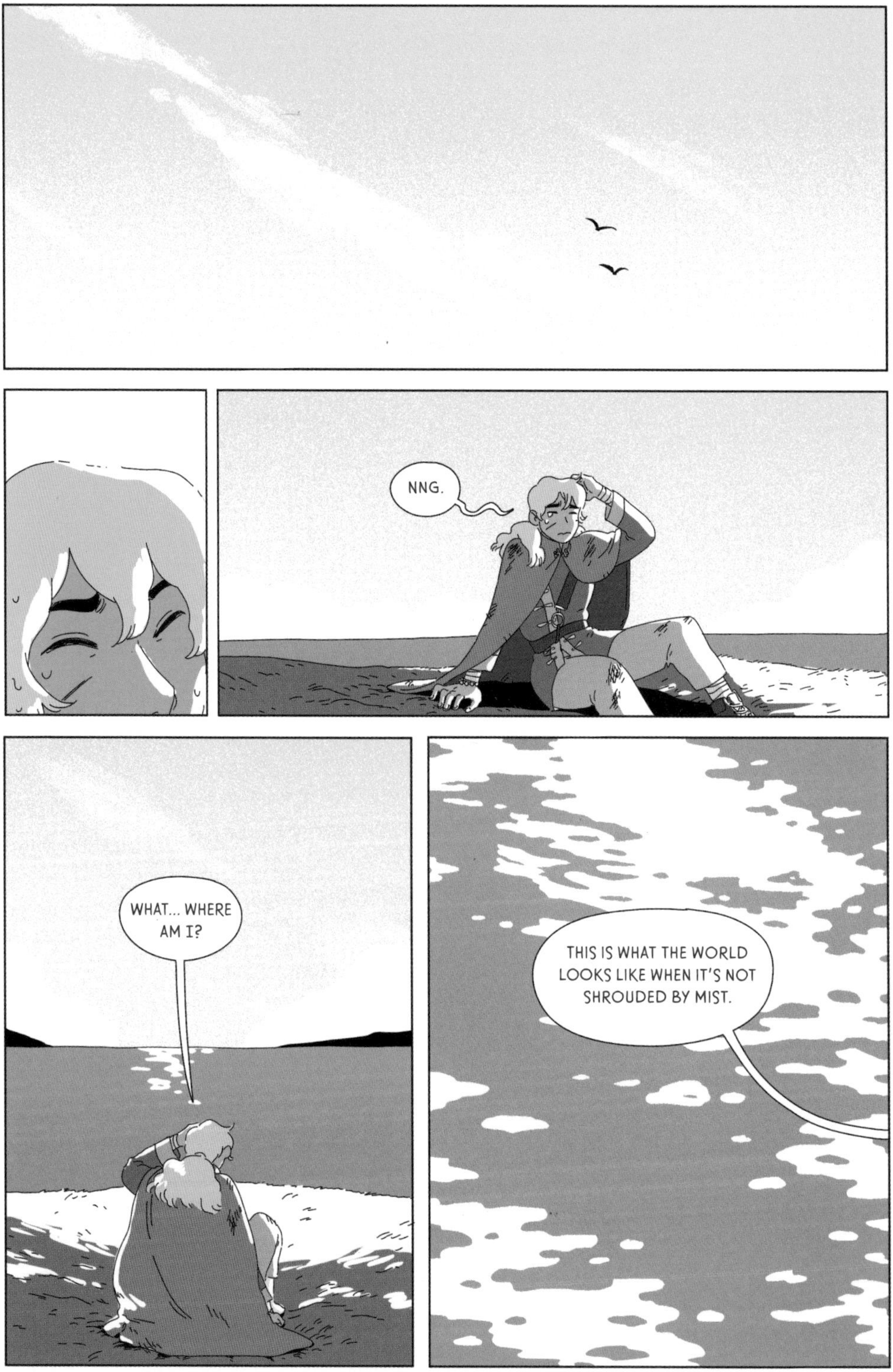
NNG.
WHAT... WHERE AM I?
THIS IS WHAT THE WORLD LOOKS LIKE WHEN IT'S NOT SHROUDED BY MIST.

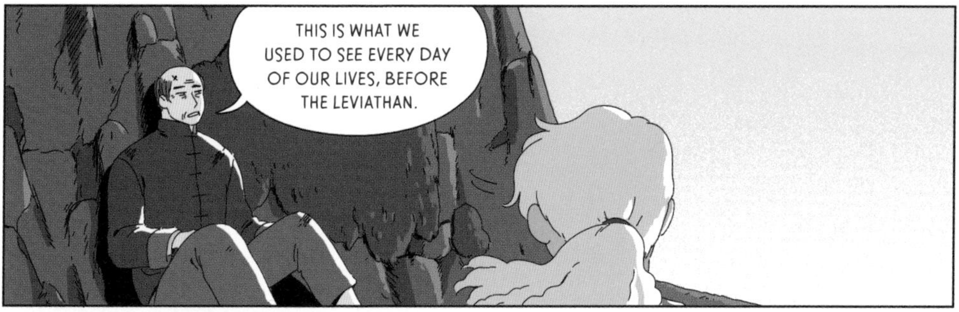
THIS IS WHAT WE USED TO SEE EVERY DAY OF OUR LIVES, BEFORE THE LEVIATHAN.

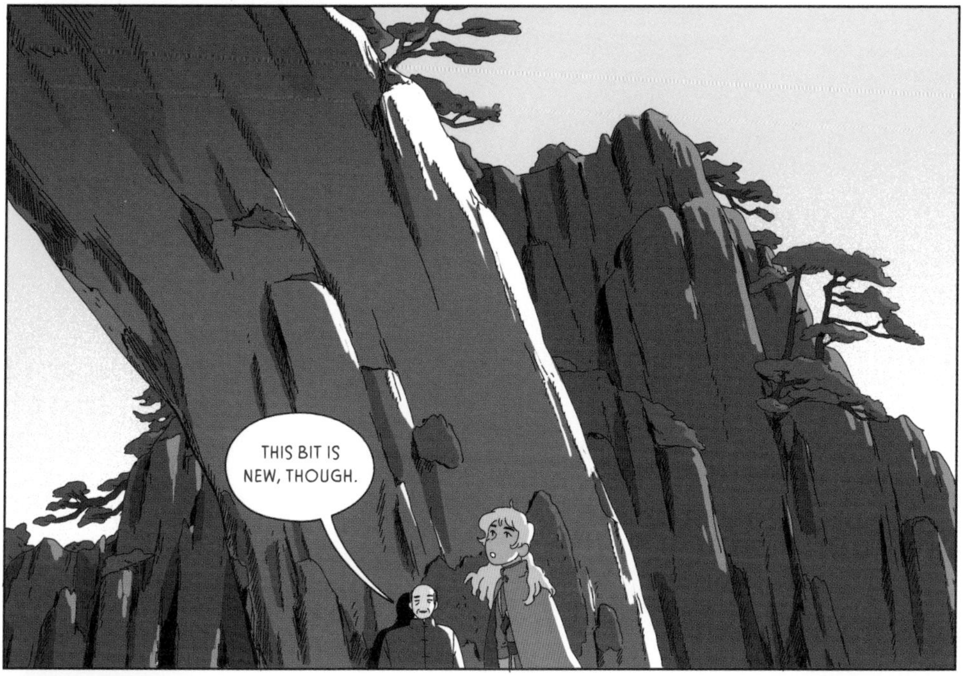
THIS BIT IS NEW, THOUGH.

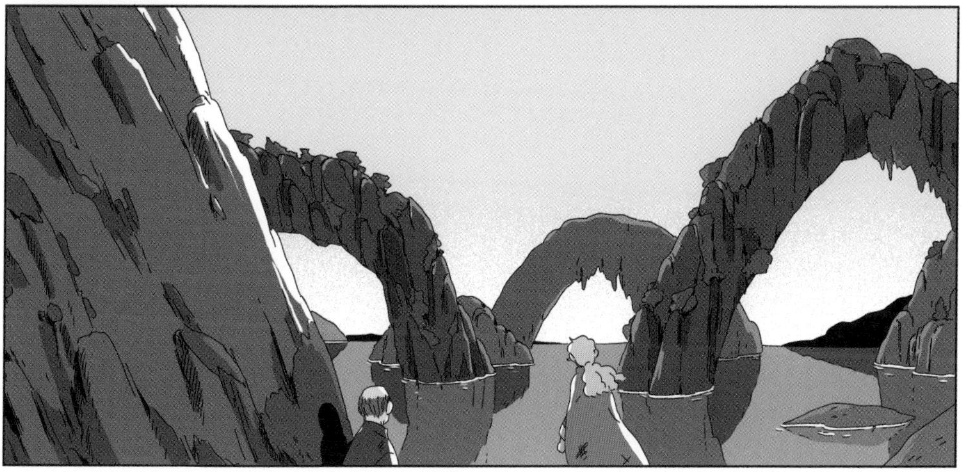

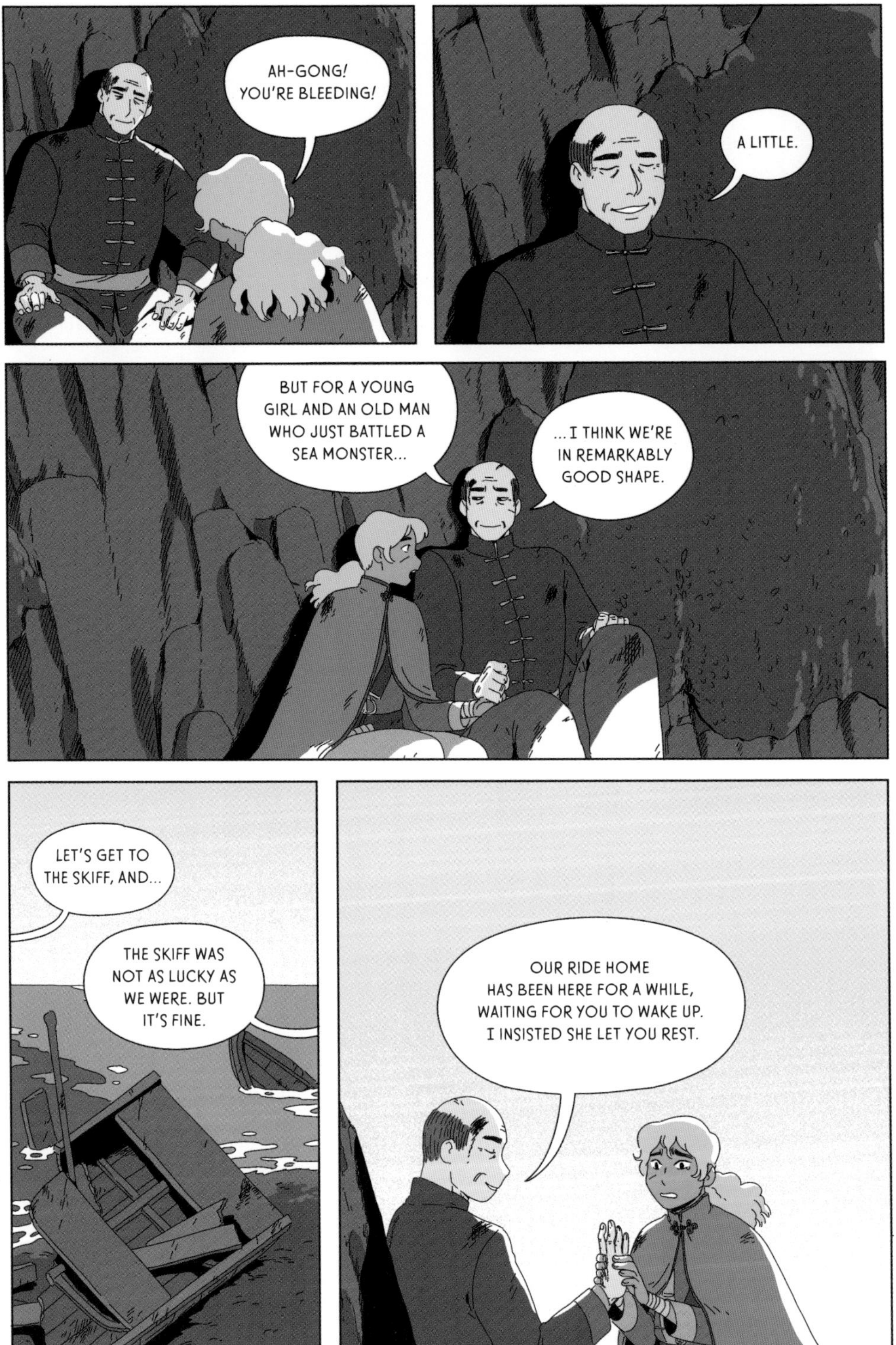
AH-GONG! YOU'RE BLEEDING!
A LITTLE.
BUT FOR A YOUNG GIRL AND AN OLD MAN WHO JUST BATTLED A SEA MONSTER...
...I THINK WE'RE IN REMARKABLY GOOD SHAPE.
LET'S GET TO THE SKIFF, AND...
THE SKIFF WAS NOT AS LUCKY AS WE WERE. BUT IT'S FINE.
OUR RIDE HOME HAS BEEN HERE FOR A WHILE, WAITING FOR YOU TO WAKE UP. I INSISTED SHE LET YOU REST.

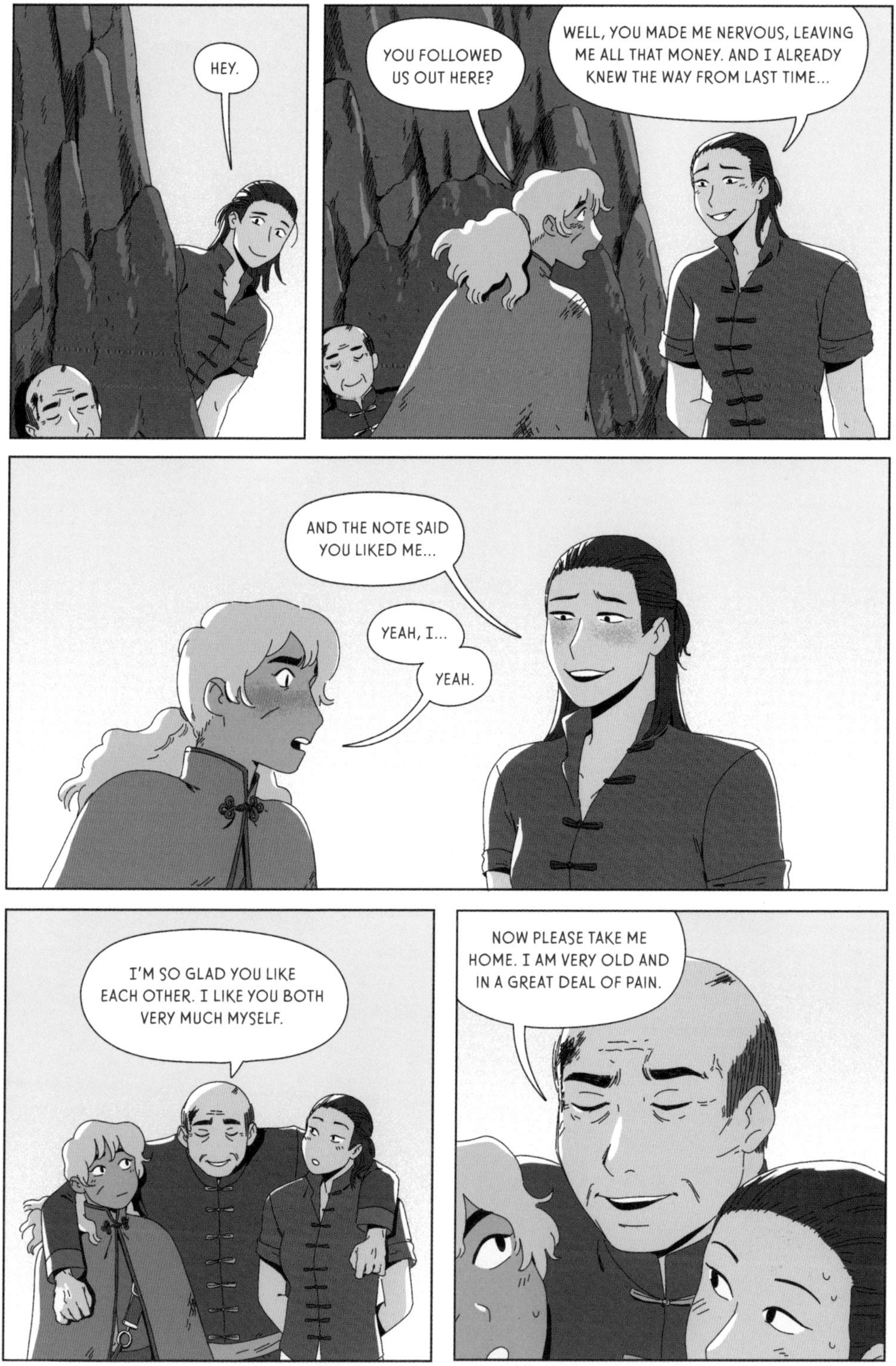
HEY.
YOU FOLLOWED US OUT HERE?
WELL, YOU MADE ME NERVOUS, LEAVING ME ALL THAT MONEY. AND I ALREADY KNEW THE WAY FROM LAST TIME...
AND THE NOTE SAID YOU LIKED ME...
YEAH, I...
YEAH.
I'M SO GLAD YOU LIKE EACH OTHER. I LIKE YOU BOTH VERY MUCH MYSELF.
NOW PLEASE TAKE ME HOME. I AM VERY OLD AND IN A GREAT DEAL OF PAIN.

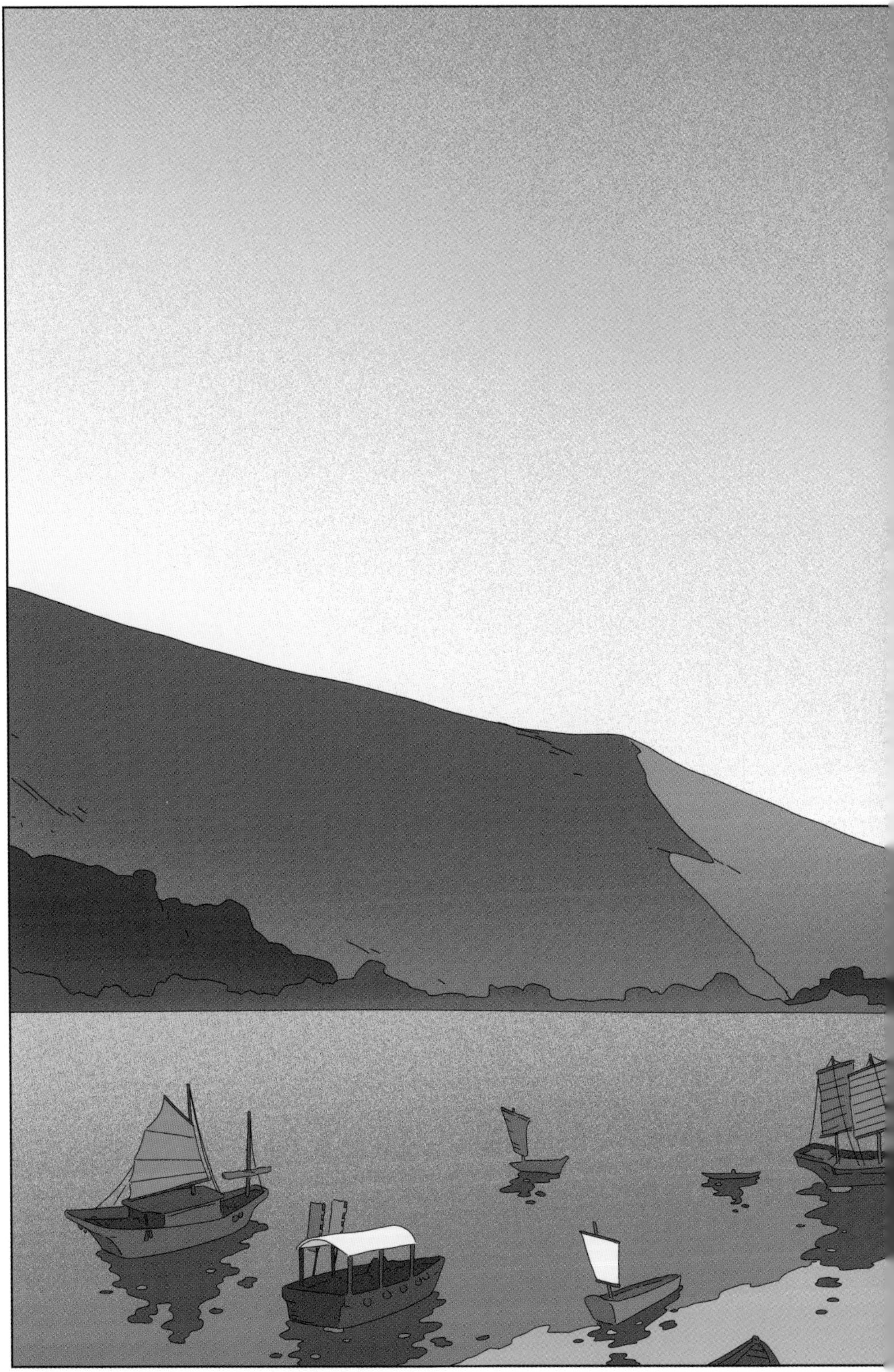

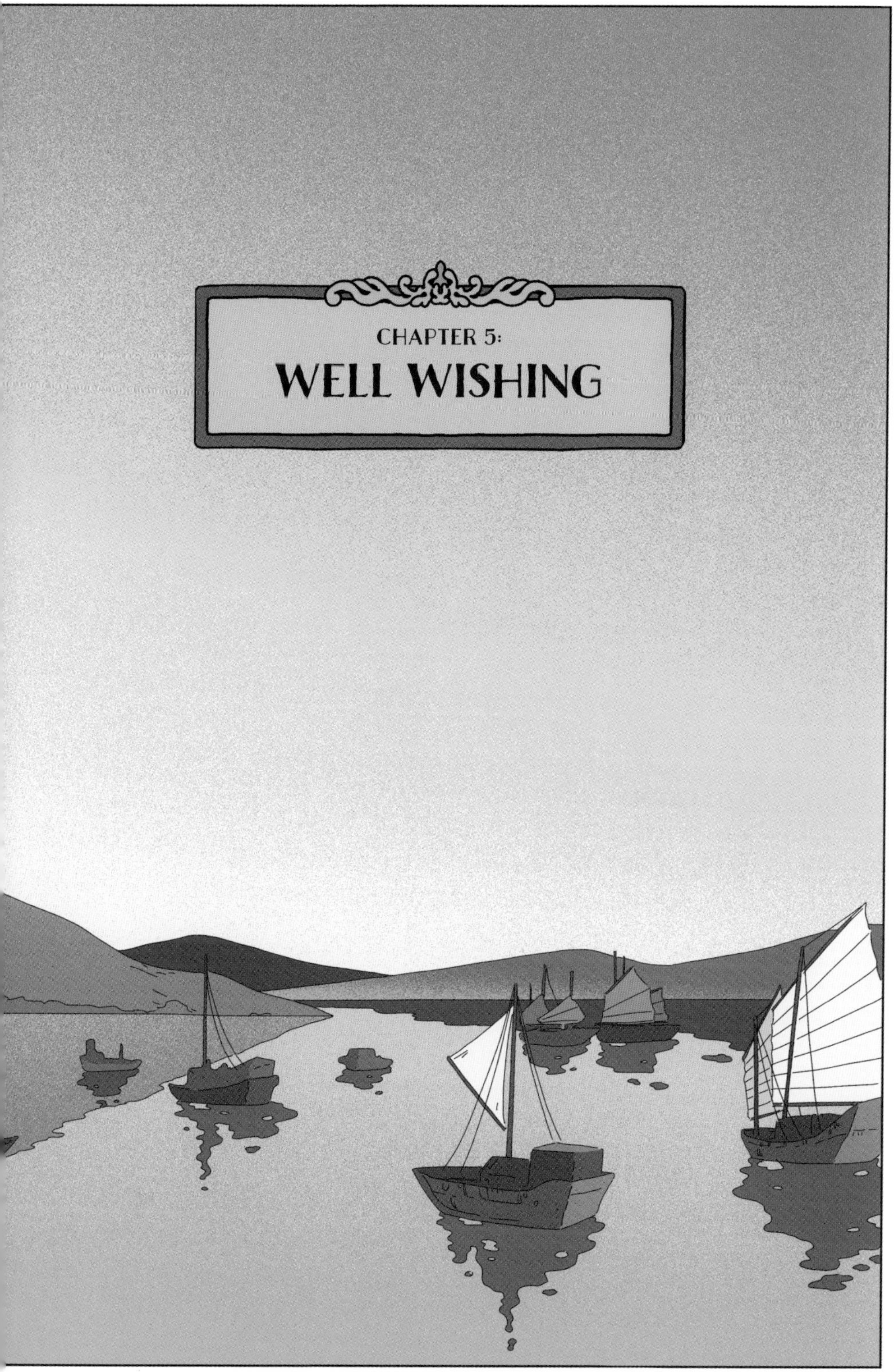
CHAPTER 5:
WELL WISHING

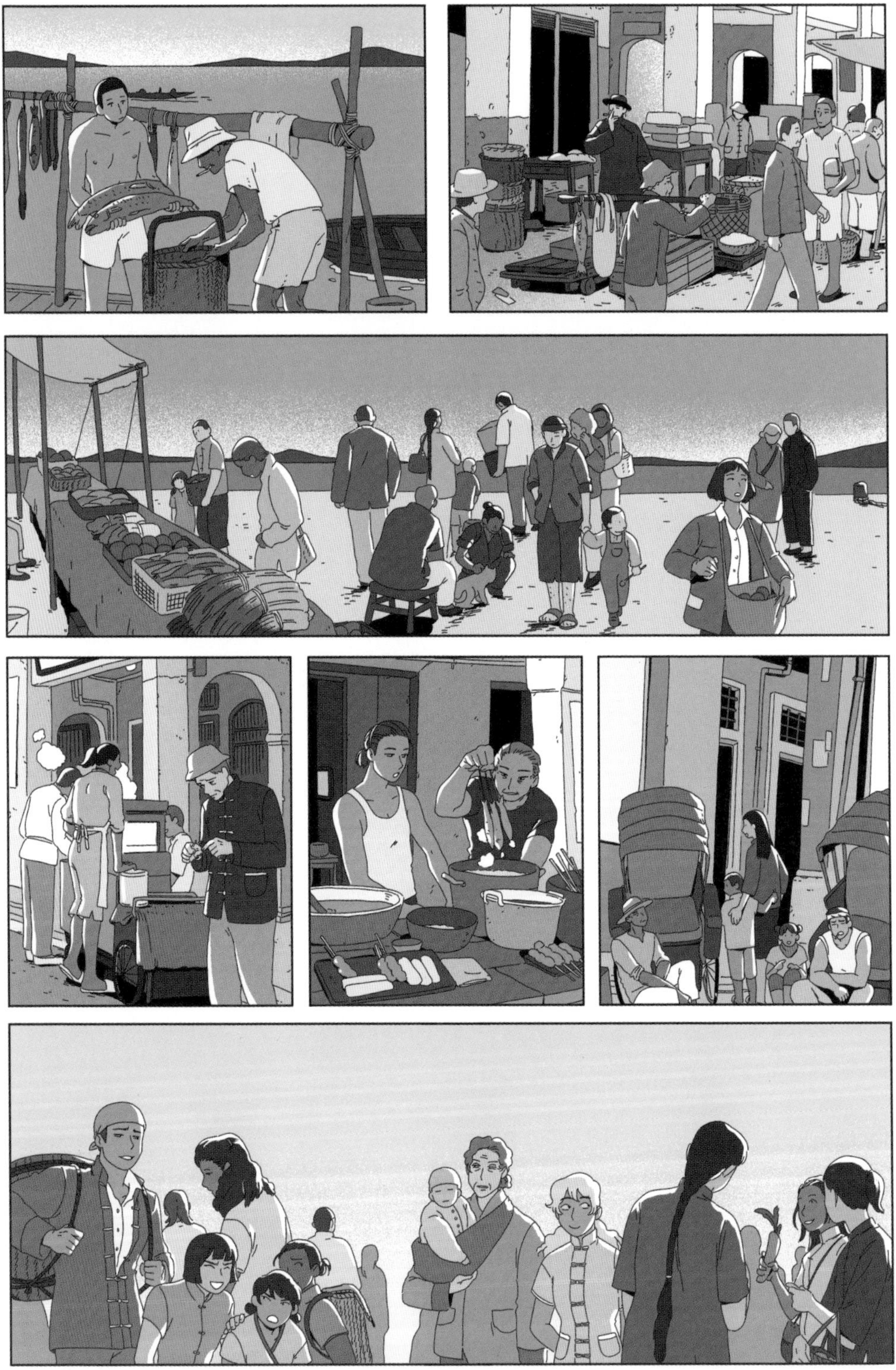

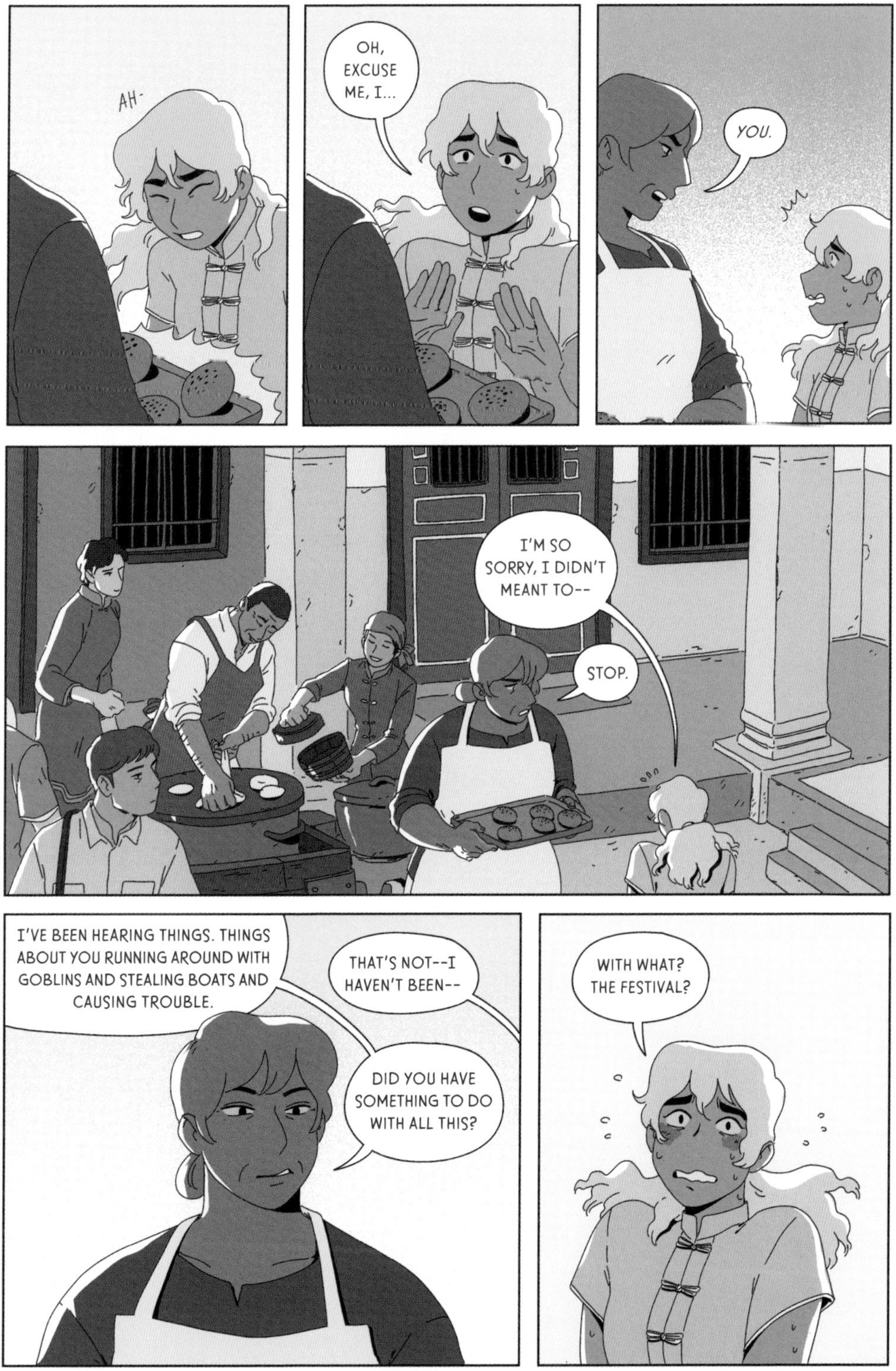
AH-
OH, EXCUSE ME, I...
YOU.
I'M SO SORRY, I DIDN'T MEANT TO--
STOP.
I'VE BEEN HEARING THINGS. THINGS ABOUT YOU RUNNING AROUND WITH GOBLINS AND STEALING BOATS AND CAUSING TROUBLE.
THAT'S NOT--I HAVEN'T BEEN--
DID YOU HAVE SOMETHING TO DO WITH ALL THIS?
WITH WHAT? THE FESTIVAL?

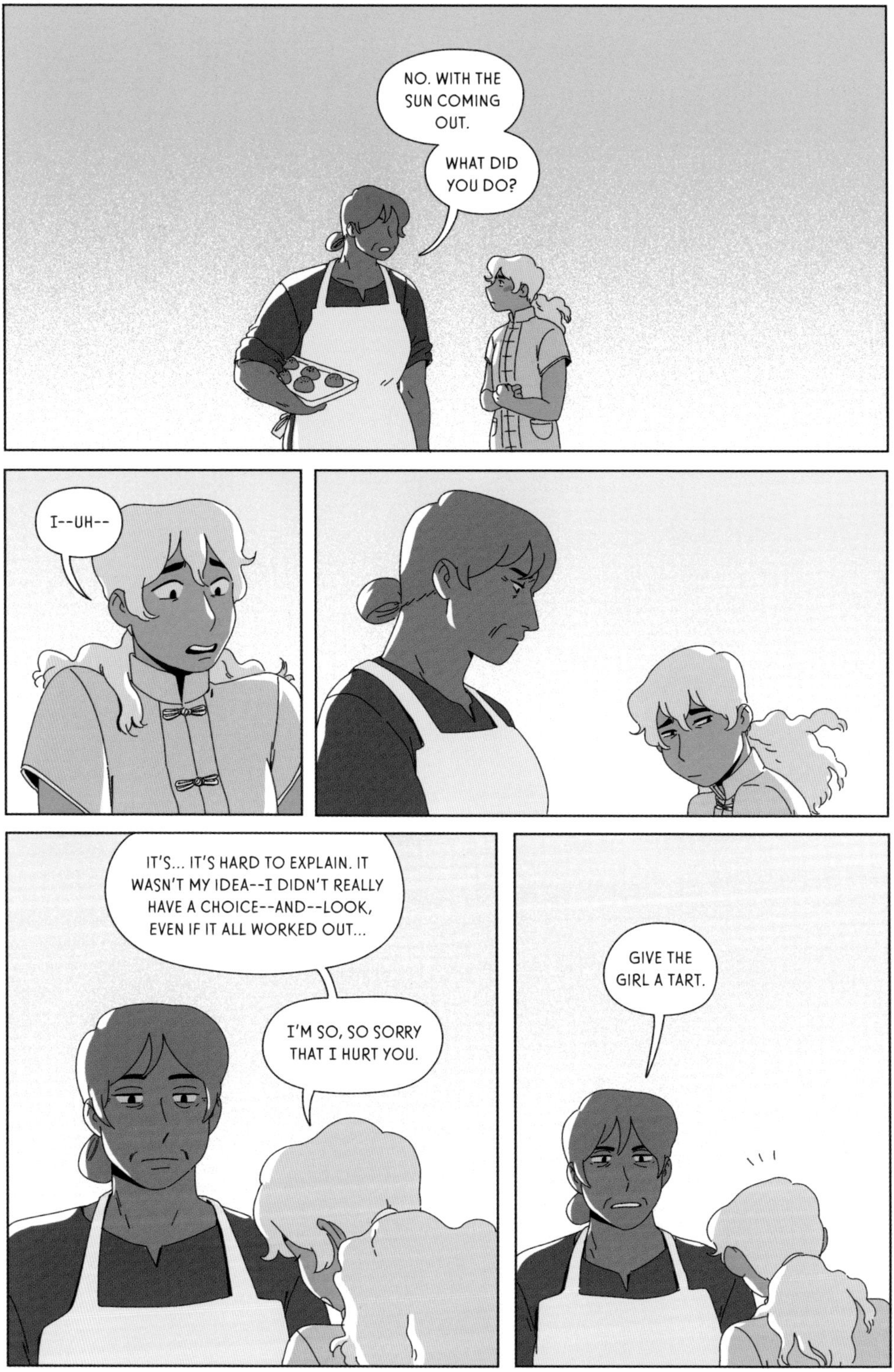
NO. WITH THE SUN COMING OUT.
WHAT DID YOU DO?
I--UH--
IT'S... IT'S HARD TO EXPLAIN. IT WASN'T MY IDEA--I DIDN'T REALLY HAVE A CHOICE--AND--LOOK, EVEN IF IT ALL WORKED OUT...
I'M SO, SO SORRY THAT I HURT YOU.
GIVE THE GIRL A TART.

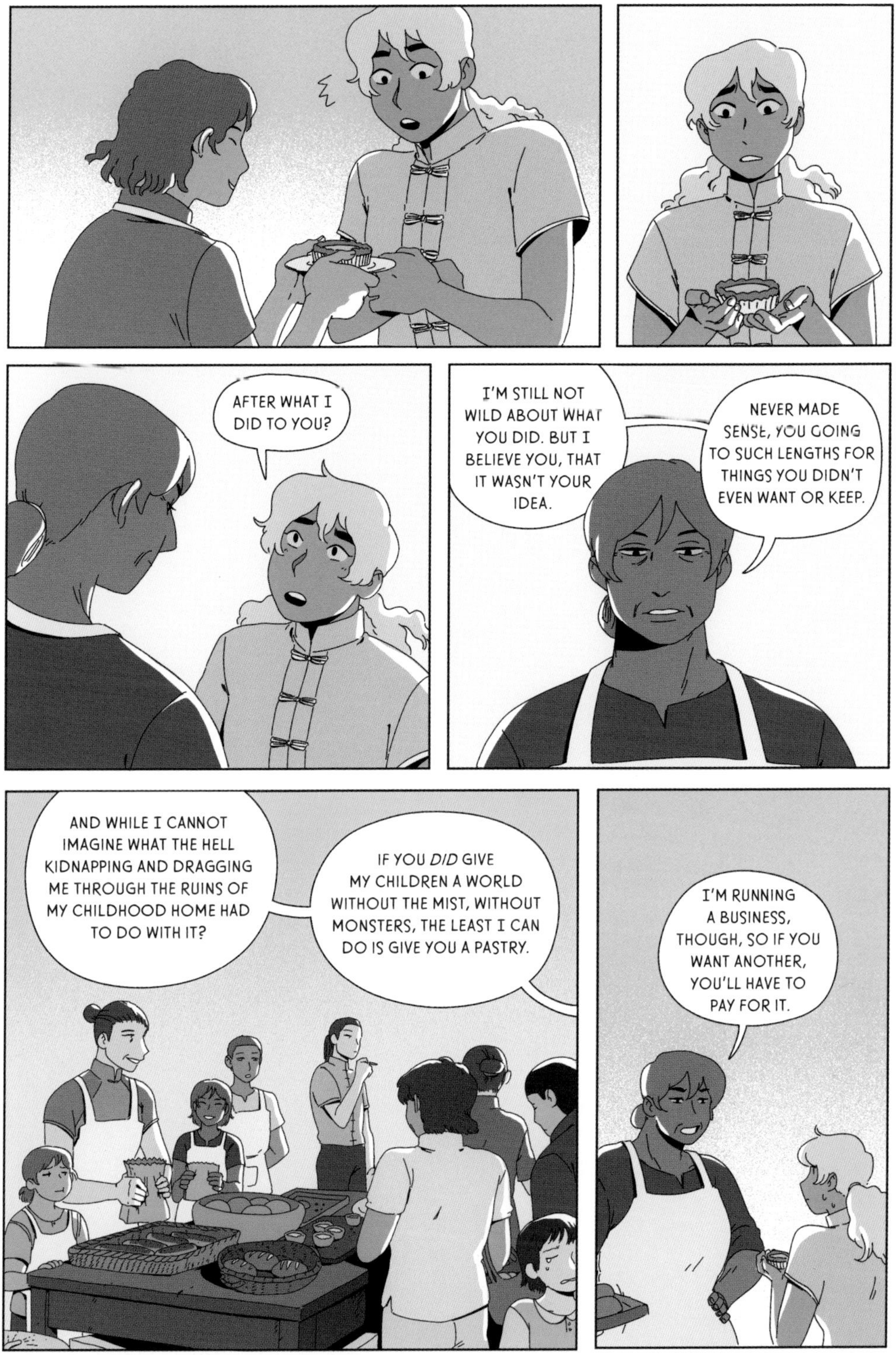
AFTER WHAT I DID TO YOU?
I'M STILL NOT WILD ABOUT WHAT YOU DID. BUT I BELIEVE YOU, THAT IT WASN'T YOUR IDEA.
NEVER MADE SENSE, YOU GOING TO SUCH LENGTHS FOR THINGS YOU DIDN'T EVEN WANT OR KEEP.
AND WHILE I CANNOT IMAGINE WHAT THE HELL KIDNAPPING AND DRAGGING ME THROUGH THE RUINS OF MY CHILDHOOD HOME HAD TO DO WITH IT?
IF YOU *DID* GIVE MY CHILDREN A WORLD WITHOUT THE MIST, WITHOUT MONSTERS, THE LEAST I CAN DO IS GIVE YOU A PASTRY.
I'M RUNNING A BUSINESS, THOUGH, SO IF YOU WANT ANOTHER, YOU'LL HAVE TO PAY FOR IT.

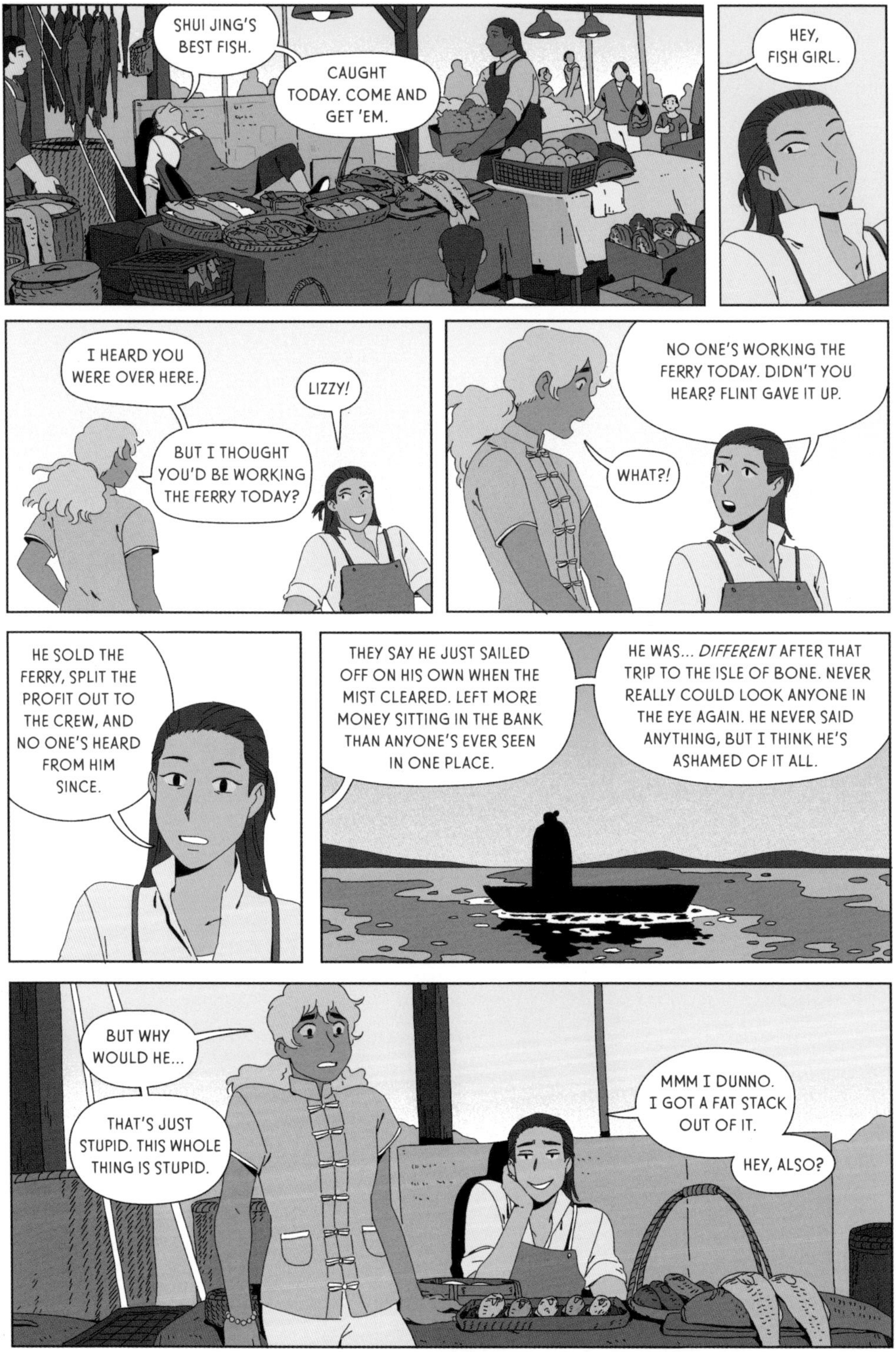
SHUI JING'S BEST FISH.
CAUGHT TODAY. COME AND GET 'EM.
HEY, FISH GIRL.
I HEARD YOU WERE OVER HERE.
BUT I THOUGHT YOU'D BE WORKING THE FERRY TODAY?
LIZZY!
NO ONE'S WORKING THE FERRY TODAY. DIDN'T YOU HEAR? FLINT GAVE IT UP.
WHAT?!
HE SOLD THE FERRY, SPLIT THE PROFIT OUT TO THE CREW, AND NO ONE'S HEARD FROM HIM SINCE.
THEY SAY HE JUST SAILED OFF ON HIS OWN WHEN THE MIST CLEARED. LEFT MORE MONEY SITTING IN THE BANK THAN ANYONE'S EVER SEEN IN ONE PLACE.
HE WAS... *DIFFERENT* AFTER THAT TRIP TO THE ISLE OF BONE. NEVER REALLY COULD LOOK ANYONE IN THE EYE AGAIN. HE NEVER SAID ANYTHING, BUT I THINK HE'S ASHAMED OF IT ALL.
BUT WHY WOULD HE...
THAT'S JUST STUPID. THIS WHOLE THING IS STUPID.
MMM I DUNNO. I GOT A FAT STACK OUT OF IT.
HEY, ALSO?

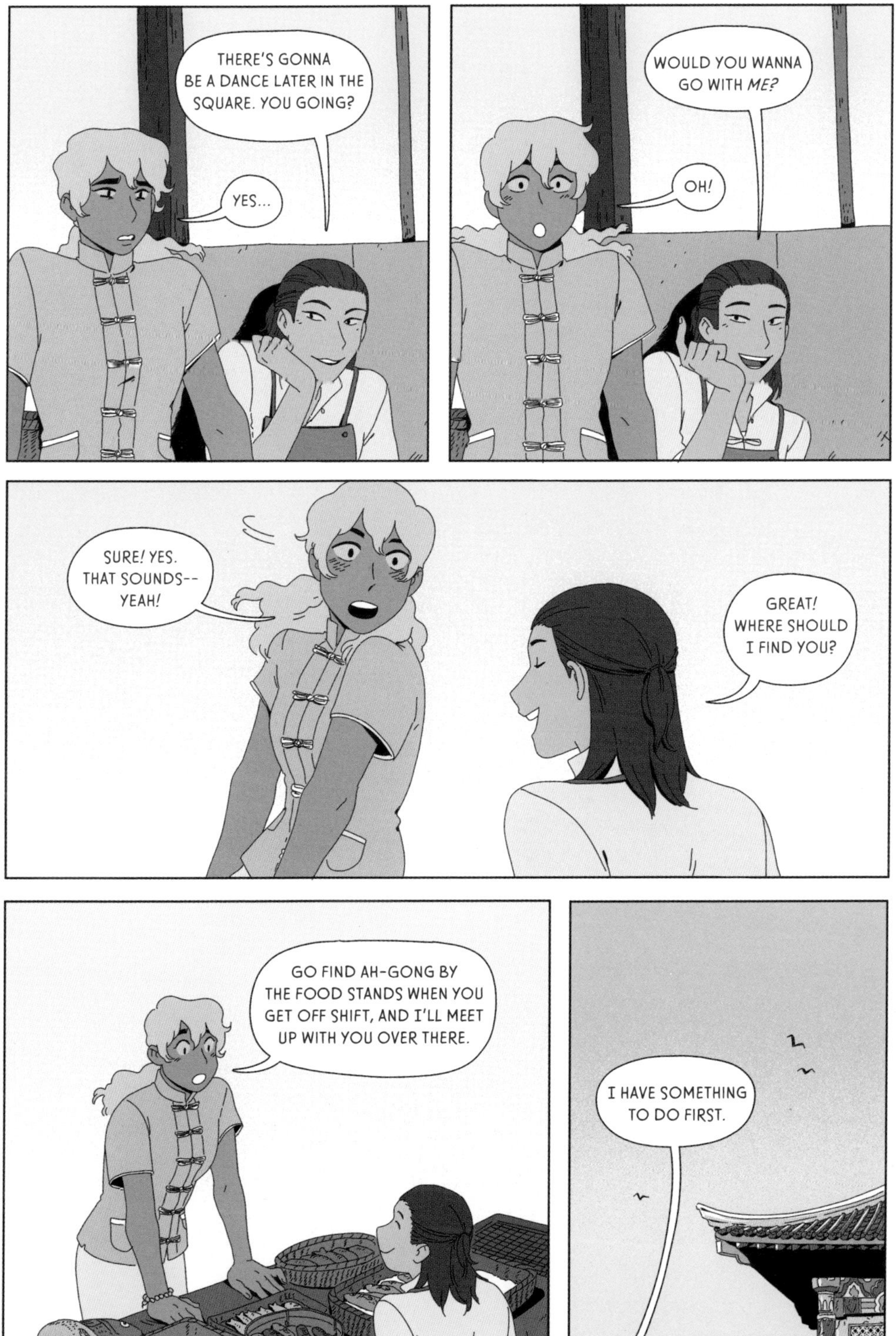
THERE'S GONNA BE A DANCE LATER IN THE SQUARE. YOU GOING?
YES...
WOULD YOU WANNA GO WITH *ME?*
OH!
SURE! YES. THAT SOUNDS-- YEAH!
GREAT! WHERE SHOULD I FIND YOU?
GO FIND AH-GONG BY THE FOOD STANDS WHEN YOU GET OFF SHIFT, AND I'LL MEET UP WITH YOU OVER THERE.
I HAVE SOMETHING TO DO FIRST.

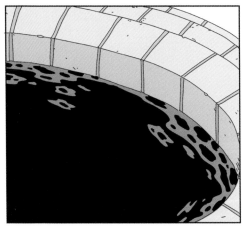

I KNOW YOU'RE HERE.

PLEASE. I WANT TO TALK.

WHAT DID YOU WANT TO TALK ABOUT?

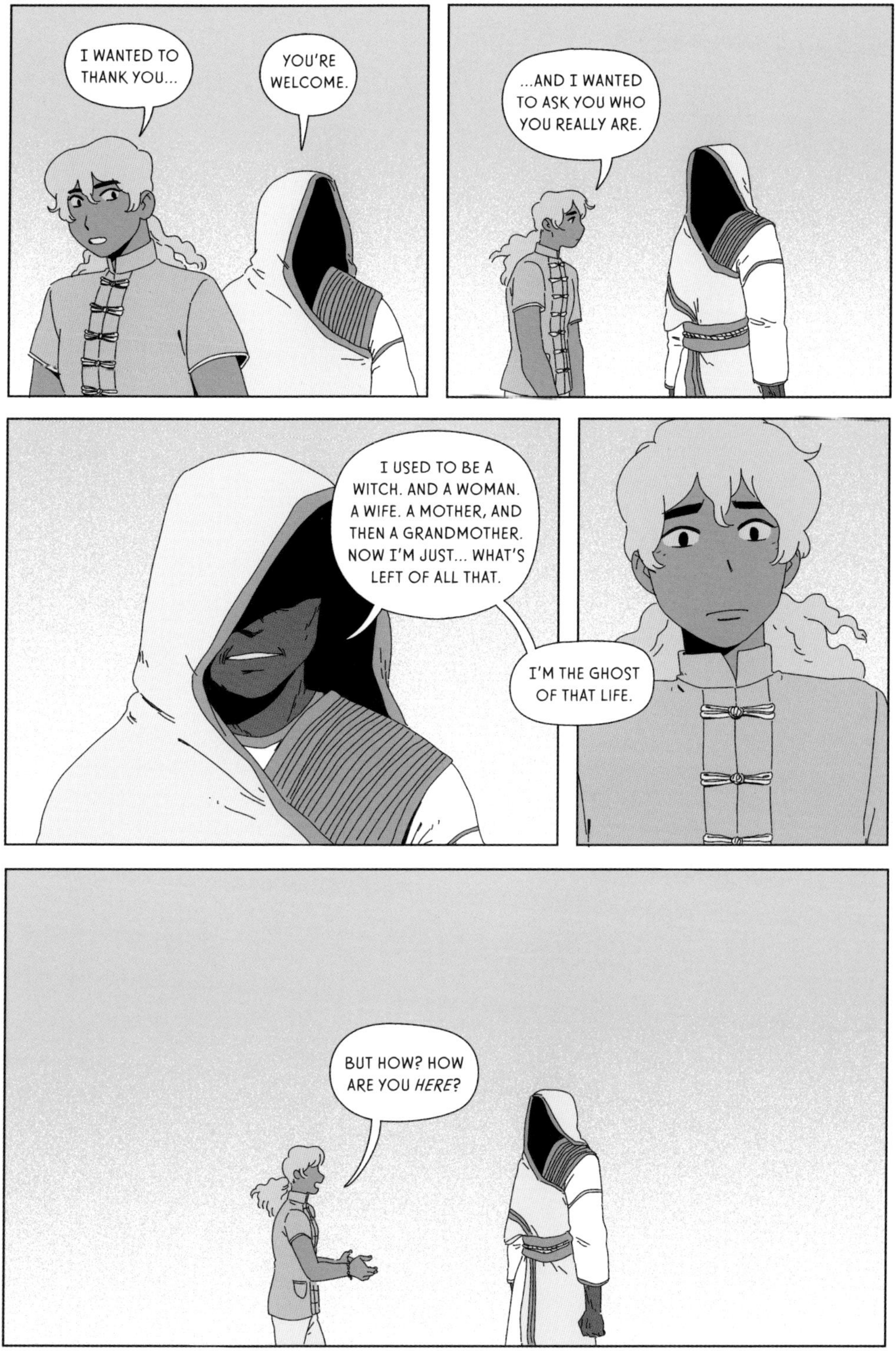
I WANTED TO THANK YOU...
YOU'RE WELCOME.
...AND I WANTED TO ASK YOU WHO YOU REALLY ARE.
I USED TO BE A WITCH. AND A WOMAN. A WIFE. A MOTHER, AND THEN A GRANDMOTHER. NOW I'M JUST... WHAT'S LEFT OF ALL THAT.
I'M THE GHOST OF THAT LIFE.
BUT HOW? HOW ARE YOU *HERE*?

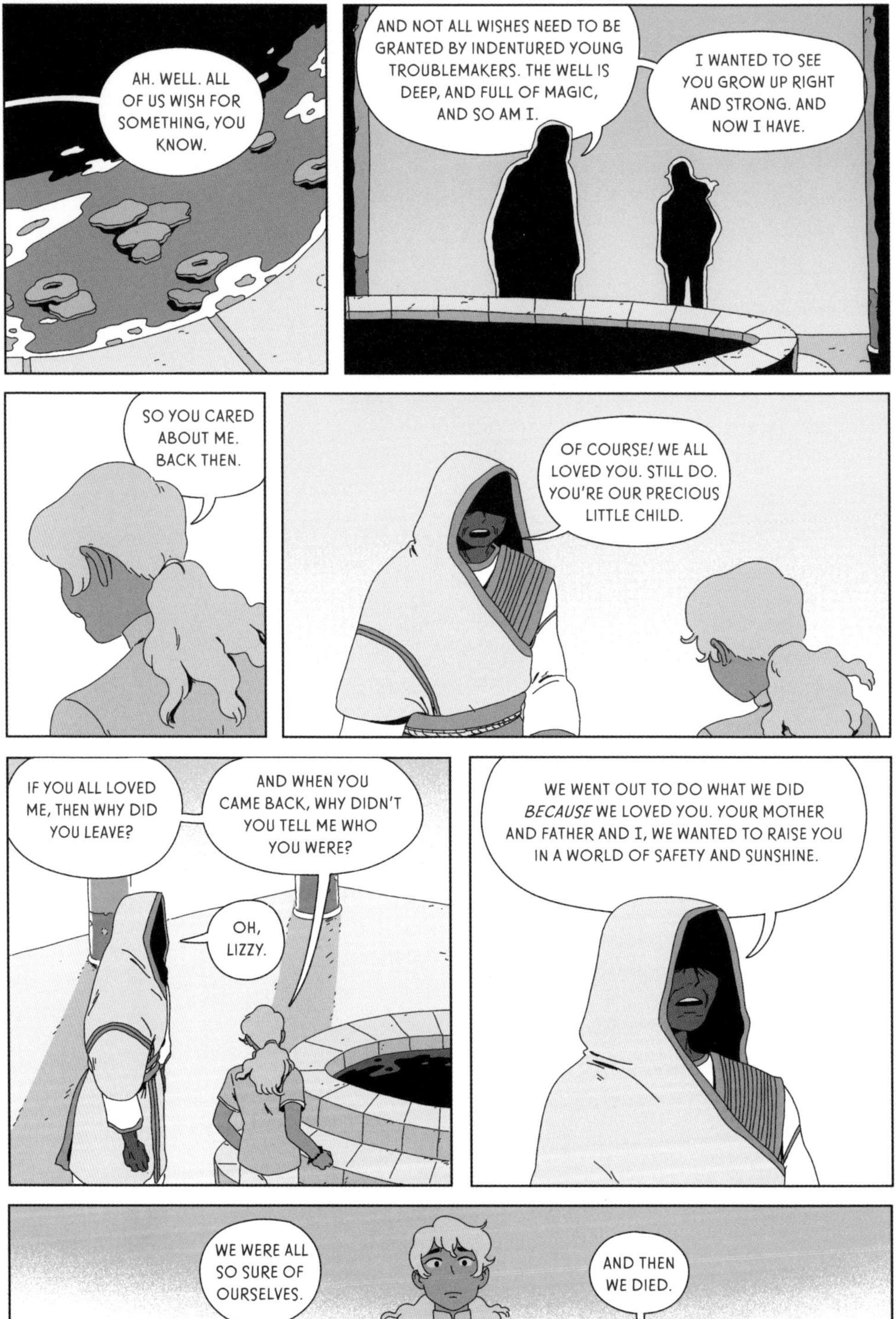
AH. WELL. ALL OF US WISH FOR SOMETHING, YOU KNOW.
AND NOT ALL WISHES NEED TO BE GRANTED BY INDENTURED YOUNG TROUBLEMAKERS. THE WELL IS DEEP, AND FULL OF MAGIC, AND SO AM I.
I WANTED TO SEE YOU GROW UP RIGHT AND STRONG. AND NOW I HAVE.
SO YOU CARED ABOUT ME. BACK THEN.
OF COURSE! WE ALL LOVED YOU. STILL DO. YOU'RE OUR PRECIOUS LITTLE CHILD.
IF YOU ALL LOVED ME, THEN WHY DID YOU LEAVE?
AND WHEN YOU CAME BACK, WHY DIDN'T YOU TELL ME WHO YOU WERE?
OH, LIZZY.
WE WENT OUT TO DO WHAT WE DID *BECAUSE* WE LOVED YOU. YOUR MOTHER AND FATHER AND I, WE WANTED TO RAISE YOU IN A WORLD OF SAFETY AND SUNSHINE.
WE WERE ALL SO SURE OF OURSELVES.
AND THEN WE DIED.

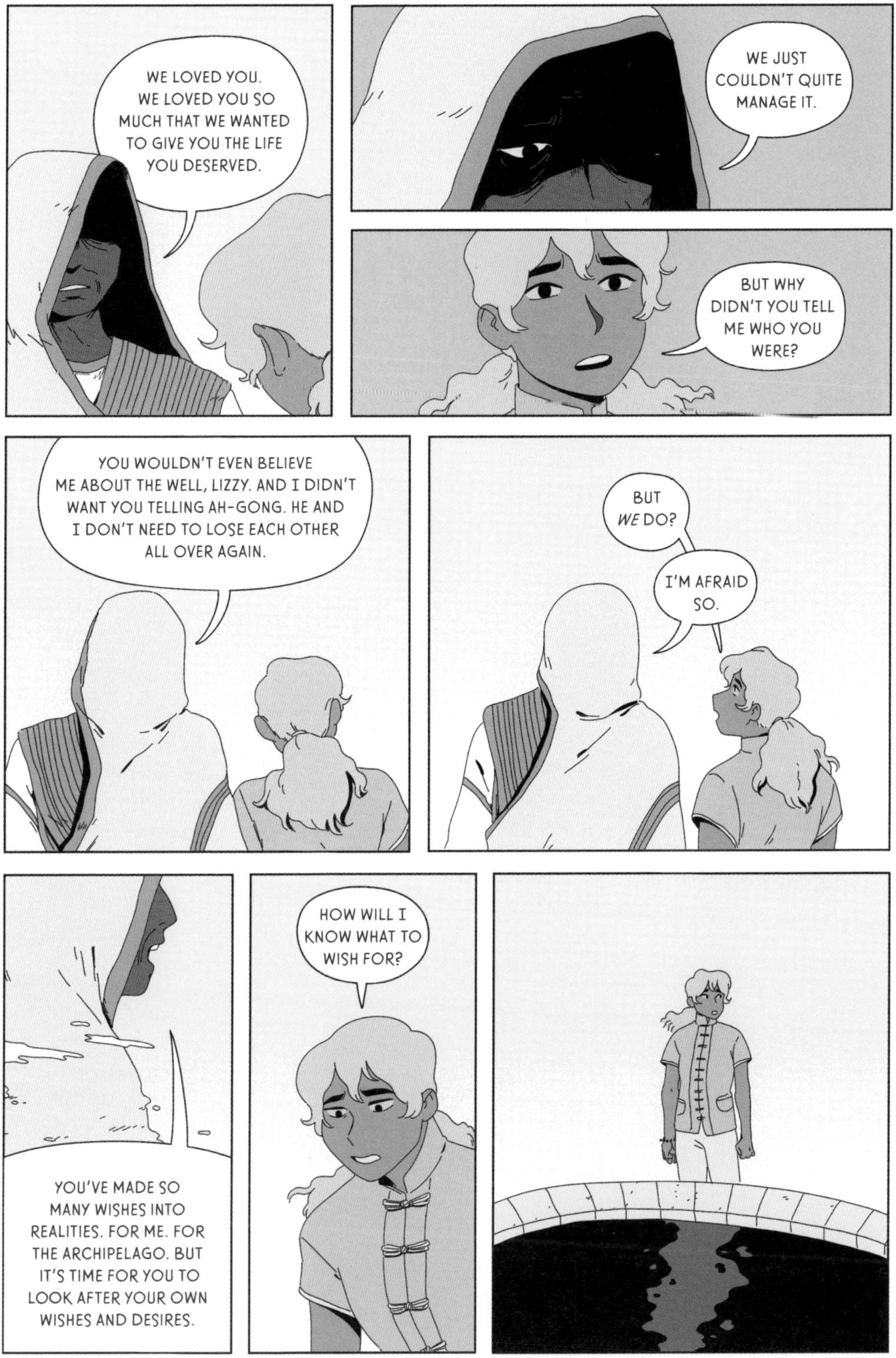
WE LOVED YOU. WE LOVED YOU SO MUCH THAT WE WANTED TO GIVE YOU THE LIFE YOU DESERVED.
WE JUST COULDN'T QUITE MANAGE IT.
BUT WHY DIDN'T YOU TELL ME WHO YOU WERE?
YOU WOULDN'T EVEN BELIEVE ME ABOUT THE WELL, LIZZY. AND I DIDN'T WANT YOU TELLING AH-GONG. HE AND I DON'T NEED TO LOSE EACH OTHER ALL OVER AGAIN.
BUT *WE* DO?
I'M AFRAID SO.
YOU'VE MADE SO MANY WISHES INTO REALITIES. FOR ME. FOR THE ARCHIPELAGO. BUT IT'S TIME FOR YOU TO LOOK AFTER YOUR OWN WISHES AND DESIRES.
HOW WILL I KNOW WHAT TO WISH FOR?

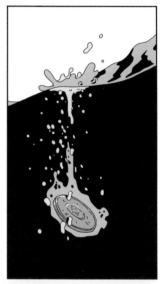

clink

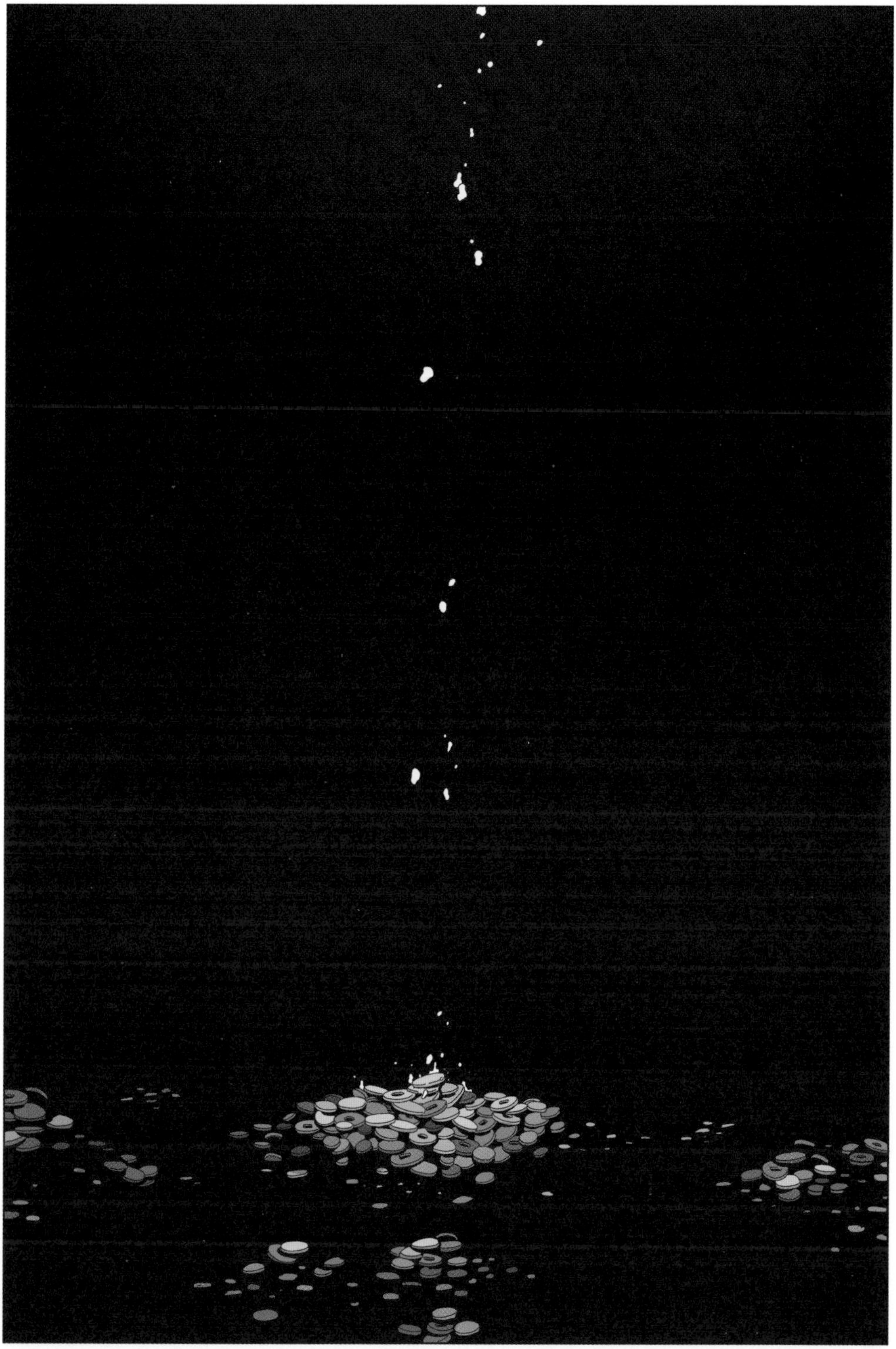

For Kat, who left the coins in the well —J.W.

First Second

PUBLISHED BY FIRST SECOND
FIRST SECOND IS AN IMPRINT OF ROARING BROOK PRESS,
A DIVISION OF HOLTZBRINCK PUBLISHING HOLDINGS LIMITED PARTNERSHIP
120 BROADWAY, NEW YORK, NY 10271
FIRSTSECONDBOOKS.COM

LIBRARY OF CONGRESS CONTROL NUMBER: 2021916664

OUR BOOKS MAY BE PURCHASED IN BULK FOR PROMOTIONAL, EDUCATIONAL, OR BUSINESS USE.
PLEASE CONTACT YOUR LOCAL BOOKSELLER OR THE MACMILLAN CORPORATE AND PREMIUM SALES DEPARTMENT
AT (800) 221-7945 EXT. 5442 OR BY EMAIL AT MACMILLANSPECIALMARKETS@MACMILLAN.COM.

FIRST
EDITION

FIRST EDITION, 2022
EDITED BY MARK SIEGEL
COVER DESIGN BY KIRK BENSHOFF
INTERIOR BOOK DESIGN BY SUNNY LEE

DRAWN DIGITALLY IN CLIP STUDIO PAINT ON AN IPAD PRO 9.7

PRINTED IN CHINA BY 1010 PRINTING INTERNATIONAL LIMITED, KWUN TONG, HONG KONG

ISBN 978-1-62672-414-3 (PAPERBACK)
1 3 5 7 9 10 8 6 4 2

ISBN 978-1-250-81652-8 (HARDCOVER)
3 5 7 9 10 8 6 4 2

DON'T MISS YOUR NEXT FAVORITE BOOK FROM FIRST SECOND!
FOR THE LATEST UPDATES GO TO FIRSTSECONDNEWSLETTER.COM AND SIGN UP FOR OUR ENEWSLETTER.

BY ART
WE LIVE